The Naked She-Wolf

Vesna Ćuro-Tomić

Translated by Ligia Luckhurst

éditions•出版社•ediciones

HARE

publishing•verlag•izdanja

ISBN: 0957254555
ISBN 13: 9780957254558

CONTENTS

ACKNOWLEDGEMENTS

I would like to thank my husband and my friends who, by reading the draft manuscript, helped this book be better than it would have been had they not done so. Those friends are Sanja Miličević-Armada, Dubravka Belas, Slaven Perović, Ligia Luckhurst and Dr Marko Ilić who provided expert advice.

They say nothing happens by chance. Who knows what the wingbeat of that butterfly from Beijing brought you; only you didn't recognise it when it came, nor did you know the turn your life would take from that moment on. What had brought on the events that happened here? Whatever happened, happened because it was inevitable that it should. The very fact that they did happen proves the inevitability of the events, as O. W. Grant, the Man Who Grants One Wish in the movie Interstate 60, *said.*

The Body

The young man in green hospital overalls rested the head of the stretcher against the leg of a chair in order to blow his cherry-red nose, already raw from a bad cold. His colleague, supporting the rear end, halted helpfully. Having dealt with the nose problem, the one with the cold applied both hands to the stretcher once more, smiling discreetly to apologise for the delay. Pale and motionless, the gathered people looked on as the two young men skilfully tilted, lifted and lowered the stretcher as they manoeuvred it between the tables and through the door. The body on the stretcher lay completely hidden under the white vinyl cover. Just as it was about to disappear through the door, its left hand slid from under the cover, swinging lifelessly to and fro as if waving goodbye.

The Diary

The hand took the black Moleskine notebook out of the desk drawer. The first page read, *"For two centuries artists and intellectuals – from Van Gogh to Matisse, from the Modernists to Hemingway – entrusted their thoughts, their sketches and their notes to these historic notebooks. The Moleskine is back now, to be passed from pocket to pocket once more, continuing its yet-to-be-written adventure. The blank pages of this diary are ready to receive and tell the story."*

The hand hovered over the first blank page, clicking the pen.

The Smell of Beauty – Friday, 30th September

The story did not start here, but this particular moment is where we join its flow.

Framed by curly hair and lit up by a smile, a beautiful female face peeked through the door and asked prettily, "May I come in?" The young woman's appearance elicited twin smiles of surrender from the two younger men in the room. The third one, older than the other two, remained serious. The only woman among them smiled too, but her smile was somewhat more reserved than that of the men.

Entering, the young woman simply confirmed what could be sensed the moment the door had begun to open: the smell of beauty. The very elements lent a helping hand: the golden rays of late September sun broke through the branches of the tree outside the window and poured light on her lovely face. Jelena took the newcomer in with her woman's expert eye. Young, slim, pretty. Gives an impression of natural freshness and artless charm. Curly hair, light chestnut in colour. A tightly fitting short light-green cardigan over a white blouse; a wide skirt in brightly coloured print, gathered at the waist. Legs bare, smooth, glossy and tanned. Shapely little feet wriggling restlessly in white high-heeled strap sandals as if echoing the nervous movements of the hands. French manicure, neatly finished with milky white varnish. "Good morning," the girl said to no one in particular. "I'm not interrupting anything, I hope?" Turning to Andrej, the oldest of the three men, she added, "There; here I am, as agreed."

Andrej got up, approached the young woman and took her hand, slowly extended in greeting. "No, you're not interrupting anything," he said. "Do come in."

"I'm sorry if I'm late," she said, adding a broad smile to her apology and completing it by sweeping the other three people in the room with a panoramic glance.

"Do come in, please; sit down," Andrej repeated. "Let me introduce you. This is Nina Ivezić, everyone... our new colleague... we've discussed her appointment. Nina, this is Jelena."

Jelena extended her hand, and Nina smiled shyly. Jelena's smile was reserved and her look curious and slightly ironic; the irony, however, was meant for her male colleagues and not for the pretty newcomer.

"You're Jelena Turkalj, the art critic?"

"I am," said Jelena.

Nina's eyes halted on the handsomest man in the room.

Andrej said, "This is David," and David said, rising: "David Antolić, books."

Smiling sweetly, the girl offered her hand and said, "I know. Nice to meet you." She did not withdraw her hand when he held on to it. "Congratulations on the award. When is the presentation?"

"Tonight at seven at the Journalists' Association. You've just been invited."

"Thanks, I'd love to come, I really would, but I won't be able to make it... I'm really sorry."

David nodded his understanding.

The youngest of the three men came closer and said, "It's no big deal for him. He is the stenchmark of Croatian lit crit:

columnist of the year for two years in a row; the star of Croatian journalism, respected by the males of the profession and lusted after by the females..." Nina chuckled, reclaimed her hand from David and gave it to the young man who, imitating David's manner, said, "Mario, television and entertainment. In a word, paparazzo." Nina laughed again; the others chimed in and the shared laughter helped melt away the formality of the introductions.

"People often dislike me; but then, some say I'm the double of Spikey from Notting Hill." Nina laughed; Jelena turned her face away from the attention-seeker. "The Boss you already know, that's obvious." Mario indicated Andrej with a sweeping gesture.

Andrej said dryly, "As of today, Nina is member of the editorial staff. Since we're already Friday, she'll be starting on Monday. As you know, she'll cover theatre." He made a limp wavy gesture with his right hand. "Monday first thing, editorial staff meeting at ten."

Twirling a pencil between her fingers, Jelena watched the young woman with interest. Her shapely figure in the door had been, in the meantime and in stark contrast, replaced by Dora, the secretary, whose voluminous hips took up the width of the door frame. "Dora, our secretary," intoned Mario. "Nothing physical – that is, of the body – or psychological – that is, of the soul – escapes her penetrating attention."

"We've already met," said Nina.

The secretary giggled; the joke was obviously lost on her, but she enjoyed having the attention she deserved. "Want me to make you a coffee?" she asked Andrej, showing off her intimacy with the boss and her domination of the others for the benefit of the new staff member.

"No, thanks," Andrej replied dryly, stepped into his office and closed the door.

"Firm but fair," Mario commented with a wink towards the Chief Editor's door.

News Desk trainee Ivana burst into the office mumbling through her wad of chewing gum something to the effect of,

"Hi guys! Am I late? Has the boss clocked me?".

"Are you late?" That was Mario. "You've only managed to be on time once since you started here!"

Ivana shrugged. She had spotted the new face, but no one was offering to introduce her. "Have I missed something?" She got no reply.

"I've cleared a desk for you, dear," Dora said to Nina in a brisk, business-like tone. "If you need anything else, just let me know. I'll sort it." For the supremely self-important Dora, everything happened in the first person singular.

"Thank you," said Nina. The desk was by the window and, as she went up to it, the young woman found herself framed by the window as if in a portrait, placed there to give everyone the chance to examine her thoroughly once more. The sunlight had turned her hair into a glowing halo.

The Devil himself could use such an angelic face, the thought came to Jelena out of nowhere.

The Police Inspector

"You're an odd bunch," the Sergeant said as his glance travelled over the people seated before him. The Inspector gave him a barely perceptible nod and the Sergeant fell silent. Taking a seat at the desk next to his governor, he reached into the inner pocket of his jacket and produced a well preserved, much cherished old *Pelikan* fountain pen and a yellow, meticulously sharpened HB pencil. His side pocket yielded a small notepad of the no longer obtainable *Lipamil* brand, probably found in the forgotten warehouse of a long defunct factory. His left hand sported a large *Doxa* watch. The whole of him spelled decades of dedicated service in the Force, each decade marked by an official gift: a watch, a fountain pen...

His preparations done, the Sergeant leaned forward and planted his elbows on the table.

The Inspector cut an altogether more sophisticated figure: young, slim, tastefully dressed, with an up-to-date haircut and a pleasant demeanour.

The handsome man offered him a hand. "Who'd have

guessed we'd meet under such circumstances."

The Inspector nodded again. "Who'd like to tell me what happened here yesterday? Any volunteers?"

The gathering before him probably did not see themselves as an odd bunch: had someone asked them, they would have said they were ordinary, normal people, only, perhaps, unhappier than average.

The Editorial Office

The new member of staff smiled again at her colleagues, sat down at her desk, hung her handbag on the back of her chair and repositioned slightly the monitor and the keyboard of her computer. Slowly, with barely a sound, she opened her desk drawers and inspected the mesh pen holder containing a few pens, the scattered paperclips and the scissors she found inside. The drawers were dusty; the young woman shook off her fingers and delicately rested her elbows on the ancient Formica desktop with frayed edges.

"That used to be Piljek's desk, but he's now moved to my room and got a larger one," said Dora bearing an armful of office equipment: a small, hard-cover notebook, a notepad, yet another pen, a Sellotape dispenser complete with a Sellotape roll, a stapler and a box of paperclips – the regulation kit of the modern Croatian journalist.

Little if any journalistic work was being done at that moment in the editorial office of *The Herald*, one of the two highest-selling dailies in the country: everyone's eyes were on the pretty new colleague. Having stowed away Dora's welcome gifts, she switched her computer on. Mario was ready: "There's no password, just click OK." She nodded and thanked him, continuing to manoeuvre the mouse on the mat while gazing intently at the screen for some minutes. Her mobile rang; she answered in a low voice so as not to disturb the others. All in all, she could not have spent more than fifteen minutes in the office. She got up to leave, and this time everyone watched her quite openly. "That's my work done for today," she said, pulling a funny face.

"Off so soon?" said Mario quickly.

"It was lovely meeting you," said Nina, keeping her funny face on and looking straight at Mario which made it look as if she had meant him alone. She had marked his intrusiveness and was poking gentle fun at him, which drew a smile from everyone in the room. "See you Monday."

"We could pop out for a coffee," Mario spoke up again. "My treat."

Jelena and David exchanged glances and Ivana winked.

"You're on," Nina said. "And I propose that on that occasion we start saying 'thou'[1] to each other." This time, she looked at Jelena too, and then at David. They responded with a friendly nod.

When the door closed in Nina's wake, the tension in the room dropped almost audibly as the men finally exhaled the breath they had been holding since she had first entered the room, the fact that did not escape Jelena's attention. With a good-natured if slightly mocking smile, she regarded her favourite colleague, David, whose desk faced hers. He did not need to see her in order to know how and why she regarded him at that moment and intentionally did not look back. Smiling and nodding approvingly in Jelena's direction, he gave her a one-handed thumbs-up sign instead. This naturally meant: yup, the wench is well fit; but it could also have meant: okay, okay, you're right—I fancy her.

The office took on its usual dull appearance again. A moderately sized room crammed full of furniture assembled, like the body of the Frankenstein monster, from many different sources: cheap old chipboard alongside even cheaper modern laminate surrounded by walls which were, like the floor, made of prefab slabs. Amidst all that, like in a Gogol burlesque, there stood a wooden coat-and-hat stand. The atmosphere was

---

[1] Similarly to French, Italian and German, Croatian distinguishes between the singular and the plural of the second person personal pronoun. One uses the singular, "ti" (thou) with family, friends and good acquaintances. The plural, "vi", is more formal.

gloomy in spite of the large windows overlooking a busy suburban street the noise of which they failed to absorb. But for the computers on the desks, the room would have resembled any old office from communist times.

With a quiet chuckle, Jelena made an effort to return to the text flickering on her screen: a moonlighting article on wine. Six years on payroll at *The Herald*, she was getting increasingly interested in ecological topics and devoted more and more of her time to her freelance column *The Guide* in the *Health and Environment* magazine, her enthusiasm for writing about visual arts progressively flagging the while: even though art might be essential for the survival of the species, she felt, a profession which did nothing but discuss art might not be equally useful.

"Good job you're chasing the deadline;" David's laughter echoed her own. "You won't have the time to cross-examine me." Jelena did all her freelance work in the office, as her husband Bruno, a computer programmer, always seemed to be using both their desktops and their laptop simultaneously.

"What's wrong with you, why have you all gone quiet?" Mario exclaimed. Jelena sighed: no proper writing today, then. "That babe's kickin' fit!" He made a slurping sound as if smelling a tasty steak. Nicknamed Dipsy in the office, Mario Strvinić had been with *The Herald* ever since the first Croatian celeb-tracking mag, *Eye To Eye*, had folded. Behind his back, however, they called him Carrion, because of his personal "professional code of conduct" rather than because of his surname[2]. "The fact is," he would say, "we're all the same: all journalism is, essentially, vulture-work. What's the difference between gossip and news from the Parliament? Shall I tell you? Gossip tells it as it is." Whenever he ran out of fresh gossip, he told jokes. It was hard to tell whether he was amoral because he was a paparazzo, or if he had become paparazzo because of his amorality. His favourite saying was, "Better a cunt for a moment than a mug for life."

"You must like her a lot if you're prepared to buy her a

---

[2] Carrion is 'strvina' in Croatian, and Mario's surname is Strvinić.

coffee," Ivana prodded. "You've only just tied the knot, and you're already lusting after fresh meat. Your poor wife, I feel for her."

Mario had married an heiress; a post-war jet-setter and the daughter of a war profiteer. She frequented the places he visited in his professional capacity; that was how they had met. "We deserve each other, eh?" was Mario's comment at the time. "That's what you're all thinking, innit?" Now he snapped back at Ivana: "She doesn't go short when I get a bit on the side."

Insensitive to rudeness which was the norm for her generation, Ivana did not reply, staring listlessly at the work schedule she had prepared for going out on the beat. "And your BF?" Dipsy asked.

Ivana had recently "found a serious boyfriend", a colleague from Classifieds. She seemed to care for him, to the delight of the entire editorial office where everyone hoped the "kid" might "settle down".

"What about him?"

"You'll let him carry on drooling over that baggage from Common Services with whom he lunches every day in the canteen?"

"So what? She's my mate," Ivana replied.

"My sweet, sweet child," said Dipsy, "have you not heard that old adage, 'Come to me sweetheart but don't bring your mate; for her I will kiss and you I will hate?' A good one, eh? Huh?"

"Ha-ha." Ivana shrugged, feigning boredom. "We have a *ff*-relationship, I'll let you know." She covered her mouth with her hands as if to stop the others from overhearing and said in a loud whisper: "That means, *fuck & fun*."

"Never heard of it, to be honest."

"You couldn't have. I made it up."

"Congratulations, baby. In that case, let him drool."

"Whatever," Ivana said, rising. "I'm off to the Assembly[3],

___

[3] The Assembly of the City of Zagreb, an elected representative body vaguely similar to a borough Council but without executive functions.

then home."

Youngest by age and by years of service, she was still external correspondent in *Zagreb Today* section of the paper. "I got so wasted last night that I'm still picking myself off the floor. Ah well, what the fuck" she added, speaking to everyone and no one, although no one had asked her a question. "When are you supposed to get shitfaced if not when you're young?"

"I got it!" Dipsy called after her. "That's where f-floozie comes from."

"Eh?" Ivana gave him a blank look.

"From *ff*, no?"

"Leave the kid alone," said Dora protectively. She always fought a woman's corner, unless the woman in question threatened her primacy.

Dora despised Dipsy for his eternal cadging of cash which he never remembered to pay back and for the way he incessantly rummaged through his pockets for loose coins. "That shows you what sort of a man he is;" she would say, "it tells me all I need to know." One could say that it was the case of the pot calling the kettle black: because of her tendency to save money at the expense of others, she was nicknamed Dora Gimmeyoura. She, too, forgot to contribute when coffee for the office espresso machine was being ordered. Not that she had coffee often, but she made one for Andrej at least once a day, mainly using David's or Jelena's stock. "Gimme some of your coffee, kids, just one tiny sachet," she would plead shamelessly on a daily basis, convinced that, in her privileged position, she should not be expected to sink so low as to pay her share. Andrej always took his coffee alone. He never took part in communal coffee-and-snacks sessions, claiming he only ever had coffee first thing in the morning and never ate between meals. One could nevertheless sense that he wanted to keep his distance, not just towards his subordinates but towards people in general. Hearing that the new colleague was being discussed, Dora sashayed in from her foyer, watering can in hand, pretending she had come to water the plants. "Buff lassie, ain't she?" she said, moving towards the flowerpots on the window sill. "Have you noticed she says 'thou' to the Boss?"

"We have," Dipsy replied. "Everyone knows he's a letch." His voice dropped on the last word, hearing Andrej's door open. Andrej always looked as if he had just caught everyone misbehaving, so it was not clear if he had heard what Dipsy had said or was simply wearing a sour expression for no particular reason.

"Dora", he said tersely in his pleasant, educated voice: "I'm going out. I'll be back at some point, don't know when." An attractive fifty-seven year old, he had a fine, delicately shaped face, a bit like John Malkovich with paler eyes and more hair. He left with a nod. As the door closed behind him, Dipsy said: "Even *my* blood runs cold at the sight of him. A man of ice. Has any one of you ever seen the Boss laugh?"

His coldness and reserve had earned Andrej the nickname "Fish", used by everyone in the office – everyone except Dora, that is. She halted in the door and cast a reproachful eye at Mario, while saying to everyone: "Did you know that, as a young man, Andrej used to be so handsome that men, women and children in the street turned to look at him?"

"He's still handsome," said Mario, "*and* a dandy, *and* a letch. Only, he doesn't give shit about anything; he'll end up in the Ministry of Culture like his predecessor."

"You really *are* a pig," Dora said. "Andrej is a superb journalist, I'll have you know."

Andrej Martić had started his journalistic career as literary critic. When Croatia achieved independence, he became the editor of a new weekly, created to fit the new government. When the weekly folded because of insolvency, Martić was placed with *The Herald* as the editor for cultural affairs. There, he wrote the editorials and interviewed the giants of Croatian music and literature from time to time. He was highly esteemed.

"If you say so," Dipsy replied.

"It's weird how no one knows anything about him;" Ivana barged in, "what his private life is like, his favourite food, whom he likes to... y' know."

"A miracle! Someone about whom Dipsy didn't manage to dig anything out," Dora mocked.

"Well, in my book, *nothing* is a relative concept. I know he's married to Helena Šoljan, the famous theatre and film actress, who used to be so gorgeous once that all Zagreb called her *la belle Hélène*. I know he's got three daughters from three different marriages. They say that he doesn't even know the eldest daughter, that the middle one is a junkie with a criminal record and has in any case disappeared without trace, and that the youngest one is *disturbed*... Never mind his private life, though. The fact that he never said anything about this new chick is a more serious matter. He didn't even mention she looked divine."

Jelena and David, as if by mutual agreement, resisted being dragged into the conversation.

Shrugging, Dora said sagely, "It doesn't have to mean anything. It's a question of taste."

"Whose taste wouldn't include that babe?" Dipsy smacked his lips voluptuously. "Where was it she used to work before?"

A laptop bag appeared in the door, followed by Piljek, whose desk the new colleague had inherited. Until recently, Piljek used to peer suspiciously through the door before entering. Since he had been given the laptop, his pride and joy, however, he had taken to thrusting it through the door first as the living proof that upward career moves affected human character. His expression said, *I've just been to an important meeting*. Of late, his career had been advancing in leaps and bounds, and the acquisition of the said laptop marked the most notable step. It was given him when, having had mastered the basics of accountancy, he had wormed his way on board the paper's restructuring project and began rubbing shoulders with the senior management. "Piljek's been honing his arse-licking skills," Dipsy had remarked at the time. "Have you heard the one about the cannibal who'd eaten a Croatian manager..."

"Ah, you're here," said Dora.

"Yep," Piljek snorted. "'Nuff meetings for today." He had a droll habit of saying "Yep" by way of greeting: every time he met someone, he would bark out "Yep." In his absence, the entire staff of the *Herald* greeted one another with yeps.

"Dear me, Piljek, you've wasted away and gone all grey from toiling on that project of yours," said Dora, not without rancour. She could say whatever she pleased to Piljek, even now that he outranked her: he was still, as he ever had been, her personal assistant and amanuensis and was known to pop out to *Cvjetno*, which had the best shish-kebab in town, to fetch a spot of lunch for the two of them, laptop or no laptop.

Piljek nodded importantly. "Not easy, not easy at all…" Almost as a reflex, he raised his hand to his heart.

"… for a delivery man in evening literacy classes to rise to be Accounts Manager," Dipsy continued on Piljek's sentence in a low whisper. "One has to eat a lot of shit to get that far… and what is a man but what he consumes? *Garbage in, garbage out.*"

Piljek did look more tired and more worried with each passing day, but also more and more pompous. The way he clung to his laptop, clutching it with eyes full of feverish greed and ambition, reminded Jelena of Gollum when he found the Ring.

"We have a new colleague," Dora announced eagerly.

Piljek nodded. He never asked about anything lest someone thought he lacked information. Dora knew his weakness and explained, "Nina Ivezić. Andrej brought her in. She'll do theatre."

Piljek nodded again. "I've written down your messages, they're on your desk," Dora told him in an intimate yet portentous tone.

"Fine," said Piljek.

In addition to greeting everyone with "Yep," Piljek never said "thank you" but always expressed his gratitude with "Fine", which he modified in tone and pitch according to the situation: a short, flat bark for his peers, and, for the objects of his adulation, a long and braying one: "Fiiiiiine…"

The Inspector

The Inspector gazed pensively at the top of his desk, tapping it silently with his fingers as he awaited an answer to his question. His Sergeant rapidly took notes with his well-sharpened pencil, underlining with a fountain pen a word here and a word there, bent over the desk with concentration like a pupil jealously protective of his work: one could almost see him sticking out his tongue and biting its wiggly tip to aid his efforts. This all-too-human weakness was a comfort to those whose statements he was recording; his zeal, which in other circumstances they might have found comical, eased their tension.

The Annual Award for Journalism Ceremony – Friday, 30th September

"It gives me great pleasure to announce that this year's Annual Award for Journalism has again been won by our colleague –" the President of the Association of Journalists paused dramatically " – David Antolić! (Applause in the auditorium.) In addition to his regular column in *The Herald* and his texts on the recent literary and dramatic production, David has published a book of essays entitled, significantly and poignantly, *Push Harder.* This exceptional work heralded in a new climate and even set new standards for our journalism, a fact which was duly acknowledged in our literary and journalistic circles. Although I believe that the book needs little introduction since it has already been so extensively reviewed, I'd still like to say that *Push Harder* represents more than just a collection of essays. This book reflects the Croatian society today and provides a shrewd analysis of our contemporary art and its audience, delivered with surgical precision but also with humour, in a pure, economical, almost sparse idiom utterly free of sentimental bathos and didacticism. I congratulate the author in the name of the Association of Journalists and – to cut the long story short – I'll take the liberty of quoting from the first page of *Push Harder: Cut the romantic crap and let's get down to business!*"

Laughter rippled through the large Hall of the Association as the winner of the award mounted the stage and approached the microphone to thunderous applause. Antolić gave the speaker a firm handshake and then, while being congratulated by the Moderator, a young and very pretty female colleague, smiled quite unprofessionally and blushed as their cheeks came together in a colleaguely kiss.

"What can I say," he began in his trademark relaxed and somehow amused manner, or so it seemed to those who knew him, which, in effect, included the whole town. "I'm well chuffed about the award. It's beginning to be a bit embarrassing, really – three years in a row... There's something suspicious about it. (Laughter in the auditorium). Some say that an author's greatest achievements hardly ever win recognition in his lifetime and that awards tend go to approachable work that most people can understand. (Two or three lonely chuckles could be heard; one never knew what David was going to come up with next.) But you know all that anyway. I might add that I found a publisher at the first attempt which, they say, means that something must be wrong either with the book or with the publisher. Allegedly, you're not a great writer if you don't get at least five rejections. (Relaxed laughter in the auditorium.) My conscience is, however, clear: the award does not involve any cash, and, should the jury change its mind..." He bowed and stepped away from the microphone, to applause.

Journalistic circles knew that Antolić always dared speak his mind: the general consent placed him somewhere between an arbiter and an *enfant terrible*. His column touched on totally unrelated topics, ranging from Nobel Prize to abortion rights. Ten years of exercising a prominent public voice and winning distinguished awards gave him the power to initiate trends and the reputation of being unbribable made him a rarity. The award for his book of essays *Push Harder,* published by the Croatian Association of Journalists, merely represented the latest confirmation of his status.

Jelena had been trying to persuade David to put together a selection of his writings on theatre, film and literature and publish them as a book for a long time. "Every single one of your texts is an essay," she'd say, "while so many idiots publish books!"

He wouldn't hear of it out of sheer laziness, until Buba, his ex-wife, joined Jelena's campaign. "It'll make the kids happy," she said, "that their daddy has a book." Thus, once he had consented, everyone pitched in: Jelena went through literary reviews, and Buba and the children – Matko and Hana – through all the other texts. They delved through archives, cut, pasted, photocopied and, from time to time, got David to choose a suitable text for the book. At first he just shrugged off their efforts, believing their enthusiasm would soon wane, but they never gave up, which, after a while, made him take the whole affair more seriously. A few months into the operation, he wrote an introduction and took over the helm. The book was set and published in record time. David's colleagues praised it and even the critics could not bring themselves to criticise it.

The people surged towards him, congratulating, thrusting cameras and microphones at him. Loud questions mingled with the clicking of cameras: "Did you expect such a success? Why did you wait until now to publish a book? Are you writing something new?"

David answered the questions smiling, gesticulating and charmingly pushing his hair away from his forehead. From time to time, he would cast an imploring look towards the small group of his friends waiting for him at the far end of the table by the door, as if asking to be rescued. "Someone has worked out that you reviewed more books written by women than by men, and that you covered more typical women's topics. Why is that? Do you find the feminine way of thinking closer to your own?" a reporter asked. David laughed and pointed at his company of friends. "There, look – my best friends are women. That's why I know everything about women, and women will always be central to my work... and not just work."

The group David was indicating consisted of Jelena, her husband Bruno and Ana, their mutual friend. Jelena watched David with a broad smile, as did Bruno. Only Ana's smile was a restrained, close-lipped one. Although she was no less fond of David than Jelena, Ana was more agitated than happy; she was envious and ashamed of being so. She, too, wrote. Not only did she write, but she would have considered herself a *writer* were she successful in making a living from her writing. Since she wasn't, she considered herself a failed writer, just as she believed herself to be a failure at many other things.

"You're being silly," Jelena would say. "You're forgetting that you live in Croatia. If making a living from writing were the criteria, Croatia would have the total of one single professional writer: Ariana Čulina."

Ana could imagine herself in David's place, there at the flower-bedecked table, but could not rejoice at his success.

The media beast sated at last, David waved to his friends and pointed at the other door, bringing an imaginary glass to his lips and tipping it, which meant "I'm off through the other door; meet you at the bar."

"Man, that was intense," Jelena said, embracing David and kissing both his cheeks.

David laughed, showing a row of even teeth.

"You've got star potential." Jelena patted his shoulder.

Unobtrusive and distant as ever, Ana gave him a hand with her usual reserve. David nonchalantly took her whole arm, flung it over his shoulders and pulled the young woman into his embrace, laughing heartily. "Go on, relax a bit! You look like a victim of child abuse, nursing terrible traumas. I assure you that Earth won't leave its orbit if you smile."

Ana frowned briefly, shook her head and then, as if roused from a dream, smiled absently and brushed David's cheek with a clumsy kiss. "I congratulate you with all my heart," she said.

David drew Jelena and Ana close, one to each side, and embraced them, one arm each. "Bruno, let's get out of here, what do you say? Let's find somewhere normal and have a drink."

Taciturn as ever, Bruno was hard to fathom. He could have been lost in thought or merely uninvolved. When they first met, Jelena was mesmerised by his voice, which was bizarre when one considered how seldom he said anything. Be that as it may, his voice had captivated her like siren song. "No one has a voice like yours," she'd rave, "except Farkaš, the TV presenter... only his is marred by a lisp, and yours is simply perfect." Perhaps that was the reason behind Bruno's silences; he didn't want to dissipate his magic and attract what he did not solicit, Jelena thought at the time. However, Bruno, the man with the golden voice, was the only one in their circle who had nothing to do with language, speech, writing or art of any kind. He was programmer with HT, the Croatian Television, and occasionally undertook large projects for other clients. "With the two of us by your side, you ask the only other man present if he'd like to go for a drink. What do you take us for, your *go-go* girls?" Ana said, trying to be funny, but since she didn't know how to, and never looked relaxed, she sounded like a strict teacher telling him off.

David shook his head several times. "Ana, Ana, you'll never get married, girl", he said, pinching her cheek.

"I have to get up early tomorrow, so I'll give it a miss," Bruno said, "but I'm leaving you Jelena and the car so as not to spoil your evening."

"We could go to *Movie Pub*, then, what do you think?" said David.

"Or simply home," Jelena replied. "I'm tired. This has gone on longer than I expected. That's what you get when you're charismatic."

"And I have a headache," said Ana.

"We're celebrating with a dinner next week anyway, remember?" said Jelena.

"All right, we're going home," David conceded.

At the Club door, they almost bumped into a markedly handsome man, the like of whom was under normal circumstances seldom to be found among journalists unless one counted David in. With a woman's lightning speed, Jelena noticed that the man's eyes smiled like those of Jeff Bridges, were warm like Bill Pullman's, moist like Tom Hanks' and dark blue like Nicholas Cage's. Did he really look into her eyes long enough for her to see all those details, or did she imagine it? Meanwhile, the man greeted David warmly. "Well done!" he said, squeezing David's hand.

"Hiya," David replied cheerfully. "At last! A man of law in the Association! I haven't seen you for ages." He introduced the handsome newcomer to Jelena, Ana and Bruno. "This is Pero Kovačić, a police Inspector, would you believe it." He turned to Pero again. "I hope you're here to pick up a girl and not a corpse."

Pero laughed, revealing a row of white teeth. "Actually, I was hoping to come to your presentation but didn't make it. My congratulations!"

"This, folks, is the best-read policeman you're ever likely to meet" David said. "He was our colleague at the Uni, but then realised that he preferred his *Crime and Punishment* first hand and went on to study criminology..." A police Inspector, Jelena thought, surprised; I'd never have guessed. Not only are his eyes beautiful, his *hardware* is perfect, too. Why did I think of *hardware*; because it's ambiguous? Or because it's a term used by Bruno, so I'm taking his sceptre away, so to speak? And why *sceptre*? Would Freud say it was because of its phallic shape? Would the word *hardware* bear the same connotations of sex and perversity if the man in question was a skinny, rickety miserable almost-man with his Adam's apple protruding over the edge of a greasy turtleneck, a specimen such as frequent this Club? My God, Jelena, stop; what is wrong with you, she checked herself. The higher tier of her consciousness admonished the lower one: don't be silly, be sensible! She smiled as someone who had woken up with a scream having had seen a horrifying vision in a dream, hoping she hadn't been staring too long and too obviously. She glanced at the handsome Inspector: his eyes gave nothing away. She looked at Bruno next: he seemed to be anxious to leave and had not noticed anything. Ana appeared indifferent. Only David gave her a quick warning look. "My lovelies," he said to both women but seemed to be leaning more towards Jelena, "I need to warn you that Pero is the toughest law enforcer for ladies."

Everyone laughed; Jelena was the last to do so, absentmindedly and in a strained manner. Her mind was like a crowded tram, with someone from the front of the carriage calling out, "Hallo, come up here, there's an empty seat available." The seat had been vacated by Bruno who had got off at who knows which earlier stop, and was now being offered to someone called Pero, who had just boarded the tram.

"Leaving already? Shame," said Pero.

Did he look at me again just now, Jelena wondered. Of course it's a shame we're leaving. She automatically fluffed up her fringe a bit with her hand and raised her chin. But he *really* is a dish! Maybe that's why my imagination has gone into hyperdrive? As they took their leave, her hand was hot and pulsing inside his like a live sparrow. His hand was warm and enveloping.

Her inner monologue flowed on like a torrent carrying everything off in its way. What was the name of that illness, when thoughts kept on coming without any control? Logorrhoea of the mind? Maybe it didn't have a name because it was silent, and people didn't want anyone to know. Outside the main entrance, Ana, David, Jelena and Bruno went their separate ways. Jelena and Bruno made for the car park in Palmotić Street. On the stretch between the National Theatre and Nikolić Street, they were accosted by three different beggars, all three of them young and reasonably good looking girls, spaced along the road with approximately ten metres between each two. Each of the three demanded one kuna to buy a sandwich. "This is a new phenomenon," Jelena told Bruno.

"Eh? What's that?" As usual, he hadn't noticed anything.

Jelena ignored the first beggar, and said to the second: "I'm not giving you money. I'll buy you a sandwich instead."

"Okay," said the girl, and Jelena took her to *Nice n' Fresh*, ignoring Bruno. Muttering his disapproval, he followed.

"Choose what you like!" She sounded harsh and arrogant. The girl chose a slice of pizza. While ordering and paying, Jelena watched the girl's comely face reflected in the mirror behind the counter: her lips were smiling, but her eyes had a sly and peeved look. When at the end of Masaryk Street the third beggar girl came up to her, Jelena repeated her offer: "I can buy you a sandwich over there in the bakery." Bruno said, "Oh come on, please...", and the girl replied, "Auntie, I don't fancy such a long walk."

When they'd put some distance between themselves and the girl, Bruno said, "What is the matter with you tonight?"

"Why? Isn't that a cool way to deal with beggars?"

"No, since you're asking. Imagine if everyone gave them sandwiches – what would they do with all that food?"

"Yeah, but a mobile phone engineer, a Patriotic War veteran, who didn't want to register as PTSD[4] victim but had chosen to open a small business instead, although he would have been given benefits straight away, considering he'd gone to the front at the age of 24 and watched his mates drop around him like flies – and you want to see how he reacts when you tell him that the charger you bought in his shop two weeks ago had already gone wrong: he becomes absolutely livid, which means he probably does have PTSD..." Jelena noticed she'd gone off track. "Never mind all that now, the point I'm making is that this bloke has been through hell and back. He used to hang out with Gypsies, and he says that if you ask a Gypsy for one kuna, or twenty, or fifty, he'll never give you the actual money, but will want to know what you need it for, and will then buy you the most expensive cigarettes if that is what you need, or a foot-long sandwich, or whatever you care to ask for, but the money – that he will not give. Gypsies are smarter than us..."

Jelena had bad conscience because of the impression Pero Kovačić had made on her. Since she had got together with Bruno, she had never fancied another man. That was why she was talking more – but not much more – than usual.

Seven – Friday, 30th September
Going home at last, Jelena sighed. She darted a quick surreptitious glance at her husband's already somewhat softened profile (like in that commercial where the egg got *softened*; what on earth made her think of that crap, she

---

[4] Post-traumatic stress disorder

wondered). The profile of a well preserved forty-something. *Hm, interesting* – her thought meandered off again – softened – mellowed; mellowed – yellowed; yellowed – wed; wed – *dead...* Marital transpositions and transformations. If I was the editor of the Puzzles & Pastimes page, I'd propose the following task: develop a train of synonyms starting with *softened* to describe the feelings of a husband towards his wife after fourteen years of marriage.

He can sense I'm watching him, only pretends not to so that he doesn't have to react, she thought gloomily. Softly dead or deathly soft – the syllables had lost their meaning and become meaningless sounds — he still looks great, she thought; better than me, in any case. She looked through the car window. The traffic on the bridge to New Zagreb on the other side of Sava River was light. Midnight. Tomorrow is Saturday, she thought; at least I'll catch up on my sleep. The weekend.

The weekend. For the last six or seven years, the weekend had stopped being something to look forward to. Instead, she welcomed Mondays. "It's actually quite normal," David told her. "They say that after seven years all the cells in our body get replaced, which is why the seventh year is the critical one in every marriage. In the seventh year, the new cells probably wonder, 'Ugh, what am I doing next to this strange creature? I'd better get out of here as fast as I can!' No one can predict how the new cells will react to each other. In theory, a new she and a new he could like each other as much as their first editions used to. But I've yet to see it confirmed in practice."

Jelena smiled, remembering David's childish delight in expounding his theory for her but also for his own benefit. Bruno looked at her.

"What," he said.

"Nothing", said Jelena, trying to sound neutral. Her bodily cells do not know Bruno's any more. And the second seven-year cycle is nearing its end; that probably counts as well. Still, the next cell match might work again, who's to tell? What could be the probability that it would? A gazillion gazillions to one? And what is it with number seven? What do the numerologists say?

And the Kabbala? It pisses me off sometimes, that I can be so ignorant. The number seven is important in psychology: allegedly, non-verbal signals get the message across seven times faster than words. That's why lies run on short legs[5]. And that's why seven seconds is time enough to judge a person. Everything that comes afterwards merely confirms the first impression.

Two years earlier Jelena persuaded Ana to join her in having a go at becoming a financial advisor which started by experts advising candidates on how to get the most out of their own money: where to invest, how to claw money back from the state instead of handing it over to it, and so on. The introductory lecture was given by the Managing Director of the franchisor. At the end of the lecture, he said to the candidates: "You've already made your opinion about me. I don't really want to know whether you like me or not; all I need you to tell me is how long it took you to assess me?" "Ninety minutes," said a young lad. "Half an hour," a young woman said. "Well," grinned the MD, spreading his arms with professional theatricality, "let me tell you that you're lying, the lot of you. You needed exactly seven seconds; no more, no less. Seven seconds is enough for you to form an opinion about me. Not rationally, of course. Are you familiar with the theory about seven parts, or the theory about icebergs? Only one seventh of any iceberg can be seen above water." Would that not by any chance be one eighth, Jelena had wanted to ask, but then thought the man probably knew his stuff. "The theory about seven parts relates to man, who is built on seven to one ratio. The head, for example, represents one seventh of the bodily length of a human being." The MD drew the side of his palm across his neck as if slitting his own throat.

Jelena's thoughts wandered as they usually did just before falling asleep: 7 days, 7 mountains and 7 seas, 7 wonders of the world, 7 samurai, the magnificent 7, 7 brides for 7 brothers, that scary movie *Seven*... Seven deadly sins. How did they go

---

[5] Croatian proverb, meaning that lying will not get you very far

again, the deadly sins? Pride... greed... lust... envy... gluttony... wrath... sloth. Cruelty is not on the list, though. Cruelty is the foremost human characteristic, the most important one and the least discussed. Except when it erupts and surges like an uncontrollable wave gushing forth over the edge of a dam. Shed' once read about a man who'd tied a puppy to his car and dragged it around the roads of New Zagreb. The people stopped him only when the puppy was all but unconscious and bleeding out of many wounds. He'd been punishing the puppy, the man explained, as a revenge for bursting into his garden and scaring his kids. Poor kids, with such a father. Cruelty, then, is quite self-evident. She could however never understand why wrath should be on the list. Was it really such a sin? And what was the meaning of wrath, exactly? Rage, or ordinary anger? And what of jealousy? Was jealousy not a mortal sin? Maybe it went under 'envy'. But it cannot be one and the same thing: envy is when you covet the possessions of another, and jealousy... when you don't want others to acquire what is yours.

"Sleepy?" she heard Bruno say.

"As if! When am I ever sleepy?" she said cantankerously. "You're the Sleeping Beauty, not I." She envied Bruno's ability to fall asleep in the midst of a most blistering row. That would always remind her of the moment in *The Sleeping Beauty* – the most fascinating moment in the story – when the Princess pricks her finger on the spindle and everyone suddenly freezes: the cook, knife in raised hand, just as he is about to slaughter a chicken; the housewife about to swat a misbehaving servant with a wooden spoon; the Queen with her hand in the air, holding a comb. "Of course, that must be it," she went on, almost cheerfully. "Perhaps you're actually asleep. You have been cursed with eternal sleep by the Wicked Fairy – myself – and now you're waiting for a princess to wake you up." Bruno completely failed to demonstrate that he had heard what she'd said.

She felt weepy. The PMS, she thought, or the depression of a lonely person on the eve of a warm and sunny weekend.

Someone (Woody Allen?) had correctly remarked that holidays were sad because they only made happy those who were already so, while adding to the unhappiness of the unhappy ones, as they were expected to be happy on a holiday... or words to that effect. He had put it much more elegantly... Now I know why they say that thoughts drift, she thought sluggishly. Like a ship with no captain and no crew. The car turned towards Utrine.

The Horn of Plenty

"People are either protagonists or spectators," Jelena said to David.

"Really?" David raised his eyebrows with affectionate but ironic curiosity. Jelena was always coming up with fresh theories about human nature.

"Yes, really. You, for example, are a typical protagonist."

"Yeah?"

"Yeah. Protagonists are always at the centre of events, all eyes are on them as if on the lead actor on the stage; they're in the spotlight literally and metaphorically. They get things moving."

David laughed. He looked more like a Hollywood star than a columnist. His face was handsome, neither cute nor of the type they called "too beautiful for a man", but rather good-looking in a typically masculine way: with a firm jaw-line sporting a three-day-old stubble, and a straight, symmetrical nose. He wore Rip Kirby-style black horn-rimmed glasses, not the tiny narrow metal-framed ones that were currently in fashion. His forget-me-not blue shirt brought out the colour of his eyes. He had no tie on and wore one only if he absolutely had to, and the same went for suits. He preferred black or brown velvet or corduroy jackets, avoiding those with elbow patches so beloved by intellectuals. His whole appearance exuded natural calm, ease and self-confidence which showed in his gestures, expressions and the way he ran his fingers through his hair. He was very charming.

Jelena watched him with a smile. The sight of his shapely figure always cheered her up. They had known each other for almost twenty years. They met when Jelena was in her first year of Art History and Comparative Literature and David was the most attractive fourth-year student of Sociology and Comparative Literature. Confused as she was and awed by the very fact of being a student at the Faculty of Philosophy, she was chuffed to be noticed by the popular male colleague who was not only permanently surrounded by gaggles of prettiest girls, but had also been offered the Assistant Lecturer position with the Department of Sociology: in a word, handsome *and* clever. For some obscure reason, however, their mutual chemistry did not develop towards love. David had once, in jest, said that, at the sight of Jelena, a long-dead Mediterranean ancestor of his whispered inside his head, "Leave that one alone, she's a respectable girl." On her side, Jelena had never felt desire for David; she might as well have desired to live on the surface of the Sun. Thus David became Jelena's best friend, closer than any of her girlfriends. He differed from most men insofar as, secure in his unchallengeable manliness, he dared to be tender and sweet. He enjoyed female company and took part in women's conversations, learning from women themselves how best to please them. He addressed all his female friends as "Jozo[6]". Even though it would have sounded like mockery in anyone else's mouth, they liked it because they felt good, cherished and cosseted in the intimate company of this attractive man. For better or for worse, he gave himself and his attention fully to any lover, even if their relationship did not and was not meant to continue beyond one night. From time to time, his passion would erupt and he'd enter a phase he'd dubbed *Cosmic Eroticism*; at such times, he was capable of abandoning all his other preoccupations in order to be with the girl who had captivated him.

"Cosmic Eroticism; yeah, right," Jelena teased him good-naturedly. "Each womaniser has his own theory."

Quite simply, rules were for others, but not for David. Had he respected them, he would have been like a giant accepting

---

[6] Joe

the chains that bound him when it would take but a simple stretch of his mighty body to shatter them to pieces.

"You can see how it all fits together," Jelena went on with her theory of protagonists and spectators. "For protagonists to exist, there must be an audience of spectators."

David laughed. "Must there?"

"You and I, for example. You're one of the most attractive men in Zagreb's cultural circles. If one were to make a chart of desirability, with marks for looks, intelligence, honesty – not that anyone cares for *that* particular virtue – education, talent, sex-appeal, humanity – you'd achieve top score in all those. The horn of plenty. Not only do you have everything, you bestow bounty on everything you touch. That's what a protagonist is: the one breathing life into things, like Pygmalion."

"I'm perfect only in the eyes of a favourably inclined beholder," David laughed again. "I have my black holes, like everyone else."

"Perhaps, but smaller ones... And do you know how you can recognise spectators? Spectators are usually single, childless people of fairly acceptable but inconspicuous appearance, in whom everyone confides while they dispense wise counsel in full awareness that it is not wise to do so. They always understand things better than the general majority, not because they're smarter but because they haven't got a life and consequently have much more time at their disposal..."

"Wait a minute, I'm single too."

"No, not single: divorced; that's not the same. What's more, it is not surprising that you're divorced; the miracle is that, being who you are, you managed to stay married for eleven years. And the name of that miracle is Buba." David shook his head. "Brrr. It's better to be protagonist than spectator."

"Yes, only people have no say in the matter; they are what they are. I'm pure spectator."

"But you've got a husband."

"Aha! That's the only difference you can spot."

David laughed. "I wanted to see if you'd fall for it."

"True, I have a husband, but my husband is... emotionally

unformed." She didn't explain further. David regarded her seriously now. "Why do all your theories come out badly for you?" Jelena didn't reply. "Is Bruno protagonist or spectator?" David asked.

"Protagonist who, choosing the line of least resistance, tied himself to a spectator, thus losing protagonist power. It will return one day, when a lady protagonist turns up and manages to wake him up without scaring him."

"Wow!" "I'll need a few minutes to process this." He went on, in a more serious tone: "You think too much. It's all a lot simpler: people are either plus or minus types…"

"What, a black-and-white split?"

"Quite simply, you look forward to meeting some, and avoid the others."

"You come out well in that division," Jelena put in.

David merely waved. "Plus people do well and positively influence others."

"And nature," Jelena added again.

"They influence everything positively because they have good intentions."

"I, too, have good intentions, but I can see myself leaning towards minus, somehow."

"Perhaps one should pardon one's minuses if they're out of character, and yours must be, since you're aware of them. Make an effort; plus and minus require the same amount of it."

The Inspector
"Please stick to the facts," said the Sergeant importantly, turning over a new sheet in his notepad. The Inspector's glance roamed the room but did not probe people's faces, as if avoiding a premature answer to his questions.

The Seminarian – Friday, 30th September
Buba and the children had not attended David's Award Ceremony because of Buba's mother Mira's memorial service the same evening, the first anniversary of her death.

Nan Mira used to live with Buba and David while they were

together, and later with Buba and the children. Then Nan died. Buba and David got divorced. Matko was now seventeen, and Hana fifteen years old.

Buba missed her mother. She missed David even more.

The mass was impersonal and uninspired. Bored, the children squirmed in their seats and had to be given warning looks like when they had been little. Buba's own attention wandered, examining insignificant details of her surroundings: the arrangement of objects on the altar, the dandruff on the shoulders of people in front of her…

The officiating priest had an assistant. "The seminarian will assist me during the communion," he explained. When the mass was over, Hana said, "I know this boy, he used to go to my primary school. I recognised him by the mole under his eye; I always used to think it looked like a tiny tear. His mum had died and I always thought he was crying for her. He used not to be all that good looking; he looks a lot better now… He's actually very good looking now. Only, why did the Reverend call him Simeon when his name is Mario… I don't get it."

"He didn't say Simeon, fathead," Matko taunted, "he said *seminarian.*"

"Simeon, siminarion, what's the difference, you stupid git?"

"You're totally dense. Like when you thought that Bin Laden put bombs in bins."

"Yeah, and? How do you know he didn't? I bet there are bombs in bins all over the place there!"

"And where is 'there'?"

"That's enough, kids," said Buba.

Matko, always keen to show he knew more than his sister, explained with feigned boredom that seminarian was not a name but a man studying to be a priest.

"Poor Mario," Hana said, "I don't understand why he decided to become a priest. How sad."

This time Matko agreed with her. "Yeah, imagine having to attend mass several times a day."

"That's not the point," Hana replied. "Obviously, the point is he's not allowed to have a woman, ever, or even think about women."

Buba joined the conversation, confirming that celibacy was indeed a major problem for young priests.

"Why does this rule exist at all?" Matko asked.

"Primarily so that church property doesn't get scattered among heirs," Buba said.

"If it's all about property, then it can't be sinful to have a mistress," Matko concluded.

"There's also the matter of loving God above all else. And no one who has children can love any god more than his own child," Buba added.

"Jesus, I'd never be able to live like that! If I knew I'd have to become a priest, I'd have a fuck three times a day every day before they priested me in," Hana exclaimed.

"Hana!" Buba cried, horrified. Matko grinned happily.

***

"The discussion we had after the mass! If the Reverend heard us..." Buba told David the whole story when he came round the following day. David laughed to tears, and Buba did, too.

"I'm sorry I couldn't be with you," he said.

"So are we, not to have been with you," said Buba. "Particularly Hana. You know how much she loves social life, just like you..." She laughed. Buba had the beautiful face typical of voluptuous, well-rounded women, dominated equally by full lips and large brown eyes. Her ad in the Lonely Hearts column, had she had placed one, would have read, "harmoniously built curvaceous brunette, of lively and cheerful character..." Since her divorce, she had gone out on several dates, but did not like any of the men she'd met enough for a serious relationship. As far as her children were concerned, they acted all tolerant and grown up, pretending to nag her to *find someone for herself*, but Buba knew that, if she did, deep in their hearts they'd see that as treason; Hana in particular.

After the divorce, Buba and the children remained in the large apartment in Laginja Street, while David took a flat a short distance away, in Tomašić Street. They spent quite a lot of time together; almost more than before. That could have been the reason why the children took it all in their stride. David enjoyed Buba's company. Divorced for five years, they still understood each other so well that there was hardly any need for words between them. Buba did not burden him with guilt. She reminded him of Inspector Banić's ex-wife in Goran Tribuson's novels: she had matured into a warm, patient woman full of understanding. She was the soothing mother rather than the exciting mistress.

Efficiency was the bane of Buba's life. She believed efficiency to be a dangerous, specifically women's illness that needed treating. Efficiency, she thought, cost her her marriage as, over the years, she became ever more adept at juggling work, children, home, speed, the desire to please, to do everything on time, to be perfect. To be *efficient*. She worked as theatre script editor and phonetician and enjoyed her job. She even met David in the theatre: he was a young critic and she a free-lancing editorial assistant. Both before and after her divorce, Buba was universally admired by friends and neighbours for her time management and her responsible attitude towards everything. In the last few years, however, she had begun to realise that her responsible attitude was, in reality, compulsion: her plans *had* to be fulfilled. The editing task she brought home to work on had to be completed, the ironing had to be done, the dishes had to be washed, she had to find the time to read at least a few pages of a book, and to have a chat with the kids... The day would be wasted if the plan wasn't realised, and for the plan to be realised, she'd often go to bed at two or three in the morning, gradually becoming more and more tired and irritable. Her character demanded that she present a calm and content face to the world; this required additional energy. She believed that her sense of responsibility was responsible for her divorce.

While she was being efficient, David was relaxed, fresh, in a good mood, full of life – full of lust for life. As she became more efficient and more dissatisfied, he became ever more relaxed and contented. They were like two cars, one of which drove at manic speed while the other one rolled along calmly and elegantly, managing somehow to arrive at the traffic lights at the same time. The difference between them grew; Buba became faster and faster while David slowed down even more and leisurely surveyed the surrounding scene. This went on until she started feeling uncomfortable being seen naked by David, and he began pretending to be asleep when she crawled into bed next to him.

Now, after the divorce, everything had become normal again: they were good friends and good parents.

"And how are you," David asked. "Are you better?"

Buba knew what he was referring to: she had recently started taking Seroxat, the new generation anti-depressant which was, the pharmacists said, completely different from the usual tricyclic and tetracyclic antidepressants. Ana had told her that she'd even read about Seroxat in an English novel; the heroine related how she couldn't shake off her depression for years, until the discovery of an antidepressant which only affected serotonin. With its help, she was well again. And there were no side effects. The blurb on the box said that it would take between ten to fourteen days for the medicine to become effective. The instructions explained that it worked by inhibiting the storing of serotonin in brain neurons, since the storing of serotonin caused depression and the obsessive-compulsive disorder... whatever that meant.

"Much better, thanks." Whenever he asked her how she was, Buba unconsciously tried to sound better than she was and to suppress the rancour which she did not acknowledge even to herself. "It's working."

"You're sure it's not addictive?"

"They say it isn't. Allegedly, it simply substitutes natural processes, just like vitamins substitute food."

"I'd rather you got off it as soon as possible just the same."

Me too, thought Buba.

Seroxat
Before she started taking Seroxat, Buba had asked Jelena for the

full low-down.

"You too," Jelena said sententiously. "If even *you* need it, it's small wonder I do."

"One can be depressed and cheerful at the same time," Buba said.

"I know," said Jelena. "Perhaps you're manic-depressive. Just kidding."

"Well, maybe I am. And maybe I'm the sort of person who eats herself from within."

"It's called introdepression," said Jelena.

"What, it actually exists as a named illness?"

"I've made it up. But it might exist, who knows? Like introspection."

"Or intro*section*," Buba made her own word up.

"All bad things are *intro*, *inter* and *entero*," Jelena said and they both laughed.

"Brrr, I feel worse now," Buba said.

"You say *brrr* like David," Jelena remarked. "You two will get back together one day, mark my words."

Buba laughed. "You're mad." But she was secretly pleased with Jelena's comment.

It took some three weeks for Buba to feel any effect from the tablets – or what she believed to be their effect. She reported her findings to Jelena: "Is it working? You tell me: I laugh more than ever, occasionally I experience moments of immense joy, and then I think that, when I die, the neighbours will say, 'Shame, she was so happy and full of life!' I cry less, I rage less, I'm more diligent, I mostly do everything myself and don't yell at the kids when they forget their chores... If I think about it, it looks like they benefit from my Seroxat more than I do."

The Inspector

"And you are – ?" the Sergeant asked haughtily. The Inspector regarded the young woman who tensely sat on the edge of her chair. Her back was straight and her face expressionless.

Ana

"A born writer", David had said of Ana. It was hardly enough to say that Ana wrote: writing was the only thing that really interested her. Unsuccessful as writer, she discussed her passion only with Jelena and David because she knew they would not laugh at her. They both thought her gifted. She had always been considered *promising*: her compositions were read at school assemblies, she was in the Journalistic Group in secondary school, and she wrote short stories. She even published some while she was at the Uni: one of them won the *Evening Gazette's* Best Short Story Award. She had studied psychology and literature. Having completed her studies in record time, she got a job at *The Herald* straight away. There she met David and Jelena and was content because she believed that journalists were the closest thing to writers. However, she failed to progress from general duties including anything and everything from culture to politics and, having realised that a journalist, unlike a writer, had to work with people and, even more importantly, had no free time left for writing, she left *The Herald* after one year. She applied for the position of editor in *The Children's Book* publishing company and stayed there for the next nine years. Her job mainly entailed trying to squeeze some money out of the Ministry for Education and the Ministry for Culture. During the Patriotic War[7], they only published school textbooks ("better than switching to arms production," the Managing Director had remarked), so the bankruptcy and the demise of *The Children's Book* at the end of 2003 came as a relief, even though her workload as editor did leave her enough time for writing. She got herself the position of Pedagogue[8] in a newly opened private secondary school. She was reluctant to submit her application ("What's got into you,"

---

[7] Croatian War of Independence, fought between 1991-1995 between Croatian Government forces and the Yugoslav People's Army, following the Croatian declaration of independence from Yugoslavia

[8] Something like Child Welfare Officer, Head of Achievement and SENCO combined

mum had said, "you haven't got first clue about children. All your education won't help you a bit there; you need to know about real life") and, when the stern Head Teacher dryly informed her that the school had selected her for the job, accepted the appointment with trepidation. But she liked children much more than adults and she told herself that all would be well.

The work was quieter – at least it appeared to be so in the beginning – and she had more free time than before. She needed the surplus time for the novel she had decided to write. If in a good mood, she attributed the fact that she could not make a living by writing to the poverty of the society in general and the anomalies typical of a plundered, corrupt state. Whenever her spirits were low, however – which was often – she blamed herself and herself only, and not just for her failure as writer. Nothing made her envious, except the success of other writers. That was the reason she did not enjoy David's Award ceremony.

The Hand

The hand wrote into the Moleskine notebook: *The headlines and the articles have been selected purely by chance.*

It slowly glided over the neat pile of papers on the left side of the desk, took a newspaper from the pile on the right, opened it and slowly turned the pages, one by one, from back to front.

THE BACK PAGE: The thick, soft, luxurious, perfumed, colourful modern toilet paper threatens the collapse of sewage systems

Threatens (us) with the collapse of sewage systems, perhaps?
CULTURE: Marcel Duchamps's *Urinal* voted the most influential work in modetn art, according to the results of a poll conducted among 500 British art experts. Picasso's *Demoiselles d'Avignon* ended up in the second place and Warhol's *Marilyn* in the third.

The hand folded the finished paper neatly in half and placed it on top of the pile on the left. On the next blank page of the notebook, it wrote down: *A coincidence: in the same day, two important pieces of cloacal information: toilet paper and urinal.*

It then took another unread paper from the right side of the desk.

The Naked She-Wolf

Ana was quickly accepted by the children. It was as if she was one of them, and just as unfinished. They seemed to share the understanding of the tortuous, painful process of human completion, the moment of breaking the hard shell from within, the shell at the other side of which, perhaps, nothing good awaited them, bar hope. "You know," she told Jelena, "I am aware that in many ways I don't exactly fit within the parameters of normality. So I did ask myself if I should be working with children at all. Then it occurred to me that it was actually a good thing, me being the way I am, because I'm able to sense a lot more than *normal* pedagogues; my range is broader, the same as with singers: the wider the range of the voice, the better the singer. What I'm saying is… whatever the trouble they're in, I'll recognise it at once because I've been through the same, from end… to end."

Jelena regarded her silently, not keen to find out what *end to end* might signify. With Ana, everything was torment.

"From ordinary trouble to… trouble with the law," Ana concluded absently.

Jelena shuddered discreetly, hanging on to her silence.

Ana was so happy during her first year in the new job that she wrote at full pelt; the novel seemed to grow all by itself. She called it *The Naked She-Wolf* and finished it in less than six months, but it took her more than a year to show her work to Jelena and David. The previous year, at the start of summer, she had handed them a copy each to read while on holiday. "No obligation," she told them. "If you get bored, stop. And do tell me if it's rubbish." To Jelena, she said, "I know it sounds stupid, but I feel as If I've finally *realised* myself."

***

In sweltering Zagreb heat, alone with her grumpy mother who had little understanding for "scribbling and bookishness", Ana anxiously awaited Jelena's and David's reaction. Meanwhile, she spotted an ad for *a Luxor ring which brings luck and success to the wearer*. The ad contained the confession of a Polish woman who, on the verge of despair, bought the ring only to find her career, her finance and her love life suddenly blossom. Ana bought the ring and wore it on her pinkie, upside down so that people wouldn't know what it was, half-believing and half-disbelieving its powers. Whichever was the case, after a few weeks things got moving. To begin with, Jelena called: "Ana, this is fantastic. I only started reading it two days ago, I couldn't find the time any sooner, but then I couldn't stop until I finished it. Man, you're phenomenal!"

"Nah," Ana said, with a kind of happy trepidation, "please don't tease. You know important this is for me."

"Seriously, it's the best thing I've read in the last ten years or so."

"Since you last read *War and Peace*, then," Ana joked lamely, her throat contracting.

"Awesome, awesome, awesome," Jelena enthused.

"But don't you find it drawn out, you know, in that bit where…"

"No, no, everything's perfect… Frankly, I didn't expect something like that… And the title is brilliant, *The Naked She-Wolf*… A title like that can mean a solid piece of pornography, a literary masterpiece, a crime story, a horror story… makes you think of *The Woman who Runs With Wolves*… It can mean anything."

"Yeah… *homo homini lupus*. To the naked she-wolf, man is wolf… She is not a she-wolf who changes her coat but not her disposition, and definitely not a wolf in sheep's clothing," Ana explained, "Like a she-wolf, she relies on her inner strength in her struggle, and not on some outer garment such as beauty, for example. A hairless – naked – she-wolf is by definition an ugly freak and the pack will reject her; that is why she must be strong and brave. Have you ever experienced the feeling of not wanting to go outside because you don't wish to exhibit your *inappropriate* body?"

Moved but also angry, Jelena said nothing.

Ana added, laughing: "The naked she-wolf definitely doesn't get told by her mum, 'do something with your hair and your face, you look a mess!'"

Jelena laughed at this too.

"Because her mum abandoned her long ago."

Jelena sighed.

"But that's not the point. The most important thing is that, even when she gets turned out of the den, the naked she-wolf still belongs to the wolf species. Some members of the pack pity her, others won't let her near, but none have need of her. The problem is, they know they have too much in common with her to be able to forget her. And what they have in common is pain, huge amounts of pain..."

"You're winding me up," said Jelena cheerfully although she could feel her skin crawl. "You must be talking about some other book. What you're saying sounds morbid, while your book is funny, full of life and above all unputdownable..."

"Funny doesn't always have to make you laugh; funny can be witty. Full of life doesn't have to mean cheerful, and Steven King's horror novels are also unputdownable. The subject is morbid because life itself is morbid... A good title, *Morbid Life...* is there enough contradiction in it for a proper oxymoron, I wonder?"

"Quite enough," said Jelena dryly.

"I mean, life is morbid but various paths of survival can be funny... at least in fiction." Ana laughed. "In any case, the naked she-wolf *does* survive."

Jelena laughed, too. "There you are, then."

But Ana had more to say. "You know what I've realised? A book doesn't have to have a theme, because life itself doesn't have one. Life is everything and contains everything, sand as well as gold. Life is like a river... I know, not very original. When the prospector comes, he scoops up a tin pan full of sand just like I scooped up a bookfull of life, and then sifts, and sifts, and sifts until he finds gold. Gold is the best thing that he can find but it is not the theme: the theme is the whole content of the pan. More often than not there isn't any gold in it at all."

"Impressive," said Jelena. "You worked it out all by yourself?"

"Of course."

"Luckily, the book is less complicated than you'd like us to believe. Be that as it may, a first novel of this magnitude, wow. You really are a born talent, David was the first to realise that."

"I haven't heard from him yet," said Ana with unease.

"He's still on the yacht with those girls from *Elle*, all fours in the air. He rang me yesterday and said he was like a pig in clover. I know what he'll tell you when he's read the book, though, and so do you."

Indeed, David phoned a few days later, just as overwhelmed as Jelena had been, and taken by surprise: he "hadn't expected to see writing of such maturity... interesting, with perfect dramatic structure and memorable characters which carried on living in one's head, a gripping story, effortless flow of action, simple, sagacious..."

"You wouldn't joke about such matters, would you?" Ana asked warily.

"Now that I've read it, I'm convinced your perpetual insecurity is pure affectation," David said in reply.

"Your brutality makes you convincing," Ana said, laughing excitedly.

***

Ana's self-confidence soared, her expectations grew and she glowed with contentment. In September she took her manuscript to *Argus*, a publishing company belonging to her former colleague from *The Chidren's Book*, not because she was hoping to get privileged treatment but because, going to him, she felt the least embarrassment. "Be objective," she told him. "I'm not looking for favours. Or rather, don't be objective, be ruthless. If it isn't any good, well, it isn't any good."

"No worries, darlin'. I don't need to tell you what you

already know: nepotism butters no parsnips. This business is my living," the enterprising Herzegovinian owner, Dujić, replied. He had a reputation of being smart at sniffing out profit or at least at avoiding losses.

It took him a month to read the manuscript. When he finally did phone back, he was brief: "Your book's all right, darlin'. We're going ahead. Come to see me; we must sort out the contract."

The editing, the paging, and the proofreading were finished by the end of November. All the while, a thought kept revolving in Ana's head: oh my God, I'm having a book published! I can't believe it!

"Oh my God, I'm having a book published! I can't believe it," she said to Jelena.

Jelena laughed. "You remind me of me in the first few weeks after I got married. I used to wake up in the middle of the night, check that Bruno was really there in bed next to me and say to myself: 'Oh my God, I've got a husband! I've got a husband!'"

She didn't quite believe the book was happening even when she received her contract (an edition of 2000 copies, large for Croatia, at 95 kuna each, of which 10% went to the author) and the advance: nine thousand kuna before tax.

The Naked She-Wolf was in the bookshops in time for Christmas. The book looked good: an outline of a woman's face, half-hidden by shadow, on the background the colour of milk chocolate, with large red letters over it: *The Naked She-Wolf*, and, above the title, *Ana Marton*.

Many of Ana's acquaintances got in touch, praising the book. Unknown readers contacted her, wanting to meet her. This encouraged her to expect positive reviews, but only a few short and unremarkable comments came up in the press. The top critics were silent. "It doesn't happen so fast with books," Jelena said. "It's not a movie which you can see in two hours and rattle off a review the same day; it takes time to read three hundred pages."

Ana blamed Dujić for failing to promote her book.

"Darlin'", he said instructively, "word of mouth makes for best promotion." What does he care, Ana thought; he must have received a grant from the Ministry for Culture anyway for publishing a novel that is not a translation of a foreign bestseller – and by a new writer at that. He's not counting on any sales, and if by some miracle they do materialise, so much the better. An edition of two thousand copies wasn't going to make him a fortune in any case. Dujić's joke, that he'd "published her and was thus a publican" struck her as being in poor taste. He did, however, seem to be right about *word of mouth*: a few dozen copies circulated among Ana's friends, friends of friends, their acquaintances and colleagues. They recommended it to one another, saying it was new, fresh, original, unexpected and witty, but most of them did not *buy* any books because they could not afford them. As far as David was concerned, Ana had strictly forbidden him to review her book.

"You're nuts," Jelena told her. "If he were to write a review, everyone would follow suit. You'd be a hit in three days flat."

"That's why I don't want him to do it," Ana replied.

"You know he wouldn't praise the book if he didn't think it merited his praise. He'd merely help your novel get the exposure it actually deserves."

But Ana refused grumpily. "I know, but then I'd never know if the book was really that good, or if people just thought it was because David had said so. And what if we're found out to be friends, and there he is, praising my work!"

"Everyone knows that David is incorruptible."

"That may well be so, but it is still easier to drag others down than be raised by someone!"

The Naked She-Wolf was given a cold shoulder across the board by juries. It did not make the selection for any of the literary prizes. It got no public recognition whatsoever.

***

Ana knew why the general public did not take any notice of her novel. Why would it? Who was that nondescript, mousy young woman anyway? As soon as the book had come out, Ana's mum said, "Buy yourself a nice little suit, girl, and get your hair done. The way you are now, people will think you haven't got a clue…"

Mum is always right, Ana thought. She remembered reading a description of a portrait of Chekhov (in a story by V. Tokareva, the only one capable of writing such a thing): *there he was, in that picture, a lonely, hunched man; his fame and his talent had been left behind, in some other place* – or words to that effect, only much better put. Who was Ana Marton? A hunched, stooping creature with no literary reputation. Where had she suddenly appeared from? What was she like? Which circles did she belong to? Was she important? Beautiful? Was she loved? By whom?

"Why do you waste your time scribbling?" her mum said. "Who reads books these days?"

"I haven't read such a good book for ages," David said. "And whoever reads it will say the same. The majority of people, however, don't read books that haven't been recommended by critics. And most critics are, essentially, bureaucrats. If you bring them a stamped certificate that you're a writer – well, then they'll acknowledge you in their column. If your work is entertaining, they won't know how to deal with it. If it's boring, they'll be on safer ground: a boring book can't be commercial, and if has been published in spite of being non-commercial, it follows that it must be of artistic value; in that case, one must treat it seriously and with respect. The critics appreciate books which are like neatly trimmed poodles or like muddy, scruffy, disobedient strays. Your book, on the other hand, is… like a Rhodesian ridgeback. Have you girls ever seen one of those?"

Jelena and Ana shook their heads in unison.

"There's only a few of them in Croatia, that's why people don't know about them. A ridgeback is lean, graceful, strong, handsome, powerful and noble… Never mind. Your book, too, is a rarity, so people don't understand it. Given the time, they will."

"Van Gogh only sold one painting in his entire life," said

Jelena.

"Yeah, posthumous fame." Ana sounded bitter, how else.

Her book seemed artless, almost folksy in its simplicity, non-conceptual and non-trendy; even those who did notice it felt that it would not profit them to say so. It reminded Jelena of Jagoda Truhelka's books which she enjoyed even as an adult. At the time of *The Naked She-Wolf*'s publication, women's literature was no longer in vogue and kitchen sink realism had been replaced by genre, only to make an unexpected comeback in books written by men: imitating successful women writers, men had begun writing in the "feminine" way, "directly from life", in a simple and entertaining style, about love and everyday life. And they did very well, particularly those belonging to well-known cliques. The publishing world was in upheaval; newspapers got onto the game and more than thirty novels came out that year. The literary locomotive chugged merrily ahead, pulling a train loaded with brightly wrapped parcels, but Ana alone had no place on any of its carriages. She was invisible, inaudible, unread.

"How absurd," Jelena said. "Your book will have its own fan club some day, like *Lord of the Rings*, but no one knows about it because you can't be found in literary reviews."

Early in the New Year, the book vanished from shop-windows. In bookshops, it got moved from top shelves to the bottom ones, and the sales dried up. The only good news came from libraries: several of them reported a waiting list for *The Naked She-Wolf*. "There you go then, what did I tell you!" Jelena said.

Once, in Pula for a seminar, Ana dared enter the largest bookshop in town and ask for *The Naked She-Wolf*, knowing she wouldn't be recognised. The shop assistant raised her eyebrows hesitantly and then searched the *Domestic Fiction* section of the shop. "No, we haven't got it," she said.

They haven't got *it*, Ana thought. As if *it* was a *critter* from outer space. "You haven't got *it*?" she echoed. The assistant shrugged indifferently, not noticing Ana's caustic tone.

Ana's well-trained eye spotted the red-and-chocolate spine

at the bottom shelf of *Domestic Fiction*. "There it is," she said.

The shop assistant turned lazily in the direction of her finger. "Oh yeah, we do have it. Would you like a bag?"

"Do I get author's discount?"

"Sorry?" the assistant said, puzzled. "Only the author can have author's discount."

"I know. I *am* the author."

The assistant took her time getting her head round this, then said, "You're the author?"

"Yes."

"Aha." Unsure of what to do, the assistant was playing for time. "Well, then…" she shrugged, "then you'll have to show me your ID card."

There you go, that's the sort of crap writer I am, Ana thought. Instead of being pleased to have the author in person on the premises, she's checking my ID.

The shop assistant sensed she'd overdone it and added, "It's because of the Accounts, y' know, so that I can justify the discount."

When Ana moaned to Jelena about the incident, she said, "You're not a crap writer. It's the way we treat books and writers here that is crap, because we only respect money and everyone knows that writers are poor."

Unwilling to admit she was still hoping that someone from the *official circles* would finally deign to comment, Ana followed all book reviews. Only one prominent critic, writing for the weekly magazine *Global*, did reflect on *The Naked She-Wolf. (…) all in all, Ana Marton would do better to stick to psychology which is, according to the back cover blurb, her original profession. Her style is nothing to write home about.* Ana was hurt, but one particular sentence made her realise that the distinguished critic had not read the whole book: *The author seems incapable of separating her personal reality from the subject matter of her work, which, put another way, means that she has not yet reached the level of literature in its proper sense.* Ana had herself made a similar statement in the book, but the critic had evidently not read it.

"Like all high output critics, he'd obviously read the beginning and the end, and rifled *diagonally* through the middle." David laughed and waved a hand. "Take no notice; he, too, needs to make a living."

For the same reason she followed the reviews, Ana watched the flagship culture programme on TV, the one which focused on publishing and featured a weekly top-ten list of bestsellers. She read or at least tried to read all the books from the fiction top-ten. One Friday, *A Woman is a Sea-Shell*, a novel by Maja Kelčec, an unknown author, came up as the number one. The very next day Ana did the round of bookshops in the city centre – the ones mentioned in the closing credits of the programme as the source of the sales data. "Have you got the novel *A Woman is a Sea-Shell* by Maja Kelčec?" she inquired in each one and was delighted to discover that none of them either stocked the book or had even heard about the book or its author. Jelena and David were right, then: a book's fame had nothing to do with its quality. My absence from the public eye, she thought, doesn't mean that my book is rubbish. The sleaze and the corruption she had discovered in the programme mattered to her only insofar as they explained the lack of exposure her book had received. Later, she heard that publishers sniggered at top-lists because the information they provided was meaningless.

"They snigger, yeah," said David, "but they're very pleased if they make it onto the list. Television is power. That's why we have so many stupid books no one reads. The Ministry would be much better off giving the grants to the author, not the publisher, and in advance, so that the poor sod can write without worry."

The final blow for Ana was the news that her book had got into the hands of a mortally ill woman, her mother's friend. She started reading and liked the book very much, but then she suddenly went downhill to the point when she could no longer read. She said she was so close to death that she hated everything that would remain alive once she died. She did, soon, and the book remained unfinished. Ana was shaken to the core.

"I don't understand you," Jelena said. "It makes no sense. People simply live shorter than books. How many people died reading the Bible? I can't see why you should get so upset."

"I don't know," Ana said, "but it's not good news."

The Hand
October

CULTURAL EVENTS: Why do 250,000 Croats own only the first part of Don Quijote? Because *The Morning Chronicle* gave away 300,000 copies of the first part for free, and charged money for the second part, which came out a few days later. Only 50,000 copies of the second part were sold.

THE BLACK CHRONICLE: Let us remind ourselves that on 31st May at 8 PM, Index.hr announced: *We have a porn movie with Severina*. In the next few days, from webpage to webpage, Severina's film spread over the entire country. Severina demanded that an injunction be issued banning Index from showing the controversial material, as it was her intellectual property and her creation...

The hand picked up the pencil and the *Moleskine* and swiftly wrote down:

Severina is sexy. Severina is also smart, yet she had to resort to such a stupid argument: intellectual property.

The hand put the pencil down, closed the Diary and fastened it with the signature Moleskine elastic band. Then it replaced the Diary into the desk drawer.

Editorial Staff Meeting – Monday, 3rd October

On Monday it rained. Damp, cold and greyness seeped in through the window. By the time David arrived, Jelena had already read the papers and had surfed the internet. Before he sat down, David collected his copy of the paper from Dora's desk, opening the Cultural Affairs section first. "Just look at this... the Annual Award for Journalism ceremony... nnn... to David Antolić, the author of *Push Harder*... blah-de-dah... this year, for the first time, the Award comes with a prize, which is of importance in the current sorry state of our culture, and particularly from the point of view of our intellectuals who vegetate at the bottom rung of the social ladder. The value of the prize is *fif-ty thou-sand ku-na!*"

Jelena looked up from the paper she was reading. "Really? Awesome!" Then she saw the impish glitter in David's eye and his grimace. "It's gone to your head at last, eh?" she said with a touch of spite. "Everyone loves you and your book so much I'm starting to feel resentful –"

"What do you think, did Oscar Wilde collect his own quotes, or did others do it for him?" Davis asked, laughing. "I mean, if I'm to do it all myself, I ought to start now…"

Just before ten, Dora strolled in regally, swaying her hips proudly like a pregnant elephant, panting and blowing with self-importance rather than from exertion. Dipsy was usually the last one to arrive, "straight from the night shift", as he used to say. This morning, he was early and very excited about the list of known Croatian homosexuals that had turned up on the internet. He was all but slavering as he anticipated the pleasure of examining it closely. Full of inspiration, he said directly as he came in; "If all Croats are paying VAT, what do all Croatian homosexuals have to pay?" Met with indifferent silence, he triumphantly answered his own question: "AAT, of course: Anal Activity Tax. Good, eh? Topical, no?" Then he remembered David's award: "And how is our award-winning colleague? The ceremony was well attended, I hear, the hall was stuffed to the sphincter – full marks!"

Monday would have been a washout had Nina not arrived in Dipsy's wake. Ivana came in straight after her, but hardly anyone noticed. Nina entered to the sound of clicking heels and sweetly wished "good morning to everyone". All the faces lit up at once and the whole Editorial Office got brighter, as if all of a sudden the day had turned sunny and the air had been filled with morning freshness. Nina traversed the path between the door and her desk with an almost levitating grace. Dipsy and David watched this poetry in motion with unblinking rapt attention. Homosexuals fled from Dipsy's mind; if he thought of them at all, it was to marvel at their stupidity: how could they not fancy a vision like this? Lovely as sin. Nina seemed unaware of the many eyes that followed her. Moving naturally, without any coquetry, she sat down, took some papers and the notepad from her bag and arranged them on her desk, ready for work. She reached for a pen, wrote something into her planner and only then placed her hands on the desk and looked around. The whole sequence took some ten seconds if that, and yet it appeared to be a meaningful and thrilling whole, like a film. The moment she glanced around, everyone looked away as if on cue; even Jelena, a woman. Nina smiled, continuing not to notice the attention she commanded (she's got to be pretending, Jelena thought, what woman would fail to notice that?), and then repositioned her telephone and other objects before her. "Staff meeting in ten?" she said to no one in particular, glancing at the clock on the wall and comparing it with her wristwatch. Everyone nodded.

"Yup," Dipsy said. "At *ten hundred zero five.*"

Nina gave him the broad smile of a happy child. Seated with her back to the window, she could see everyone clearly whilst they saw her as a shadowy silhouette. This enhanced the unreal, movie-like quality of the scene. Jelena remembered reading somewhere that whoever sat with the light behind their back dominated the room.

The meeting took place every Monday at five past ten. Punctual as clockwork, Andrej would arrive at ten on Mondays, and at eleven for the rest of the week. Muttering his usual short, dry greeting, he made straight for his office where he always spent the five minutes between his arrival and the start of the meeting. At five past ten, he re-emerged and perched on the edge of the small table wedged between his door and the door of the office as was his custom. On the wall behind his back hung a still life with a blue fish in it. Cold Fish and a dead fish – everyone wickedly enjoyed the juxtaposition. Dora brought him coffee.

The meeting was brief as usual. As usual, David was the first to announce what he was planning to cover that week; as usual,

Jelena was the next one to speak.

"Nina?" Andrej asked.

"I think we ought to do the Students' Centre," Nina said.

"Good," Andrej nodded.

"I'd start with *ITD Theatre*[9] and Zuppa[10], but I propose to interview Nataša, Martić and Vaki as well. I'll leave the actors for the end of the week."

Andrej nodded again.

"For next week, I've been planning to tackle the financial situation in *Gavella*[11] and the *HNK*[12]. For the *In Focus this Week*, I thought I'd question if that car dealership was going to move to the premises of the Students' Centre, the *ITD* and the gallery. I could speak to the Managing Director…"

"Good," said Andrej.

"Teacher's pet," said Dipsy. Only Nina laughed.

"Zuppa needs to be at the airport at noon," she said to Andrej. "He promised me an interview if there's time." She glanced at her watch. "I ought to leave now, actually." Andrej nodded. Nina collected her things from the desk and put her voice recorder, her notepad and her mobile into her bag. As she spoke to Andrej and got ready to leave, David's eyes followed her every move. Jelena thought she ought to tell him this made his eyes so very blue, blue like the deep blue sea, bright like the sea shimmering in the sun. His beautiful eyes. An eruption was imminent.

"That would be all, then," Andrej said and withdrew to his room. "Dora," he called out, without looking back, "call Matković at the Academy for me and ask him to confirm Vienna."

Dora was already on the phone. "Haloooo," she was saying

---

[9] ITD is Croatian for "etc" – etcetera, meaning "and so on". Etcetera Theatre, then.

[10] Vjeran Zuppa (Split, Croatia 1940 -), critic, poet, translator, playwright and the Artistic Director of the ITD Theatre in Zagreb

[11] A Zagreb theatre

[12] The Croatian National Theatre (Hrvatsko Narodno Kazaliste)

in her affected drawl which could string a word over two octaves if the situation demanded. "That's greeeat, thaaaank you soooo much," she sang out and put the receiver down. "Just done it," she said to Andrej's back, proud for remembering to call before being told. "It's all been confirmed. You can collect the tickets for the concert from the press centre, and the interview has been scheduled for the next morning."

Andrej half-turned, just enough to indicate he'd heard her, and waved a hand. "All right, thanks."

Dipsy rose, sat back down and scratched his hair Spikey-fashion, trying but failing to attract Nina's attention. Exiting, she told him: "No coffee for us today, then – for me, at least. But we're saying 'thou' to each other as of today." She said goodbye and left.

The Hand

30/12: THE PRESIDENTIAL CANDIDATES' DEBATE ON TV

Ćiro[13]: I consider Croatia to be already in Europe. I believe Croatia is aesthetically – I emphasise, AESTHETICALLY – handicapped."

Anto Kovačević: "Croatia would happily put itself in jail if that would get it into the EU."

Mikšić, an entrepreneur from America: President Mesić feels that he's been given the role of a potted plant. It's sad that he's fighting for yet another mandate as a potted plant."

31/12: THE BACK PAGE:

McDonald's plan to use gas for slaughtering chickens.

The Inspector

The Inspector listened to the young woman who spoke

---

[13]Miroslav "Ćiro" Blažević is a Croatian football manager. His most successful period was with the Croatian national football team, which he took to quarter-finals in the 1996 European championship and also won the third place in the 1998 FIFA World Cup (Wikipedia)

succinctly, in a clear, pleasant voice that didn't hesitate. Mechanically, he glanced at his watch. The Sergeant did the same, nodding disapprovingly, probably in an attempt to ingratiate himself with his boss.

The Planner – Monday, 3rd October

The afternoon had hardly begun when Jelena decided to write the day off as a dead loss; and since it was a dead loss, she thought she would use it to request a planner for 2005, encouraged by Dora's request that she speak to an Englishwoman on the phone instead of her.

"Listen…" As ever, Dora avoided addressing Jelena by name. "You understand a bit of English?"

"A bit," Jelena said, not daring to reply as she would have liked to, "For Pete's sake, you've heard me speak English at least a hundred times!"

"Me too, but that woman on the phone speaks very poorly; I'm worried I might get something wrong."

"Right," said Jelena, "put her through."

It turned out that the woman who spoke poor English was a Londoner whose educated voice carried no trace of the Cockney twang. Maybe I've earned my planner now, thought Jelena and launched her attack. Acquiring any item of office equipment was a feat for her, and the said planner had grown into a symbol of impotence. Each year the same pathetic little drama with the planner as subject played itself out between Jelena and Dora. The first time round, Dora didn't even know what a planner was and naturally couldn't order one. The following year she told Jelena that she, Dora, needed to know exactly what was required if she was to order it; a year later, Jelena's request had come too late even though it was made at the very beginning of December. Jelena wrote into her planner: next year, ask for the planner at the end of October / start of November.

She went round to Dora's desk. "Dora, I'd like to order the planner for 2005."

"*You'd* like to order?" Dora squinted at her. "You mean

you'd like to make the order *yourself?*" Whenever Dora dropped the 'thou' with someone younger than herself, she was about to give that person a hard, hard time.

"No, of course not," Jelena stuttered. "I mean, I'd like you to order..."

"Aha." With a business-like air, Dora glanced at her desk calendar and exclaimed, "Lordy, girl, what's the matter with you? We're only October!"

"I know, but last year you said..." Jelena was already on the edge of tears, cursing herself for not leaving the stupid planner alone. Dora regarded her triumphantly. Jelena, however, wasn't going to give up now. "Last year I asked you to order it at the start of December, and you said I was too late."

"I haven't even thought about next year's ordering, child! I don't propose to bore you with the details of my workload, but trust me, next year's planners are the least of my problems," said Dora importantly. "Here, for example: we're about to approve mobile phones for some people..."

We're about to approve, Jelena thought, *we're about to approve!* Against her will, her mouth contracted into a hard lump, like molten plastic that had hardened into an irregular shape. Stupid, what else; they've stultified me to such an extent that I can't help acting like an idiot: ordering next year's supplies in October! She's right, of course. But this time I'm not giving up! "Perhaps you wouldn't mind making a note in your... planner... (she couldn't resist the temptation to be a bit sarky) to order it when the time is right?"

"You know what, why don't you remind me in a month's time, or even better in a month and a half," said Dora in a bored voice and looked away: end of discussion, go away, you boring gadfly. "I've got to clear it with Božo."

"Božo? Božo who?"

"You really ought to learn the names of the people you're working with," said Dora. "Božo Piljek."

"I've forgotten his name is Božo," said Jelena sheepishly, and then mustered the courage to say, "You have to clear my planner with Piljek?"

As if he'd been listening behind the door, Piljek put his head through it. "Clear what? What's the problem?"

"There isn't a problem," Dora retorted, waving a hand as if swatting a fly.

"It seems that I'm the only one needing a planner in this office," Jelena said, unable to contain herself, "but it looks like *The Herald's* budget might not be able to stretch that far."

"It's not a problem," said Piljek quietly and slowly as was his usual manner, "but I, for example, keep all that in my laptop." He lifted his chin self-importantly.

Jelena felt like giggling aloud. Like she needed *Piljek* to explain computers to *her!* But she clenched her jaws tightly together: why give the enemy the satisfaction? "You mean, you've got your planner in the laptop?" She tried not to sound spiteful.

Pleased to be given a chance to lecture, Piljek nodded gravely. "Here, I can show you..."

Jelena went over to his desk and bent over the open laptop.

"You need to go to *mail...*" Piljek said importantly and opened *Outlook Express.*

"You mean, *Outlook?*"

"Yeah, that one," Piljek said instructively, "and there you've got... wait a minute... yes, yes, there it is... it's quite simple, only you need to know how to use the thing... you type in the date and the time of your meeting here... look, I'll write in '12.00'... and then it reminds you, whatever you might be doing at the time..."

"Yes, but isn't it simpler to have a tiny diary with the calendar, so you can see at once... "

"Don't know, maybe; I find this to be the best way," said Piljek as if he'd invented ICT.

"And if someone phones you at home, say, and wants to know if you can meet up the next day at noon, don't you find it easier to open a tiny notebook than switch the laptop on?"

"So, you're saying you'd actually find a notebook more convenient?" Piljek nodded as if seriously considering the problem.

"Oh, never mind," Jelena said. "I'll buy myself a planner, although I've vowed not to spend any more of my own money on *The Herald*."

"Listen, Božo," Dora called out, "that guy Ševenda wanted to speak to you again. He wants to know when he can expect his fee."

"That correspondent from Karlovac?"

"Yeah, the one. He wanted your mobile number but I refused to give it to him, so he asked for your e-mail address, but I couldn't remember if your name on it was Božo or Božidar, so he'll be ringing you again tomorrow."

"Božidar, *bozidar dot piljek,*" he said triumphantly, proud to have an e-mail address. Jelena was flooded by a feeling of impotence and revulsion. You stupid arsehole, she shouted silently, you ignorant imbecile! She always walked away defeated from an encounter with Dora and even Piljek and, however small and unimportant those miniature fiascos might have appeared to be, she felt that those tiny (tiny?) frustrations remained forever in her system like stinking gobs of slime circulating through her organism, unmetabolisable, indigestible and undefecatable.

"How can you let those primates upset you, silly," David said later.

"How? Next to them I'm dumb and confused; they always manage to make it appear as if I don't know what I want; I look sheepish and stupid and I never know how to hold my ground. Where does their strength come from?"

"From their limitations. They never doubt themselves."

"Even if I'd never met her before," Jelena went on, "that one sentence she said – *we're about to approve mobile phones for some people* – would tell me all I needed to know about her. *We'll* approve! The vanity! And Piljek, now there's a specimen. Once upon a time, Vanity and Ambition got married…"

From the moment she met her, Jelena could sense Dora's hostility towards her. Little by little, she understood its cause: until Jelena's arrival, Dora had been the only woman in the Editorial Office. In spite of her poor education and lack of sophistication, she had been ruling all the male subjects in her own little kingdom since forever. The queen bee. Jelena could clearly sense that female superiority. Next to her, she felt puny and anaemic, like a vegetarian vegetable broth next to a hearty beef stew full of chunks of red meat. Still, weak or not, she was another female in the den and Dora sensed her as an enemy.

"You exaggerate," David said when she described her relationship with Dora in those terms.

"I don't. Look at Piljek, his relationship with Dora is almost sensuous… He told us many times how 'all the lads used to be in love with Dora and put fresh flowers on her desk every day'. She's still his ideal of beauty, in spite of being over fifty and weighing ninety kilos at the very least… even Fish looks more human when he talks to her. That whole lot seem to me like a weird sect keeping a secret from us…"

"What could they be hiding? Only the secret of their youth we didn't witness. We first met them in their middle age, and they remember themselves as young, more beautiful and happier than they are now; that's all there is to it."

"Perhaps. But she has the same effect on you: stupid, petty and boring as she may be, she never annoys you as much as she ought to. Or take her: whatever you may say or do to her, she won't get angry with you. Her reactions are those of a female of the species. It doesn't matter that you'll never impregnate her; the instinct is there. And if I as much as look at her in the wrong way, she'll be ready to sting me with her venom."

"She's quite legitimately jealous of a younger woman."

"I am younger, yes, and smarter… I'm faster than her: in the time it takes her to waddle down the corridor with her fat thighs, I'm already at the tram stop. Only… she probably emits more pheromones."

"Ah, biochemistry, your hobby-horse," David laughed. "But you may have a point when you say that she's a female of the species to whom males inevitably react. The evolutionary stage we're sadly striving to overcome."

If I was a proper female of the species, Jelena thought, perhaps my male would not be able to do without me.

David seemed to be reading her mind. "You're on a slightly higher level of development; you're more complicated and your instincts are therefore more repressed. But that makes you intriguing and complex..." He ruffled the hair at the back of her head and rested his hand on the nape of her neck as he always did when he sensed that Jelena's spirits were low or when she confided in him or was, perhaps, rather obviously trying to hide whatever was troubling her. He seemed to be offering his palm for her head to rest on, as solace and comfort. Jelena loved it when he did that; it calmed her down and gave her a wonderful feeling of closeness. She felt uncomfortable for letting David into Bruno's intimate life. As self-excuse, she said, "I recently read something worth keeping in mind: about an investigation into the causes of longevity. You know what they found out? That people with friends lived longer. Friendship turned out to generate more contentment than family, husband, kids or art... I mean, I'm not saying that because I don't believe in marriage and stuff like that..."

"Why, then?"

"I used to think that career, stress, rat-race and so on were the worst. Like Piljek. And then his very example made me realise that it was all about friendship, or rather lack of it: he's pursuing his miserable career so hard he hasn't got the time to sit down and take a proper breather, never mind have the time for friendship.

"I really don't feel like wasting my time on Piljek," David said. "Shall we go for a coffee before going home?" Jelena knew he was aware of something troubling her and was offering her a shoulder to cry on.

"I can't, I'm going to *King Cross* with Bruno," she said.

The Victim

The Inspector knocked and, not waiting for a reply, entered the spacious, cold autopsy room, waving a hand in response to the pathologist's greeting. The latter stood leaning on the edge of the autopsy table, next to the body's feet. His sleeves were rolled up and his mask was hanging from around his neck; he had just exhaled a trailing plume of cigarette smoke with a deep sigh of pleasure. "My first since I got up this morning," he said, "and this one, too." He indicated a steaming cup of espresso by the corpse's knee with its death-darkened skin.

The Inspector laughed. "If you're trying to shock me…"

"Oh no, far from it. After Ovčara[14], this is a real picnic. A doddle compared to piecing body parts together and hoping they all belonged to the same person. The guys I get here are never innocent anyway."

"And? Have you got something for me?"

"Patience, man," said the pathologist. "I've barely started."

The Social Climber

Andrej Martić was only 22 when he married his first wife. A young graduate from Dalmatia in Zagreb (a *Vlaj*[15], said those who knew him from before). His landlord had a daughter, Janja, a quiet, demure girl a year or two younger than he. The girl was not pretty, but, strictly raised in a traditional Catholic family with a Herzegovinian father and a mother from Posavina, she poignantly reminded him of his own mother and sister. Under her serious and severe appearance, the girl's swirling hormones, activated by the thought of the handsome student separated from her by no more than a thin wall, fired her imagination. Although she wasn't much to look at, she'd pointedly sneak past Andrej's half-opened door scantily dressed, or knock on it all tarted up and offer him cakes baked by her

---

[14] Ovčara is a location near Vukovar, where around two hundred men, prisoners from the Vukovar hospital, were massacred by Serbian forces on 20 November 1991. (Wikipedia)

[15] Vlah is a blanket term covering several modern Latin peoples descending from the latinised population in Central, Eastern and Southeastern Europe (Wikipedia). Here, it means "member of the Serb minority in Croatian Dalmatia and therefore by definition an inferior sort of creature" In the Croatian region of Dalmatia, Vlaj/Vlah (singular) and Vlaji/Vlasi (plural) are the terms used by the inhabitants of coastal towns for the people who live inland, and is often intended to be pejorative, as in "barbarians who come from the mountains." (Wikipedia)

mother. Penniless and determined to graduate as soon as possible, Andrej spent most evenings in his room. Little by little, the two found it more and more pleasant to spend night after night in the same bed, uttering muffled sighs and moving cautiously on the creaky springs of the old mattress.

When Janja became pregnant, Andrej did not dare return *damaged goods* to old Škoro. When he asked her reluctantly for her hand ("We ought to get married…"), Janja blissfully threw her arms around his neck as if in a movie, said *yes* and kissed him. She walked out of college in her fourth year of business studies. As soon as the clandestine liaison ended in marriage and the couple began openly living together, the princess of the night transformed once more into the ugly frog. Six months into the marriage, Andrej stopped making love to his wife. She did not complain. Back then, the church did not condone sexual pleasure even for married couples, and Janja was going to church every Sunday with her mum and dad and defending her profligate husband before her parents. Škoro and his wife watched their daughter dry up and wither, but in a married woman it didn't really matter.

Six months after the wedding, Janja gave birth to a daughter. Škoro's family added up the months, but Janja's mother tirelessly kept spreading the news that Janja had given birth "to a healthy premature baby girl, praise the Lord." The child was not yet two when Andrej left, unable to stick it out any longer. Janja's parents could not bring themselves to forgive him and would not allow him to see their granddaughter under their roof. Thus, initially, Janja took her daughter to the Zoo on Sundays for a stroll with her father, while she killed time walking the deserted streets of east Zagreb and halting before the shop-windows of closed shops. All her life, before and after Andrej, seemed to boil down to shop-windows of closed shops.

As years went by, Janja became more and more devout and the atmosphere in the parental home grew ever gloomier. Considering it his duty to help, old Škoro bought her a flat and paid for a hairdressing course to give her the means of earning a living. And then, went the talk in the family, Janja completely lost her marbles and married another penniless, jobless wastrel who subsequently moved in with her. When Škoro heard about it, he summoned her to his presence, asked if the rumours were true and slapped her face. "That's for what you did before," he said. "You are my shame and my disgrace." Janja never came round again and never again brought her daughter to see her grandparents. Allegedly, her husband drank, beat her and abused the child.

The child was strange and always depressed. Neither Janja nor the child ever saw Andrej again.

No sooner had he left Janja than he married again, this time a woman slightly older than he – she was 30 while he was 24 – and very solvent. Her name was Magda; she was very beautiful, with a barely noticeable limp caused by a childhood bout of polio, and she was an old maid. She was however a Zagrebian born and bred, with an apartment in Radić Street[16] and a solid business: she owned and ran a well-established fashion salon with premises on the ground floor, directly below the apartment. Although a seamstress by trade, Magda was Andrej's equal in sophistication and erudition; it was she who taught him the art of elegant comportment that became his pride. Magda's family – two elderly aunts, an uncle, and two cousins – turned their backs on her because of her marriage to Andrej. She was the only one not to realise that he had married her purely for gain. After the wedding, things apparently began to work out for him: he landed a full time permanent position in the newspaper, the Chief Editor praised his work, he was well thought of by his colleagues, his salary was good... Magda, too, gave him a daughter. He did not spend much time with this second daughter either: as his social position improved, life with Magda became less and less tolerable. He was no longer a provincial, an upstart or a bare-arsed bumpkin. He lived at a respectable address. He not only belonged to the city's society

---

[16] A prestigious and expensive shopping street in the old centre of Zagreb, inhabited by and large by the oldest and wealthiest Zagreb families.

but was on the way to its top.

Like he had done with Janja before, he left his second wife when their child was two. He had decided that he was done with marriages, wives and children and was going to live alone. He pampered himself, enjoying a well-earned peace. Many years later, he heard that his second daughter was on drugs, a heavy junkie, and that her mother was powerless in the situation. Only once, however, did Magda come to him for help.

With Helena, it was completely different. When he saw her for the first time on stage at the HNK, he began to hope that he, too, might finally get to experience that hitherto unknown feeling: love. She was surreally beautiful; he thought it might have been the play of light and shadow on her makeup, but when he met her backstage after the performance, he was stunned by the allure of the gorgeous actress with her husky voice and throaty laughter. For him, she represented the symbol of the great, high, distinguished, glamorous, idle world he aspired to be part of. It took almost half a year for Helena to agree to date her relentless suitor. She felt an innate resentment towards ambitious migrants from *thin soil*[17] who were prepared to deny their roots and sell their own mother in order to worm their way into Zagreb's social elite. In the end, she came to believe him – as women, in the end, always do – when he claimed that she was the woman of his life and that he would never desire another.

They, too, had a daughter, Andreja.

Now, fifteen years later, the only difference between his marriages with Janja and Magda and the one with Helena was that in the last one Andrej stayed put long enough to see his daughter grow up and doted on her while he hardly knew the previous two.

---

[17] The reference is to the red soil of the traditionally poorer southern mountainous regions of Croatia. It thinly covers the rock underneath, whilst the soft, black soil of the richer northern regions lies metres deep.

The Inspector

"Right, that's all for today. We'll continue tomorrow," said the Inspector, rose from his desk, put his chair back and made for the door, nodding goodbye. The Sergeant collected his notepad, fountain pen and pencil and put them in his pocket. Then he, too, got up and followed in the Inspector's wake, repeating with an air of importance: "We'll continue tomorrow." Exiting, the Inspector nearly bumped into a slim, nervously moving young man. "Oh, sorry," said the young man, "and sorry I'm late." He stepped aside courteously to make way for the Inspector. "I'd just like you to know that I'm at your disposal whenever you need me; something like this doesn't happen every day." Without a reply, the Inspector made a non-committal gesture with his hand and left.

La belle Hélène

Helena did not know Andrej's previous two wives nor did she know much about them. Had she known them, though, she would have doubtlessly thought that Andrej possessed a kind of *wife-deadening* poison. That he was Bluebeard. In the beginning, young and beautiful, inundated by offers and roles, popular, famous and always reaping the longest applause, Helena was all carefree laughter. She could not yet sense the coming of the years on the other side of youth. The roles of mothers were yet to come. When they did, at first they were of troubled mothers who had a child very young, or had abandoned their children for the sake of their lover, or were more beautiful than their daughters. Later, there came the roles of proper, good mothers who had nothing else but their child to devote their life to.

As husband, Andrej had long since become cold towards Helena. She was aware of it and had been for a long time. When she saw him one evening with an extremely beautiful and self-possessed young woman, it was just an image for Helena, a soundless one, with no smell or emotions about it, at least no emotions she would not have been experiencing for a while: the feeling that the connection between her and her husband was no more. The girl reminded her of herself twenty years ago, in her casual conviction that the magic mirror on the wall would forever keep saying, "You, o Queen, are the fairest of them all."

Helena had been attracting admiring looks since as far back as she could remember. From the time when, as a little girl, she had her cheeks annoyingly pinched by her mum's friends who gazed at her in wonder, right up to... not so long ago. When did I *actually age*, she asked herself. At forty five, a gorgeous, sensuous raven-haired beauty, she still caught the eyes of men, but she could hear the ticking of the life clock inside her head: not-long-now, it's-all-up, not-long-now, it's-all-up...

When she was little, she had burned the tip of the middle finger on her left hand. The burn was quite bad; her mum said that fingertips were very sensitive and that she would probably remain scarred for good. For good – the thought was abhorrent. That something should forever remain on her body, something that should not be there, something that was not her own. She felt the same way towards the wrinkles on her skin – that they were not her own. She had seen an old lady scratch her neck once: she had taken her loose skin between two fingers and was rubbing it as if it were a sheet of paper, while the skin drooped and dangled. Helena thought she would vomit at the sight.

In any case, it just wasn't worth it, getting old. Much better to die young, beautiful and loved. They said that one lived as long as the memory of him or her lasted. If that was the case, why not be a beautiful memory? The thought was hardly original: be a beautiful corpse. A more original one, then: be a corpse.

Actually, she thought with increasing frequency, it might be best to go mad. A solid, well-rounded madness with not a ray of reason breaking through – wouldn't that be a perfect way out?

The Hand

Old newspapers found in the storage room (February 2004):

ECOLOGY AND STATISTICS: A Croat consumes around two kilos of assorted additives a year in bread alone.

November 2005:

The eco-test law amendment postponed.

FRONT PAGE: Croats own more credit cards than EU citizens.

Josip, 11, dies in landmine explosion 300 metres from home.

Karma – Monday, 3rd October

Jelena and Bruno usually did their main weekly shop on Mondays, in the afternoon, not so much to avoid the weekend crowds in shopping centres as to convince themselves that they were able to save their weekends for more pleasant exploits. When Jelena phoned him to remind him of *King Cross*, Bruno muttered grumpily, "Oh, no, do we have to…"

"It's Monday, isn't it?" said Jelena.

"I know, but do we really need stuff?" Bruno replied.

A row was on the horizon. "Of course we do," Jelena said. "It's two weeks since we've last been. You don't remember because it's my job to think of that sort of thing …" At least don't ask silly questions, she told him silently in her mind. Stop right there, she then said to herself, this is not good. But she still went on. "I told you a hundred times that, while to you it doesn't matter when we do things, me, I'm… dunno… limited, perhaps (that was a conscious concession) and when I lay out a route, I have to traverse it, or I become frustrated (a massive concession) which spoils the rest of my plans (true) and, as you know, I've got many of those because I have too many obligations! (A truth she'd be unwise to stress.)" Bruno continued to communicate by coughs and sighs. "I mean, this is not a discussion to have over the phone, but…" Jelena was trying to sound tolerant and *civilised*, "we have to acknowledge the basic difference here: it really bothers me that you never listen to what I'm saying, and it annoys you when I remember everything you say and then hold you to your word. I was assuming we'd agreed to go to *King Cross* today; you've either forgotten or are trying to wriggle out of it."

"Okay, okay," said Bruno as if giving up trying to convince a moron. "We're going."

"I see," Jelena carped on. "That means, I'd rather go than have to listen to you." Mistake! Don't badger him! She made herself sound cheerful. "Anyway, how do you know you won't have a wonderful, life-enhancing experience in that very place, this very day, an experience you can't afford to miss?" She still wasn't pleased; what she said sounded ironic. But Bruno did seem to be less irritable when he repeated, "Okay, okay!"

They left the city by the motorway. It took them nearly half an hour to get from Savska to Remiza. The stench of exhaust fumes wafted at them. "I think ours is an exhaust-karma," said Jelena, trying to get her own and Bruno's mood up. Bruno smiled faintly but did not ask for an explanation. "It is our karma to drive behind the smelliest cars. I only wonder how, in those ancient days before the time began, such karma could have been put together for us tiny atoms in the universe, when cars didn't even exist. What a mighty *configuration* it must have been," she finished, using Bruno's terminology. Bruno laughed. He liked it when Jelena joked although that didn not guarantee she would not flare up in anger or burst into tears a minute later.

At *King Cross*, Jelena was driven up the wall by the shop assistant in *Ipercoop* uniform. The girl did not know where to find fructose powder. "Don't you work here?" Jelena asked.

"I'm in the Technical Department," the assistant said flatly. "Ask my colleague in Foods."

"And where might I find your colleague in Foods?"

"In Foods, innit?" the girl said and vaguely indicated some thousand square metres of shelving laden with food.

"If I worked here, I'd know what was where," Jelena said to Bruno cantankerously. Bruno did not reply. She experienced his silence as intolerable disloyalty. "I can see I'll end up being the troublemaker here!" Again, Bruno said nothing, following her listlessly. She halted by a shelf displaying a large *special offer* sign over an array of dozens of plastic bottles full of ruby-red liquid. On the label, under the product name, *Multivit Juice*, the caption NO PRESERVATIVES caught the eye. Jelena inspected the back of the bottle: no mention of ingredients.

There *was* print there, but so tiny that she could not make it out even with the aid of the magnifying glass she always kept in her bag. "Look at this!" She tugged at Bruno's arm. "It says here, *no preservatives*. You know how much sense that makes? They might as well have written it on a tin of bicycle varnish, because this has nothing whatsoever to do with juice; this is a toxic mix of chemicals, artificial dyes and artificial flavourings. They didn't even call it fruit juice, they wouldn't be allowed to, but they do want the customers to assume that's what it is. And there is no law against writing *no preservatives* on something that doesn't require any." She looked pointedly at Bruno, but he said nothing. "You don't care," she said. "Right, that means that my karma for today consists of car exhausts, Doras and a husband who doesn't care."

There was more: rummaging in her bag for the note with the number of the lipstick she wanted to buy in *DM*, Jelena discovered her purse was missing. It contained her ID card, her business cards, till receipts and around three hundred kuna. The rest of her documents she kept in a wallet, and her credit cards in a different purse, smart woman that she was. Yet Bruno chided: "How do you manage to keep losing it? I don't get it…"

"Is there anything about me that you do get?"

She glanced at a young couple approaching them. There was something peculiar about them that Jelena couldn't quite put her finger on, and then she understood: the wife, really still no more than a young and delicate girl, was pregnant and already had the heavy waddle of pregnant women. And her husband – a slim, handsome young man – waddled alongside her in solidarity, with the same slow rhythm. That's how Bruno once used to walk, in the same rhythm with her; they would do the chores together, he'd look forward to shopping with her. It's more like being on a seesaw with him now, she thought, we're out of synch and one of us is always heavier than the other; perhaps we really ought to get off…

In the wine department they communicated very well, discussing which wine to buy. The shop assistant waiting to help them would never have guessed it was their first harmonious conversation in the last 36 hours. But one need not marry for the sake of wine…

***

"Hi!" A cheerful face appeared before her: Nina. A pretty, smiling face among the gloomy, nervous shoppers milling around *King Cross.*

Jelena tried not to look morose: it would not be polite. "I just lost my purse," she said, in case she did look morose after all.

"I'm sorry," Nina said. "Was there a lot of money in it?"

"Three hundred kuna. But even if it had been fifty… I hate losing things."

"I know; me too," Nina empathised. "How about a coffee to make you feel better, what do you say? On Jolly Saucers Square. The coffee isn't great, but the name of the place is so lovely it always makes me want to go there." She laughed, looking at Jelena, then at Bruno and back.

Jelena looked at Bruno; he nodded assent. "Nina, this is Bruno, my husband," she said. Even Bruno, always 85 percent absent when Jelena's friends were in question, thawed up in Nina's lovely presence.

No sooner had they sat down when the tannoy announced, "Would Mrs Jelena Turkalj please go to Customer Services Desk… Would Mrs Jelena Turkalj please go to Customer Services Desk…"

At the Customer Services Desk, a friendly little old man handed Jelena her purse. The contents were intact, including the money. Jelena thought it embarrassing to offer the old man a reward; instead, she thanked him warmly and squeezed his hand between hers.

"You've got the power; you've just altered my karma for today," she told Nina cheerfully as she got back to the table, waving her purse to show what she meant. She did not even glance at Bruno.

Nina's laughter rang merrily. "What a nice thing to say," she said.

As they talked, Jelena noticed that Bruno's eyes had come alive, lit up by the lovely sight of a beautiful girl having a relaxed chat with his wife.

"Tell me what sort of editorial office I've joined. I don't know anyone there except Andrej," said Nina.

"Hmmm… And I was just about to ask you for your first impressions," Jelena replied. She found it embarrassing to ask Nina how she knew Andrej.

"David is handsome and clever, Mario shallow, Dora imposing, and Ivana daft," Nina laughed.

"That's pretty much spot on. Mario is shallow and unscrupulous, walking over dead bodies to get information. Nothing is taboo to him but, by the same token, nothing is sacred to him either. Dora is the queen of our little realm, and she's very vain, so tread carefully. If you don't give her due respect, you'll be down without ever knowing what hit you. You must mind your Ps and Qs with Piljek as well. He's none too bright, but is nevertheless in charge of our daily allowances, expenses, fees and overtime. He's Dora's lackey; if she hates you, he'll hate you as well. Me… I'm not a bad sort, only I'm moody and I'm often gloomy."

"Really?" Nina laughed. "Well, yes, those involved in healthy living and preservation of nature can't help being gloomy from time to time. That makes sense."

"How do you know what I'm involved in"

"Dora told me in strict confidence." Nina laughed.

"With an expression on her face suggesting that I was a bit eccentric?" Jelena laughed too.

"And what might be the suitable occupation for an eccentric journalist's husband?" Nina wanted to know.

"You'd better ask what sort of a wife it takes to stick it out with an addict," Jelena said. Nina winced a bit and gave her a serious look. "A *computer* addict," Jelena added.

"I'm a programmer," said Bruno who had just finished ordering their coffees.

"Are you really? In that case, I have a favour to ask," Nina laughed.

"I propose that you two should say 'thou' to each other for starters," Jelena said.

"Sure," Nina agreed. Bruno nodded his consent.

"What do you think of her?" Jelena asked him as they drove back. "Isn't she wonderful?"

"Yeah, nice girl," Bruno said. Coming from him, it was an outpouring.

"That's the new colleague I told you about." Bruno was listening. "Everyone likes her. Even Dora likes her." Bruno laughed. "Just seeing her cheers you up. Doesn't she look like some supernatural being that somehow got into a human body though, the body of a beautiful young woman? See, she's so wonderful I'm not even jealous although I can see you like her."

Grown wise through long connubial experience, Bruno did not reply.

***

That evening, having got home, Jelena phoned Ana to find out what sort of a weekend she had had and to check on her mood. Her mood turned out to be bad. To cheer her up, Jelena told her she had a new colleague, "a very nice girl; her name is Nina and she looks a right cupid."

"Nina?" Ana asked sharply. "baby-faced, curly-haired?"

"That's the one."

"Nina Ivezić?"

"Yup."

"Do you know who she is?"

"Who?"

"She won the Writers' Association First Novel Award. I didn't even make the selection." There was a yapping tone to Ana's voice.

Jelena said, "Have you read her novel?"

"No," Ana snorted. "She's a translator as well, you know," she added. "She translates novels for the *Female Soul* series."

"Ah, that's why her name sounded familiar," Jelena said.

"I've known her for ages; by sight. And she used to freelance for *Argus*. She's always been somehow special, people have always talked about her as if there was a mystery of some sort there... beautiful people fire imagination... they even used to say she'd had a difficult childhood..."

"Well now," Jelena laughed, "when it comes to imagination, it looks like she'll be firing it up in her new workplace, too. The men are already busy imagining, including David. Beautiful, clever, talented – to all appearances, perfect..."

"A successful human specimen, eh?" Ana said. "Perfection doesn't exist, though, and so I wonder..."

At that point Jelena understood that Ana was going to spoil her mood sooner than she could improve Ana's, and ended the discussion.

The Hand

The hand flexed its fingers as if about to play the piano. Its knuckles crackled. It got the Moleskine and the pen ready. From the pile on the right, it pulled out a newspaper, randomly, as if picking a number in a prize draw, and slowly began turning the pages.

INTERVIEW: Branko Čegec: The collapse of Croatian publishing – the consequences of the incursion of newspaper publishers into the book market and their unrestrained rampage therein.

"(...) Taking those publications seriously as books is something of an insult to anyone in publishing; not only do they not react against it, however, but often themselves participate or at least do their utmost to get in on this inconceivable trivialisation of their own existence and basic cultural standards. (...) I cannot understand some very prominent people who are prepared to see years of their work and experience devalued in exchange for less than '100 minutes of fame' of highly dubious provenance.

(...) We are a country with no literary criticism and no serious reflection on books in our press which has so far not managed to produce a single prominent critic capable of writing a thousand words about a book that would make sense, since the current cultural imperative requires trivia and truffling out juicy details about the writer.

(...) When Edo Popović publishes a serious novel, it doesn't even get a mention (...) because Edo Popović's scandal potential is poor. At the same time, we are served endless interviews with tiddlers, ladies whose contributions to world literature consist of clichéd bonking and literary wanking."

The fingers of the hand twitched slightly, and then it wrote down on a blank page of the notebook:

I don't know... This rant about the exclusivity of book publishing reminds me of the already lost war the expensive original CDs and DVDs waged against their pirated copies with equal quality of picture and sound. Quite simply, cheap technology makes democracy happen. Books are now bought by people who shunned bookshops as they would shun the temples of some alien religion, fearful of not knowing what to do there and how to behave.

As far as tiddlers are concerned, not every tiddler is a piddler. Some of them are scribblers.

The hand pushed the notebook aside, folded the finished newspaper and, hovering briefly in the air, took another paper, the one from the top.

The Inspector

"Right," said the Inspector. "If you have things to do, go and do them. We'll interview you one by one. Who wants to be first?" The Sergeant moved his stern glance from one person to another, like a teacher deliberating which pupil to pick, aware that crafty pupils would look him in the eye, hoping to convince him that they had done their revision and therefore did not need to be picked.

Statistics

Ana was not beautiful. She had never been beautiful, except as a baby, according to her mum. People say that those born beautiful grow up ugly and vice versa; that ugly babies become very beautiful adults. She was thin, bony, with a cutting look in her eyes and lips pursed tightly together, twisted out of their true shape. In secondary school, she looked like a slender green sapling that could grow into a beautiful tree. But the sapling had not thrived; it remained as it was, slight, with buds that failed to open. Pale, without a trace of makeup and with nervous hands, she wore slouchy trousers and oversized jumpers, resembling, in her thirties, the ugly duckling that never became a swan. Yet she wasn't ugly at all: she had what the English call *fine bone structure*, a well-shaped face and a harmoniously built body, if far too skinny. She never tried to improve her appearance: she neither cared nor believed it could be done.

Ana's friends believed her main problem was her dominant and cold mother who was the cause of Ana's lack of self-confidence. Ana knew she lacked confidence: she even courted the favour of her neighbour's chickens. Of late, since her mother had become unwell, Ana took on the task of mowing the lawn. Their neighbour's chickens, acquired to subsidise her meagre pension, became agitated and threw themselves at the fence as chickens do when they smell freshly mown grass they'd like to peck. Ana would then turn off her lawnmower every few minutes and throw some grass over the fence, so that the chickens wouldn't have to wait, wouldn't be dissapointed, would remember their benefactress and would therefore next time welcome her with even greater adulation.

Having had read the interview with Sandra Bagarić[18], the young soprano, Ana noticed an intriguing parallel between the two of them: the singer had described herself as coquettish; her husband, she said, had told her that she was forever seducing everyone and everything around her – children, adults, animals… That, Ana thought, is the good, life-affirming aspect of coquetry, spontaneous and unplanned. The singer is coquettish because she enjoys being liked by all and sundry, while I do it in order to ingratiate myself – not even with

---

[18] Young and extremely attractive Croatian soprano, famously outspoken on the subject of sex; on one occasion she said that, had she been a man, she'd have "****ed half the world".

people, I haven't got that far yet – but with my neighbour's chickens.

Indeed, she was never courteous or friendly towards people; on the contrary, she was brusque and withdrawn, like orphans who, raised in a home, had never known tenderness and don't know how to express it. She was reserved, highly talented and extremely antisocial. Jelena teased that she was like Elfrida Jelinek, another extreme case of hypochondria, anxiety and assorted fears. She kept having all manner of tests done: a blood test several times a year, the complete and the differential one; more than one gastroscopy, abdominal ultrasound and mammogram (regularly), and a thyroid test. She had had a colour Doppler flow analysis of her arteries, ovaries and her uterus done, as well as a brain CT scan, EEGs and ECGs (several times). She had also had a colonoscopy, a fibroscopy of ear, nose and mouth, a mole removal procedure and various dermatological examinations.

"You're only thirty, girl," Jelena told her. "Consider the statistics! How many thirty-somethings do you know that have all those illnesses you fear?"

"Statistics, you say?" Ana repeated. "Statistically, every fifth woman gets breast cancer. Let me give you some statistics: one of my friends has got it; if I have roughly around fifty friends and acquaintances, that is one in fifty. A neighbour's got it: that's one in hundred, which is the number of women in my street. Among my schoolmates, one: one in six hundred. At work, there is one, already older than thirty – that makes one in 1500. Among relatives, none. All in all, if statistics tells us that every fourth or fifth woman gets hit, my personal statistics doesn't put me out of the danger zone. And do you know what the ultimate consequence of statistical thinking is? You end up wishing that someone close to you would get ill to make you feel safer... and you can stop giving me that reproachful look."

"Doesn't the fact that there are no cancer cases in your family make you feel better?"

"No; the most recent research shows that cancer is not necessarily inherited: it's more the matter of lifestyle, environment, food – generally the things we enjoy, perhaps… Although, from time to time, they do discover genes responsible for cancer; they found the one for breast cancer and the one for colon cancer, I think. Whether they can put them right, though, is another thing." Ana stared into space, deep in thought. "Genes are a very big deal. I often imagine that once upon a time there was a sad, narrow-shouldered and long-nosed girl given in marriage to someone who didn't even like her, like in *The Birch Tree*[19]. She bore him children, gave them her genes and sent them off into the future, all the way to me. And with me, those genes will now disappear from the face of the earth." She fell silent, thinking. Then, "Aren't you curious about whose genes you inherited and whom you're going to pass them on to?" She paused, remembering Jelena had problems getting pregnant and said *sorry*, with no real empathy, immersed as she was in her own thoughts. Although she never spoke about it, she often thought about her father, regretting never having known him, or anyone on his side of the family.

Jelena shrugged. "To return to… I won't say statistics, but the probability that you might get all those illnesses you dread—"

"That's got nothing to do with it," said Ana. "I have a concern, a *disquiet*. And, because I have this disquiet, I fear what it might portend. Why am I concerned and you are calm? Perhaps because something in me senses that my life will be short? I may have unconsciously read the omens pointing to my final destination."

"It's a common neurosis. What's more, if you're worried about dying young, you're already late," Jelena laughed. "You've outlived two of your consultants, one GP, a radiologist, an orthopaedic surgeon…"

Ana ignored her. "If only some soothsayer could tell me I'll live to a ripe old age, I'd be happy and calm. But, like this…"

---

[19] A novella by the Croatian writer Slavko Kolar (1891-1963); later a film (*The Birch Tree*) directed by Ante Babaja (1967)

"Wouldn't we all," Jelena shrugged.

The Hand

The hand snapped its fingers: *This could come in handy.*
WHOLE BODY HEALTH CHECK IN 15 MINUTES:

A magnetic resonance imaging (MRI) scanner with the brand name of Avanto became operational yesterday in Zagreb at *Diagnostic 2004,* the private polyclinic for radiology, neurology and nuclear medicine. The scanner is the first of its kind in this part of Europe and one of only ten such machines in the world. It uses TIM (Total Imaging Matrix) technology which can produce a top quality image of the patient's whole body in just fifteen minutes. (...) Moreover, this newest MRI makes it possible to diagnose cancers and their metastases, wherever they may be located in the whole body. (...)

"Metastases, wherever they may be located in the whole body!" That reminds me of that film critic who always wrote that "the film had won multiple awards."
A FRESH SCANDAL FROM THE COURTROOM: THE PRIEST AND 15 VIRGINS

The Zagreb District Ecclesiastical Court has issued a non-custodial sentence to Čuček, the parish priest who, during RE lessons, liked to dandle little girls in his lap – girls so young they still played with dolls and sneaked into mummy's and daddy's bed at night. As he spoke to them of God and his Angels, he put his hand into their little panties and felt for the clitoris; he also groped under their white blouses, where tiny nipples had barely began to bud. The Court was of an opinion that a jail sentence would have been too severe a punishment for a crime the victims of which suffered no long term consequences.

The female journalist who wrote the article took great trouble with her descriptions; her text is exciting in the pornographic sense.

The Butterfly Effect

Apart from being a hypochondriac, Ana was also superstitious, although the word did not exist in her vocabulary. Instead, she spoke of omens. She'd say that hypochondria and superstition were logically connected, as both had to do with fear of the past rather than fear of the future: the past already pointed towards what we feared in the future, and that is why we feared. If she feared the results of a medical test, and had received a negative omen on the day of the appointment, she wouldn't go.

"I don't get it," said Jelena. "If you're healthy, the results of the test will say so even if you receive negative omens."

"No, you're wrong," Ana explained. "If I'm healthy, there won't be an omen."

"I still don't get it. Are you saying that if you do get one, it means you're ill?"

"No, only if I find out the result. If I don't go, I may have succeeded in switching to a different chain of events. Each event is preceded by another specific event – not any old event but a specific one. And it is followed by an equally specific event. Those events form a chain. Bad omen, visit to the doctor, illness. Good omen, visit to the doctor, good health. Bad omen, no visit to the doctor, the chain breaks; I now switch to another chain, where a visit to the doctor is not yet due, and in that one, I'm healthy."

"Right, I get it now," said Jelena. "But that means you might jump over too many chains and turn into someone else… There's that muddled-up movie, *The Butterfly Effect*, which is about something like that…"

"No, please, don't start about movies again," Ana cut in. "But yes, it does mean I could change radically, and even become someone else, only in that case I wouldn't remember myself the way I was and would have no idea of what sort of a person I used to be."

"Yeah. But doesn't that mean you should be able to change things backwards?" Jelena said.

"You could say that. If we could interpret events in our lives more accurately, we'd know exactly what we should do. And what's in store for us. From that very first tiny point of emergence, our birth. I'll tell you another story…"

Jelena sighed.

"A boy developed brain tumour. The tumour was benign, but the boy died because he was misdiagnosed and then treated for atypical epilepsy for years, during which time the tumour spread until nothing could be done to save him. Had he been treated correctly from start, he'd have been hale and well a few weeks after the operation. Now, three doctors of the four involved in his treatment have already died... can you guess of what? Brain tumour. The fourth doctor was diagnosed with brain tumour, too, but he's still alive. A coincidence, or a curse?"

Jelena shuddered.

Ana had recently begun noticing that her periods of fear had become almost a continuum, and periods without fear had virtually disappeared. After completed tests and subsequent negative results, instead of relief and joy, she would feel, albeit distantly, vaguely and only for a split second, that she was missing her fear. It felt as if she were naked or had, on a winter morning, got up into an unheated room from under a warm duvet. And that was not all: she felt that her fears were an excuse for her not to do what she ought to be doing; not to be what she could be. How is it possible, she asked herself, to miss unbearable torture? Does that prove that my fear is, after all, in itself an illness? And if I'm aware of it being one, how come I can't rid myself of it? Why should someone be born to live only to flee from life into fear?

"Psychology can explain that," Jelena said. "People find it hard to give up their troubles because they experience them as part of themselves. That's why you, too, miss your fear because without it you're not yourself. But, you know, it's actually quite good not to have a serious illness. Try it."

The trouble was, she feared most when she was without fear. She was afraid when she felt fine. For some reason she believed that a strong person could endure anything; so, to a strong person, everything eventually happened, even the things he or she feared.

"It's the other way round; everyone says fear is bad because you attract the things you fear," Jelena insisted. "That's why you need to erase such thoughts."

"I don't think fear is dangerous if it is accompanied by humility and sadness," said Ana. "It is dangerous when I think, I'm all right, I'm strong…"

"All you're doing is finding excuses for your fear. And fear is exhausting. And, if it's true that our subconscious follows commands, that means it is trying to create what you suggest."

Ana became thoughtful. "Yes, perhaps… I used to think it was all rubbish they keep telling us in order to make us feel responsible for everything, but… Have I told you about that man whose daughter was gravely ill…?"

Jelena shook her head; another of Ana's stories she preferred not to hear was looming.

"The man kept repeating, "I'd give my right arm for her to get well." Lo and behold, in the end he lost his arm in an accident, and his daughter got well."

***

"I'm worried about Ana," Jelena said to David. "I'm beginning to believe it would have been better for her if her book never got published. She's getting darker and darker. No one cares about her book, she says, just like no one has ever cared about her."

"Who doesn't care?"

"Don't know… the critics, the public, literary circles, whatever."

The book was a kind of Ana's inverted mirror: the vibrant, cheerful side of gloomy, wretched Ana. Sarcastic in real life, she was witty in her book. In real life, she suppressed emotion, freeing it in the book. Freedom, that was it: in her book, she was free from all her misfortune, her fears, her impotence and dissatisfaction.

The Hand

The hand stretched its fingers, rubbed the other hand, rolled up the sleeves and reached for the newspaper on the top of the neat pile on the right side of the desk.

CULTURE: Regarding the publication of *Antigone, Oedipus Rex* and *Medea* by a newspaper: "It was said that classical Athens used to spend more public funds on its theatres than on its fleet."

ZAGREB NEWS: Dangerous asbestos got left behind around the Faculty of Philosophy following a water pipe replacement.

The Forum

David proposed a panel discussion on *The Naked She-Wolf* to his colleague Tanja, who hosted Thursday Forums in the Press Club. "*The Naked She-Wolf?*" said Tanja. "I've read it; a strange book. I asked around, but couldn't find a soul who knew Ana Marton... I haven't got a clue who that woman is, and yet she writes so well!"

"I know her," said David. "She's our colleague, a journalist. A friend of mine. She's a bit peculiar, but very interesting. It might turn out to be a great discussion, particularly because the critics took no notice of the book."

"Yeah, I see," said Tanja. "But she did come down pretty hard on the literary circuit, and on the critics, *and* on the journalists. And on the Chairman of the Journalists' Association."

"Correct. It is, apart from anything else, the best current cultural satire around," David said. "Even though that's just the background, given in broad strokes. The most important aspect of the book is the love story, an unusual story..."

"All right, give me her number," said Tanja. "We'll put something together. But promise that you'll be the one to present the book." She smiled coquettishly.

The panel discussion was a success. The Little Hall at the Journalists' Club was packed with Ana's friends and friends of her friends. The Journalists' Association was officially represented only by Tanja and her ageing colleague Barić, who wrote for the journalists' trade monthly, *The Journalist*. David read extracts from the book. Each extract earned him a fresh bout of applause. Barić gave a formal address, speaking on behalf of the Journalists' Association of Croatia. He emphasised the need to encourage the creativity of women, mentioned the fact that the Association had been the launching point of many a successful career, and, just falling short of invoking the memory of Marija Jurić Zagorka[20], expressed his hopes that their colleague Ana Marton was already writing another book. He cadged a signed copy of *The Naked She-Wolf*, promising a review in the very next issue of *The Journalist*.

A month later, Ana visited the Journalists' Association website and looked up the contents of *The Journalist*. There was no mention of her in the *Books by our Colleagues* rubric, nor was there any the following month. David enquired with Tanja why there had been no review. Tanja asked Barić, and Barić said he hadn't had the time to write one. Thus this review, too, bit the dust.

"Of course," Jelena said to David, "it was to be expected: she sneered at the literary and journalistic circles. For male readers, the book is too much of a love story and too feminine; for women's magazines, it's not trivial enough; nor is it dull enough to be considered a classic. It doesn't belong anywhere."

Everyone Has One Good Story

Ana believed that every person had one good story, *own* story, their own unique story, which was their best story. Other than that one story, whatever else one wrote was merely recycling. Or simply work. Some people began by writing their own story, others wrote it last. Either way, once written, it couldn't be mistaken for anything else.

The Naked She-Wolf was Ana's story. She was delighted when the novel got published and believed she'd be content whatever the reactions turned out to be: she'd got her story out;

---

[20] Marija Jurić Zagorka (1873 – 1957) was a Croatian novelist and dramatist, and the first female journalist in the country's history. (Wikipedia)

that was all that mattered. Many people did indeed contact her, men and women, the very young and the old, saying that the book had encouraged and liberated them, that it had helped them... and yet she was hurt by the lack of interest by the critics. She felt humiliated, as if bringing out the best food and drink she had to offer to a valued guest and seeing her offerings scornfully snubbed without even having been tasted. The worst of all was that she felt she had soiled her book by publishing it. Who cared?

"Let it go; write another book," Jelena pestered. "You must write. Forget the critics: they come and go, and books remain."

To get Jelena off her back more than for any other reason, Ana started writing her second novel and found herself struggling. The first one had been easy. Her own story, it flowed of itself. The second novel did not flow; she had to invent and construct. She carried on writing only because she hoped that, if it got published, someone might pull out *The Naked She-Wolf* and say, "See, this was an excellent book. The second book by the same author is, however, a disappointment..."

The Hand

The hand slowly turned the pages. Each time, it would pedantically moisten a finger on a wet sponge.

THE PAPER OF 17TH DECEMBER: Severina loses her case: the court rejects her porn movie authorship claim. Severina's lawyer will appeal.

THE FRONT PAGE: Part one of *Moby Dick* as free supplement with each copy of *The Morning Paper*

CROATIA WILL HAVE TO TREAT GOTOVINA[21] AS A TERRORIST.

---

[21] General Ante Gotovina, indicted as war criminal but lauded as hero of the Patriotic War by the Croatian people, spent four years in hiding before his capture in 2005. In 2011 he was found guilty and sentenced to 24 years in prison by the International Court in Hague. In 2012, the Appeals Panel of the same Court found him not guilty on all counts and released him.

The hand slowly closed the notebook and put it neatly back into the desk drawer.

The Inspector

"That's it for now. We'll call you back if we need you," the Inspector said. His Sergeant licked a finger, turned a blank page in his notepad, stood up and called out through the door: "Next!"

Double Delight – Friday, 7th October

Leaving work on Friday, Jelena felt just as depressed as the day before, all the worse for having slept poorly the previous night. Deep in thought, she walked past the glass window of the reception without a glance, although she never left without saying a friendly "good night" to Anđelko, the amiable middle-aged Bosnian receptionist. A Banjalukan, he fled to Zagreb with his family in nineteen ninety, while his Serb neighbour moved into his house in Banjaluka[22]. Although it was officially claimed that after the war all Croatian houses and flats in the region snatched by Serbs had been returned to their rightful owners, Anđelko was unable to get his house back in spite of all the connections he could muster, all the lawyers and long drawn-out court cases. Anđelko believed that the generous size of the house, its central position and the fact that it was new and beautiful were the reasons for his failure. "Going home already?" Anđelko said. Jelena waved. "I've had enough for today. See you tomorrow."

Bruno was waiting by the parked car. Jelena noticed he was not looking towards the reception, safe in the knowledge that she who he was waiting for would arrive. And before, he used to wait for her staring impatiently in the direction she was too come from.

"Do you need anything?" Bruno asked before the turn-off

---

[22] That means that Anđelko was a Bosnian Croat. In 1990, just before the war in Bosnia and Croatia formally began, the less formal but equally atrocious hostilities at local level made many families flee their homes.

for the market.

"Lettuce."

"Don't we need any bread?"

"Yes, if throwing away a whole loaf of white bread and half a loaf of brown isn't quite enough for you," Jelena retorted abrasively. Bruno always stockpiled food in huge quantities. During the first seven years of their marriage (the seven fat cows), she fondly called him Bear because of this habit. Come to think of it, during those first seven years, he used to stockpile less than in the following seven. Perhaps that, too, was a symptom of something?

"I just fancied freshly baked bread," said Bruno.

She pursed her lips together to avoid making a comment. "You get the bread; I'll get the lettuce," she said coldly. She watched his receding figure as he went down the aisle. Actually, he was still a fine figure of a man: tall, slim, with a nice tight arse. A real intellectual type, with glasses and without muscles. His best feature could only be seen face front: the eyes. The beautiful, limpid, blue-grey eyes that always appeared to be smiling, even when the rest of his face was serious. Boyish eyes, optimistic, friendly; maybe superficial. His neck's not strong, though, she thought, and smiled in spite of herself. A man turned to stare at her in passing; she averted her face and her smile vanished. My thoughts must have been written all over my face, she thought. She had read somewhere once that ovulating women, fertile and ready to procreate, fancied strong bull-necked men whom, given a choice, they would, at that time, prefer as mates to secure strong and healthy offspring. As for the rest of our monthly cycle, she decided, we carry on being happy with our reed-necked, sensitive intellectuals and don't even think of bull-necked males until the next ovulation. That would explain everything: delicate, weak, docile husbands and strong, brash, rough lovers with their thick necks.

Offspring, Jelena sighed.

She was no longer smiling. These floating states of mind, with thoughts swirling in her head like streamers in the wind – she disliked them. Gloomy mood took hold of her again until she was barely able to hold back tears. She bought the lettuce and returned to the car. Bruno was already loading the shopping bag into the boot. She remembered she'd prepared the ingredients for a new cake she was planning to try. Hopefully, it would turn out well. *Triple Delight.* A symbolic name. One cake in the place of three other delights. Or in the place of two delights + the cake? For a brief moment, she was able to rejoice in the peace and the unchangeable rhythm of life in her home. The first inkling of the forthcoming calm of old age, or perhaps the calm before the storm; she didn't even try to understand. "The years between 40 and 60 are the worst," an older, more experienced friend told her once, "because you don't see yourself as old yet and are trying to go on being young although you can clearly see that something is amiss. Once you're past sixty, you can relax and enjoy yourself." But I'm not yet 40, Jelena thought, I've got another two years... no, one and a half year to go...

Halfway through her baking session, *Triple Delight* began to get on her nerves, so she cut it down to a double one: pastry and yellow cream, without biscuits covered in chocolate. If double delight isn't enough, she thought, the triple one won't help either. Bruno dozed off in the armchair. As soon as he had nodded off, she fell ravenously to. Later, she would again be able to tell him she was getting fat because she was using food to fill the emptiness in her life.

In the bathroom, Jelena stood a long time in front of the mirror. She brushed her hair, brown, heavy and straight, cut to chin length in a straight line. She had been wearing the same hairstyle since secondary school. She parted her fringe, regarding her relaxed face, careful not to arrange it into an expression or tighten any muscles. She did not like the look of her face when it was relaxed, which was why, in front of the mirror, she always mechanically arched her eyebrows and pouted her lips, unaware that she was doing it until one day Ana, standing beside her, copied her actions. Since that moment, Jelena avoided looking at herself in the mirror in the presence of others, lest she began pouting and arching her eyebrows. She was ashamed of arranging her face. Relaxed on purpose now, she checked if her lips pouted, her eyebrows arched or her chin jutted. She stretched her lips into a smile. Objectively, I'm not ugly, she thought, only I ought to laugh more. David had told her that she resembled Julia Roberts when she laughed. Her laughter was loud and natural. Her hair was chestnut, semi-long, with a fringe. What do I look like to Bruno, she wondered; does he see me objectively, from distance, like I see him, now that I no longer feel he loves me?

Men liked Jelena. Ever since Uni, she had not gone short of suitors. David told her that her main attraction was her femininity rather than the plain, vulgar sex appeal. "That doesn't mean you have nothing to offer," he laughed. "On the contrary, like the real woman that you are, deep inside you keep the fire burning for one man, and one man alone." She laughed, pleased with his comment. David's authority in these matters was considerable, and he would not lie to her.

Everything might have turned out better if Bruno and she had had kids together, she thought. It would have definitely been *different*. Perhaps now she wouldn't have any time to lose in front of the mirror, she heard Jelena Number Two say.

She had suffered when, five years into her marriage, she found out that most likely she would not be able to have children. For Bruno, it was even harder. She postponed proper medical examinations. She kept persuading herself that there was still time, that it was too early for radical solutions. Of late, she repeatedly ran into articles, films and interviews mentioning the biological clock, as if sounding a warning. Her mother proposed artificial insemination; Jelena shunned the thought. She feared violation of nature. Can any violation bear good fruit? Is it violation or is it progress, perhaps even evolution? She was more in favour of adopting a child. But what would children made by artificial insemination say to that? Or the children born to raped Bosnian women? They should take no offence; it's just the opinion of a neurotic woman. Or an excuse. Actually, she thought, still gazing at her reflection in the mirror, maybe it's better that we can't have children. It makes everything a lot easier.

She looked around with the feeble intent of attacking the chores in her two-bedroom apartment which was due for a complete renovation. It was given them by Bruno's mother: after her husband's death, she had swapped her huge four-bedroom apartment for a two-bedroom one plus compensation for the difference in size. She lived comfortably and without worries on her pension and the compensation money. She had moved to the old people's home of her own accord. The home was privately owned and run, and she needed to supplement her not insignificant pension earned as the financial analyst at INA[23] from her savings to make up the home's monthly 600 euro charges.

Mum Dubravka, as they called her, lived pleasantly in the home situated in the city centre. She was mobile, not all that old (68), and she kept herself occupied by numerous activities: she was a member of a chess club, a GONG[24] volunteer and a freelance journalist for Radio Zagreb's Programme 2. It was as if she was finally able to live her life the way she had always wanted to. Bruno and Jelena rarely visited her at the home; more often they would meet up with her in town: she would usually take them out for dinner to one of the better fish restaurants. Jelena liked Dubravka's self-sufficiency and her independent ways, although she would sometimes feel chilly apprehension when she saw the traces of that very same self-sufficiency in Dubravka's son. Mum Dubravka never moaned about not having grandchildren and did not miss being Granny Dubravka one little bit.

***

A night without a touch, sleeping back to back; a silent morning smelling pleasantly of coffee. Jelena stared through the kitchen

---

[23] INA - Industrija nafte, or INA for short, founded in 1964, is the Croatian national oil company. (Wikipedia)

[24] GONG, formed in 1997, is a Croatian non-governmental organization that oversees elections in Croatia.

window while Bruno read the previous day's papers. People read today's paper only in American movies, because a little boy tosses it onto their front lawn as he speeds past on his bike, or he stuffs it into their tunnel-like mailbox. Yesterday's paper is as good as today's if you didn't manage to read it yesterday. Jelena cast discreet glances at her husband, wondering how long he would be able to last in such a marriage... a relationship involving few conversations and little touch. He seemed tranquil enough.

After coffee, the bathroom. "You first?" "Nah, you go." "Okay, I won't be long." Not counting the "good mornings" on rising, up to nine o'clock they'd uttered the total of those – how many were they? – ten words.

After the bathroom, the market again. "Shall we?" Bruno asked.

"I don't fancy going," said Jelena. "We don't need anything in particular anyway... You go."

"All right," Bruno said. "What should I get?"

He's not trying to persuade me to go with him, thought Jelena. We've reached yet another new marital stage, then. "Dunno," she said. "Get whatever you like. Chicken breast fillets?"

"Okay."

"In that case, get some cauliflower too, and I'll braise it."

"Wicked," said Bruno. "With breadcrumbs?"

Unfailingly, he perked up at the mention of food, as ever, Jelena thought. Husband: a ridiculously simple mechanism.

She dragged herself listlessly around the flat, starting a number of chores: collecting dry laundry off the radiators, picking up dirty clothes strewn over the bathroom floor, scrubbing coffee stains off the hob, making a 'to do' list for Monday. She did not finish any of them.

Bruno got back in no time at all, pink with the cold outside air and altogether refreshed. He looked almost cheerful, as if detoxed, Jelena thought. Dejelenised, dewifeised, demarriageised.

The marriage trap. No way out. Divorce is not a way out

either – it brings no satisfaction. At least, the *thought* of divorce brings no satisfaction. Once you get stuck in a marriage, there is no best solution. Jelena shook herself a bit to stop the thoughts. That was where the "Move away from the spot" superstition came from, the one about erasing something bad one had just said.

***

After lunch, she phoned her mum: don't leave for the weekend what you can do today.

"Ah, how are we, how are we…" Mum repeated Jelena's question. "Like two savages, that's how we are. Whenever the doorbell rings, we dash around madly because we're never properly dressed. We freak out as if Martians were at the door. And if it isn't Martians, it can only be you two… or beggars."

"Why don't you go out somewhere nice?" Jelena carried on with the dialogue they had had so many times.

"You know what your dad's like: he doesn't need anyone and he doesn't feel like going anywhere. All he wants to do is sleep, and I keep stuffing my face because I'm bored. What about you two?"

"The same," said Jelena gravely. Her mum laughed.

"I didn't get any sleep again last night; it must be the full moon or something. Dad was snoring away like a chainsaw as usual…"

"How's dad?"

"How? Fine, how else would he be? Sleeps like a top all night, and there he is, on the sofa again… you know what he calls it: being in a doze-phase. And Bruno?"

"Bruno is in a doze-phase too, thanks," said Jelena, trying to sound cheerful.

"You're coming for dinner tonight; you haven't forgotten, I hope?" mum said.

"I have," Jelena said.

"Mr Josip is coming…"

"Which Mr Josip?"

"My ex-friend Biba's ex-husband. He lives in America; he's

just come to visit his daughters."

"Don't know about that," said Jelena unenthusiastically.

"Don't *I-don't-know* me," mum said. "It'll be more fun if we have company. And why cook when I'm cooking dinner anyway. Stuffed peppers, your favourite. I bet Josip could do with a few stuffed peppers too."

"All right then," said Jelena. "It's a deal."

She could still hear her mother speaking as she put the receiver down, but she pretended she could not.

Dinner at Mum and Dad's, with Mr Josip – Friday, 7th October

They rang the doorbell and mum opened the door, flushed and perspiring. The rich aroma of stuffed peppers wafted from inside the flat.

"Ah, good that you're here at last," she said in a hushed voice, panting. "I've been running between the kitchen and the sitting room; the man's sitting there all alone, and your dad's behaving... like a common hippy."

Mr Josip turned out to be a pleasant gentleman, no more than moderately snooty for being a visitor from the richer, more developed world. Dad had indeed loosened up beyond all boundaries of acceptability. When he pulled a pair of white ladies' knickers out of his pocket and proceeded to spring-clean his specs with them, everyone pretended not to notice. Perhaps Josip was not even able to make out clearly what sort of an unsightly rag dad was using. Jelena was familiar with her father's theory that only the cotton cloth used for knickers could clean glasses properly. Fortunately, mum was in the kitchen at the time. She always fought with dad about those knickers, offering to cut them up into smaller pieces and hem them to hide their origin, but he wouldn't hear of it. He must have been drawing at least some pleasure from taunting her.

"Mmm, the peppers are really lovely," Mr Josip said politely. "I must admit it's not likely I'd find such food over there..."

"That's what I thought," mum said hurriedly, "which is why I made them…"

"So you're not very ajur-fed up there, then," dad said. Josip gave him a blank look.

"Dad's joking," Jelena said, holding back laughter. "He meant, ajur-vedic."

Mr Josip said nothing. Mum looked daggers at dad, sweating profusely.

Josip turned to Jelena. "Your mother told me you're interested in ecology."

"I am, a bit," Jelena said. "I write a weekly column about ecology-related topics."

"I must tell you I was very surprised last night when I took off the shirt I'd put on clean in the morning and saw that it was all black around the collar."

"What ho, Mr Joe, didn't you wash properly around the neck?" dad barged in.

"Nooo," Josip laughed to show he understood banter. "But it made me realise that the air here is much more polluted than in Boston, although I expected it to be the other way round. You know, there, when I take my shirt off in the evening, it is almost clean enough to be worn again in the morning."

"Who'd have thought it," muttered mum, flashing her eyes angrily at dad, "that Zagreb's more polluted than Boston."

"It's because of catalytic converters," said Jelena. "Until people are forced by law to have them, we'll go on being poisoned. Kids in particular…"

"You haven't got any kids anyway," said dad. Mum glared threateningly.

Taking no notice of her father's remark, Jelena went on: "It's been officially established that the lungs of Zagrebians are in worse condition than the lungs of smokers."

"Jesus, are they really?" mum said.

Dad waved casually. "As if it mattered. If it did, journalists would write about it in the papers…"

"*I* write about it," Jelena put in.

"I'm talking about important journalists, the ones who write about home affairs, on the main pages of dailies. Or the ones that make TV-documentaries. But they're not interested. They think it far more important to educate us Croats about the traditional techniques of wool processing in Transylvania; I've just seen a programme on telly. Is there a dessert?"

"Patience," mum hissed through clenched teeth, hamming discretion. "Wait for the man to finish his meal!"

"You know what Arsen[25] said," dad began, with mum already protesting, "that after a while love begins flowing in through the stomach and that he and Gabi[26] are so rotund because they still love each other a lot. Like you and I. And there you go, shouting at me!"

Once Mr Josip had gone, mum asked anxiously, "Did he wipe his specs with my knickers in front of that man, I daren't even ask?"

Jelena and Bruno burst out laughing.

Dad waved his hand dismissively and went back to the sitting room to join Bruno who was sitting in front of the television sipping wine. "How are you coping with your wife?" he asked compassionately.

"Fine," Bruno replied.

"Yeah, you're still a gunman in your prime."

"A gunman?" Bruno laughed.

"A man with a working gun," dad said. "And me, my wife moans at me because I think of nothing but food. Once your gun stops working, you're no longer a hunter; you eat what you've got. And no one needs you any longer; that's how it is..."

"What are you on about?" Jelena asked, entering. "What gun? What hunter?"

Bruno laughed. "Your dad has just come up with another metaphor."

Jelena went to her father and embraced him: "My darling hedgehog."

---

[25] Arsen Dedić, (1938 -), Croatian composer, singer, poet and author
[26] Gabi Novak, (1936 -), Croatian singer, Arsen Dedić's wife

The Wave – Tuesday, 11th October

On Tuesday morning, as usual, David burst like a gust of wind through the door of the half-empty, still sleepy *Little Café*. Jelena was waiting, nodding over her first coffee of the day. David halted in the open door, ran his hand through his hair and smiled broadly, waved to Jelena, winked at Šime the waiter, nodded to Dipsy who was standing by the bar, got to Jelena's table in a couple of long steps, took his coat off, slung it over the back of a chair and sat down, followed by the looks of everyone in the café. Apart from Jelena and Dipsy, that meant two surly young colleagues and a retired journalist who was practically part of the furniture. From his position at the bar, Dipsy waved to David. "Good morning, esteemed colleague."

Jelena glanced contemptuously in Dipsy's direction: *colleague!* He had to be kidding. David grinned at him and flipped him the finger teasingly.

"Thank'ee, thank'ee," said Dipsy. "Esteemed colleague, even when you flip your finger, you do it not like a Balkan yokel, but the cool American way. Respect!" Like an air hostess showing how to use oxygen masks to instruction from the loudspeakers, he demonstrated both finger-flipping styles as he spoke: the middle finger of one hand bent towards the palm, the middle finger of the other one pointing upwards.

David waved his comment aside and sat down next to Jelena at their usual table at the front by the glass wall panel, facing the pavement seats outside and turning his back to the bar and Dipsy. Šime the waiter approached. A living legend in many Zagreb cafés, from *Corso* and *The City* to *The Old Clock*, a figure of fame for generations in Zagreb cultural circles, he had retired two years ago and had since been freelancing in the *Little Café*. "You'll 'uv yer usual, wi' 'ot milk?" He always spoke in dialect with his regulars. "And yous could mug us ter mark yer award."

"You're the best informed waiter in town, to be sure," said David. "What'll you have?"

"I'll 'uv me Vecchia[27], only a bit ron," Šime replied, vanishing behind the counter.

"A real Dalmatian drink," David said and picked up the paper Jelena had just put down.

When Šime returned with David's coffee, Jelena produced her little sugar container and measured two spoonfuls into the cup. Šime halted and said: "There yous go again wi' yer jordan. Wa' did yous say it wuz, saccharose?"

"Fructose," Jelena said. "What's a jordan?"

"Eeeh... a jordan is... wha' is it yous call it here... crappot? Poopot?"

Jelena laughed.

"Potty," Dipsy threw in.

"Me sugar's not sound 'nuff fe yous, is it?" Šime went on. "Yos would be a bright kind o' sugar, like? Eh? It's all one and the same thing; come 'ead, yous can't live forever."

"Come on, Šime, hasn't she told you a hundred times that that stuff is good for men?" David laughed.

Šime laughed too. "Away wi' yous, yous jonalists think up such squallies. Yous think yous can live forever," he repeated. "As if you'd be missed if yous didn't."

"Fame hasn't changed you, I see," Jelena said when Šime moved away from their table.

"I had my mobile off all weekend."

"People like hanging around winners, regardless."

"Precisely, regardless! But only exceptional people and exceptional, world-changing books should win awards. And the world can quite easily survive without my book." David propped himself on one elbow and brought his face close to Jelena's. "Enough of that; tell me first how things are with you." He ruffled her hair gently.

"You're the only man I know who can ruffle a woman's hair without her fussing about her hairdo."

"Don't change the subject."

"I'm not. I'm fine. Let's not talk about me now." Jelena

---

[27] Vecchia Romagna, an Italian brandy popular in Zagreb

moved her face away from his. "You know a better book that should have won the award instead?"

"I'm sure there must be more than just one," David continued seriously. "In any case, there can't be much difference between my award-winning one and those that didn't win anything. They're products of the same epoch, all of them."

"Yes, and?"

"Awards should mean something, but they're given out for wrong reasons. Something ought to change."

"That's utopia. What could possibly change?"

"You know what Ranko Marinković[28] said twenty years ago? That Arsen Dedić was our greatest poet and would be the only one to remain so, only people weren't aware of that yet. And he has remained so; he's greater than the poets who, at the time, were deemed real poets, unlike Arsen who was a *singer-songwriter*... Today there's Hus[29], Marijan Ban[30], Edo Maajka[31], the one from Cold Beer[32], Gobac[33]..."

"Particularly Hus," Jelena put in.

David went on: "They're so talented they work with total ease, and when something is easy..."

"... it is not hard," Jelena laughed.

"That's right, and it's perceived as lacking gravitas. But when someone comes up with a concept made to measure for culture vultures, they declare it to be proper art."

"Correct," Jelena agreed. "That's why I like *Steamroller* –

---

[28] Ranko Marinković (1913 – 2001), Croatian author. His best known works are the play *Glorija* (1955) and the novel *Kiklop* (1965) (Wikipedia)

[29] Husein Hasanefendić-Hus, one of the founding members of the *Parni Valjak* (The *Steamroller)* rock group

[30] Croatian poet and songwriter, singer with the group *Daleka obala* (*The Far Coast*)

[31] Edin Osmić, stage name Edo Maajka (1978 -) Bosnian rapper

[32] Hladno pivo (= Cold Beer), Croatian punk rock group established 1987

[33] Davor Gobac (1964 -), Croatian singer-songwriter, leader of the *Psihomodo pop* rock group.

no concept whatsoever, just words and music, simple love songs, or life songs – as you wish... And I like Neno Belan,[34] who always makes one smile. I went off painting because of concept. You heard about that rich bird last summer who bought a *sculpture* somewhere at the coast and forked out several thousand euros for it? The sculpture consisted of three old books about art tied together with a rope and suspended from the ceiling. And what happens now? When she puts it up at home, suspended from the ceiling, she'll have to keep explaining to everyone it's art. When he made *David*, Michelangelo didn't have to explain anything to anyone. And I'm not buying 'our time' as an excuse; those three books are not the art for our time. They are not art at all, plain and simple. I mean, painting a moustache onto Mona Lisa is not the problem; the problem is painting Mona Lisa in the first place."

David laughed. "Do you remember that story from Don Quixote, where a lunatic goes from village to village with a hollow reed and blows up dogs? When they ask him why he's doing that, he says, 'Do you think blowing up dogs is easy?' You're the same: 'Go paint Mona Lisa if you can!'"

Jelena made a hurt face, but laughed anyway. "Mona Lisa is not the same as a blown-up dog."

"You know what I mean. Critics, too, believe that only the hard stuff has value. It would be stupid to try and paint Mona Lisa in this day and age. In the 16th century, we had Leonardo and Mona Lisa; in the 20th Duchamp and Mona Lisa with moustache painted on; in the current century, who knows what she'll look like... And you're forgetting the element of play."

"I know; creativity is in the play, but..."

"That's right, the effortless quality of play can generate confusion which is why, as I already said, it doesn't get taken seriously. Culture vultures, too, value ready-to-wear and scorn unique originals."

"You've lost me now," Jelena said. "What are we actually discussing and who is claiming what?

---

[34] Croatian rock musician

"We're talking about my award not saying anything about my book, either good or bad. In any case, who can say what's good and what isn't?"

"It's good in my opinion, if it means something to you. "

"That may well be so, but you're not the decision maker here."

"I did contribute to the general climate of approval for you and your work," she laughed.

"Exactly; you belong to my circle. That's how it starts…"

"I know; now you're going to tell me about the wave again."

"Of course. Look what happens…" David immediately began gesticulating. "Every time you're told how someone is marvellous, fascinating, beautiful, clever, you are disappointed when you see that person and believe that it is so because you've been expecting too much. You're right, but that's not the whole story: whatever you were told about someone was wrapped in the image that circle of people had of that person." Animatedly, his hands described circles in the air. "That means that, more than just being himself, he is also their image of him, an image comprising all their individual contributions, making him more beautiful, smarter and more important than he would be outside that circle. That is not to say that people do it with a goal in mind; they don't. Mostly, they simply go along with the prevailing opinion. Liking comes in concentric circles. The family is the first circle. If a child is liked by its family, there is no damage to the 'me', the ego. The school is the second essential circle, then the university, the workplace… Those are the social circles. Simultaneously, one passes through the circles of time: child, teenager, young adult, adult… Here's a good example," he laughed. "Each time I had a new girlfriend, she'd already know of all the hot chicks I'd dated and I'd grow in her regard because of that. Get it? So it all becomes like in the movies: I like the one who's never heard of me and therefore sees me as I am, with no concentric circles involved. Or like when you're rich and think that women only want you for your money, so you hide the facts from some poor, naïve girl who doesn't know how rich you are, and she falls in love with you anyway and you with her because of that. The same thing happened with Buba: she was not impressed by my context. And with jobs as well; whenever I started in a new job I already had a reputation, so no checks were made. And it is no different with awards: in my circles, people believe I deserve the award and the circle spreads out like a wave."

"Wave, right," Jelena said. "I'll give you that. In your case, however, there is also synchronicity."

"Synchronicity?" David looked at her, his eyebrows raised.

"By pure chance, you're handsome and talented. By more chance, you're a journalist, and you just felt like writing a book..."

"That's not exactly what Jung had in mind when he spoke of synchronicity. At best, those might be ordinary synchronisms," said David, his glance skimming the newspaper headlines.

"Whichever way you look at it, you're the public's favourite," Jelena went on. "Whatever you create will be accepted."

"It's my duty, then, to come up with something against culture vultures... And you?"

"What do you mean, me? I'll follow you. At the end of the day, you're the sociologist here."

"That's not what I meant. I notice you haven't been in a good mood of late."

"Oh, that. Nothing special. My husband takes me for granted." Again, she reproached herself for including Bruno when speaking about herself: the betrayal of loyalty, the most important of marital vows.

"Pardon?"

"You know how politicians speak? For example: *decisive measures will be taken*. When you hear stuff like that, what do you do? You don't listen, you switch off. And that's how Bruno switches me off."

"Jozo, you're taking the mick," said David. "...or you're a retard. You don't expect your husband to be in love with you after so many years? If he didn't love you as much as he does, he'd hardly be able to bear you."

"I must be retarded, then," Jelena said. "I know he loves me. He loves me the most anyone can love one's own wife of fourteen years. And he'll love me until he falls in love again. When he does fall in love, with some other woman or man, he'll go on loving me, in the same way he loves mum Dubravka: he'll look after me, visit me once or twice a week... How I rattle on! Shall we go?" she said, picking her handbag up from the chair. "Oh yeah," she suddenly remembered as they waited for Šime and the bill, "who's that Pero Kovačić you introduced us to at the Awards Evening? Where do you know him from and what's he doing in the Journalists' Association Club?"

"Aha! I noticed he'd caught your eye. Mirela, the animator in the Club, that nice young poet, that's his girlfriend. But as I told you then, the man's a ladykiller. And so, I don't know what you might be planning..."

"Please...! Have I ever planned anything?"

"Why do you ask, then?" said David, shrugging.

When David got up, Jelena remarked, "Am I imagining things, or have you indeed got yourself up nicer than usual?"

"I'm still the laureate, aren't I?" David winked.

"And there's also our new colleague," Jelena said. "All Zagreb swoons at the thought of you, and there you are, about to be foxed."

"Don't rush ahead," David replied good-naturedly. "And don't hex."

"Graft me regards ter dat Bosnian o' yos," Šime said as they were leaving. Dipsy followed them. "You're off tew, pretzel?" Šime asked. Pretzel was his word for paparazzo.

"I'm meeting a lady client," said Dipsy, winking. "And speaking of Bosnians," he put in readily, "I've got a Bosnian one for you..."

"You're always on about Bosnians."

"I'm not a nationalist; I'm fair and abuse everyone equally. Here, for example: do you know who Croats' ancestors are? *Cro*-magnons. Geddit? And fancy one about

Herzegovinians[35]?" Mario laughed at his own joke, in advance. "Do you know the name of a building company from Šuica[36] that works according to the principles of feng-shui? Feng-shuica. Good, eh?"

Even David and Jelena laughed.

When they got out of the café, they spotted Ivana in the distance entering the reception of *The Herald*. "There's our Ivana," said Dipsy. "That moron of hers lunches with that bottom-wiggler every day..."

"Let them be," said David. "Tell us instead how your marriage is doing."

"Chugging along nicely," said Mario. "But," he went on, "have you seen that jumbo poster on Držić Street: WGW JEBENO DOBRO[37]? In emulation of the American *fucking good*, of course. And on the telly, they advertise *Helf – sweet down to your balls*! I'm expecting to see an ad for, say, Diesel: NOT WEARING DIESEL SUCKS DICKS." He fell silent for a moment, then added: "And there you go, accusing me of using vulgar humour."

"Do you know what the most popular advert was between the two World Wars?" David asked. "*Dora* soap is best, the rest you can forget."

"Ah, the unexpected reversal: you expect it to rhyme and it doesn't... Phat! That's real wit, not *fucking good*," Dipsy waffled on. When they entered the office, he asked, "Where's our Beauty?"

Ivana was already in. "I'm here," she said.

"Not you," said Dipsy with brutal sincerity. "The new one."

"Uh-huh. She comes in late," said Ivana. She did not look hurt. "She's the boss' pet."

"Nothing to do with being the boss' pet," Jelena said. "It's

---

[35] Herzegovinians are usually presented in jokes as cunning, ruthlessly exploiting the naivety of others for their own gain.

[36] Šuica or Šujica is village in the municipality of Tomislavgrad, Bosnia and Herzegovina

[37] Croatian for 'fucking good'

the nature of her work. If she has to go to a performance in the evening, she doesn't have to show up here at nine."

"I'm only saying," Ivana said. "That woman goes on my nerves."

"Why?" asked Jelena, surprised.

"Because she burst into the loo just as I was wiping myself, pardon me... The lock was out of order." Ivana shrugged. "In any case, I feel handicapped next to her."

Everyone laughed. Jelena said, "You're right. Being caught in an embarrassing situation is reason enough to dislike the intruder."

When Nina arrived, everyone forgot Ivana's toilet tale. "We could finally do that coffee today," she said, looking at David and Jelena.

"All right," Jelena said. David smiled, not as seducer but as one seduced.

"You wrote a novel and won the *Tin Ujević* Award for it, haven't you?" asked Jelena as Nina began arranging her desk.

"Yes," Nina replied, pausing. "How do you know?"

"Your name was familiar, and then a friend reminded me... a colleague of yours; she's also written a novel."

"Yeah? What's her name?"

"Ana Marton. She's written..."

"I know: *The Naked She-Wolf.* I've read it. An excellent novel."

"I'll tell her; she'll be pleased."

"What's the title of your novel?" David asked.

"*The Angelic Trap.*"

"Autobiographical, then," said David, smiling.

Once more, Nina limited her response to a smile. Jelena laughed. Dipsy did not get the point.

"We must read it," David said.

Nina smiled impishly. "You must."

Following which everyone got down to work. Most likely on account of Nina's presence, David did not exchange regular daily comments on the articles in the papers with Jelena, or poke fun at Dipsy. Dipsy was rather more dignified than was his custom. When Andrej arrived, he gave everyone a dry nod as usual, and a separate one to Nina. "Everything all right?" he asked. Nina nodded: "Everything's fine."

An Idea – at the *Little Café*, Noon, 11th October

Strangely for October, the *Little Café* was bathed in sunlight. All the tables under the red-and-green striped awning were occupied. David, Nina and Jelena waited for Šime to clear a table. "'Ow can the state 'ope ter escape ruin," Šime said, "when yous, instead o' 'av'n a lunch break 'ave a werk break!"

As they each sat down, David chivalrously pulled out a chair for Nina.

He asked her about her book. "I haven't read it yet, I'm sorry; I'll do it as soon as I get a chance... What's it about?"

"It's a love story, of course," Nina laughed. "And a crime one." David and Jelena were listening attentively, so she went on. "The heroine is a young drug addict who experiences love only once in her life, for a young lad who is also an addict. When they first meet, they both appear to be losers. From that moment on, however, the girl is happy, comes off drugs, everything seems to be working for her, her zest for life returns, she wants happiness, while he sinks ever deeper into the mire. When he dies of an overdose, she takes revenge on everyone she holds responsible for his death..."

"Sounds interesting," Jelena said.

"That's just the beginning," Nina laughed. David and Jelena laughed too. "I'm not telling you the rest, in case you ever decide to read it."

David could not take his eyes off her and most likely failed to hear quite a bit of what she had said.

"Interesting," Jelena said. She had a feeling that Nina believed she'd been expecting something like *Eighteen* or whatever number of *Strokes of the Brush Before Bed*[38]. Perhaps she did. It would have been the crack on the face of

---

[38] *One Hundred Strokes of the Brush Before Bed*, erotic novel by Melissa Parente (Serpent's Tail, 2004)

perfection… She remembered Ana's contemptuous snort. "We'll read it," she said.

"And how is it doing, the book?" David asked.

"I'm quite happy," said Nina. "I got three good reviews. In women's glossies," she said with a touch of irony. "Two were neither here nor there, but I learned the third one by heart, that's how good it was." She laughed melodiously. "This is how it goes: *The novel reminds one of a stranger in a strange land the language of which he doesn't understand, but nevertheless manages to communicate perfectly using all available means: hands, gestures, pointing at things and onomatopoeia, all the while charming the head off anyone he meets, unlike the boring nerd who has learned to speak that foreign language to perfection, without any accent, so that no one even notices that he is foreign, nor is there anything in his speech for people to remember… The novel* Angelic Trap *could be defined as inspired naïve work by an exceptionally talented young author whose second book we await with interest…*" She was enchanting as she recited without any affectation. "I had to boast a bit," she finished, laughing. Jelena listened with interest and sympathy; David was spellbound.

When Nina announced she had to leave, David rose at once and Jelena said, somewhat brusquely, "I haven't finished my coffee."

"Of course, sorry," said Nina. "There's no need for you to rush."

David sat down again and said, "Okay, we'll stay on a bit."

Nina said goodbye and left.

"I appreciate your sacrifice," said Jelena testily.

"You're heavier than an elephant," said David. "Poor Bruno."

"I'd like to finish my coffee in peace like I do every day, like I'm used to doing; what's heavy about that? I thought you liked it too. However, you men only need to see a pretty woman and you…"

"You and your male-female clichés!" David waved a hand. "Obviously being close to an attractive girl affects one's behaviour; it's normal for people to affect one another. It's not merely natural, that's how human society is organised."

"Yeah, yeah, all according to regulations. You must think I'm mean," Jelena said. "But you men always take sides with the prettier woman. She can be a courtesan, an adulteress, a blackmailer, a murderess, a schemer; anything can be hiding behind her pretty face and everything is forgiven. What am I saying: forgiven! She'll never even be suspected of anything."

"That's right. As they say in American movies, no one says that life is fair."

"I mean," Jelena went on, not looking at David, "I understand what it is you get off on: a lovely girl, alluring, yet innocent like a little child... I believe that little girl in the body of a grown woman is the very thing you fancy... Ana is right: you're all paedophiles!"

"I was just about to say that you sound like Ana," David said. "And the second person plural you keep using is the worst of all... As for Nina, she is a young *adult* woman, at an age when she is attractive to both fathers and sons, without father having to be a paedophile or son suffering from the Oedipus complex."

In a bad mood, Jelena was on the verge of tears. "You have a way with words," she said. "I told you this has nothing to do with Nina; you don't have to defend her."

"Nor do you have to accuse her. Don't introduce her to your husband, problem solved!" David replied, laughing.

"I already have; I told you we met her in King Cross. But I believe that I irritate Bruno so much that I've put him off the female sex for some time to come."

David shook his head in comic disapproval.

"Perhaps I ought to find a lover," Jelena said. "What about that Pero of yours?"

"Aha, so you are interested in him after all?" David looked at her suspiciously. "Can't say I'm surprised; what's more, believe it or not, I not only saw you look at him, but also him looking at you... I shouldn't have told you that, it might give you ideas. Watch out, Jozo!"

"Oh, please, I'm 38 and a half," said Jelena impatiently.

"The most dangerous age. Biological clock ticking. Husband asleep. Collagen reserves running out, new ones not being made…"

"You're a real mate, thanks."

"You know my view of the matter: *carpe diem*." He ruffled her hair smiling broadly.

Jelena moved her head away from his touch, but then she, too, laughed. She went on seriously, "That story of Nina's, it doesn't sound bad at all."

"Not bad at all," David agreed.

"Ana is convinced Nina won the award only because she's young and beautiful…" Jelena paused. "I've got an idea! What do you think: could we pay a pretty young woman to let Ana publish her second novel under her name?"

David regarded her with raised eyebrows.

"Hmmm, yes… wait, that reminds me of something… but of what? Oh, yeah, there was this Slovenian winemaker who produced a perfect *pinot gris* – I discovered that while researching my article on resveratrol – and he wanted to enter it in an important European competition, but knew that, as a Slovenian, he had little chance of winning, regardless of the quality of his wine. So he registered it as an Italian wine and won the first prize. Receiving it, he said, 'Yes, but I've got to tell you it's really Slovenian, this wine.'"

"And?"

"And they didn't disqualify him. His vineyard was next to the Italian border, so they didn't have to be strict. He was able to keep his prize, and now he's so renowned that he doesn't have to cheat any more."

"That's right; he's being carried by the wave."

"So could Ana… only…" Jelena frowned "…if the book were to succeed under the name of a pretty author, Ana would be mortified, because, you know, no woman really believes she's ugly, no matter what she says. And one should never be sincere about a woman's looks, if they're not great…"

David agreed.

"Wait, I've got a better idea!" Jelena exclaimed. "How about publishing her book under your name?"

David stopped in mid-gesture to listen, his hands still in the air. "Wait a minute, wait a minute," he said slowly. "That's not a bad idea, not bad at all!" He laughed and grabbed Jelena's shoulders. "You're a genius! That's it! It's got to work. Quite right, quite right; it's my duty, now while I'm riding the wave." He clapped his hands, rubbed them together and then crossed them at the back of his head which he threw back with an expression of delight. "That's going to work! Wonderful, Jozo, absolutely brilliant!"

"That means, we're going ahead with it. The long period of boredom is finally to end. I mean, that's not what's important, but..." She looked at David. "You're not even listening to me. What are you thinking of?"

He waved his hand absently. "If you knew, you wouldn't think me perfect any more." He laughed.

Discussing Ana and awards had made him remember his own *black hole*. Fifteen years earlier he had taken part in a serious award fraud, a fraud which, unlike the one they were planning would, did actually harm someone. Due to circumstances, he had done it in collaboration with and on the instigation of his current editor, Andrej Martić; this, however, did not exonerate him in his own eyes, nor could his youth and inexperience do so. Andrej, who at the time had excellent relations with colleagues in high places, got nominated as member of the jury for the highest literary award in the country. One of the ten jury members, at Andrej's own suggestion, was young David Antolić. When David told them which novel in his opinion was the best, Andrej had a private chat with him and explained that it would not be opportune to give the award to a Serb author. Under ordinary circumstances it wouldn't have mattered, but then, in the midst of war, with unbearable tension everywhere, with neighbour turning on neighbour, such a move could stoke up passions and set people against the entire profession. The young man in question was talented, he said; his time would come sooner or later... He proposed that the award be given to another novel, almost as good as the first one; it would cause no problems and the award would not go to an undeserving author. At the end of the day, who was really capable of assessing art... David consented. It seemed that Martić may have got his way with several other jury members. The Serb never won the award, and Martić's career remained politically spotless. When he and David found themselves working together for *The Herald*, neither the one nor the other mentioned the episode.

"Shall we?" He could hear Jelena's voice.

"I believe your idea might give me a chance to atone for one of my old sins," he said.

Jelena did not ask any questions. She knew him well enough to tell when he was in a serious mood. They got up. David put an arm around her shoulders. Leaving, they did not hear Dipsy singing to Anđelko the receptionist through the window: "*Carpet woven all in squiggles, come my love and make me wiggle...* One of your folk songs, to ease your yearning..."

Moving away from him, Anđelko said, "You know so many things, Dipsy old son, and none of them useful."

The Hand

October 2004

NEW UNIVERSALISMS – IT'S HARD TO BE GLOCAL

From a text by Prof. Bruno Latour, Paris: "The universal used to mean something fairly simple: the further away you were from the local tradition, the more universal you were. It would appear that the usual line of development ran from the local towards the global (...) Things have now changed considerably. (...) According to a number of anthropologists, the situation is becoming ever more confusing as people invent new localisms faster than the globalisation can destroy them. New traditions are discovered every day, whole new cultures spring into being, new languages are created. (...) The root metaphor seems to have been turned on its head: the more identities are being uprooted by modernisation, the stronger they hold on. That is the reason behind the success of the word 'glocal', confirming that labels cannot be safely arranged along the old scale of growth ranging, with continuous additions, from the most local to the universal... With the compass of modernisation spinning so madly, how can we tell legitimate glocal additions from the illegitimate ones? (...) That cosmoses are objects up for grabs is a new and disturbing idea. How is it possible to bring those different cosmoses together in a future unity shared by all? A future common Domus?"

That means: the glocal = the local, resisting the global. That is why ethno and the fashion for neo-Nazism, anti-modernism and the creation of mini-states are so popular.

October 2004

INTERVIEW: Ive Šimat Banov, art historian: "I enjoy my work and, like Barthes, I feel relieved not to be obliged to be modern any more. I have the right to complete my homework."

Coincidences – Thursday, 13th October

Ana rushed to finish her shopping before her rendezvous with Jelena. *Merkator's* checkout was not too busy. The cashier pressed the button by mistake and started the conveyor belt too early, making the next customer's shopping tumble onto Ana's cottage cheese, fettuccine, mayo, *Twix* and bread. The customer, a young woman with beautiful silver and onyx pendant earrings, laughed, scooped her purchases up and said, "Oh dear, sorry," and Ana smiled back with a cordiality unusual in view of her perpetual gloom. Surprised by her own reaction, she said, "It doesn't matter; actually, I could use those biscuits of yours."

She had arranged to meet Jelena in *Golf* on the Flower Market. When she entered, it took a few moments for her eyes to get used to the light. All the tables were full. Someone waved at her from the one closest to the bar. Ana went over, and the woman who had waved said, "We're just going." Ana recognised the silver earrings with the onyxes and said, "Haven't we already met today, in the shop?"

The woman remembered at once. "Oh, yeah, in *Merkator.*"

"What a coincidence," said Ana, genuinely intrigued.

But it did not end there. Before Ana had properly sat down, the young woman returned and asked, embarrassed: "Sorry, aren't you Ana Marton?"

"I am," Ana replied, astonished.

"I recognised you from the photo on the back cover of your book," said the woman.

"Eh?" Ana bucked up at the mention of her book.

"Yes. I'm Mirta Gluhak."

"Really? I can't believe it!" Ana exclaimed so loudly that people at other tables turned to look at her.

A few months after the publication of her book, Ana was informed by a young and therefore still conscientious employee at *Argus* that a number of female readers had phoned, wanting to get in touch with the author of *The Naked She-Wolf.* The staff at *Argus* refused to give them her number. One reader, however, thought of e-mailing a letter which eventually found its way to Ana, with a few weeks' delay. The letter was lovely and Ana put it into the thin scrapbook David had given her as a present when *The Naked She-Wolf* had come out.

Dear Ana,

Reading your book, I felt such closeness between us that I had to get in touch. I don't know where to begin, perhaps with the moment a faaaat book with an interesting title caught my eye in the shop-window. I'm not much of a reader, a book a month, sometimes more. I believe you'd like to read my impressions. The first page already promised interesting reading. Pages followed one another without a break. The first impression remained unchanged right to the end. Engaging, tender, familiar, warm, funny. Do I make myself clear. That is the reason I address you as Ana and say 'thou' and feel that you'll easily get my meaning.

All your stories happen around us, to you, to me, to our friends.

From the middle of the book onwards, I carried on reading it as a morning ritual, before going to work, greedily, because I was in a hurry and didn't want to be late, yet I needed to find out what happens next. But you might not care to know where my morning ritual takes place ☺

I talked about your book so enthusiastically that soon there was a whole list of people who wanted to read it, mainly women. I was surprised the other day when a friend, a young actor spoke to me about your book and recommended that I should read it because it was entertaining and true to life! I wasn't surprised because of the book but because of his age. I'm explaining so much to you, things I normally wouldn't explain, because I fear that yore mistrust might take the wrong direction.

I've muddled everything up now and I'm not even going to read what I've written. If I read it, I'd probably shorten the letter to the size of a greeting card or would not send it at all. Sorry for all the illiterate bits.

Thank you for your book and thank you for writing. I wish you a new book, and to get rich from writing.

A hug from
Mirta Gluhak

Mirta Gluhak was in a rush, or she may have felt uncomfortable, like Ana did: what could they talk about, the two of them, close to each other through the book and the letter but strangers in all else, in a conversation that had to be short, and would be awkward if it got too serious. Meeting and getting introduced to each other was enough. They exchanged telephone numbers and promised one another to stay in touch.

Of late, Ana had been dogged by coincidences.

When Jelena arrived, she could not wait to tell her what had happened. She spoke breathlessly.

"You're always so fascinated by this sort of stuff," Jelena said.

"I can't understand why you aren't," said Ana. "Isn't this an incredible thing to happen? Consider: it happened in Merkator, in Vukovar Avenue, five kilometres away on the other side of town, three hours ago. Two women who'd never met before, two tiny specks in the Universe. What chance brought them together in the same place twice in one day?"

"One doesn't say the world is small for nothing," said Jelena

Ana went on, ignoring the comment: "And they may never meet again afterwards. Even that would already be something. But then it turns out she's read my book and that we're, in effect, connected. And that she is the one who's written to me – the first response ever to my book, and you know how much it meant to me at the time."

"You've got artistic imagination," Jelena said.

"Artistic imagination! It annoys me when you're so superficial. You're not even trying to see the connection. I'm not discovering anything new by saying that all events are connected; nothing happens just like that, everything is linked, everything leads somewhere. For example, I've asked myself a hundred times what my life would have been like if my bicycle hadn't been stolen..."

"Bicycle?" Jelena repeated. "Is that a story I don't know?"

"It's not a story. Simply, I lost my bicycle. When I was little, I couldn't roller-skate, climb trees or ride a bike. I was a clumsy wuss. For my sixteenth birthday – imagine, as late as that! – I asked mum to buy me a bicycle. So she bought me a blue Pony. I practised first in the courtyard, then on our street which was most of the time free of cars back then. After a few days, I mustered enough courage to venture into Vukovar Avenue. I was doing really well, except for falling off my bike whenever a large lorry approached from the opposite direction. Nevertheless, I rode that bike all right, moving smoothly and keeping my balance well. Two weeks later I was using my bike to go to the shops and was immensely proud of myself: cycling was the first sport I'd ever mastered. And then one night someone stole my bike from the yard. Mum refused to buy me another one because I'd been negligent and didn't store the bike away in the shed. So from then on, I never rode a bicycle again. I probably wouldn't know how to ride one now. If one could rewind the time, however, and the bike hadn't been stolen, what would've happened? I might've ended up in excellent shape, tough and muscled; I might've met interesting cyclists and struck friendship with them. Evenings, we'd go down to the banks of the Sava[39] perhaps, sit together around the fire, roast sausages, play guitars and sing. A boy might have got interested in me one such evening and seen me home. I might have fallen in love and got married. I might not have had time for writing because I'd have had two kids straight away; maybe we wouldn't be sitting here talking now, maybe we wouldn't even have liked one another. Perhaps I'd have become neither a psychologist nor a writer, but, say, a painter."

"A human being is born to an infinite number of possibilities. It's impossible to anticipate all the combinations in that cosmic game of chess, so why bother? What practical gain can you have by being aware of living only one of those possibilities at this moment?"

"Maybe such awareness does have some use, maybe it can help one avoid trouble. Have you heard about the ninth symphony curse?"

Jelena shook her head.

"Do you know how many composers died while writing their ninth symphony? Or that Jan Sibelius wrote only eight symphonies, refusing to write the ninth one because he was afraid to, even though, after his eight one, he lived for another thirty years?"

"I didn't know that. And do you know that Maksim Mrvica's first name is Maksim, and surname Mrvica[40]? I'm kidding, I'm kidding; but just imagine how witty his parents must be..."

Ana gave her a black look.

"It was a joke, sorry," Jelena said.

"Have you read about that Croatian boy from Germany who savagely *like a beast* killed his girlfriend and her mate, dismembered them and stuffed their body parts into black binbags?"

---

[39] The Sava is a river with a source in the Slovenian Alps, running through Zagreb and joining the Danube at Belgrade in Serbia.

[40] The name translates as Maxim Speck. Maxim as in 'the biggest' (maximus) and Speck as in 'tiny' (a speck).

"I have, what horror!"

"Do you know where his father came from?"

"No," said Jelena, surprised by the question.

"From a place called Zvjerinac[41]," said Ana triumphantly.

"You get mad at me when I say that you have artistic imagination," said Jelena, "but you simply must write."

"Why should I write?" said Ana gloomily.

"Where else can you offload all this stuff? It's too much for one soul. A book is your natural extension. That's probably the case with all born artists." She thought that publishing Ana's second book under David's name may not be such a great idea. It could be too schizophrenic, too risky for Ana, unstable as she was. She had no intention of telling her anything; it would be best if David did it.

Thoughtfully, Jelena contemplated the narrow, sombre face, the gaze devoid of curiosity, the pursed lips. No one would rush to read anything by this dour, anxious lass. Her lively, entertaining, funny, insightful, erotic, exciting book – who knows where she'd pulled it from! A bright potentiality might have broken into it from Ana's unrealised parallel life. "Perhaps your book is your second self," she said. "Ana – Mr Hyde; *The Naked She-Wolf* – Dr Jekyll."

Ana smiled faintly. "I've just been thinking the same thing."

"There you go, then; that's why you must write – to stay healthy. To start with, such talent is not born every day. Don't wave your hand, I think you know that too. You've read what other people write. Secondly, if you don't write, that darkness of yours will devour you. Your autoimmune enemy."

"Look what happened the other day," Ana said. "The father of one of my old schoolmates died. They found him on the shore; the sea had washed him out. He hadn't drowned; he'd died of a heart attack. He fell into the sea and the sea carried him a few kilometres away. All his life he'd lived in Brodarica

---

[41] Translates as "Beastville".

near Šibenik[42]. And you know what was strange: he'd never been to sea, in a boat. He'd never even taken a walk by the sea. He didn't like the sea."

"If he never walked by the sea, how did he fall into it?" Jelena asked.

"He liked drinking. Every evening, he'd follow the same route: a walk through the town, a glass of wine and water in the pub and then back the way he came. It was a cold evening with thick fog. He probably couldn't see his way very well – he was old, in his eighties – and might have wandered onto the jetty unawares."

"So?"

"Don't you get it? He'd feared the sea all his life, kept away from it – only to die in the sea."

"So?"

"Is that a mere chance or is the Universe organised in such a way that he always knew he'd die in the sea? I mean, he didn't die in the sea because he'd feared it but he feared it because he knew his death was waiting for him there."

Jelena was silent.

"So now," Ana said, "I worry that it proves I'm going to die of what I fear most, and at the same time I'm happy that my book's theme has passed the reality check, see?"

"I see," said Jelena. "In that case, write."

"To what purpose?"

"To put it your way: we can't even imagine the number of lives which might have taken a better direction thanks to your book. The life of a book is long; give it time. Give time to your book and to yourself. Write more books instead of strangling this one. You're a born writer; no one can take that away from you."

"Like hell they can't. No matter what I write, a handful of addlepated nitwitcrits are able to smear their narcissistic spit over everything that means something to me. To me, writing is

---

[42] Brodarica derives from 'brod', the word for 'boat'. Šibenik is town on the Croatian coast.

paramount to all. I live to write, because if I wasn't alive, I couldn't write. An example: when I went to that lecture about *Biology and Healthy Nutrition*, you'd have thought I'd gone for the sake of my health. But no, I barely had the time for a sandwich because of that lecture, and went because I needed information for my book. It was important that my heroine listens to the lecture, not I. What she eats matters to me, not what I eat. And all that so that some fop can write: 'Another unremarkable book'. Yeah?"

"That's all insignificant."

"I don't mean to say that my book must by definition be good but that, be it ever so good, they would destroy it. The critics are pests and parasites. If I were to write *Hell*,[43] I'd put them in the seventh circle."

Jelena laughed. "You exaggerate," she said.

"Tell me, what are critics for? When were they invented, as a profession, I mean..."

"I know that already in the 18ᵗʰ century, Samuel Johnson wrote about Shakespeare. There must be earlier stuff, I'm sure..."

"Right. They've been studying him for some three hundred, four hundred years and have now found out that Shakespeare was too lazy and too poorly educated to have had written all that by himself. Whereas at the end of the day it's not important at all whether the author of those plays was Shakespeare or whoever, what matters is that nothing better has ever been written."

"Without critics, would you have ever heard of Doris Dörrie? Or of Tokareva, with whom you were just as delighted?"

"Okay, you may be right to a degree... I heard of Doris Dörrie on telly. I read about Tokareva in the papers; I doubt that I'd have found her by chance. Russians have no American style marketing. And it would have been a pity not to have found her."

---

[43] Ana is referring to Dante's *Divine Comedy*.

"There you go, then" Jelena said. "One needs critics like one needs... insects. All insects are harmful to something and good for something else. Nature arranged it that way. Statistically speaking, a critic is more likely to come across good things and write about them than cause valuable work to remain unnoticed. That means they're more useful than harmful, on the whole..."

"Although it might have been better for me not to have read either Tokareva or Doris Dörrie," Ana interrupted her.

"Why?"

"Because... why do something when you know that others have already done it better? It's pointless."

"Rubbish," said Jelena firmly. "Your book is excellent. In any case, who says that bad books, too, haven't got a purpose? You're the one who believes that everything is connected."

"That doesn't mean I want to write bad books!"

Jelena didn't feel like carrying on with the discussion; with Ana, it usually ended up in a blind alley where arguments meant nothing. She changed the subject. "Have you read that young Spanish or Basque author everyone's talking about, her name is Echeberia or something like that..."

"Lucia Etxebarria. I heard of her but I haven't read her yet."

"I watched her the other evening on the telly. She spoke about capitalism grinding us down and persuading us we needed unnecessary things in order to make us shop crazily, and in order for us to shop crazily, we first have to be made miserable; they make us miserable by frustrating us with images of ideal life we ought to aspire to, but it is an unattainable goal because it is unrealistic. Such life doesn't exist. Great love, for example, doesn't exist. Yet we all spend our entire lives awaiting this great love and are miserable because we believe that life is meaningless without it. She took Victoria Beckham as an example. That woman, she says, has had cosmetic surgery done from head to toe in order to attain some impossible ideal; her husband is cheating on her, she's unhappy, there's not a moment of peace and happiness in her day. And she's rolling in money..."

Ana nodded absently. "Yes, yes, I'm sure she, too, writes well. In fact, there's no reason for me to compare myself with all of them. Shakespeare is enough. After his writing, mine resembles the heavy footfall of an old elephant."

Jelena regarded her silently. She'd read somewhere that hypochondria went together with illusions of grandeur. She kept that to herself and said instead, "Ana, pride is a mortal sin. Just think, no one has surpassed Shakespeare for half a million years!"

Ana shrugged.

The Hand

A VUKOVAR WOMAN SPEAKS AFTER 13 YEARS The Serbs who raped me in the concentration camp still stroll through Vukovar

KIKLOP, THE FIRST LITERARY *PORIN*[44]: This year entered 248 titles by 55 publishers. All professional associations involved with book publishing took part in the selection: The Association of Publishers and Booksellers, the Authors' Association of Croatia, The Croatian Association of Children's and Teens' Authors, The Croatian Association of Librarians, The Association of Croatian Literary Translators, the Literary Department and the Social Sciences Department of HAZU[45] and cultural commentators in the press as well as literary critics. The selected titles will compete in 12 categories.

The year enters titles? Which are by publishers, rather than authors? Will the journalist who wrote this have a say in choosing the winning title?

Thursday, 13th October – Buba encounters Helena

David took care of Buba and the kids no less now than he used to when they were still living together. He didn't pay alimony set by the court and didn't even know the amount. Buba still

---

[44] A Croatian music award

[45] Hrvatska akademija znanosti i umjetnosti – the Croatian Academy of Sciences and Arts (Arts and Sciences)

shared his bank account and was a joint cardholder, even though she never used her card without consulting David. Only, he seldom had the time to shop with his family.

As always when in town, Hana stripped her mum of cash with lightning speed: she dragged her into *Diesel* in Frankopanska Street "just to see what trousers they've got". "Mum, these are only 800 kuna," she said, beaming, so Buba ended up buying them and moaned afterwards as was her custom: "Sometimes it really feels as if you two are sucking me dry... like dementors."

"Speak in the singular, please," said Matko.

"If you intend to torment me," said Hana with dignity, "we'd better take the jeans back right now."

"Sure," said Buba. "You say that because you know we can't take them back, only exchange them." But later she gave Hana a peck on the cheek and said, "I'm sorry. You're right, if I bought them for you, I have no business tormenting you for making me do it. And you do look nice in them." She could not tell Hana that her obsession with clothes did not trouble her because of the money they cost, but because of Hana's tendency to invest clothes with the power she should have found in herself: new clothes gave her short-term confidence to compete with *popular* girls and feel beautiful. Buba knew that because her own adolescence, too, had been a painful one.

Comfortable about himself and therefore more modest in his demands, Matko completed his shopping quickly and, since he wore his clothes until he grew out of them, relatively cheaply: 600 kuna for Doc Martens', and a mere 350 kuna for a new pair of Rifle jeans in a sale. He did mention a "real bomber jacket" – 1000 kuna – even as he chided his sister for her greed. "You're a pain in the fundament," he kept saying to annoy her.

Hana could not resist shops and shopping. "Wow, look, I read about this..." she cried outside *L' essence de Provence* shop-window.

"What sort of stuff have they got?" Buba asked.

"You can buy me natural soap against acne here; it's made of clay, olive oil and lavender."

They went in. Hana flitted from glass shelf to glass shelf. "Look at this body milk with grapefruit essence... and this is just perfect, orange... and look, a body exfoliating scrub..."

Rolling his eyes upwards, Matko said gravely, "They've got shampoo, too; we haven't got any at home."

The young assistant pointed at a whole shelf full of shampoo.

"What are they like?" Buba asked. "Have you tried them?"

"Well, I use the olive oil one," the young man replied, "and it's great."

The larger tube cost 69 kuna, and Buba asked about the half-size one. "Do you happen to know how many hair washes one can get out of this one? Are these shampoos good value, or...?"

"I don't know about the small one," said the young man who was, to be honest, completely bald except or a few tufts of hair behind the ears. "I use the large one and it lasts me, like, ages." Buba heard Matko cough to hide his laughter.

"If only we could win 20 thousand kuna on Lotto," said Hana as they left the shop with only the shampoo.

"Yeah," said Buba absently.

Hana muttered, frowning, and worked out sums with her fingers. "No, it wouldn't be enough. We should ideally win 30 thousand," she finally said.

In front of the shop, they nearly bumped into a beautiful woman. Before Buba recognised her, the woman laughed and said, "Buba Antolić, always in a rush... I like this shop too".

It was Helena Šoljan. Apart from working in the same theatre, she and Buba had known each other from early childhood – they used to live next door to each other in the same apartment block, at number 33, in the former Končar Street, now re-named Tratinska Street, and they went to the same primary school. Helena was a few years older and, as far back as she could remember, Buba looked up to her and saw her as a model. She used to be the prettiest girl in the whole school, so pretty that boys did not dare call out after her.

Around the time she started secondary school, Helena

moved to Ribnjak with her parents. Years later, she and Buba met again in *Gavella* Theatre, where Buba had become script editor while Helena was the lead actress.

For the last six months Helena had been on sick leave. One day, during a rehearsal, she suddenly burst into tears and left the building. A few days later, she returned, but not for long. Her second breakdown was worse than the first: out of the blue, they said; she just sat there, they said, speechless and motionless, unblinking. The ambulance took her to the Crisis Clinic where she remained for three weeks. When she finally contacted the theatre, she said she was well and receiving medication, and that she'd been told she'd soon be fit to go back to work.

"Well, and how are you?" Buba asked with genuine interest.

"All right, I expect," Helena shrugged. "Better. I don't know when I'll be back, and I'm not in a hurry, to be honest."

"How about dropping by for a coffee?" Buba asked.

"Dunno… I don't go out much. Actually, I hardly ever go out. I'm calmest when I'm at home. I went out quite by accident today; Andrej is concerned and tries to make me go out whenever he's at home with our daughter…"

"Do keep in touch," said Buba, leaving.

"Who's that?" Matko asked.

"A colleague from work, Helena. She's also dad's boss' wife. And a famous actress… a fact you wouldn't know since you don't go to theatre. And she's my childhood friend, from primary school."

"How can you even remember you went to school together after all this time," Matko said without a trace of irony.

"She's very beautiful," Hana said. "Was she beautiful before?"

"Yes, always. She was the prettiest girl in our school."

"And were you friends with her?"

"I was, for a while."

"How does it feel to be friends with someone who is so beautiful, and knowing everyone likes her better than you?"

Buba could not summon up a clever answer. "Everyone is

beautiful in someone's eyes," she said. "Someone who really likes you won't even notice Miss World standing next to you. And beauty isn't everything."

"Yeah, tell me another one," muttered Hana, glancing sternly at her mother.

Hana's questions were, to Buba, always revealing of the fact that her daughter pondered subjects a contented child would have no reason to ponder. Alas, Hana did not inherit her father's charm or her mother's generous flexibility. And she hadn't yet learned to accept herself as she was, as Buba had learned, but not before she'd met David.

Hana asked Matko, "Matko, would you prefer a beautiful stupid girlfriend or an ugly clever one, if you had a choice?"

"You're nuts," said Matko.

A question straight out of *Alan Ford*[46], Buba thought. "No, really," she said seriously, to support Hana. "What would you rather have: an ugly, clever girlfriend or a beautiful, stupid one?"

"Dunno," Matko said indifferently. "If she was ugly, I'd never get together with her in the first place."

The Hand

The hand stretched its fingers as if limbering up for a piano recital. The Moleskine notebook lay open before it in readiness, and the pile of newspapers on the right side of the desk was somewhat lower than it had been the last time. The neatly stacked pile on the left was now higher.

CULTURE: The novel *Cracked Wheat* by Davor Špišić

---

[46] *Alan Ford* is an Italian comic series created by Max Bunker (Luciano Secchi) and Magnus (Roberto Raviola) in 1969. It is a satirical take on classic secret agents full of surreal black humour. It never gained fame outside Italy, except on the territory of former Yugoslavia, where it became a point of reference. The appearance of the hero of the series, the bumbling spy Alan Ford, was based on the actor Peter O'Toole. Buba is here referring to Bob Rock, one of the main characters, who famously states that "it is better to live a hundred years as a rich man than a day as a beggar."

has won the VBZ[47] competition

2/12, Thursday

THE FRONT PAGE: The Government is doing its utmost to arrest and hand over Gotovina.

20/12

Miss Plastic Surgery: 6 Operations So Far

Friday, 14th October

"Friday, at last" Jelena sighed.

"I thought you liked Mondays," David said.

"I like fewer weekdays with each passing year."

"Where were you last night? I called you."

"Why?"

"I can't remember." David smiled a broad and cheerful smile, leaning back into the leatherette armchair at the *Little Café*.

"Ana and I went to *Golf* for a drink," Jelena said.

"Adventurous ladies," David laughed.

"I thought we might find you there," Jelena sighed. "Ana is getting really difficult. She's self-obsessed, and obsessed by her book. She is full of spite, she's gone all mystical; she feels to me as if she's turning from a living being into some kind of a weird tangle, as if she's fading and disappearing into the distance, or something. She's obsessed by critics ignoring her book."

"She hasn't yet realised that one mustn't take them seriously."

"Yeah, like when Chabrol quotes Balzac or Racine or something in the opening credits. When they asked him about it in an interview, he said, Well, I have to think of the poor critics, or else, what would there be for them to do? This way, at the start of the movie, they see 'Balzac' and say: 'Aha, a Balzacian film!' That way they're satisfied and I can do what I like."

David laughed. "Critics love being able to recognise things: *this* comes from *that* tradition; *this* respects *those* conventions;

---

[47] A Croatian publishing company established in 1991

that is such-and-such movement or style. That way they can show off their knowledge; they can measure, weigh and sort things like a butcher in his shop: a first class top round steak, a shoulder, cut-offs for mince... That's why they didn't grasp the quality of Ana's book."

"You try and convince her!"

"She might become standard for writers in the future, but for the time being, she is one of a kind and critics don't know what to make of her."

"Yeah, a Rhodesian ridgeback," Jelena said. "At what stage do we tell her about our plan?"

"At dinner, when the atmosphere is good."

"So when are you taking us out for dinner?"

"Tomorrow. I've already told them to reserve the best shanks they can lay their hands on."

The Hand

11/02

EVENTS OF THE DAY: Eighth form biology to include lessons on contraception

CARDINAL BOZANIĆ: DO NOT ALLOW THE POISONING OF CHILDREN'S SOULS. Cardinal Bozanić called on parents to monitor carefully the programmes offered to their children. Officiating at the mass for Stepinac Day in the Cathedral last evening, he called for consensus between the Croatian public and the politicians, and a dialogue on the issue of artificial insemination, as essential questions of human dignity were, as he put it, at stake.

CHRONICLE: PHEROMONES AFFECT SEXUAL ORIENTATION "What are pheromones? Pheromones are the means of communication within an animal species: they carry chemical messages, warn of danger, indicate the way to food and advertise sexual interest. A bitch secreting pheromones, for example, can attract a male from more than two kilometres away. Men and women both secrete pheromones in a volatile, odourless form in order to attract the opposite sex. In the nose, pheromones are picked up by the so-called vomeronasal organ (VNO), far better developed in animals than in man. The VNO system consists of a network of tiny pheromone-detecting receptors which then pass their message in the form of nerve impulses to the hypothalamus, the part of the brain where the centre for emotions is located."

Saturday, 15th October, *The Old Fiacre*

David celebrated all his awards in *The Old Fiacre*, the restaurant that had been his favourite since youth and even more so since he had become single again: he indulged in black pudding, sausages, štrukli[48], sauerkraut, sarma[49], potato halves[50] and other rustic local dishes on *Fiacre*'s menu. This time he had reserved shanks with roast vegetables which had already been prepared by the time the diners arrived.

On her way to the *Fiacre*, Jelena bought a beautiful arrangement made of small flowers only, and placed it at the centre of the dining table. The waiters understood that something was being celebrated and were particularly keen to please, expecting above average tips.

Apart from David, no one seemed to be cheerful. Buba was downcast although she tried to hide her mood. She had been to see the gynaecologist the day before and was told that she was most likely starting her menopause. "Is that normal?" she asked, disappointed. "I'm only forty."

"My dear madam, I've got patients who've been on HRT since they were 35. By the same token, I'm treating an 8-year old girl who already has periods. The boundaries are shifting. That makes your case perfectly normal, considering you started your periods at 11, and your monthly cycles being short, a mere

---

[48] Štrukli is a traditional Croatian dish of filo pastry with a cheese filling. It can be boiled or baked.

[49] A savoury dish of rice and mincemeat rolled in sauerkraut leaves on a bed of shredded sauerkraut. In Bulgaria, it is made with fresh white cabbage leaves, while in Greece vine leaves are used. Middle-Eastern variants are known as "dolma".

[50] Potatoes cut in half and simply roasted in the oven

23 days. The ovaries don't last forever; they're good only for a limited number of ovulations."

"That's news to me," said Jelena when Buba told her the story in a low voice to avoid entertaining the whole table with it.

"To me as well," Buba said. "Essentially, a healthy woman has around 400 to 500 periods in the course of her fertile life." She whispered even more quietly, "I simply used mine up early. Maybe that's because I do everything quickly, three things at once; it might be like the four-stroke engine: a fast burnout. I'm all accelerated; even my periods are shorter than normal..."

"Slow down," Jelena said.

She glanced at Bruno. He was playing with a glass. Instead of the table, she saw emptiness between the two of them.

Ana looked anxious, huddled, hunched.

"If only they'd invent pills for optimism," said Buba, to no one in particular.

Towards the end of the dinner, just before the dessert, Ana took a book out of her bag. Everyone craned their necks to see what it was: a paperback, a pink-and-white cover: *Nina Ivezić, The Angelic Trap.*

"You bought it?" Jelena was surprised.

"Yes, I accidentally spotted it in the shop-window on my way to work," said Ana.

"In the shop-window? It's not recent enough to be in the window," said Jelena, speaking before thinking. She didn't particularly wish to catch Ana lying.

"When the author is pretty, the book is always on display," Ana replied.

David took the book from her and opened it randomly. He began reading aloud: "*The woman looked at the young man's excited face and then at the man who was waiting for her at the door...*" He carried on reading silently.

"Hey, you're not going to read this now, are you?" Ana reached for the book.

"She writes well, good sentences... And it sounds interesting," said David and glanced at Ana.

"You don't have to feel guilty, it's not as if you were singing in a dead man's home."

"Where do you always pull these morbid associations from!" David sounded cross. "This book is very good, but not in the same league with yours," he added, with consideration, almost with tenderness. Ana's expression almost unnoticeably softened.

"If I'd said that, she'd have accused me of duplicity," Jelena put in.

"You people in soft professions are all vain to the point of sickness," said Buba. "That comes from never having pulled your weight."

"Yeah, whilst you toil in a coal mine," David and Jelena said, almost in one voice. Buba picked up the book and looked at the back cover. She gazed at the photo of the author.

"That's our new colleague," said Jelena. "She'll be covering theatre."

"That means, she's working with you?" Buba asked David.

"No, I'm done with theatre, she's taken it over."

"What a lovely girl; it's weird that..." Buba stopped in mid-sentence, embarrassed.

"Please continue. You meant to say, it's weird that she's a writer," said Ana.

"No, I meant to say," Buba faltered slightly, "it's weird that David still hasn't bagsied her. Unless he has," she finished unconvincingly.

David laughed, and Jelena winked. "Well... let's say she hasn't escaped his attention."

Buba said: "It actually bothers me that nowadays they always put the image of the author on the cover, or you know him or her from the papers, or you've seen him on the internet or on telly. It spoils my reading. If I were now to read this book, I'd definitely imagine the heroine as her."

Ana was nodding her agreement. "True, true. My book would perhaps be more successful without my image on the cover. Like this, people imagine my heroine as me and don't like her, and wouldn't like her even if I was the greatest of writers. My books should be free from me..."

"Guys," Buba said to change the subject, "guess whom I met the other day? Helena Šoljan, your boss Martić's wife."

"What is she like?" Jelena asked.

"You don't know Helena?"

"Only from theatre and television," Jelena replied. "I know she's very beautiful."

"Still one of the loveliest women in Zagreb," Buba agreed. "But the word in the theatre is that she's having psychological problems of sorts. She did look a bit strange, absent, but she still has... that natural majesty. A real diva. Only now she resembles a great tragic heroine." She thought that, in addition to her ovaries, meeting Helena might be reason for her bad mood. They both had a common denominator: ageing.

"With a husband like hers, I'm not at all surprised she looks tragic," Ana said. "He's your typical parasite, looking for the organism most suitable for symbiosis."

"How do you know?" Jelena asked.

"Doesn't he look cold and slimy?"

"They say she's had several breakdowns," said Jelena. "Meanwhile, her husband is in top nick, attracting young women."

"Which young women?" Buba asked.

"All of them. I won't be surprised if he casts an eye at our new colleague, the author of this book, as well, if he hasn't already done so," Jelena said. "He seems to be attracted to beautiful women."

Buba gave another look to the photo at the back of the book. "She really is very beautiful. She looks like..."

"Like an angel, doesn't she?" Jelena asked. "That's what I said." She thought of Nina, and then, unwittingly, of Pero Kovačić as well. Confused, she glanced around as if someone was stalking her.

"All men are like that," Ana barged in. "That's their original sin, that no man desires the same woman all the time. He craves freshness and youth, like a vampire craves fresh blood..."

Bruno stared expressionlessly ahead. Jelena knew that, within himself, he was silently protesting: he hated such discussions. She said: "There's no mystery there. It's all down to chemistry. Simply, women have a surplus of some elements which makes them want to stick to the same man longer than he wants to stick to them. Men, on the other hand, have different elements…"

"That's our Ninotchka[51] all right," David laughed. "Love is a capitalist fabrication; it all boils down to chemistry."

"That's why it is totally wrong to say that tastes vary," Jelena went on, prompted by the three glasses of wine she had had rather than with the subject. "For example, the other day I read about the results of a large survey: Croats find Angelina Jolie the most attractive of all the world-famous beauties, and Severina of all the Croatian ones. And so does my husband." She didn't look at Bruno, not wishing to see the reproach in his eyes. "I'm convinced that that specific physical type – a generous mouth, full lips, large breasts – will one day be proved to provoke a particularly powerful discharge of testosterone in men. Or it might be established that women belonging to that type possess particular chemical properties – manufacture more pheromones, for example, which are a direct invitation to mate…" She avoided looking at Bruno again. "Now, the fact that neither Severina nor Angelina will remain attractive to their husbands much longer than us ordinary women is neither here nor there; at least they'll have had their moment of passion… We, however, who haven't been born Angelinas or Severinas, we'd like to be loved with equal passion just the same…"

Bruno regarded her silently. She wished he wouldd take her by the hand and say, "To hell with Severina and Angelina! You're mine and you're the one I love."

"You're a bit tipsy," David said, "but it is true that ours is the age of curvaceous, voluptuous women with fat lips. Dear girls, you philosophise while you ought to purr like cats.

---

[51] *Ninotchka* (Ernst Lubitsch, 1939), a film in which Greta Garbo plays a stern, rigid, scientifically minded Soviet special envoy to Paris where she eventually gets seduced by its delights.

Content, well rested, well nourished and nicely groomed wives please their husbands better than scowling, hungry, nervous manageresses. And pleasant women go down well, like a good massage, a warm bath, quiet music and fine chocolate. Geishas. Odalisques. Courtesans. I know I've just signed my death sentence and mortally insulted you, but... I told Jelena only the other day that all women should be the followers of Žuži Jelinek.[52]"

Everyone laughed.

"And I think that a woman can only be attractive until she's forty. After that, no male passer-by seeing you in the street is likely to think, *If only I could lay this babe!*" Jelena said.

"What about *Sex and the City*?" Buba asked. "At forty, you feel like thirty. I think the cut-off point should be at least forty five."

"No worries, you'll always stand a chance with your exes." David winked at Buba. Buba laughed and blushed.

"I've read somewhere that fireflies have hormones too. It's because of those hormones that they shine. A firefly with more hormones shines brighter. And they shine to attract males. The brighter they shine, the more attractive they are," Jelena said.

"Damn," said Buba quietly, "this kills me more than anything else I've heard about female hormones tonight!" She, too, seemed to be emboldened by wine. "Other tables will think we're a bunch of salacious libertines." She glanced around.

"Like we care," Jelena said.

The waiter who'd come for the empty plates interrupted their conversation.

"It's unfair, the inequality of men and women," Buba said.

"But we all share the same human soul, though," said David.

"Which one of you could try and reveal," Ana retorted cleverly. "I could use that for my male characters."

---

[52] Žuži Jelinek (1919-), legendary Croatian fashion designer and bespoke tailor for women; also columnist and social commentator. She published a number of books advising women on how to be happy and successful, using their femininity

Bruno was silent. Bruno would not lend his soul even to the noblest of artistic causes, Jelena thought. A good title, she thought, *Soul Donor*. Really, I never seem to get around to registering as organ donor. So I'll get a dog-tag like soldiers in movies. I have to find the time, or I'll die before I manage it. I don't want to be indolent like Bruno who postpones everything and will never be a donor, either of organs or of soul. Oh yeah, she remembered, has it not recently been announced that anyone who hasn't explicitly refused would be considered a donor? That means I'm not late. And, equally, Bruno's soul must be available until he explicitly forbids it.

"Everything's better than an unconvincing story," she heard Ana say. "Like an Eskimo writing about African desert. Or that novel by Nick Hornby, the one about divorce…"

"You mean, *How to be Good*," Jelena put in.

"Yup, that's the one: there, he describes the thoughts of a woman about to separate from her husband. To me, it feels masculine," Ana said.

"You're right," Jelena agreed. "Now that you mention it, it does seem to me to be rather atypical of women. She's brave and knows what she wants, like a man… and women mostly hang on to their marriage for fear of solitude."

"Have you noticed what we're discussing the whole evening?" Buba said, again in order to dispel the tension. "Of men and women and nothing else. The only subject that is never boring."

"Essentially, what else is there?" Jelena said. Ana gave her a silent look.

David readily said, "OK, let's change the subject!" He turned to Anna, announcing pointedly, "Jelena and I have cooked up a plan for you that'll solve all your problems and do something useful for the whole society as well."

Everyone listened with interest. The waiter interrupted them again: "Ladies and gentlemen, would you like a dessert?" Many voices rose drowning each other but Jelena broke in, hushing them down. "Stop – wait a minute. This calls for something special. You won't be cross?" The question was for

David. She turned to the waiter. "What dessert wines have you got?" she asked.

The waiter said, as if stating the obvious, "We've got prošek[53]."

"Have you by any chance got Kozlović's or Kabola's Momjan muscat?" enquired Jelena, trying not to sound as if she was putting on airs.

The waiter waved his hand.

"And Tokay?"

"No."

"Port, perhaps?"

"We haven't got any."

"In that case... could you please bring us some... Don't know... What shall we have?"

"What an expert!" said Buba.

"I'm preparing an article about wine, and I've spent months researching and... tasting. I've discovered the world of dessert wines. I mean, I've finally found drinks that are pleasant to drink and not just the means for getting drunk. Sweet wines are the drink of paradise. *Recioto*, *Aleatico*, *Sauternes*, Torres' *Moscatel Oro*, *Somos* – the inexpensive yet wonderful wine of Greek peasants, Batič's *Valentino*, Paul Jaboulet's *Muscat De Beaumes-de-Venise*..."

"Wow," said Buba, impressed.

"What makes the sweet wines sweet?" Ana asked. "Is something added to them?"

"No, they're sweet because they're made from semi-dried or dried grapes. For the *'Ice Wine' Traminer*, for example, the grapes are picked in the middle of winter when they're almost completely dry. It's hardly surprising that three decilitres of that wine cost five hundred kuna: a bunch of such grapes will yield, perhaps, a single drop of wine. Have you heard of resveratrol? No? Resveratrol is what makes wine healthy; it's a

---

[53] Sweet Croatian dessert wine often confused with Italian prosecco with which it has no similarity whatsoever as prosecco is a sparkling dry wine similar to Asti Spumante.

sort of substance on the skin of grapes that protects them from mould. It is allegedly an anticancerogen as well. In any case, when a wine has up to five percent resveratrol, that's considered very resveratrol-rich. And *'Ice' Traminer* has fifteen percent! What's more, it is the most sublime drink I'd ever tasted, something absolutely fabulous, fabulous... I've tasted all those wines; the only one I'd still love to try is the sauternes *Chateau D'Yquem*, the most expensive sweet wine in the world... Breathe!" said Jelena to her friends who'd been listening, entranced. "And now," she said to David, "over to you."

David coughed as if about to deliver an important speech. "It's like this," he turned to Ana. "You'll publish your book under my name." He paused dramatically to give his words time to sink in, but no one reacted, including Ana. They were obviously missing the point. He went on, "I'll sign the contract, give interviews, visit libraries, read extracts. We'll enter it – I mean we won't, the publisher will – to compete for the most important literary awards: *Ujević, Matoš*[54]..."

"And for *Uliks*[55], that's a new award," Jelena threw in.

"When the book wins the awards, only then we'll tell them it's yours," David said.

Ana's mouth was open; she was truly surprised. "Eh? What? What are you talking about?"

The others, too, fell silent.

"About your second book. Listen," David explained animatedly. "In the first place, you'll avoid comparisons with your first book..."

"As if anyone's ever heard of it," said Ana. "I don't understand you..."

David ignored the interruption. "Secondly, it won't be ignored because it was written not by an unknown woman author but by a multiple award winner, journalist David

---

[54] Awards named after Croatian poets Tin Ujević (1891-1955) and Antun Gustav Matoš (1873-1914)

[55] A literary award named after the novel *Uliks* (Ulysses) by Croatian novelist Ranko Marinković (1913-2001)

Antolić..."

"It'll be the first fiction book by the talented blah-de-dah... so everyone – and the greatest experts will be the first to do so – will say that they are not surprised, that they were expecting this kind of development..." Jelena put in.

"And when it has bagged all the awards and they find out who the author really is, they won't be able to take their praises back," David finished.

"Aha," Ana was beginning to understand. "How do you know it'll win the awards?" she asked.

"I know because you write brilliantly, and..."

"And you are liked," Ana completed his sentence. "It's clear to me now."

"That's why we're doing it," David said without much emotion.

"Jesus, you're out of it," Buba said.

"Just imagine the *shock*," Jelena said. "If that won't be a lesson to all those pretentious nincompoops, then I don't know what will."

"And imagine the moment of revelation: 'Look, this is the real author!'" said David. "It would be best if it happened in the middle of the award ceremony, if we do win. The whirring of the cameras! I believe it will be long remembered."

Even Ana started laughing. "All we have to do is choose the publisher," she said.

"How about staying with *Argus*," said David. "It'll make the joke even better: to show that even they were nicer to me than they were to you, because I'm *established*."

"It's a deal," Ana agreed. "It's much saner than my own idea..."

"What idea?"

"Never mind. If you knew, you'd only say I was being morbid again."

"Morbid, morbid and morbid again," said David.

"Coconut, coconut and coconut again," Buba and Jelena said together, quoting from a boring TV-ad.

"What about the legalities?" Buba asked seriously. "It all

looks a bit too childish to me. I have a feeling you'll wake up tomorrow and realise it's impossible."

"Forget the legalities," Jelena said. "It's such an unheard-of precedent that no one will know what to do with it. It's not a theft of manuscript; law doesn't even cover our case."

Buba laughed. Everyone looked at her, so she explained: "I just remembered.... Nothing to do with this... When Ringo was a puppy, he used to sit in my lap as I drove. He'd crawl all over the steering wheel, so David got cross and said that the police would have me for that, and I said there couldn't be a law against keeping puppies in one's lap when driving, because no one had thought of it. David then said there couldn't be a law against keeping a cow in one's lap when driving either..." She laughed. "And it's the same with your proposal: not a puppy, but a great big cow..."

David nodded, agreeing. "Exactly, a cow behind the wheel. And by the time they get their heads around it..."

"I wouldn't mess with it," Bruno said.

"You *would* say that, wouldn't you," said Jelena, a bit sadly rather than derisively.

"Let's do it," said Ana. "I've got nothing to lose anyway."

The Hand

Friday, 14th January

THE FRONT PAGE: Parents abandon little daughter in the middle of her hernia surgery to take part in the RTL show *Wife Swap*. The cameras captured the medical examination of the child.

Željko Vukmirica put it well when he, in Sanja Doležal's talk show, speculated that the next step in the development of television will be to place cameras into the stomach of a member of the public to see what was going on inside.

27th January

CULTURAL AFFAIRS: Syria nominates Vesna Parun for the Nobel Prize

Monday, 31st January

THE FRONT PAGE: Investigation within the Church in

Croatia: 42% of priests claim: Marriage would not interfere with our office

CULTURAL AFFAIRS: Ephraim Kishon, the famous satirist, dies

Tuesday, 1ˢᵗ February

LIFE: The jury selection for the trial of Michael Jackson commenced yesterday in the Californian town of Santa Maria

Fairytales and Mothers

Ana was raised by her mother. Her father died early in Ana's life; when she was five, her mother told her. "And it was good riddance, Lord forgive me," she'd always say when Ana asked questions about him. Ana memorised that sentence, *good riddance, Lord forgive me,* long before she became capable of understanding its meaning. "What's there to know?" mum would say gruffly. "You look the same as he. Take a look at yourself – that's him. A largish nose, but that looks good on a man's face. He was handsome, the devil. You inherited his allergy to penicillin. The palaver I had running round hospitals with you whenever you had common tonsillitis! He, too, was allergic and always took care not to get ill."

Ana couldn't recall daddy's face; she only remembered that he was very tall and smelled nice. Only a few of his photographs were to be found around the house: group portraits with mum, Ana and family, their figures barely discernible.

When Ana was eight, a tall, corpulent man smelling strongly (of tobacco?) began visiting their home. He'd laugh loudly, click his tongue and lick his lips. Mum told Ana to call him *uncle*. She, Ana, thought his face resembled the snout of a wolf. Mum was happy when she gave birth to a child, a boy, even though he cried all the time. A few months later, he died in his sleep.

Whenever mum was not in the room, the tall man would look Ana over, pinch and pat her. When she was nine, she told her mother that "uncle had been tickling her tummy and her weevie". Mum said, "You dirty little slut, always making up stories!" and she slapped her. Since then, Ana didn't tell her anything any more. When she was thirteen, she said to the man, "I'll kill you sooner or later, pig!" The man drank more and more and his rows with Ana's mum got nastier and nastier. During one such row, Ana's mum shouted, "You disgusting scumbag, you're sick, you should be locked up in a loony bin. You're maaaaad! Maaaad! Good job that poor mite died. I've had enough of rotten fruit!" He swung out an arm as if to strike her, but Ana's mum stood straight, holding her ground, and said, "Only my father ever hit me, once. No one else ever hit me again and no one ever will!"

When Ana was fifteen, her stepfather was found dead in the apartment. Ana's mother was at work and Ana was at school. The neighbours had smelled smoke and burning roast. As no one answered the doorbell or came to the door when they banged on it, they called the police. The body lay on its back on the kitchen floor, with a bloody wound at the base of the head. It was not clear whether the injury was the result of the fall or a hit by a blunt object. The man's mouth reeked of alcohol, and the oven belched black smoke: the roast had already been carbonised. The death was officially declared to be the result of a mishap, but the neighbours talked, saying great many things which mostly boiled down to the drunken fool having had got his just deserts. They also said he often used to nip back home from work when Janja was not in and then strange noises could be heard in the apartment, as if he had brought another woman around. But they never told the police about it; it was best not to have anything to do with the police. Mum was questioned several times by the police and Ana was sent to a *team of psychologists* for treatment. Ana liked the way the psychologists questioned her and decided to be a psychologist there and then; she admired them when they guessed right and had fun leading them onto a false trail: she felt proud of herself whenever she managed that. They asked her how her stepfather had been treating her; she said she'd never had a special relationship with him, that he'd never attempted to take her father's place and that she'd never particularly wanted him to. That was all. She continued being sent for treatment for a while, but as her behaviour showed no disturbing traits and as she was doing as well in school as ever – an *exemplary* student, as her form tutor would say – the conclusion was reached that the dire events in the family did not leave a significant effect on the child.

Mum did not appreciate Ana's good grades; she reproached her for not taking care of her appearance, nagged her to go out, saying she wasn't exactly the regular kind anyway. She would often wrench books out of her hands – Ana used to read a lot – and tear them up in front of Ana's eyes. After such an explosion of fury and scorn, she would burst into tears of remorse, and Ana would comfort her. She feared for her mum. Mother would remain thoughtful for a few days, and full of consideration, as if tiptoeing around someone who was ill, and then everything would go back to normal. Ana dreamed of moving out as soon as she got a job and received her first payslip.

After "uncle's" death, mother sold the apartment and moved with Ana into much cheaper small bungalow with a garden in Trnje. She put the remaining money in a bank and withdrew it sparingly as required. "I won't be able to work for much longer," she'd say, "my legs won't hold me. I've washed enough heads in my life, me." She worked as a hairdresser at *Studio Estetic*, formerly *Bratstvo*[56]. "I've worked and suffered enough in my life. This money is my only security... What if I were to fall ill, who'd help me?" mother would say to Ana in defence of her avarice. Luckily, Ana was not the demanding sort.

Only much later, she understood her mum had changed when she lost the child. And what rotten fruit meant. And what fairy tales were about: stepmothers were really mothers all along...

The Report

"I haven't had such a well preserved body for a long time," the pathologist said, rummaging inside the body's wide-open abdominal cavity with concentration. He scratched his forehead

---

[56] Formerly: before Croatia became independent. Bratstvo: brotherhood.

with his left pinkie, the only finger that wasn't covered in blood. "It's clearly due to healthy life, care for the body, wholesome food. Shame we can't snatch such bodies away while they're fresh, there'd be a glut of organs for transplants. Like this… it's just another pointless death."

"It may have made the world a better place, who knows?"

"Oh, I can see you're a poetic soul," the pathologist laughed.

"When can I have the report?" the Inspector asked.

"Tomorrow. It's almost finished. You know we're always faster than you guys."

The Beauty and the Beast

Looking back, it seemed to Helena that Andrej's admiration had lasted about as long as that of passers-by, and much shorter than the admiration of the audience. Life with him was all lazy lounging and reckless squandering. Her earnings were large and money was not a concern. They renovated Helena's parents' spacious, beautiful apartment in Novak Street, a quiet street of rich villas and large gardens; in the city centre, yet tucked away from the tumult of the crowds and the claustrophobic new-builds. They furnished the place together. Andrej chose the furniture, the carpets and the paintings with more care than Helena. A diligent learner, he had a cultured, sophisticated taste completely free of the in-your-face ostentation of the nouveau riche, but also devoid of imagination and freedom. Helena casually added cheerful bits and pieces, creating a home. Andrej wanted beauty, Helena comfort. In the end, the apartment turned out both comfortable and beautiful.

Once Andreja was born, Andrej started going out more and more often, but when he did stay in, he gladly occupied himself with the child. To be precise: at home, the child was his only occupation. He didn't flinch from nappy-changing and botty-washing. To Helena, he spoke less and less. She had begun to grasp the fact that he was less than perfect as husband, but at least he was a good father. Her milk dried up after six months, and, as she was no longer nursing, she went back to work.

Whenever she was rehearsing or performing, Andrej minded the child.

After childbirth, Helena had no desire to sleep with Andrej for nearly a year, nor did he come to her of his own accord. And when she desired him again, he didn't come. On Andreja's first birthday, after the festivities and a bottle of wine, awkwardly and with some embarrassment, they found themselves in each other's embrace. They tried only on one other occasion since; one fine summer night, on their tenth wedding anniversary. On that last occasion, Helena's desire was immense, more powerful than ever, while Andrej's caresses were tepid and without passion. Under the palm of her hand, Helena could feel his member twitch into a feeble erection. She clung to him with her whole body, enfolding him with her arms and her thigh. She sought his mouth. He averted his head. She drew back, humiliated and ashamed. They never spoke about that night. Five years passed.

Contrary to the popular concept about actors, Helena was devoted to her home, her child and her family. It wasn't much of a family, but it was the only one she had. Helena cleaned, cooked, took Andreja for walks.

Devoted mother and housewife by day, she would metamorphose into a diva in the evening. She all but fitted the old formula for a perfect woman: a housewife at home, a lady in public… Only in bed was she alone. The most terrible of it all was the look in Andrej's eyes: empty, impenetrable, his eyes appeared to be shut even when they were open, for fear that, if he opened them fully, he might see Helena the ogre, and that she might touch him, as if the Beauty and the Beast had switched roles.

For years she seldom went out, and when she did, it was never with Andrej. She was listless and morose. In the last two years she had developed serious problems, which began with a panic attack one evening before a performance, and it was not even a premiere. As she was about to enter stage, her heart began pounding and a choking sensation overcame her. She could not move from the spot. When they came for her, she did not speak, but tears began rolling down her cheeks. The ambulance took her to the Crisis Clinic, where they diagnosed a panic attack, anxiety and depression. She spent three weeks in hospital. Fifteen days into her stay, she smiled for the first time when Andreja was allowed to visit. Three months later she was back at work. From then on, she felt brittle, like a hollow bone. She feared it might return, that terrible emptiness without beginning or end.

In Andrej's circles, the rumour was he had a "flaky" wife who never went out. From time to time only, if she felt particularly well, she would take a walk with her daughter in Ribnjak Park. But even when feeling exceptionally well, she could not free herself of fear. She feared everything: she feared when the phone rang, she feared the doorbell; whenever Andreja was due back from school, she would imagine seeing her all covered in blood at the door. Sometimes she didn't even dare open the door but would hide in the bedroom. Only when Andreja had herself unlocked the door and when she would heard her say "Hiyaaa, I'm home, mum!" would she emerge from the bedroom, still a bit fearful: perhaps Andreja was only pretending she was all right in order not to scare her.

Less than six months later, they took her away again.

The Inspector

"And you are...?" said the Sergeant to the handsome man, nibbling the tip of his pencil, looking as if he might be about to tuck it behind his ear. But he did not; he wrote down the man's name and placed both his hands on the table in a tidy fashion. The Inspector nodded a greeting.

The Hand

Wednesday, 2nd February

FRONT PAGE: Sanader and Mesić: We demand Gotovina's arrest

FRONT PAGE: Carla del Ponte on the statement of the Heads of Government: I am confident that Sanader will now arrest Ante Gotovina.

EXCLUSIVE: Zagreb Bank reported banknotes stolen in Belfast: The pounds from the robbery of the century are being "laundered" in Zagreb. *Zaba*[57] spotted serial numbers of banknotes from the list detailing the numbers of £26.5 million stolen from the Northern Bank on 20th December 2004.

That's what I call globalisation.

Well Established – Tuesday, 18th October

Having only just sat down in front of the computer, David glanced at his watch and slapped his forehead: "Oh man, I completely forgot! I have to see Pavličić and I'm late with the Book Fair piece!" He grabbed his coat and called to Jelena, exiting: "Back in 45 if anyone wants me."

When he got back, he returned to the text with a deep sigh. "Hang on, what's that?" he stared at the monitor, perplexed. "Hey, I'm a genius! I've got two finished pages here, and I thought I'd barely started!" He ran his fingers through his hair and, raising his arms above his head and stretching with pleasure, began reading the text in a low voice: "*One might say that the actual current moment has, in our real actuality, arrived at the point that could be considered a turning point in the current situation of our society, in this moment when fledgling democratic habits are in the process of formation and the foundations of better understanding not just of the current cultural moment but of all our cultural assets are being laid...*" He paused. "What the hell is this? What is this shit...?"

Unable to hold back any longer, Jelena burst out laughing so loudly that Dora sauntered in to see what was going on. David's hands mimicked strangling Jelena. "Your work, yeah?"

"Well... you know girls always write boys' homework, and boys then become directors, presidents, academics..."

"Very funny, a very clever trick, a great trick... but you know what, Jozo?" David slammed his palms on the desk and squinted. "I'm going to hand it in as it is. Fuck me if I won't!"

---

[57] Zaba = Zagreb Bank

He pushed the hair out of his face with both hands, nodding: "Yup, that's right, it's going straight to print... I'll just add a few names as examples."

"You're bonkers," Jelena laughed. "Come on, don't be silly. The whole text is like that..."

"It'll be a fantastic experiment! Care to place a bet? A hundred kuna says everyone will keep schtum!"

"I'm not betting and this is no longer fun. You're really nuts. You're prepared to lose face just to prove something," Jelena said.

David only smiled.

"I think you're making up metaphysical excuses because you're *indolentius vulgaris.*"

"Perhaps. But it also leads into Ana's book thing. The first rehearsal.

Jelena did not reply. After a pause, David went on, "I'll get away with it because I'm well *established.* When you're established, your crap can change someone's destiny. Politicians, critics, media moguls, chief editors... me, you..."

"I don't feel established."

"What do you think, how many people get a chance to present their views to the public? Do you know how hard it is to worm your way into *Readers' Letters,* never mind anything else? If we manage not to stray from the path, and if we so desire, in the next phase we could have real power."

"We're not like that, we're good," Jelena said. "We wouldn't want power."

"Statistically, we have no reason to believe that we necessarily have to belong to that nice two percent of mankind. We have no way of knowing what we would be like if we had the opportunity. To be influential and not allow yourself to be castrated by it would be the ideal to aim at: as soon as you accept power, you're castrated because there are always more powerful ones whose orders you must obey. When you're influential, you can afford to be extravagant."

"Extravagant?"

"Extravagance is nothing other than freedom to be yourself,

to have your taste, your opinions, to be able to judge the work of others regardless of fashion or the prominent critics' preference, or cliques..."

"We don't have enough thinkers to have cliques; cliques need leaders. All we have is an army of intellectual robots. I call them *cultural shopaholics*," Jelena put in.

"Yes, you're right; hired hands and shopaholics, no different from that mass of grey faces milling around huge shopping centres, only these race one another through bookshops, book promotions, first nights, openings, columns, TV-reportages. We really need to bring all that down."

"You're the sociologist. Work out a plan and I'll follow you, " Jelena laughed. "But first finish your text." She picked up the newspaper. "Look: they've announced the selection for the *Uliks* prize," she said, reading. "15th of December is the deadline. We don't have that much time, you know. The nominees will be named at the beginning of January..."

"Ah, the new mega-award."

"The very one. Meant to become the most important and the most influential one. There won't be a jury; instead, the best books will be chosen by all the most important cultural associations and all their members. Get this, all! That means, all the members of the Writers' Association..."

"If only we were a normal country with one writers' association; but no, we've got four."

"No kidding; which four?"

"Let's see: The Croatian Authors' Association, the Croatian Writers' Association... or perhaps the Association of Croatian Writers and the Association of Croatian Authors? And the other two... I can't remember what they're called, and there's also a children's one..."

Jelena laughed. "Whatever. All the writers, then, all the members of the Critics' Association, the Translators' Association, and of Matica Hrvatska[58], HAZU's Literary

---

[58] *Matica hrvatska* (Latin: *Matrix Croatica*) is one of the oldest Croatian cultural institutions, dating back to 1842. It is the largest publisher of

Section and who knows what else – they all get to vote. Imagine how long it'll take all those people to read all the books published this year, from fiction to faction, plus all the translations. We must hurry with the publication if we're to enter the competition on time."

"Tell Ana to finish up."

"I think she's finished, she's still well motivated. But it would be wise to hurry up because of her as well: you just never know when she might suddenly decide it's all crap and that a full rewrite is in order."

Their conversation was cut short by Andrej's arrival. Trailing close behind the boss, Dora the secretary sailed majestically in like a ship on calm seas and asked: "Coffee?"

"All right," replied Andrej carelessly entering his office.

Dipsy rushed in without saying hello and almost smashed into Dora in the doorway. She slapped his shoulder affectionately. *Eeuw*, Jelena thought.

"One for the girls, shall I?" said Dipsy. Dora halted to listen. Not waiting for the answer, Dipsy went on: "Why is it so hard to find a clever, handsome and sensitive man?"

"Not a clue," Dora said.

"Because they already have boyfriends. Good, eh?"

Andrej emerged from his office, came up to Dipsy and, standing behind his back, said with a frown: "If you've finished, colleague…" He turned to Dora. "Dora, get me Tarbuk on the phone, please." He went back in and shut the door.

David and Jelena, too, turned to their monitors.

"Done," said David some half an hour later, smiling his broad smile.

"You've kept my bit?"

"Of course."

Jelena shrugged and shook her head. "Wait for me; I'll be finished in a minute. We can go out together. I'm meeting Ana in town for a coffee; she's free the first two periods."

Croatian language books. The organization also organizes cultural events, symposia, round-table discussions and theatre. (Wikipedia)

"All right," said David and reached for his newspaper.

He'd barely opened it when Nina appeared in the door, breathless from running up the stairs and pink from fresh air – in a word, pretty as a picture. "Great, you're still here," she said instead of a greeting. "It's not nice to come in and find no one around." She sat down at her desk and took out her notepad. "What a boring press conference."

David was not even aware he was gazing at her. Nina glanced at him and smiled. Jelena sensed more than she saw them exchanging looks, and suddenly thought of Pero Kovačić.

"When do you have to hand this in?" Jelena asked.

"Saturday," Nina replied.

"Why not leave it, then," said David. "Jelena and I are going out for a coffee; you could join us."

Nina looked at him, her hand hovering over the keyboard. "All right then; I really don't feel like writing." She turned to Jelena. "I keep forgetting to ask you, would it be possible for you and me and your husband to get together one Saturday, to sort out that software, if you can find the time…"

"No problem," Jelena said. "On Saturdays, all we have to do is go to the market. Let's go, shall we?"

The Hand

December

THE FRONT PAGE, CULTURAL AFFAIRS: *The Eighth Commissioner* has won all the literary awards. *Has Baretić really written a great novel?*
22/12

EVENTS OF THE DAY: In his Christmas Message, the Archbishop of Zagreb, Cardinal Josip Bozanić, makes a dramatic appeal: "Croatia is being corroded by the sins of corruption and lack of solidarity…"

Same day, same subject:

GFK[59] has investigated the public opinion on corruption, social problems and solidarity: every second member of the public bribes someone, and every third believes such behaviour to be normal. *Aha! That means that some of those who bribe think it's normal, while others don't. A list of professions, ranked by the amount of bribing practice:*

1. Health & Medical (35%)
2. Legal (24%)
3. Customs & Excise
4. Civil service etc

Nina and Ana Meet

Ana was late. They waited for her in *Tolkien's*. She approached their table with a frown. Jelena wasn't sure whether it was on account of the smoke-filled, murky atmosphere in the café – the choice of venue had been Ana's – or of the fact that Nina was with them. It was quite like Ana not to bother being polite when she was in a bad mood.

"This is Ana, our friend and former colleague from the editorial office," said Jelena. And then, to Ana, "This is Nina, our colleague. And yours, as writer."

Ana extended her hand as she took her seat, and Nina politely half-rose from hers, smiling. "Nice to meet you," she said warmly. "I'm a fan of yours."

Ana gathered her eyebrows darkly in response, and then half-heartedly raised them, indicating a question. "Yeah?" she said. She did not like it when clearly superior people conspicuously stooped to her level. "I've read your *Naked She-Wolf*," said Nina.

"What, the whole book?" asked Ana rudely, feigning boredom.

Nina nodded as if to say, *I know where you're coming from*, laughed and said, "The sceptical author... I've read the whole

---

[59] GFK (Growth from Knowledge), established in 1999, is the Croatian national agency for the investigation of public opinion, like GALLUP or MORI.

book. Devoured it. It's marvellous. It's unfair that it didn't win any awards... although it's perhaps understandable. Your book only seems naïve and artless, while it is, I believe, at least ten years ahead of its time..."

Ana looked surprised and, by a few degrees, warmer. "Thanks," she said, this time without sarcasm or scowling. She didn't mention she'd bought Nina's book, and hoped that Jelena hadn't told Nina that she had. The truth was, she hadn't yet started reading it: she didn't like reading whilst in the middle of writing a book.

"Shall we say *thou* to each other?" Nina proposed.

"All right," Ana nodded. "I think we already met in our salad days. In the times of *Zdenac*[60] and *Corso*[61]."

Nina was surprised. "Yeah?" She didn't pretend to remember and was not embarrassed by not remembering: with her, everything was light and natural. Ana noticed this, too, all the more for never having been light and relaxed herself.

"The Aljoša Luženski crowd," she said flatly.

Nina laughed with a wave of the hand. "Oh, yes, Luženski, that pompous poet. I remember his fingernails were so filthy I used to gag when he lit my cigarette."

"I was in love with him" Ana said.

"Really?" Nina regarded her, still with no discomfort in her look. "You were young," she laughed.

"Very," said Ana. "But he fancied *you*."

"I had no idea; I don't remember," Nina laughed again.

David and Jelena listened to their conversation with interest. They were both watching Nina: her face attracted their looks. Ana could feel that too. She thought how Nina most likely never had problems with boys; they wouldn't have dared play their rude pranks on her. "Have you ever had a nasty

---

[60] Zdenac means 'well' (as in water). *Zdenac* is short for *Zdenac života, The Well of Life*, a famous sculpture by Ivan Meštrović, where traditionally young people gather in the evening before heading off for clubs and cafés.

[61] A well-known café in Zagreb, close to *The Well of Life*

experience with a man?" she asked.

Nina looked at her with serious eyes. "Do you mean in the human sense, or the love sense?"

"I mean, with a boyfriend."

"No," Nina replied simply.

"I have, many times," Ana said. "With Luženski, among others."

"I'm sorry," said Nina. "I must have been lucky."

"Nothing to do with luck," Ana shrugged. "Most likely there's a natural selection going on around you that you're not even aware of, because nasty types know you're not for them... Sorry, I don't know how to say things in a roundabout way."

"That's all right," Nina said. "One should only ever speak plainly. But you exaggerate."

She laughed and looked at Jelena and David, as if asking for help. They were both smiling. Jelena glanced askance at David. He looked bewitched. Jelena thought how Nina was indeed extraordinary; exceptionally beautiful, exceptionally artless; someone who simply could not be associated with ugly things and bad people any more than a butterfly could live in a pool of mud.

"Yes, yes," Jelena could hear Ana say, "they probably just adore you from afar."

Nina laughed. "Perhaps it would not be a bad idea if they came a bit closer sometimes."

"Maybe, but that would be another story," Ana said. "Shall we?"

They got up to leave, each of them with their own body, thoughts and life.

The Hand

December

CULTURAL AFFAIRS: *Kiklop*, the first literary *Porin*, to be awarded today at the 10th Book Fair.

CULTURAL AFFAIRS: The *Jutarnji List*[62] Award: Who

---

[62] The Morning Paper. The name of a newspaper.

has written the best book of 2004? The reign of non-fiction and faction is over. This year, it's a potpourri of genres, with a marked tendency towards horror.

Shopping for a Birthday Present for Dad – Monday, 31st October

On Monday, Jelena left the office earlier than usual. She got up from her desk, took her coat off the hanger and waved to David. "I'm off. You're still at it?"

"As on this occasion you didn't help me, I'm not quite finished."

"Please don't; I had nightmares about that stupid thing. I even dreamt you were tortured like in war movies, by the Gestapo or something, to confess who'd written your text."

"That means you don't quite believe your own theory about culture vultures."

"I do believe it, but what I wrote for you was grotesque... And you really say that no one asked you what had got into you to write something like that?"

"Yeah, there was this girl from *Glorija*[63] who told me I'd written a wicked analysis of the Fair..."

"Ah, well, if it was a girl..." Jelena laughed.

"I thought you and I could have a spot of lunch somewhere but I forgot you guys do your weekly shop on Mondays."

"I feel like my mum when you say that," Jelena laughed. "I'm sorry I can't come with you; I could use a bit of light relief," she sighed. She'd had yet another incident with Dora which had left her, as ever, in a state of helpless turmoil. Dora had forgotten to give her the message about a postponed meeting and Jelena had only found out about the cancellation when she got to the place. Back in the office, she said, "Dora, how come you didn't... (hm, that's too wishy-washy) ... Why didn't you tell me the HDLU[64] had phoned? You'd have saved

---

[63] One of Croatian women's glossies
[64] Croatian Association of Artists

me the hike all the way to the Mosque[65] for nothing." "Whaaat? What's that about the HDLU? I didn't tell you, did I? Ah well, I've been rushed off my feet today so much I'm sick of it all," Dora replied indifferently, without a trace of apology. Jelena just stood there, trying to think of something authoritative and dignified to say. Should she say, *Next time, please,...* or perhaps, *I'm warning you I'll have a word with Andrej about this...* or even, *What sort of indolence do you call this; please do the work you're paid to do!* Instead, she repeated sheepishly, "I've wasted two hours on nothing..." Dora shrugged and returned to her paperwork, saying, "And they could've given us a bit more warning, couldn't they?"

Jelena shook herself to drive Dora's image out of her mind.

"Dora again, eh?" she heard David say. "How does she always manage to derail you like this? How on earth can you feel overpowered by someone you deem so inferior?"

Jelena shrugged. "Probably because I'm not all that *superior*. I've got to go now. Apart from the *weekly shop*, I've got to get a prezzie for dad," she said. "It's his birthday tomorrow. Trust *him* to be born on the Day of the Dead, of all days."

"All Hallows Day, not the Day of the Dead," David said.

"I know, but he loves the birth-death paradox. He's still not got bored saying that one man's misfortune is another man's gain every time."

Jelena was not in a very good mood. David laughed. "What's bugging you, other than Dora?"

"Bruno has been more and more insufferably nervous while shopping lately, and so..."

"And so you're cross in advance?"

Jelena shrugged. Her interpretation of Bruno's nervousness

---

[65] The popular name for the current HDLU building and the surrounding area. Completed in 1938 from designs by Ivan Meštrović, it was originally a gallery for the promotion of Croatian art. In 1941, it was adapted into a mosque; hence the nickname. After 1955, it became the Museum of the People's Revolution. In 1993, the building's original purpose and function were restored.

went as follows: if nervous when shopping, he'd be nervous doing anything else with her; if nervous whenever doing something with her, he didn't love her, and if he didn't love her and they stayed together in spite of that fact, they had to be cowards and boring, middle-aged people who expected nothing more of life.

***

Getting a present for dad was a hard task. She had planned to get him a safe; he had always wanted one.

"Excuse me, do you sell safes?" Instead of showing surprise or at least some curiosity (people did not buy safes every day), the young woman in a white protective coat gave her an indifferent look and replied languidly, "Saaafes? Noooo."

"And lockable cash boxes?" Jelena enquired, ignoring the blinking and the rolling of eyes.

"Sooorrry?"

"Cash boxes, have you got them?"

"Nooo, ma'aam, we haven't."

"You see, that's where you're wrong," Jelena said triumphantly. "You've got them, up there on that shelf." She was convinced she'd managed to get the better of at least one little pig, one little Dora who'd grow to be a great big Dora some day.

"You should've said you wanted toys in the first place," the shop assistant said, not in the least confounded.

"What do you mean: toys? You've got a proper cash box there." Instead of stopping there, she added unnecessarily, "And you said you didn't. If you have a cash box and believe you don't have one, you might even have a safe even though you told me you didn't have one. Had you just said you didn't know, I'd have asked someone else. Like this, believing you knew your business, I could have gone away without buying what I was looking for…" By then, she sounded confused and spiteful even to herself: what an evil old hag had a go at me today, the girl will tell her friends later.

"That's multimedia; you should have asked the colleague in

the multimedia section," came the assistant's cool reply.

"So why didn't you send me over there at once, instead of telling me you didn't have any safes?"

"You don't have to shout at me, madam."

"Madam wasn't shouting at you at all," said Bruno who had until then merely stood by and listened to the exchange. "It is your job to give her the right information. But you're not doing it properly."

"We ought to report you," said Jelena, less crabbily but with more confidence. Bruno's protectiveness had warmed her heart and filled her with tenderness; she nearly kissed him in front of the frosty shop assistant.

The girl all but spat in their wake. "Go on then, report me," she said defiantly.

They left, united against the common enemy.

Dad's Birthday – Tuesday, 1st November

"Come off it, girl, what pleasure can you possibly find in wishing a happy birthday to an old donkey like me?"

"Oh dear, dad, what a welcome," Jelena groaned. "However... I wish you good health, long life, lots of joy, to love your wife, to be loved by your daughter, to lack nothing..."

"Enough, enough! You chant like a Gypsy," her father said.

"You really are a boor," Jelena said, hurt, and turned her back on him.

"You know that an old stump carries no leaves; all it has is its thick, ugly bark."

"Oh dear, no, here come your instructive garden metaphors."

"Garden is the spring of life, my darling. People with gardens survive hard times. You know what it used to be like in Sarajevo during the Siege[66]? People hauled boxes of soil up onto their balconies and grew lettuce. Most of them survived on pasta, flour and ancient tins from the humanitarian aid.

---

[66] April 1992 – February 1996.

Children sickened because they didn't have any vitamins and minerals in their food. Do you know how many Sarajevans became ill with cancer? Those with gardens, however, ate anything that would grow there: carrots, lettuce, chard, dandelions... and stayed healthy. Do you remember *Soylent Green*? When they sell vegetables through metal bars, as if they were expensive jewels. And how much they pay for two tomatoes and a carrot."

"What's that, what green soviet?" asked mum from the kitchen.

"Soylent, not soviet. It's food from the near future: green nutritional tablets made of human flesh, of dead people, because there is no other food left on Earth. Everything is encased in concrete; people sleep in the street and in stairwells..."

"Yuck, just as we're about to eat," mum cried. She came to the door, drying her hands with a tea towel. "Sit down, never mind him. He's worse than usual tonight."

Jelena was in a bad mood too. When mother asked her what was wrong – like any mother would, she knew by the look on her face that something was amiss – she told her about Dora and the shop assistant. Even as she spoke, however, she felt she was lying. She should have said: I'm not happy with Bruno and that's why any stupid little shop-girl can fuck up my day – that would have been the real truth of it.

"Dora Gimmeyoura again?" dad asked.

Jelena nodded.

"You know what weeds are?" dad asked.

"Dad, please..." Jelena said.

"Weeds, my darling, are fitness trainers for useful plants. The useful plant struggles against the weed for dear life. If it survives, it is stronger than the weed. If the weed defeats it, the plant cannot stay alive. So what's it to be, then: are you going to moan or are you going to fight?"

"Dad, please..." Jelena said.

"Don't *dad-please* me, but mind what I say. I've always been telling you that. And you know what else I'll tell you? Do you know why weeds are strong? Of course you don't know, why should you…"

"I don't know," said Jelena, irritated. "I'm not a farmer."

"Neither am I, but I learn from nature. Now then, why is it that the weeds are so resilient? What gives a weed its strength? A weed doesn't know it's a weed. It believes itself to be as valuable and beautiful as a useful plant. No one thinks of oneself as a weed."

"I might be a weed, then, and she might not," Jelena said. "I wouldn't mind, if only I wasn't trying to treat her as an equal because I don't want her to feel bad about herself for being crude and half-literate."

"That's exactly the point," her father said. "Have you heard of bindweed?"

"I think so," said Jelena, shaking her head in disapproval but knowing resistance would be useless.

"Bindweed is a weed, a sort of creeper. It can wind around a branch of a fruit tree and force it to bend down to the ground. The bottom branches usually are the ones bearing the most fruit. It weighs them down even lower. And that's where bindweed lies in wait. Snap! It winds around the branch and drags it down, taking its light and air, growing and rising to heights it never even dreamed it could reach. What can you learn from that?"

Jelena shrugged.

"If you're smart, you'll learn something. It means, the more fruitful you are, the more you attract creepers. And the more you bend down to their level, the easier it'll be for them to grab hold of you, feed on you and strangle you, depriving you of what is rightfully yours. That's what creepers are like: you mustn't bend down to their level but handle them nicely from above, and then they can do you no harm. Stay in your proper place, like a fruit tree, tall and proud."

Jelena laughed. She revelled in her father's firm conviction that she was worth more than Dora, that she, Jelena, was a fruit tree and Dora was bindweed, and that that was the only reason Dora always managed to wind around her, suffocate her, drag her down. Dora, the fat slag.

"Go on, girl, laugh. One day you'll understand my words."

"I understand, dad, of course I do. You're right," Jelena said.

"The hell you do," dad said. "You don't even know that bindweed is the easiest weed to remove. You simply pull it by the stalk and lift it off the ground. All creepers are easy to uproot."

"Fine, okay, I get it," said Jelena. Then she related how they wanted to buy a safe but didn't find one, and got 12 year old *Ballantine's*, a set of whisky tumblers and five pairs of cotton socks instead. The socks had no elastic around the ankle because dad hated socks with elastic, claiming *they stopped the little circulation he still had left*. "It's not a very imaginative present," said Jelena.

"A safe would've been better."

"Just as well you didn't get him one," said mum. "He's getting meaner and meaner as he gets older anyway."

"Just as well you didn't get me one," said dad. "Your mother has made sure I didn't have anything to put in it anyway. She thinks my pocket is bottomless, a *pockpot*."

Wednesday, 2nd November, *Pizza Box*

On their way home from work the following day, having had got to New Zagreb[67], they went their separate ways: Bruno went straight home, and Jelena picked up her mother and drove her to Kruge, to her tailor. Once her mum had got out of the car, Jelena drove around the area to pass the time. She was hungry, weary and gloomy. Entering her apartment later, she sniffed the air, disappointed: she could detect no smell of food, although Bruno had been in for ages. "You could've thought of making something to eat," she said in an even, balanced tone of voice, trying not to hiss or sound irritated. I ought to be amiable, she thought, but how to ask amiably why he hadn't prepared a meal? *Ha-ha, hee-hee, my dear hubby, I thought*

---

[67] The part of Zagreb built in the sixties and the seventies on the undeveloped south bank of the Sava River.

you'd made us some noshy-wosh. Your little kitten is hungry and tired... He'd kill me after two days of such drivel, she almost laughed inwardly. Inwardly, I do everything inwardly, she thought. She washed her hands and, stomping her feet loudly on purpose, made for the kitchen. Loudly, she rattled the dishes and slammed the drawers and the fridge door. Bruno had the hard look of an indifferent culprit in his eyes; a culprit aware of his guilt, yet unrepentant. "You could've felt moved to rustle something up, if only scrambled eggs. Out of charity if not for love. I always make you something," Jelena said. "And, actually, that has nothing to do with either love or charity; it's simply not fair on the basic human level. And it's cruel." She'd gone over the top again in her choice of words and knew that Bruno would simply ignore her again. "You know which concept is the opposite of love?"

"What's the matter with you?" said Bruno. Was that vexation she'd heard in his voice, she wondered.

"The opposite of love is not hatred, as is generally believed. No, it's something far worse: indolence."

She was right: Bruno had decided to ignore her challenge to fight.

"I've been planning to have those frozen squid for supper..."

"Yup, but, as far as I can see, you haven't taken them out of the freezer. You're welcome to eat your plan, then, and I'll have eggs and salad," she replied harshly. She'd spotted a rolled-up pizza box in the dustbin. He'd phoned for a pizza, then, and eaten it in her absence. This unforgivable treason hit her harder than anything.

At bedtime, while Bruno was taking a shower, Jelena phoned Buba to find out the name of the new anti-depressant she was on. In the morning, she went to see her GP and asked for a prescription.

"Are you sure you need it?" the doctor asked.

"I'm sure. I can't change my husband, my job or my flat... I can't even change myself. The only thing left for me to do is to look for a medicine that will make it more pleasant."

"Be careful, that's typical addict motivation", said the GP, a woman of Jelena's age who had been her "family doctor" for a decade.

"You know I never take anything, not even Persen[68]," Jelena said.

"Okay, try it," said the doctor. "But if you're not happy with it, stop at once."

The Hand

Thursday, 27th January

THE FRONT PAGE: 30 banned additives found in ice cream, biscuits and juices

THE DAY'S EVENTS: Of more than 300 food additives approved in Croatia, one third (110) can be harmful to health (...) and more than 30 of those are banned in a number of countries, mainly within the EU...

An extract from the brochure "What Lurks Behind the E-numbers" by Dada Lerotić and Ivana Vinković-Vrček (published by the Association for Democratic Society, in the name of open public access to information and the European safeguarding principle): "The greatest number of the most dangerous additives is found in confectionery. By eating a 100 g bar of chocolate, a child will have consumed more than the recommended safe amount of additive 476, to name but one. By the same token, phosphates used as stabilisers and emulsifiers in milk-based drinks, stock cubes, desserts and non-alcoholic fizzy drinks extract calcium from human bones: German researchers have proved that they have caused osteoporosis in children as young as 10."

PAGE 22: 30 Tonnes of Toxic Waste Missing

The environmental protection inspection of the factory discovered that at Karbon Works, only one half of the factory's toxic waste was properly stored.

On page 22? Not sooner?

---

[68] A herbal antidepressant with valerian extract

Xenophobia – Thursday, 3rd November

"You're using a plastic cup again," Jelena said to David without looking up from the paper she was reading. She could tell by sound what he was doing: using the espresso machine. "Thus ingesting a fatal extra dose of synthetic oestrogen, because that cup's made of the worst kind of plastic. They call it xenoestrogen."

"I'm not a xenophobe."

"A feeble joke," Jelena said. "You obviously haven't read my last week's column, about the use of plastic in food industry: plastic crockery, cling film for wrapping food and so on."

David shook his head. "Nope, but I read the one before, about PVC doors and windows. I had no idea they were so dangerous."

"Well yes, if you have PVC windows, you inhale cadmium and practically secure some type of cancer or other for yourself and your family. But to go back to xenoestrogen, it causes breast cancer and many other cancers."

"Cancer, cancer, cancer. Even cancer can kill you but once, dammit," said David, throwing his arms up in protest. "In any case, I can't get breast cancer."

"I'm not so sure. I believe I've read somewhere that men, too, can have breast cancer, although the number of cases is small." Jelena gave him a wicked wink.

"My mother died of breast cancer," said David.

"You never told me. I'm sorry to hear that."

David waved dismissively. To defuse the awkward situation, Jelena went on talking about plastic. "Do you know that fish are turning hermaphroditic because of xenoestrogens? A massive quantity of pesticides spilled into a Florida lake once, and all the alligators became female. Haven't you noticed that men's breasts are getting larger these days?

David glanced at her and she laughed. "I made up the breast thing to check if you're listening. But I've read an article by Dr Marilyn Glenville were she says that we actually live in a sea of hormones which spread around the planet through the water cycle: people take more and more substitute hormones, excrete them in their urine, and the hormones are then absorbed by the soil... People generally don't realise that nothing ever *disappears*. Earth is not flat; it's a watertight bowl, and we keep pouring and pouring stuff into it."

"Meaning that, when 18 tonnes of engine oil suddenly spill into Neretva[69]..."

"Yup, people call that a catastrophe. But if it trickles into it for years, then it's fine."

"I'm now using fructose, which is hideously expensive, because you told me that artificial sweeteners give you prostate cancer, and now you'd have me... wash a mug five times a day to avoid plastic! I may be your most dedicated follower, but that's overdoing it."

Jelena looked back at the paper. She knew that it would take a few days for David to digest the information. Without lifting her head, she said, "It'll be just like with dioxin. You laughed at first and waved your hand at me, and later you asked, 'Jozo, which meat did you say had the most dioxin: fatty meat, or lean meat, or...?' You know what, I just might leave the Culture section after all and defect to *Health*. I feel like doing useful work and nothing but."

"Perhaps you ought to buy a farm and grow your own veg," said David.

"No need to sneer. The thought has seriously crossed my mind."

"I'm not sneering," said David. "What are you writing now?"

Jelena turned to her computer. "Today, I'm writing about Origanox."

"Which is... ?"

"Another hideously expensive food supplement. Oregano allegedly contains 42 times more antioxidants than apples, and apples are known for their healthy properties. It's a natural antibiotic and antiseptic."

"Great, at last we have something that's both healthy and

---

[69] A river in Herzegovina

tasty. Eat a pizza with oregano, and there you have it!"

"That's what I said, but their marketing lady explained that I'd poison myself with pizzas before I managed to ingest enough oregano to make a difference. Something else bothers me, though: the blurb says that a single capsule of Origanox contains 475 mg of oregano, and that you need one a day to supplement your nutrition. What does a capsule weigh? What's the rest of it made of? Why should we swallow capsules if 475 mg of oregano is all we need to take? A small jar of oregano you buy in a supermarket contains 14 grams of oregano. One gram has a thousand milligrams. If I've worked it out correctly, there's 14 thousand milligrams in that jar, which makes roughly 28 capsules…"

"How do you propose to write about it when you don't have the answers to those questions?"

"Questions are the whole point. One needs to know how to ask them. Asking questions makes one think. People should be trained to question."

"Okay," David said, "one needs to know how to question. So here's another question: why bother, when you can't avoid eating rubbish? You said that nutritionists laugh when someone mentions *healthy food*. It doesn't exist any more, they say. Indeed, the other morning on the telly I heard a nutritionist speak about *health-appropriate* milk. The presenter kept asking, 'Is that milk healthy, then?' and she kept answering, 'Yes, it is health-appropriate milk.'"

"You're right, one can't avoid it. We've already managed to screw everything up. But we could start putting things right form this moment on. Did you know, for example, that substances used in antiperspirants have been found in breast tumours? Those compounds are called parabens. There's oodles of them and their names all have something like *benzoic* or *benzoate* in them. They enter one's body through the skin and disturb the balance and the functioning of hormones. They can also be found in food products, but they're said not to be harmful when ingested: they can only enter the blood stream through the skin. British women, for example, are the greatest consumers of deodorants, but they also lead in the number of breast cancer cases…"

"I happen to know that Croatian women are second in Europe in the number of breast cancer cases," David said seriously, "but I doubt that they use deodorant more than German women do."

"Yes, you're right. It needs to be investigated. But, you know, if my text manages to reduce the danger by one thousandth, it was worth writing… Actually," she added, nodding with playful solemnity, "come to think of it, I've got synthesising intelligence. For example, when I take a shower in a hotel, I'm careful not to use more water than at home, because I'm constantly aware that all water belongs to the same planet, comes from the same pool which is not inexhaustible."

"You're showing off," said David. "Lecturing like a teacher."

"So there's no difference between Zagreb of the twenty first and Venice of the sixteenth century."

"Eh?"

"You haven't seen *The Honest Courtesan? Dangerous Beauty*[70], then? The movie? No? It's about Veronica Franco, the most famous Venetian courtesan of the period. She wasn't all that beautiful, but she was smart and well educated. And how come she was so well educated? Courtesans were allowed to use libraries, and honest women weren't, because, as someone in the movie puts it, *eloquence brought about promiscuity of mind and promiscuity of mind lead to promiscuity of body…*"

"And? What's that got to do with ecology?"

"Well, if a man were to tell you what I told you just now, you wouldn't say he was being tedious like a teacher."

"Yes, I would. Like a male teacher."

Jelena didn't think it worth her while to respond to the quip. "Let me just tell you this," she said passionately, "I'd love to meet more people with synthesising intelligence. I'd love to

---

[70] A film by Marshall Herskovitz, 1998

have a synthesising doctor who'd ask me, when I come to see him about pain in my feet, how I slept, what I dreamt of at night, if I felt happy, if I ate enough of red / green/ yellow fruit, how much exercise I had every day... and then tell me what was wrong with me. But it's a pipe dream. Even alternative practitioners send you to a mainstream doctor when things get really bad."

"All right, smartypants; I've had enough for today." David ruffled her hair. "Tell me, how are your mum and dad? I haven't seen them for ages."

"Getting older," Jelena said. "And arguing all the time. Dad's becoming impossible. The other day they had a row because mum forgot to wish him a happy birthday and he felt hurt."

"It does make a sort of sense though," David said.

"Yeah, only it wasn't his birthday," said Jelena. David laughed. "He'd simply confused the dates," Jelena went on, "and when mum proved to him that it wasn't the first of November but the thirtieth of October, he didn't calm down but told her instead that it didn't matter it was the thirtieth: had it been the first of November, she still wouldn't have remembered and was now using the two day difference as an excuse. It's pure Monty Python."

David laughed. Jelena stared through the window pensively. "I'm worried about dad. He seems to be ageing fast and losing his inner strength, no matter how hard he tries to be tough and cynical the way he always used to be..."

"It's normal, he's no longer young. How are things with Ana? Has she given you the manuscript to read?"

"Not yet. She's going through a dark patch again. She's like one possessed. She keeps going on about coincidences, particularly since that fan of hers recognised her in *Golf.* To give you an example, she's got a long list of people whose names reflect their personal traits: there's a Lucia who can barely see, and Saint Lucy protects the sight; then a nice man whose indicator was accidentally smashed by a colleague of hers and he forgave her – his surname is Dušanović[71]. Then there's a moustachioed woman whose maiden name is Brkić[72], Glavan[73] with a massive head, Vodopivec[74] who is chairman of the Former Alcoholics Association. Or Žderić[75] who is rake-thin, and Gluhak[76], the virtuoso violin player with perfect pitch…"

"She's got a point there," said David. "Nomen est omen… Zaradić[77] who is a tycoon, Zubović[78] the dentist, Večerić[79] the chef, chairman of the Association for the Protection of Birds whose surname is Grlica[80]. And what about our Piljek, who doesn't merely look but gapes[81]?

"One of his ancestors must've had gaped all the time, which produced a family gene which in turn gave rise to the name," Jelena added.

"Or that bloke from Advertising, Macan[82]: he purrs whenever he gets to work on a client or when he comes to propose an ad for one of our pages. A proper great big tom, smooching up to you when he's hungry."

"Or the Minister for Agriculture, Čobanković[83]," Jelena chuckled. "If I was the Prime Minister, I wouldn't have given him the job, with such a surname. And what about that nice girl from Accounts, Vedrana[84], always cheerful although her soul, too, must have a dark corner… And the MP whose maiden

---

[71] Duša = soul

[72] Brk = moustache

[73] Glava = head

[74] Water drinker

[75] Žderati = devour one's food in huge quantities

[76] Gluh = deaf

[77] Zaraditi = to earn

[78] Zub = tooth

[79] Večera = dinner

[80] Collared dove

[81] Piljiti = to gape, to gawk

[82] One of the words for 'tom-cat'

[83] Čoban = shepherd (pejoratively)

[84] Vedar (vedra) = cheerful

name was Knežević[85], until she became a Carević[86] by marriage (and is now a representative in the Upper House of the Parliament) – what do you reckon, what might her next husband's name be if she remarries?"

"Kraljević[87]?"

"Bullseye," Jelena laighed, then remembered Ana again. "With Ana, it's all an obsession, though."

"She's obsessive in everything she does," David said.

"Although she might be right. It could be that any little fragment of reality is the Universe in miniature. What is I-Ching? A device predicting infinite possibilities intersecting at any moment in time. Some supreme spirit could have planned it all, just like in good computer games. They, too, represent the Universe in miniature, and the supreme spirit is embodied in the team of geniuses who thought them up. Take Bruno's football game. I was surprised he'd gone so deeply into it, but he explained you could play an endless number of games without repeating a situation. The number of combinations is practically infinite. To you, it appears different every time, however, but the guy who'd thought it up can tell what's going to happen; he recognises the elements or, as Ana would put it, omens. Similarly, some wise sage can tell what'll happen to us on the basis of factors we can't put together so that they make sense... Ana could be right... If everything is Consciousness, then we are the same as words, so maybe..."

David patted her shoulder. "So maybe you ought to spend less time with her."

The Hand

5th January

TV LISTINGS: In China, an exhibition of litter collected on the slopes of Mt Everest, a small part of the total of 600

---

[85] Knez = something like a Count or Herzog; in Russian novels, usuall y translated as Prince, as in Prince Myshkin

[86] Car = emperor, tzar. Carević = an emperor's son

[87] Kralj = King; kraljević = king's son

tonnes of litter deposited by man on the roof of the world.

Fucking Good

Dipsy came in, opening the door noisily. Jelena let out a huffing breath: another hard day had begun.

"I've just been telling beach jokes to Anđelko. Wanna hear a few?" Dipsy said.

"One," David said.

"Deal," Mario replied readily, undeterred by the lukewarm response. "On the beach, a mum, sitting on the sand, calls her little son who is playing in the shallows. 'Michel, Michel!' 'Oui maman,' the little boy replies. 'Want um pie, mon bébé?' A good one, innit? I mean, it's a true story."

David laughed.

"What's the joke?" Ivana asked, entering.

"You're late," said Mario. Before she even took her jacket off, he added, "What's your take on that yokel of yours lunching every day with that buxom babe?"

"They're just friends," said Ivana gloomily.

"Join them from time to time is my advice," Mario said.

"I don't like canteen food," said Ivana, taking a small package out of her handbag. She peeled off the wrapping paper and bit into the emergent sandwich, grimacing dejectedly. "Yuck," she said and lifted the top slice to peek at the filling. "Will you look at that, the salami is leaking dye."

Jelena lifted her head, interested. "Let me see." She waved a hand angrily. "Ugh, the stuff they sell us! Bin that! They don't care, as long as they advertise it as *great-tasting homemade food…*"

"While we're on the subject," Mario put in, "they've removed that WGW FUCKING GOOD poster. Now they've put up one saying WGW JUST KIDDING."

"And they've got a poster up by *Lisinski*[88] that says, WGW BEES FUCK BEST," Ivana said.

---

[88] Zagreb's largest concert hall, named after the composer Vatroslav Lisinski

"They'll put up JUST KIDDING AGAIN later," Mario said.

When the conversation died down and everyone had got down to work, Piljek peeked into the office, paler, peakier and more pointed than usual. He went over to David's desk, clutching a few sheets of paper.

"I need a word," he said, breathing loudly and rapidly.

"Go on, then. What's up? Have you been running up the stairs?" said David.

Piljek waved a hand. "I'm dog-tired, and what with the weather change..." He beat his breast as if to stop it from heaving. In a quieter voice, he went on: "Just look at the stuff they gave me."

David took the sheets and skimmed through, frowning. "I don't get it. What is it? Take a pew."

"Fine," said Piljek, sitting down. "I don't get it either," he whispered helplessly, "none of it."

"But what is it?"

"They gave it to me to create a plan for controlling resources and making savings, filtering data by requirements, by available supplies and by human resources..."

"What for?"

"For the reorganisation project I agreed to work on."

"Why did they give it to you in particular?"

"I'm the project leader, aren't I, I have to put together a proposal..."

"I can't work it out, I'm sorry," David said. "The only thing I can think of is for you to call a meeting and hand the task over to the group, threatening you'll sack them if they don't manage to do it. Learn to delegate, that's what bosses do!"

Piljek nodded seriously. "Fine," he said. (Translation: *Thanks.*)

"Not at all," said David. Jelena coughed to hide a giggle.

After Piljek had left, Dipsy commented with ham sympathy: "Have you noticed how Piljek has shrivelled? Ambition will devour him."

Jelena didn't respond, but later, alone with David, she said:

"For the first time ever, I have to agree with Dipsy. Piljek's ambition will devour him."

David laughed. "Leave poor Piljek alone," he said. "He reminds me of our Ringo – remember Ringo? – when he was a puppy. Whenever he strained at something he wanted to snatch, his snout would become pointed and his eyes would pop out. Matko was little at the time; he'd say: 'Look how his eyes *tighten* when he strains like that!' Piljek's the same: his eyes *tighten* when he talks about something he wants, that's how badly he wants it. He should have been given two years to learn that programme, and they told him to create it instead!"

"I don't feel sorry for him at all," Jelena said. "Why did he accept? If they offered him to be head surgeon, he'd accept, and people would die because of him."

"Let him be, he's just a caricature," David repeated.

"Exactly. A caricature of ambition. I've realised that we all have a key vice that devours us in the end. Piljek's one is ambition; it's eating him up; he's all wrung out and yellow but keeps feeding his flesh to the beast. Dora is eaten up by her vanity, Dipsy by his appetite for garbage. One day he'll turn into a garbage heap; Fish will freeze in his own ice…"

"What about our vices, yours and mine? What's eating us up?"

"Contrary to Andrej, you burn with too much love for the female half of the universe."

David laughed. "And you?"

"Me? I burrow under the surface much too much… under the surface of ecology, but also of my own marriage. The way I see it, there's always something hidden under the surface. And such an attitude results in… *unhappiness*."

Chocolate with Chilli – Thursday, 3rd November

Nina came in when everyone except David had already left for their various field assignments.

"Hi! You're on your own?" she said.

David nodded and, smiling, cradled his chin in his palms, as if about to enjoy a good movie. Nina smiled back. She took off her coat, arranged her things on the desk and then knocked on Andrej's door, nodding at David. After only a minute or two with Andrej, she came out of his office with an expressionless face, sat down at her desk and worked in silence and with concentration. A while later, she took out a bar of chocolate in a pale wrapping with an image of a red chilli pepper and a brown chocolate square on it from her bag, went over to David and offered him some. "Dark chocolate with chilli," she said.

"With chilli?" David was surprised. "Jelena stuffs us all full of dark chocolate, but I had no idea one could have it with chilli."

"Oh yes. When people first started drinking chocolate – it was originally a drink – they flavoured it with chilli. Didn't you know that?"

"No," David said.

"They did. Later, I think it was the English who got rid of the chilli, added milk and started manufacturing solid chocolate bars…"

"It's their fault, then, " David said, "that chocolate is not healthy any more. Jelena's taught me what's good for you: dark chocolate, wine, apples, beer…"

"And all of it tasty," Nina laughed.

"All right then, I'm inviting you this evening for a cup of dark chocolate," said David.

Andrej came out of his office, with no more than a nod by way of greeting.

"I can't, I have to see something at *Gavella*," said Nina as the door closed behind Andrej's back. "It's preview night tonight. Saves me going to the opening night."

"Before *Gavella*, then?"

Nina glanced at the watch. "Okay," she said, "I can do that. Shall we meet in front of *Gavella*?"

"I can come and get you, just tell me where," David said.

"There's no point," Nina said. "I live in New Zagreb and you're in the centre. Why should you bother driving from one end of town to the other, in all that traffic…"

"I don't mind," David said. "I can come early; that way we'll have the time to go for a drink."

She agreed. When he came to get her at six, she was already waiting at the foot of the staircase of a modern five floor apartment block in Srediśće. The building looked lively, sporting a necklace of glowing shop-windows and cafes with neon signs in clashing colours.

"I'm sorry," Nina said, getting into the car. "I tried to call you to let you know, but I couldn't get hold of you... I can't go for a drink. I have to go to my mum's; she's not well."

Disappointed, David said politely, "I hope it's nothing serious. I can meet you after the show."

Nina wasn't keen. "I don't know at what time it ends. Perhaps some other time," she said.

"What are you seeing? *The Marriage*?[89]"

"Yes."

"Good, that's not a very long play. It'll probably finish around ten," David said. "I'll be waiting for you in front of *Gavella*. Where does your mum live?"

"In the Long Street."

"I'll take you."

"Thanks."

Driving, David kept glancing at Nina's classic profile. Conscious of his glances, she kept her head straight, sitting still like a beautiful silhouette on the dark background of the car window.

***

He waited for her leaning on a column at the entrance. He saw her come out. She looked at him and smiled broadly. Her smile delighted him. He smiled back and waved to her. Only then did he spot Buba behind Nina's back. Buba was smiling, convinced that David was waving to her. She wondered what he was doing there. The two women approached him together. Standing next to each other, they became confused.

"Nina, this is Buba. Buba – Nina," David said. They shook

---

[89] A play by Nikolai Gogol (1842)

hands. Nina went on smiling.

"And? What was it like?" David enquired, addressing neither of them in particular. Buba understood that David did not come for the show or for her but for Nina. Nina answered David's question. Buba pretended to be listening while using the opportunity to look Nina over: a young woman, most likely positive about what she wants and convinced she was entitled to happiness. Even happiness with David, she concluded.

"I'm off," she said. "I've been on my feet all day since the crack of dawn, I'm worn out. See you." She turned to Nina and said goodbye.

When Buba had left, Nina said, "Nice woman." Youthfully uninquisitive, David noticed. She faced him, smiling. "Where to now?" she wanted to know.

David thought what a sight for sore eyes she truly was. He felt proud of her, like a parent would be proud of a lovely and clever child. She walked by his side, keeping a distance as if setting an invisible boundary.

Nina suggested they went to *Tantra*. David noticed the looks which followed her from the moment they entered. Strangely, no one said hello to him, although normally he could hardly make a few steps without running into a familiar face. Nina strode confidently ahead, glancing back at him relaxedly from time to time as she wound her way among the tables. She was conscious of the admiring looks and used to them. *Tantra's* exotic surroundings enhanced her beauty: the reflection of the white canopy over the table and the subdued golden light illumined her face. She may well have chosen *Tantra* because she knew how well it suited her. She and David laughed when a waiter quietly asked two underage girls how old they were and then asked them, just as quietly but sternly, to leave. The teenagers who looked like replicants in their little blouses unbuttoned halfway to the waist and their low-riding hipster jeans got up shamefacedly, but in spite of that, exiting, remembered to thrust out their breasts and pointedly wiggle their hips, stumbling clumsily on their spiky heels.

"So," Nina said, "I now have the pleasure of being in the

company of the most coveted single man in Zagreb." She laughed. "Unless you're a dyed-in-the-wool bachelor," she added.

"I'm not," said David. "I'm a dyed-in-the-wool husband. Buba is my ex-wife."

"Really?" Nina was surprised. "She's very nice," she repeated.

"Nice, kind, pretty, smart," said David. He talked about Buba, Matko and Hana. Nina listened with interest. David thought how nice it would be to fall in love again.

The Inspector

Whilst the Inspector watched the nervous young woman with great attention, his Sergeant showed little interest as he made notes: those arseless and titless modern young women were not to his taste, not even for the sake of the investigation.

Ana's First Encounter with Andreja Martić

Before becoming a teacher, Ana had known nothing about either state or private schools, but had heard stories that gave private schools bad publicity: that they were schools for spoiled, lazy rich low ability kids who didn't need to make an effort since their parents were paying. In the conservative, strict private school where Ana worked one could find, just like in any other school, rich kids, cheeky kids, children of poor ability, untalented children with ambitious parents, serious, dedicated children whose parents were not rich but wanted them to have the best education; mostly, however, one could find pupils whose parents were well off because they worked a lot and very hard, thus having little or no time for their children. In one lesson, Ana had asked, "In your opinion, why did your parents send you to this particular school?"

"To make sure that someone is looking after us and that there's no drink and drugs," the majority of pupils replied.

In each tutor group, there would be at least one ill-adjusted child who stood out from the rest, which was obviously why his or her parents had chosen Ana's school. One could spot such children hanging around on their own during breaks, speaking only when spoken to in lessons and looking grave or sullen. Having been alone, grave and sullen all her life, Ana homed in on such children like a detector. Among them, she noticed a reticent girl with a habitual hunch who preferred to stay in the classroom during breaks. She looked her up in the register: Andreja Martić, daughter of Andrej Martić, journalist, and Helena Šoljan Martić, actress. She was surprised to discover that the girl was her former colleague's child. A colleague in the staff room said, "Can you believe that girl is Helena Šoljan's daughter? Such a beautiful mother, and look at the daughter..." She saw Andrej once at a parents' meeting. He greeted her somewhat haughtily. He even may have had forgotten that, not so long ago, she used to work with him in his editorial office. She told Buba that Andrej's daughter was in her school. Buba remarked that the world was small. "Such a withdrawn and despondent child," Ana said.

"What, in a private school?" Matko chimed in. "From my primary, only one freaky girl went to a private school..."

"Why freaky?"

"Totally fugly."

"*Fugly?* What's fugly?" Buba asked.

"Short for *fucking ugly*," Hana explained.

"What a miserable lot of colonised[90] little Croats you are," said Buba.

Matko went on: "Her parents always came to fetch her in full gear, all dolled up, and she was always, y'know, *lost.* That's probably why they sent her to a private school."

"What are you on about?" Buba asked. "It's not a Special School."

"I know it isn't. But all the ... *stunted* ones go there."

"You're such a boor," said Buba. "It's pure propaganda, spread by those who can't afford private education."

---

[90] *Freaky, fugly* and *fucking ugly* would have been inserted into Croatian dialogue.

"I'd love to go to a private school," said Hana. "Everyone can speak their mind and they don't torment students with years and wars to learn but discuss stuff instead. They respect everyone's personality there, don't they, Ana? I'd love to go."

"You're so numpty you can't tell your bum from your elbow" Matko said under his breath.

"That's enough, Matko!" shouted Buba.

Hana said loyally, "It must be a good school to have Ana working there."

Kalida

When Helena was still a young actress, a fad for consulting fortune-tellers spread among her colleagues, male and female. This could have had something to do with Kalida, the famous Zagreb fortune-teller who adored the stage and went to see the shows as often as the actors came to see her. She went for free, but charged for her consultations. Although constantly badgered to go and see her, Helena didn't want to. She wasn't exactly afraid of it, but nevertheless found the idea of fortune-telling uncomfortable. One evening, after the performance, she stayed on with her colleagues in the theatre bar. Kalida was there, at the centre of the group. When they were introduced, the fortune-teller said in her deep, dramatic voice: "Soo... that's our young beauty...You didn't want to come and see me?"

Helena didn't reply, only smiled, feeling slightly uncomfortable. Later, everyone ordered coffee and someone suggested, "Go on, Kalida, tell us what you see; just one thing about each of us." Helena didn't wish to participate, but Kalida appeared to be focussing on her. "Stay; sit down with the others," Kalida told her. When it was Helena's turn, Kalida said, "A tall man will woo and win you. To him, you'll be an ornament. He'll hold you in his hand like he would hold a beautiful rose. With him, you'll have a child..." "Helena's got special treatment," someone said. "It's a whole séance." Undisturbed, Kalida went on: "You'll bear a female child. Watch out when she is eight: she'll suffer injury. Don't worry, she won't die, but you'll have to see to it that there is no lasting damage; you'll be able to prevent that... And one more thing: be careful never to change; if you lose the tall man, you might change; if you do change, you'll never be what you were..." Everyone laughed. Helena kept convincing herself that Kalida was spouting nonsense, but she never forgot the pronouncement of the Delphic Oracle. She already knew Andrej at the time but had no idea that he would be the tall man of the prophecy.

When Andreja turned eight, not a day would go by without Helena remembering Kalida's words. One summer afternoon Andreja almost got run over by a car: she had slipped on her roller-skates and fallen. Luckily, the car barely grazed her, as they were in the low speed zone. Breathless, Helena rushed towards her, fear turning her legs into soft dough that gave under her as she grabbed the child and ran. "I'm fine, mummy, don't worry," Andreja was saying. She had only grazed her knee; that was all. Helena put her daughter into a taxi and took her to the Clinic for Trauma. "Why the panic, madam? It's just a scratch." "Please examine her carefully, check for internal injuries," Helena pleaded. But they could not find anything wrong with Andreja. They bandaged her knee and that was that.

At that time Helena's fears had already began. Fear of death, fear of life, fear of ageing, fear for her beauty, fear for her child...

Not long after the accident, Andreja went on a school trip to Žumberak[91]. A few days later, she ran up a fever. Helen thought it was flu. The temperature remained high. Andreja began complaining of headache. She vomited. Helena did not take her to the doctor because, as she told herself, she believed it was a common virus. She knew the real reason was fear, plain and simple. What if it turns out to be something terrible, something lethal, something malignant? As Andreja got progressively worse, Helena sat by her bed, motionless,

---

[91] Semi-Alpine region in northern Croatia, famed for its natural beauty

paralysed by fear. Burning with fever, Andreja was struggling for breath. "Mummy, please, take me to the doctor," she said. Helena pretended not to hear, not daring to look at her.

When Andrej got home, he rushed to his daughter, felt her forehead and said to his wife, "You crazy fool, are you trying to kill my Andreja?" He snatched his daughter out of bed, put her coat on and took her to the car. It was meningitis. She stayed in the Hospital for Contagious diseases for two weeks. The doctor there asked, "Has she recently been out in the countryside; could she by any chance have picked up a tick?" "Oh no," Helena shook her head, "she's been to Žumberak on a school trip (the doctor raised her eyebrows) but I checked her all over afterwards for ticks." "And this?" asked the doctor and pointed at Andreja's bandaged knee. "This happened before the trip?" She unwound the bandage and checked the bend at the back of the knee. She found a tick swollen to the size of a bean sitting there. Fortunately, the long term effects of the illness were relatively mild: Andreja partly lost hearing in one ear and developed a slight memory weakness. Ever since, Helena thought she could see reproach in her eyes. Her daughter had heard Andrej yell, "You crazy fool, are you trying to kill my Andreja!"

Andreja?! The sound of it filled Helena's head long afterwards. *Andreja? You want to kill my Andreja?* From that time on, Andrej spent more and more time with Andreja and became very attached to her.

The Hand

The hand slowly reached for the newspaper on its right. Before opening the paper, the hand copied into the Diary a note from a torn piece of paper that lay on the desk:
11th January

LIFE: The Aniston-Pitt divorce is one of the most reported in history.

THE BACK PAGE: A line of coke is now cheaper than a cup of coffee. The price of heroin has dropped from 920 kuna for one gram (in 1995) to 290 kuna for one gram. In the same period, ecstasy has become 70% cheaper, with a single tablet now selling for 20 kuna.

The Inspector

"All right, all right, we need to hurry up," the Sergeant said. "We haven't got all day." He said the last bit in a quieter voice, sensing his governor's glance. Leaving the room, the young woman clumsily caught her sleeve on the doorknob and almost bumped into the woman who was to be interviewed next and who, unlike the exiting young woman, did not look nervous at all.

Regulations – Friday, 4th November

"I was with Nina last night," said David to Jelena when they sat down to their morning coffee.

Jelena was surprised. "Already?"

"What do you mean, 'already'?"

"What do you mean, 'you were with her'?"

"We didn't sleep together, if that's what you're thinking of."

"But whatever you did was important enough for you to mention it first thing," Jelena nodded. "I knew that the moment I first saw her. And?"

"And nothing. We ran into Buba."

"Of course you did; it's a small world," Jelena said. "I envy you. I'm trying to remember what it feels like when a new relationship is on the horizon, you know, when you break out in goose-pimples just thinking of him…"

"I'd wish you an experience like that, if only it were sensible."

"Why should it be sensible? Life is short, you always say that. And if that's the rule for you, it must be the rule for me, too."

"Are you on about equality again?"

"No; I'm on about love."

***

Coincidence that was no coincidence did not rule only Ana's

life. Jelena, too, found herself caught in its web. Around half three in the afternoon, Bruno rang to tell her he would bring the car round and leave it in front of her office building for her to drive herself home, as he had to go to HT to patch up a damaged programme.

"Oh yeah, I'd better tell you now or I'll forget: I've arranged with Nina to meet us tomorrow after the market, so don't make other plans."

"OK," said Bruno.

Unconsciously rather than consciously, Jelena registered that Bruno didn't ask why they were meeting Nina, which meant that he remembered what she's asked him to do, and that he didn't mind doing it. Instead of going straight home, Jelena decided to go for a stroll through the town; something she had not done for a while.

"Wait, I'm coming too," said Dipsy.

"I'm not taking the lift," said Jelena.

"Doesn't matter," said Dipsy and followed Jelena down the stairs.

Jelena waved to Anđelko; Anđelko waved back.

"Hey, Anđelko, coming to lunch with me or have you had a late burek-fast[92]?" Dipsy laughed heartily at his own joke.

"Since you've got money for lunch," Anđelko, normally a good-natured bloke, replied, "you could pay me back the twenty kuna I lent you for a coffee."

"No problemo," said Dipsy, unfazed. "I only have just enough for lunch on me, though. You'll get them tomorrow, fear not."

Anđelko shrugged and exchanged a glance with Jelena. Jelena grimaced contemptuously. She said goodbye to Dipsy at the door to get rid of him as fast as she could. Luckily, he suddenly slapped his forehead having remembered he'd not made a "weensy call" he'd promised to make and went back to the building in a few springy steps. As she got to the parking area to wait there for Bruno, Jelena saw a van with *Mato-prom*,

---

[92] Burek is a filled filo-pastry dish popular as brunch in Bosnia

Self-drive Transport written on it standing there with the engine running, surrounded by a cloud of stinking exhaust smoke. She looked around hoping to spot the driver. Finally she took out a notepad and began copying down the registration number of the van and the name of the business written on it, guessing correctly that her activity would soon attract the driver's attention. Indeed, some thirty seconds later, a middle-aged man in an overall came over running from the entrance of the neighbouring building. "What do you think you're doing, lady?" he asked belligerently.

Jelena couldn't quite decide if she'd only thought about the concept or had actually read somewhere that there was a regulation forbidding one to leave the engine of a parked car running and needlessly polluting the air. "Is this your van?" she asked.

"Yeah, and? Something wrong with it?" the man asked.

"You've had the engine running for half an hour now; you've stunk up the whole neighbourhood. Why didn't you turn it off?"

"Aw, madam," the man said with a derisive smile which meant, "crazy cunt".

"Don't you know that a law has been passed according to which you could pay a hefty fine for this? Particularly if you haven't got a catalytic converter!" The man waved her off and clambered into the cabin, but did not turn off the engine. She could see him wag his head sarcastically inside.

When Bruno arrived, Jelena told him she'd have to return to the office. She didn't offer an explanation and he didn't ask, only left the car in a parking bay and walked away. When she got back to the office, Dipsy, a phone receiver to his ear, said, "We all return to the scene of the crime." Jelena shrugged her shoulders. She sat down and dialled Information to find out whom she ought to call about a parked vehicle polluting the environment with a running engine. A puzzled male voice said, "Please wait a moment," and, after a minute or two, a female voice came on saying, "I really don't know who you should call. How about trying the State Inspectorate, 2-3-3-3-7-7?" The

Inspectorate didn't know how to help and gave her the number for the Communal Inspection, 6-1-0-0-2-6-9. The Communal gave her the number for the Environment Inspection, 6-1-1-1-1-1-1. When she got through, a weary female voice told her she had no knowledge of such a regulation and suggested Jelena should try the Sanitary Inspection. Eventually Jelena got connected to the Communal Enforcement (she couldn't remember if it was the same number as that of the Communal Inspection). There, an even wearier female voice said, "Oh, my dear madam…" Jelena silently waited for her to continue. The woman finished her thought: "It's a matter of personal ethical awareness, isn't it? I wouldn't think there was a law about it… You could try the Traffic Police?"

After that, Jelena gave up. Dipsy, who had surprisingly refrained from comment until then, probably sensing he could become the target of Jelena's anger if he said something, finally spoke up: "It doesn't work like that. This is not a country with an institution for every situation." Jelena didn't afford him as much as a glance, but he went on anyway: "You know how my father-in-law would deal with this guy? He'd grab him by the collar, toss him into the van like a bag of rubbish that he is and say, 'Turn it off, you piece of shit, or I'll wring your bleeding neck.' You bet he'd turn it off double quick. And immediately develop the ethical habit of not leaving the engine on."

In spite of herself, Jelena had to admit he was right and gave him a restrained nod of acknowledgement.

**

Driving past the two "theatre" cafés, *Green Kavkaz* and *Red Kavkaz*, the latter now going by the name of *Models' Café,* she remembered how lively the spot used to be fifteen years ago. Some twenty paces away from the *Kavkaz*, in front of *The Rattle*, she had met Bruno, she hunging out with her girlfriends and he with his lads. He was handsome and quiet. She had always liked quiet men. She remembered she could look for Buba at the theatre and have a coffee with her in *Kavkaz*. She found a free space in front of the Faculty of Law and parked the car as she dialled Buba's mobile number. As usual, Buba didn't answer: her mobile was, as ever, off or dead or had got left behind at home. Jelena walked over to *Gavella*. Entering the cloakroom, she ran into someone exiting. "Sorry," she said, without looking.

Buba laughed. "How could you possibly recognise me: I have no makeup on, and you're not wearing your specs."

"I'm not at my best," said Jelena by way of apology for not laughing at Buba's joke.

They strolled over to the *Big Kavkaz* which had, Jelena noticed, become a featureless half-empty space populated by a few equally featureless faces. They sat down and ordered their coffees. Mechanically, Jelena picked up the menu. It amused her to read the colourful and often outrageously spelled names of beverages: *coffee ekspresso, coffee cream, capucino, maciato*. "Really," she said, "I don't know what to think of this spelling regulations business."

"Of course you don't know," Buba said, "because there's nothing to know. The proposed Croatian Spelling and Punctuation Standard Rulebook is just that, a set of regulations. Every language must have a set of such regulations."

"I know, but still... like this, by ministerial decree...?"

"The Minister, Mr Primorac, will be remembered as the Minister who sorted out language. Shame it's being pushed upon us in such a rushed way, but that's not his fault. His overzealous minions are responsible. They should've perhaps waited for Matica[93] to publish the Rulebook."

"I didn't even know it was being prepared," Jelena said.

"Yeah, it was. And it should have been given more time."

"And what about the spelling and punctuation rulebooks by Babić-Finka-Moguš, Silić-Anić, Novosadski...?"

"Look, no one has actually bothered to take them and compare them page by page. Believe me, the differences are much smaller than you think; they're insignificant. The only problem is that language is constantly being made a political

---

[93] Matica hrvatska (see comment on page 147)

issue. So now, with the Minister being a HDZ[94] member, the mere mention of Croatian language standards has all the cod left wing intellectuals up in arms, as well as the illiterate politicians, naturally, and none of them know what they're talking about. When the politicians trumpet the need for creating the Croatian language standard, and your equally illiterate journalist mates report this without comment, the philologists bang their heads against the wall because that means the Croatian language actually doesn't exist. The language standard is one thing and its spelling and punctuation rules are something completely different. Those rules are no more than a set of conventions you respect in order to communicate effectively, the same way you respect traffic signs to avoid a crash. My children couldn't care less whether they write *connection* or *connexion*; they're in the early phase of their learning and will learn. I'll find it hard to get used to *connexion* because I've been writing *connection* all my life, but that's of no consequence. Those who wish to be literate will have to learn the conventions, just as they'd learn driving in a driving school, and would not wonder why the blue signs mean positive instruction and red ones prohibition."

"True, you're right, that's crystal-clear: a language needs clear regulations," Jelena agreed. "If politics hadn't been using it as a tool for its own purposes, it would have developed at its natural pace like any normal language. You know, I've had it with all the Četniks and Ustašas and with euro-centrism and euro-scepticism and Bush and the Arabs and glocality..."

"You're not all right at all," Buba said.

"I told you I wasn't, didn't I?" said Jelena and asked the waiter for the bill.

---

[94] Croatian Democratic Union (Hrvatska Demokratska Zajednica), one of the main Croatian political parties, with centre-right orientation, founded 17/06/1989 by Croatian dissidents (Croatia was still part of Socialist Yugoslavia at the time) led by Franjo Tuđman.

Pero and the Crash – Friday, 4th November

At the crossing of Theatre Street and the Green Wave, the traffic lights were reduced to the blinking amber one. Without thinking, Jelena moved off in the wake of the car in front. Suddenly, she seemed to have found herself in a time machine slowing down all action: very slowly indeed, a car came at her from the Green Wave on her left. The impact was anticipated, slow and gentle: instead of metal hitting metal, she had a sensation of aluminium foil crumpling. Initially she felt shaken, and then she heard the sound: boommmmmmm. She remained seated, her palms over her eyes. She had no idea of how much time had gone by; then she heard someone knocking on the car window. She got out and stood by the car. The other driver also got out. He was yelling. "You call this driving! You... goose!"

And you're the slug the goose gobbles down! Jelena almost laughed at her own briliant unspoken repartee, only did not, because she feared people might notice the smile on her face and think she was deranged and had therefore caused the crash. They'd all then turn against her, although they weren't proper people, just a gathering of nosy Parkers...

"Who on earth allowed you behind the wheel?" said the man spitting the words contemptuously and turned his back on her.

The onlookers waited to see what would happen. The policeman asked her if she was hurt. "No," she shook her head, trying to smile, but could not because her lips were trembling. I must've got frightened after all, she thought, quite coherently. The policeman asked her another question, but she did not understand what he said. She was not even listening to the policeman, as a man approached and stood by his side, a man who... wait a minute! It couldn't be... Yes, it was Pero Kovačić! She fluffed up her fringe almost as a reflex. I hope Buba meant it when she said that my fringe had come out just right this time round. People would say, of course, that only a woman could worry about her fringe in a situation like this. Because people are not aware of the fact that women always know what's essential in any situation. Women's looks had changed history... She noticed that the policeman and Pero Kovačić were watching her curiously. Did they say something?

"Are you all right?" Pero Kovačić asked.

"Yeah, yeah," she said, trying to sound confident. She felt her neck discreetly, then her arms and legs. Nothing hurt and she could see no damage. She clasped one hand with the other and shuddered.

Kovačić wound an arm around her shoulders and inclined his head, concerned. "Are you cold?"

She shook her head and he removed his arm and withdrew politely. He's been inside my personal space, or whatever it's called in terms of body language, Jelena thought. Only, under the circumstances, it probably doesn't have the usual meaning, he being in my zone and me letting him. That is to say, I may have let him into my zone because of his looks as well as for other reasons, but not *only* because of his looks... Perhaps I ought to discuss my *enterologorrhea*[95] with a professional...

Everything was over in no time at all, or in an incalculable amount of time: the car was taken away, the incident report was made and the police car left. Jelena stood by the handsome Inspector not knowing what she was supposed to do next.

"Do you need to call someone?" Pero asked.

His voice was hoarse, excitingly so. Jelena remembered seeing a TV programme about an investigation into what kind of voice was attractive. The subjects had to listen to the voice of a person of the opposite sex and then say what they imagined the owner of the voice to be like. The results showed that husky, hoarse voices were most attractive. The subjects said that husky voices were attractive and sexy and that they imagined husky-voiced people to be very desirable. But why? Because, the researchers thought, in moments of arousal – particularly one of sexual nature – the voice tended to become hoarse, husky and deep. It was thus natural to unconsciously connect such a voice with sexual attraction.

---

[95] Inner verbosity, a word coined by Jelena

"No. My husband is not at home. He's working…"

"In that case, why don't we have a coffee somewhere? It'll help you recover from the shock… That is, if you're sure you wouldn't like me to take you to the Clinic for Trauma…"

"No, no, I'm fine, I'm not hurt at all," said Jelena. Who needed doctors, coffee was a much better idea. It was quite useful to be in a car crash before talking to someone who made you feel confused. You were entitled to appear slow, absent, confused, disjointed… your hands could quite legitimately tremble, and you could openly stare (because you were in shock). What she really wanted to do was ask him how come he remembered her.

"Perhaps you don't remember me," she heard him say.

I do, I do; how could I not remember you, she almost blurted out. She forced herself, however, to say, calmly and slowly, "I think I do… you were at David's award ceremony." She remembered how warm the palm of his hand had been, and how moist his eyes. She pulled herself together, shamefaced. She had to come up with a topic for conversation double quick, lest he noticed… the *subjectivity* of her behaviour. She barely registered when they sat down, even less where. The place was pleasantly quiet.

"To cut a long story short…" Pero said. (And bring my staring session to a premature end, Jelena added in her thoughts.)

She didn't manage to hear what long story he was proposing to cut; she must have had asked him about something earlier. Oh, yes, she'd asked him how he became a police inspector. As if such a question could be answered at the drop of a hat. And I'd actually like to know, only somehow can't follow what he's saying right now. He's cutting it short, naught to report; thoughts wove transrationally[96] in her head. He's amazingly

---

[96] *Transreason* (or transrational language) is the generally accepted English translation of *zaum*, a term coined by Daniil Kharms (1905-1942), Soviet surrealist and absurdist poet, story writer and dramatist. 'Zaum', made up of Russian words meaning "beyond" and "mind", means

handsome. If he touches my hand again, I'll kiss him.

"...decoding. All manner of skills and knowledge can be useful... For example, here's a simple perception test," Pero was saying. "Turn your face away from me and try to describe me. Whatever you can remember."

"Um," Jelena said, "this is interesting." Inspectors are so much more interesting than journalists, she thought, pleased to have a legitimate excuse to talk about him openly and without shyness. "Here goes: your eyes are blue (he laughed), your teeth are white with none missing, at least as far as I could see (he laughed again); your hair is brown and so are your eyebrows, arching outwards and upwards. Your eyelashes are long (was I right to say that, or was it too personal?), your ears close to the head. Your hair is short at the back, wavy in front, partly covering your forehead and you part it... (she raised her hands and moved them as if trying to indicate the right side)... on the right. You've got a mole like De Niro, somewhere on... (she indicated the side with her hands again) ... the right cheek, under the eye... (Have I overdone the perception thing? she asked herself) How did I do?" she asked, still facing away. She never cheated at games.

"That was pretty cool," Pero laughed. "All right, so you could be one of those people with a knack for remembering faces..." (Selective, Jelena thought, my memory for faces is totally selective.)

"What am I wearing?" he asked.

"Um, let's see," Jelena began. "A shirt? No, a polo shirt. Azzure." (She'd noticed that because of his eyes; she thought how aware he was of the incredible colour of his eyes, and how consciously he brought them out by the colour of his polo shirt. Meaning that he, like David, knew how handsome he was, and that the knowledge made him confident.) A jacket? A blazer? I haven't got a clue... A cardigan, perhaps? Of an undefined

---

experimental poetic language without definite meaning and thus not "binding", unlike everyday language we understand. (Adapted from Wikipedia)

colour? A dark cardigan? Don't know; I give up. Oh yeah, you've got a watch with a metal bracelet strap... ("Very good," said Pero.)... and no jewellery," she finished abruptly, unconsciously touching the wedding ring on her left hand, feeling guilty for mentioning jewellery. It might make him think that she...

"I must admit I didn't expect so much detail," said Pero.

He can't have worked out that I would've done rather worse with a less handsome man... can he? Jelena wondered. Still, I should have noticed less, just in case.

"I think I read somewhere that shock enhances perception," she lied. "Like when you zoom into details to enlarge them, and the whole becomes blurred..." Why, what whole am I banging about, the whole of what attracts me? I hope not... Oh yeah, I should say I had in mind the crash situation as a whole. It made me zoom in on Pero's face... "In any case, journalists need the memory for detail just as much as inspectors do," she finished, hopefully in a sober and sensible manner.

"They do," said Pero. "You work with David at *The Herald*, then?"

She described the editorial office and who did what there. He laughed when she told him about Dora Gimmeyora and raised his eyebrows at the description of Nina Ivezić (*etiam tu*[97]...). She talked about her daft father and told anecdotes about her mother. She never mentioned Bruno; that would have been in poor taste (*etiam ego*[98]...). She also told Pero about her column, *The Guide,* and how her interest in art was fading, since she discovered that not only were the art critics useless but that more crooks could be found in artistic circles than in football ones. Pero laughed. I can't talk for half a minute without tripping over myself, she thought. Glancing at his watch, she was amazed to see that it was already seven o'clock. "Is that the time? I had no idea it was that late; I had no idea what time it might be... I've got to go!" As far back as she

---

[97] Etiam tu, Brute, mi fili = You too, Brutus, my son
[98] Me, too...

could recall, she had never had worse conscience than at that moment. Ana is right, she thought, everything's connected. If Bruno's programme hadn't crashed, if the van hadn't been standing there with its engine running... But it's stupid to speculate like that; nothing happens by chance to such a degree that everything happens by chance. The notorious flower seller, known in all Zagreb cafés and restaurants (he hasn't changed at all, Jelena thought), approached their table without much expectation.

"Flowers for the young lady?" he intoned, shoving under Pero's nose a nondescript bouquet consisting of a mini-rose stem with a few half-wilted blossoms on it and a blend of dried grass and flowers.

What a stupid situation, Jelena thought; he'll buy me the nasty thing now thinking that I'm expecting him to, and if he doesn't, I'll be forever wondering whether he didn't because he didn't care what I thought, or simply because he's a man of good taste."

"Because of the crash, to make you feel better," said Pero, taking the bouquet from the vendor.

Dry flowers are not a good omen, Jelena thought, about to reach for the bouquet, when Pero carefully took the rose out and gave it to her, looking straight into her eyes. "Dry flowers are not a good omen," he said and put the remnants of the bouquet on the corner of the table. She beamed back, bringing the flower to her nose. The smooth flow of their conversation was broken.

When they had finished their drinks, Pero asked the waiter to call a cab and thrust a note with his phone number into Jelena's hand. "I'd like to know that you're all right," he said.

After they had parted, Jelena remembered she should have asked him if there was a law about parked cars with running engines; he was bound to know.

That evening, Bruno was more upset by the fact that Jelena was not upset than by the damage to the car. He did not even notice the rose, although Jelena put it at the centre of the table in the sitting room.

The Hand

3rd June

SCIENTIFICALLY PROVEN: LOVE IS A MENTAL ILLNESS

"Love is, in fact, a kind of madness, a genuine mental illness affecting the brain of those in love, according to the study by American scientists H. Fischer, L. Brown and A. Aron, published in The Journal of Neurophysiology. They claim that romantic love is a biological need, independent of sexual arousal.

Experiments have shown that two sections of the brain, nucleus caudatus and ventral tegmental area (VTA), have a role in amorous infatuation. They are populated by cells producing dopamine, the neurotransmitter linked with the feeling of pleasure, but also with addictive behaviour. Both areas are exceptionally active during gambling or in drug addicts.

Interestingly, the two 'love centres' are found in the area of the brain opposite to the sections connected with physical attraction, which invites the conclusion that love is a separate biological urge, unconnected with sexual desire. The 'love centre' is even more active in those rejected by the object of their passion. Abandoned, some people contemplate suicide or even murder: the need for romantic love can be stronger than the will to live."

Swivelling Eyes — Saturday, 5th November

"We're seeing Nina today," Jelena called to Bruno through the open door of the bathroom.

"I know," Bruno replied, toothbrush between teeth.

How does he know? Jelena wondered. "How do you know?" she asked loudly. Normally, he would need to-do lists, repeated instruction and innumerable reminders.

"You told me, didn't you?" he shouted back between two mouthfuls of rinsing water.

"I always tell you everything, and you never remember any of it," she said. He did not reply. "Could it have something to do with the fact that she's so beautiful?" A mumbled reply came from the bathroom. "Now you're making as if you have a meaningful reply to give me, only you can't because you're washing your face. It's just an excuse, though, because you don't know what to say." Some illusions should be left intact, she thought. Am I one of those jabbering women who simply cannot keep their mouths shut, and I'm not even aware of it? I won't say another word. "Have you washed your hair?" she asked just the same.

"Why do you ask?" asked Bruno.

"Because I know you'll want to look good in front of a pretty woman." He didn't reply. She repeated her question: "Well then, have you or haven't you?"

"I've washed it," Bruno said.

That's that, then, Jelena thought. "That's that, then," she said and entered the bathroom to get dressed. Bruno moved out of her way. "Kindly don't shrink away from me as if about to be touched by a jellyfish or as if a whale was passing behind your back. I'm still size 40." Why should I rack my brain at all, Jelena thought. Quite simply, I'll ask him three questions: Have you noticed we're drifting apart? Does that hurt you at all? If it does, will you strive to stop it happening? She stepped between Bruno and the mirror, and said to his reflection, "Have you noticed we're drifting apart?"

He gave her a wide, shocked look and cried, "Noooo! Why do you say that?"

"Damn," said Jelena. "I have no further questions. And I've run out of pads." Wearing only bra and tights, she got out of the bathroom and slipped her winter coat over her naked body – she never wore vests or slips: a hippie like her dad, her mum would say. Bruno watched her reflection in the mirror with curiosity rather than surprise. Aha, the *V-effekt*[99], she thought; I've got him to look at me at least.

"You're going out like that?" Bruno asked.

---

[99] *Verfremdungseffekt - alienation* or *distancing effect*, making the familiar strange; Brecht's concept within his aesthetic of 'epic theatre'.

"Why not? I'm just popping down the shop, no one will notice anything."

"You look like those flashers in the park spreading their coats open at passers-by."

Jelena halted and went back to the bathroom door. "That's that, then."

"What's what?" Bruno asked.

"That's the only association your mind can come up with: exhibitionist."

"You must admit there's an obvious similarity."

"Obvious? Why not see it as *normal* for your wife to come up with something like that... a situation where only you know that she's gone out wearing a coat over her naked body? *Basic Instinct* style – couldn't you find that erotic? You could not because, to you, it isn't. It just reminded you of a maniac."

"Come on, Jelena..."

"This particular association of yours speaks of the quality of your love for me louder than a thousand words."

"Why do you always exaggerate like that?" Bruno sounded helpless.

"So it's my fault again, because I exaggerate," Jelena said. She felt stupid in her bra and coat combo. She buttoned the coat up, put her shoes on and went out.

When she got back, she said, "You and I might soon find ourselves in a Japanese marriage." The expression of genuine and complete puzzlement on Bruno's face was comical. Jelena laughed mirthlessly. "Yes. Did you know that the Japanese don't sleep with their wives? Some haven't slept with them for twenty years, and some never did, not even when they were first married. With the Japanese, marriage has nothing to do with love. Husbands use porn and geishas to satisfy their needs, and wives had until recently kept silent about it, so the general public was unaware of the problem. Some ten years ago they began to speak up and the number of divorces soared. There's now a therapist there who treats women by renting out young men to shag them, but it's not prostitution because... don't know why, can't remember."

Bruno said nothing. He did not even show he'd heard what she said.

"Maybe it's not such a bad idea, this Japanese marriage thing, but only with the therapy included... if those poor women still have any hormones left." Her own musings sounded redundant to Jelena, but she still went on: "It would be useful to identify the optimal marriage model since you and I will never separate: you always change the toilet roll, you don't address me by my pet names in public and don't channel-surf when we watch telly."

"Hmmm??"

"Statistically, those are the most frequent reasons for divorce."

Bruno merely shrugged.

"You could have at least soaked the dishes last night, if you didn't fancy washing up. They've developed *rigor mortis*," she changed the subject. From bad to worse, as her dad would say.

"You're more and more like your dad," Bruno said.

"Sounds like it's meant to be an insult," Jelena said.

"An observation," said Bruno.

"Well, since we've opened the doors to understanding a bit," Jelena said caustically, "I can inform you that whatever is happening to us is nothing special, or even personal. Quite simply, love has transformed into a higher category, while we're growing old, with all our faults hypertrophying and our virtues... what's the word... hypotrophying. That's ageing in a nutshell: whatever is good, wanes; whatever is bad, waxes."

"Oh Jesus," Bruno moaned.

"Jesus, Jesus, Jesus," Jelena repeated, echoing him, really angry now. "Why should I rant like this anyway: you're right. Every woman has the husband she deserves."

***

They arrived at cafe *Friends* close to Utrine open air market a few minutes before noon in silence: Bruno was taciturn as usual, and Jelena was still seething. Nina appeared in the door dead on time. As soon as she spotted them, she flashed a broad smile. Unintentionally, Jelena glanced at Bruno: his face reflected Nina's smile.

"You've changed your style a bit," Jelena said.

"A bit. I felt like a change," Nina said simply, sitting down. Her curly hair was tied back into a pony tail. The severe hairdo made her regular features look timeless and romantic. Her makeup was inconspicuous: a touch of blusher on her cheeks, barely a trace of pink on her lips. Her whole appearance was delicate. Jelena studied her as she explained to Bruno that she needed subtitling software.

"I thought you translated books," Jelena said.

"I'd like to try translating movies, the money's much better," said Nina. "I need money right now. I've got problems. And you know best how low the fees are."

"Allegedly they're a tightly closed circle, those television translators," said Jelena.

"I know. Andrej used one of his connections to get me in. That's why I can't let them know I haven't got first clue about subtitling, so I need to master that software before I dare show my face there."

She's really irresistible, thought Jelena and involuntarily glanced towards Bruno who was not taking his eyes off Nina.

"I might get to translate movies for cinema release, too. David said he could ask some distributor friends..."

Jelena retrieved the mental image of Nina's first appearance at the editorial office. Now as then, she managed to be chaste and seductive at the same time.

"I've got something for you," said Nina to Jelena, taking an untidy parcel out of her bag.

"Really?" Jelena unwrapped the crumpled soft wrapping paper curiously. It contained a strangely shaped light-brown stone, its layers forming the shape of a flower. "Oh my God, it's so beautiful," Jelena said. "What is it?"

"A desert rose. I brought it back from Tunisia," said Nina. "I remembered you liked stones, and..."

"Thank you so much, you're so lovely," said Jelena. "How did you remember?" Jelena's interest in stones started when a friend brought her a piece of stone from her seaside holiday, claiming it protected one from radioactivity. The stone appeared to be quartz, although, according to published scholarship, there was no quartz in Dalmatia. From then on, whenever she went on holiday, she brought back a piece or two of that stone. She'd taken three pieces to the office and placed them on David's, Ivana's and her own desk.

"You treated us all to that fabulous dark chocolate with orange," Nina laughed. "And my chocolate memory is long", she added playfully.

Bruno coughed. Both women looked at him. "You need subtitling software, then?"

"You and Nina have agreed to say 'thou'," Jelena reminded him. Bruno nodded shyly. Nina's face became serious as she focussed on explaining what it was she needed. She inclined towards Bruno in a relaxed, friendly, intimate way. Bruno seemed bemused. Jelena was moved by his bashfulness. Shy like a little boy, she thought. She'd almost forgotten what he was like when he was being shy. He used to be shy with her in the beginning. Unlike other men, Bruno did not use conventional ways of showing a woman that he fancied her: he didn't woo her, didn't chat her up, didn't touch her up, didn't stare at her breasts, her bottom or her crossed legs. Jelena always teased him that he never experienced women by sight, hearing or touch, but rather as a kind of radiation or a chemical reaction. His reaction to a woman was soundless, like the vibration of a mobile on silent. She could feel it happening now. Am I wrong, am I imagining things because of my jealous nature, she wondered rhetorically. Or perhaps I'm not jealous by nature. Perhaps I use my jealousy to fill my emptiness; perhaps I invent reasons to justify my discontent, to justify the passing of love... Or am I looking for an excuse for Pero Kovačić? She didn't want to give in to jealousy. She picked up a newspaper on a rack. Reading newspapers in a cafe always had a calming effect on her: it felt as if she wasn't in a hurry to get anywhere and as if she belonged to a time when one never needed to rush anywhere. Bruno did not find it strange that she had chosen to read the paper at that moment in time: Jelena was always saying that she and computers were wired to opposite switches, meaning that, whenever a computer got switched on, her brain switched off. Nina understood that Jelena was simply letting her and Bruno get on with their conversation in peace and quiet.

"What have you arranged?" she asked when they'd finished.

"That you'll come to mine and Bruno will install the software," said Nina, slightly uneasy. "If it really isn't a problem," she said, glancing g at Bruno. "It's really embarrassing... I thought I'd be able to do it all myself, with instructions..."

Jelena was downhearted and ill at ease for the rest of that day. On Monday, she nearly forgot to tell David about her encounter with Pero, and her memory was just as vague about the car accident – but she did remember to tell him how she and Bruno had met Nina. The situation was stupid: she could not moan about her jealousy as it would be, in view of his going out with Nina, not appropriate to do so. "It's strange," she said, "we know nothing about Nina and yet she influences us all, somehow... You, me, Buba, Bruno, Ana, and probably even Andrej; that is to say, he might actually know something about her... She's like a cosmic force, too superior to be understood by the likes of us. Or like a character in a novel, the one whose function is to keep the story moving. The power of beauty."

David did not reply.

"What are you saying?" Jelena asked.

"I'm saying, since you've had your column, you've gone a bit too far with your analysing and drawing conclusions. You study us – including yourself – as if we were some sort of dubious produce."

"As if we weren't," Jelena shrugged.

The Hand

27th December

The hand rubbed the other hand: plenty of work to be done.

A MILLION AND A HALF OF CROATS SUPPORT *BIG BROTHER.* Intellectuals condemn *Big Brother* for fuelling false hopes of success.

CHRISTMAS TRAGEDY: More than 11,000 people killed by earthquake in South Asia

In that order: Big Brother first, then the tsunami.

28th December

The number of victims grows to 23,000

29th December

The number of victims expected to exceed 100,000

Sri Lanka: not a single animal killed by the tsunami

THE NEWS, RTL[100]: The Earth's rotation permanently speeded up and the day permanently shortened by the tidal wave.

Evening of the same day

The Journal, HRT[101]: 120 thousand victims?

The Earth's axis tilted by 2.5 cm, shortening the day by 3 milliseconds.

What is Happiness – Saturday, 5th November

Jelena knew that her mum and dad would be worried until they saw that she was hale and in one piece after the accident.

"Ah, there she is," her father welcomed her. "Lupus in troubula."

Jelena gave him a sour smile. "Or twerpus in fabula, if you prefer."

"Daddy's girl," her father said. "So, how are you?"

"I'm fine. But we're going up the wall without the car. And then, we don't know yet if we'll have to pay for the repair, in which case we'll have to wait for the insurance money, or..."

"No, no," Bruno, who was competent in such matters and therefore impatient, barged in. "The damage has been already assessed, the car is at a recommended garage; their invoice will be sent to the insurance company. That's how it works." Jelena

---

[100] Radio Television Luxembourg, Europe's largest mass media company
[101] Croatian Radio Television

thought he sounded conceited. She wanted to stick her tongue at him. Fuck your precious insurance know-how!

"You're all right though, that's the main thing," her mum said.

"That's right; I've got to agree with Kata here. You know what happiness is?" her dad said. "Happiness is when you manage to avoid misfortune. A lady journalist asked people on telly the other day what happiness was. And the people went spewing all manner of rubbish; one in ten, perhaps, said something that made a kind of sense... Had they asked me, though, I'd tell them straight away: 'There's no mystery about it: happiness is when you avoid misfortune.'"

Jelena said, "The guy called me a goose. That really hurt."

"Just take no notice, darling" mum said.

"Speaking of geese, how about some dinner?" dad asked. "There's chicken without glasses left over from lunch."

"What's chicken without glasses?" Bruno asked. Jelena chuckled half-heartedly.

"That's when I clean a chicken with no specs on because I couldn't locate them," dad said. "That means you're bound to find a feather stump or two." He turned to mum. "If they don't want chicken without glasses, perhaps you could make some of that squint tea of yours?"

Mum got up with effort. "Shall I do it?" Jelena asked. "You're not feeling well?"

"I'm not all that well today... My head's spinning... now and then, you know how it is with me..."

"She's not well, but keeps charging around," dad put in. "And if I say don't go, what's your hurry, rest a bit, she looks at me as if I were a prison guard. Weird woman..."

"I'm weird!" mum peered through the kitchen door. "I'm weird, you say? You know what happened yesterday?" She turned to Jelena. "I went to a funeral... Auntie Blanka's husband, remember... and what did your dad say as I was leaving? 'Off you go then, enjoy all the merriment, I mean internment.'"

Jelena laughed again, in spite of herself. Her father said,

"What's wrong with that? I watched you doll yourself up nicely, all in black, all elegant, like a merry widow... I'm older than you anyway; I'll be the first to go: one could see it as a dress rehearsal..."

"The things he says," said mother reproachfully and returned to the kitchen on heavy feet.

"Perhaps intelligence means finding your feet quickly in a new situation, but to take everything seriously definitely means to be stupid. The more seriously you take stuff, the stupider you are," said dad.

Jelena followed her mother to the kitchen. "Is it your hip? What did your doctor say?"

"What do you think? I've must have an operation, I've got no choice."

"Right now?"

"As soon as. You know what my friend from the choir told me? That there is a surgeon in Rijeka who is the top man for that job. He's a sports surgery specialist. My friend's son is a volleyball player, that's how she knows."

"How do we find him?"

""She's given me his number... would you call him?" Jelena nodded. "You'll drive me there, won't you?" mum asked rhetorically. "It would wear dad out, although he'd never admit it."

"But of course," said Jelena. "As soon as the car is back."

She took the teacups to the sitting room, turned the television on and searched through the channels with the remote. *CSI* on One, some kind of action movie on TV Nova, and, only on RTL, the heart-warming Croatian word: *Big Brother*. She settled for Big Brother on low volume. A girl wearing a tanga was about to take her bra off, her profile turned to the cameras. "Do they know where the cameras are?" she asked.

"Get rid of that shit," her father said.

"Let me see a bit," Jelena said. "I never get a chance to watch it."

"So you have to do it here," her father said.

"All right, if you hate it that much," said Jelena and turned the set off.

"I've got a much better idea for a reality show," dad said.

"Naturally; you have the best ideas for everything," mum said as she came in carrying a tray with a steaming jug of mint tea.

"That's right, Mrs Salošpek[102]," said dad sarcastically.

"Very funny," said mum whose maiden name was Salopek, straightening up in protest until she looked much taller than her one metre sixty five. "If there's lard on me, it's *my* lard. You could've at least come up with an original joke instead of using one from *Who Wants to Be a Millionaire!*"

"Those who appreciate the wit of others are just as witty as they," dad retorted readily.

"No one can ever out-talk you," mum said, shrugging her shoulders.

Jelena was pleased there was no further mention of the car. For her, the accident was deeply overshadowed by guilt about Pero Kovačić, and the guilt about Pero Kovačić was overshadowed by anxiety about Bruno.

The Hand

14th December

THE COLOUR SUPPLEMENT: Love is a natural opiate: looking at your beloved triggers off the same brain processes cocaine does.

"Does love have more to do with chemistry and biology than with romance?

...A young man meets a girl and craves to be near her. That is the effect created by a cocktail of hormones released by a network of neurons located between the frontal lobe of the brain and its stem. The cocktail includes phenyl ethylamine and dopamine, hormones that stimulate pleasure centres in the brain, as well as noradrenalin and adrenaline which enhance the qualities one needs when setting out to win a mate. Phenyl

---

102 Lardbacon.

ethylamine, for example, reduces appetite and the need for sleep, as food and sleep matter less in the mating period. Noradrenalin and adrenaline provide endurance, robustness and assertiveness, qualities essential to a hunter. The girl affects the young man primarily by means of visual stimuli: her face and the shape of her body are undoubtedly recognised by his brain as a potential source of pleasure. Her influence is also olfactory. Humans emit information about the levels of their sexual hormones by means of pheromones, molecules excreted by breath and through the pores in the skin, which imperceptibly penetrate the organisms of those around them. Pheromones that do not match generate repulsion.

The girl's looks and her pheromones agitate the young man's testosterone, which in turn produces desire for physical contact, amplifying simultaneously the aggressiveness he needs to eliminate competition.

Genes drive us to amorous activity through a combination of carrot and stick, pleasure and pain. This twofold strategy ensures that everyone will make maximum effort to get together with the individual who attracts him or her, Dr Robert Torre claims.

In the next phase, if the relationship is developing well, the hormone known as oxytocin, produced in abundance during erotic encounters and sexual enjoyment, gives rise to attachment.

After 18 to 30 months at most, romantic emotion, even in the most passionate of couples, loses the intensity characteristic of the initial phase of their relationship. This, however, does not mean that partners now cannot stand one another. Romance transforms into calm and comfortable coexistence, where hormones of "quiet attachment", oxytocin and, particularly in men, vasopressin, take the leading role. At the same time, the testosterone level in men drops, as there is no further need for the aggressive predation of a hunter. The euphoric romance phase can last longer than 2-3 years only in cases of unrequited love."

The Cold Gene

At home, Bruno was *independent*: he took a shower, brushed his teeth and switched on the computer...

Jelena took the meat for Sunday lunch out of the freezer, washed the cups left in the sink after their morning coffee, turned on the television and flicked listlessly through the channels. Although she tried to respect Bruno's right not to communicate, she felt anger accumulating within her. "If we happened to have children," she said before she knew she was going to open her mouth, "I'd take them to a different continent when their mating time came and do everything I could to get them to fall in love with someone of a different race and have kids with him or her."

"What are you on about?" Bruno was surprised but not curious.

"Genes. Genes are indestructible. They are worse than radiation; their half-life is not a piddling 200 years; they're not exterminated in a thousand generations and merely reappear in fresh combinations. You know those illnesses children get if both their parents have the gene for them? If only one parent has the gene, the child will stay healthy. But if both parents have the gene, the child will develop the illness. If the child remains healthy but inherits the gene, and then has a child with another carrier, *that* child will go on to develop the illness. You're Turkalj, I'm Salopek; your family is from Zagreb and Dalmatia, mine from Lika and Zagreb, but five hundred years ago, our grand-grand-grandfathers could have been brothers. That's why it's safest to mate with another race and why mixed-race people are the most beautiful."

"Yeah, and?" Bruno asked.

"And?" Jelena said. "Let's take you as an example. You're self-sufficient and cold. You might be full of coldness hormone; in that case your only problem is that you've been too long with the same woman. But it may have nothing to do with hormones; you may be carrying the cold gene you inherited from your mum. At first it was suppressed, overruled by the love hormone, by shyness, whatever. And now it's starting to surface. That's why I'm beginning to feel cold near you."

Bruno said nothing, only looked at her with raised eyebrows.

"I'll start favouring GM, crossing tomato with fish, over natural biodiversity, if biodiversity includes emotionally stunted creatures," she went on abrasively. Whenever the two of them argued, she deployed strong language as Bruno never appeared to be hurt. The first time she told him "You don't love me, it's all a farce", however, Bruno *was* hurt. He looked miserable. Jelena wondered how he managed to be so unhappy because she'd said he didn't love her and at the same time maintain such an indifferent appearance. Then she understood: he was afraid she might be right. He was afraid because he himself didn't know if she was right or not. His incomplete emotional register was incapable of measuring the difference. He imitates emotions, he wants to feel and is unhappy when she tells him he's not been successful. When did our life become like this? The only difference between ourselves and my mum and dad is in years and bodily weight. When did everything change to this? Is the change taking place even now, at this very moment? The most momentous changes are always so slow one doesn't notice them until they've happened, irrevocably so. Should one at least strive to preserve the current state of affairs, to catch and secure the running stitch before the entire jumper unravels? We'll get up late tomorrow morning, I like that. The only remaining habit from the days of our happiness: we love sleeping late Saturdays and Sundays. The rest is someone else's life."

A Ride with Dad – Monday, 7th November

Unbidden, dad phoned early on Monday morning with an offer to give them a lift into town and "deliver them to their respective workplaces", since he had to "take mum for her MOT" anyway. "Unless you still haven't washed sleep out of your eyes and aren't even planning to go to work today," he added caustically.

"We've washed it out," said Jelena. "We've already had

coffee." She tried to sound cheerful and amiable, although she was too glum to even open her mouth, never mind reply to dad's jibes.

As was his custom, dad swore outrageously at all the drivers in front, behind and alongside his car, flailed about, made atrocious faces and tapped his forehead, signalling madness. Jelena worried that one day, distracted by the weird old man's pantomime, someone might actually crash into him. He behaves as if he had Tourette's, she thought. "Come ON, drive, you dung-beetle!" her father said to the driver ahead of him.

Against her will, Jelena burst out laughing. "How do you manage to come up with such stuff?" "There's plenty of inspiration," dad said proudly. "Look how slow that geezer is." He turned to look through the window and waved at the dung-beetle. "If you find the meaning of life in being survived by your car, seeing you're so protective of it, your life can't amount to much!"

Bruno laughed, too. "One could write a comedy show based on your adventures."

"Thank you, son-in-law," dad said.

"I didn't mean it in a bad way," said Bruno. He laughed. Jelena could feel his breath on her face. She felt a sudden urge to kiss him. She touched his shoulder discreetly to silence him. While her dad was working his way round the dung-beetle, a bloke in an old BMW with a Split registration plate changed lanes, overtaking them at the same time. "These louts, why do they do it," Jelena said, to prevent her father from racing the lout rather than to vent her nonexistent anger. But dad could not resist the challenge; he slammed his foot on the accelerator and shot after the BMW. In spite of his vile tongue, he drove like a gentleman: he let a boy run across the road, and allowed a vehicle from a side street merge in. "If everyone gave way to just one car each, there'd be no jams, but those bullocks fear their horns might drop off if they do." He indicated a black Audi that was blocking him from changing the lane. "From Split, that one, natch," he waved a contemptuous hand.

Jelena noticed a tin of shoe polish and a brush wedged

between the front seats. "Why do you drive your shoe polishing kit around?" she asked.

"To polish my shoes," her father snapped.

"Stop showing off. Why do you keep it in your car?"

"You know full well I do everything in my car: eat, read the papers, polish my shoes. You should have seen that guy in Siget gape when I, queuing for the MOT, got my kit out and polished my shoes."

"Dad, you're terrible," said Jelena laughing. She didn't like the idea of being with her father; she wanted to be with Bruno, so she said, "I'll be getting off here as well, I've got something to do in town."

"Suit yourself," dad said. Jelena knew he was sorry to see her leave so soon.

Bruno gave her a surprised look.

"He's very demanding; I don't think I could have lasted much longer. He's permanently in fifth gear," she said once her dad had driven off, threading her arm through Bruno's. The moment of intimacy they'd shared in the car had passed, but Jelena was still in a good mood. She wondered if it wasn't *Seroxat* finally taking effect. That morning she went to renew the prescription. She'd finished the first pack.

"And?" her GP asked.

"Well," said Jelena, "I laugh more than before, I feel motivated to go to the hairdresser's, I'm not happy but sense a possibility of happiness at some point, I make plans for the future but not a very distant one... My marriage has yet to improve, however, and I still haven't got the guts to go for a breast examination."

"And the side effects?" the GP asked.

"Haven't noticed any. I've got so many allergies, numb spots, tremors and other symptoms that I stand little chance of registering side effects."

"All right, here's a two months' prescription," the GP laughed. "So you don't have to keep coming back."

They stood outside Bruno's workplace. Jelena didn't feel like leaving Bruno's company. "Shall we go somewhere for a coffee?"

"Can't, I'm late," he said. "We can go after work, if you'd like."

"Dunno, I'll ring you later," she said, disappointed. She stood on her tiptoes and kissed his cheek. "Ciao, then."

"Ciao," said Bruno and light-footed it up the stairs leading to the main entrance.

Jelena strolled down to Zvonimir Street, halted before shop-windows, ate two perfect schaumschnitte cakes at *Jakšić's* and, with her stomach full, boarded the tram to Sava Road at the Mosque.

"You're late today," said David when she entered.

She shrugged silently. Ivana greeted her from her nook. No one else was in, that was nice. When her phone rang, Jelena thought it wasn't likely to be Bruno, and that it was shame she did not expect any exciting calls. I tell a lie, I'm hoping it might be Pero. But he hasn't got my number. When the phone rang for the fourth time, David looked at her questioningly. She picked up the receiver. "Hello, Jelena Turkalj, *The Herald.*"

"Hello. Pero Kovačić, remember...? I just wanted to know how you were."

Suddenly overcome by nerves, she still managed to think clearly, or so she thought: to start with, he has taken the trouble to find her number; secondly, he is not a snooty dick who thinks it a law of nature that I should remember him, but asks me nicely if I do. "Of course I remember," she said. "It's kind of you to ask. I'm fine." Her voice was not exactly firm and steady, but she hoped he would not notice; they did not know each other that well after all.

"I'd like to ask you out for a drink," Pero said simply.

Jelena stayed silent. So what, she thought, we're adults. Then, with forced laughter so that David and Ivana would not think she was being serious about it, she replied, "Haven't I told you I was married? And that you were dangerous ground for me?"

"You're refusing me, then?" Pero asked.

"Alas, no," Jelena said. Is he going to lose interest in me

because I was too quick to agree? The babe was willing?

"Excellent!" Her ears reverberated deliciously with Pero's rich voice. "What are you up to this afternoon?"

"Can't make it today." A short postponement.

"How about tomorrow?"

"Tomorrow? Tomorrow... What's tomorrow, Tuesday? No, I can't make it." More postponement.

"Wednesday, then?"

I hope I'm making him wait long enough, she thought. "Yes, Wednesday is fine," she said.

"Would you like me to call you Wednesday morning to arrange the time?"

"All right," she said.

"Great. Till Wednesday, then."

"Okay," she said and put the receiver down. It was moist where she had held it. She did not look at David but could feel his eyes on her.

Over their coffees in the *Little Café*, David asked her from behind his paper, "Was that Pero earlier?"

From behind her paper, Jelena replied, "Yup."

"Need advice?"

"Not yet."

The Hand

3rd January

NEWS: The number of victims in South Asia reaches 150 thousand

HTV, AFTERNOON NEWS PROGRAMME

A famous Indian clairvoyant predicts an even bigger tsunami for 2005. "Whenever I hold my pendulum over a map, it comes to a standstill over the Caribbean," the prophet said. That particular tsunami will hit Spain and France as well. Many other clairvoyants predict similar events.

The Inspector

"Unfortunately we're not quite finished yet," the Inspector said.

"I must ask you to reconvene tomorrow at... let's not make it too early... at nine AM?"

The Automated Answering Service at the Psychiatric Hospital; Anton Gets in Touch – Tuesday 8th November

Of late, Ana had become less and less willing to communicate, even with her closest friends. She refused to cheer up. She spent more and more time at her computer writing, and when not writing, she surfed the internet. She read tons of stories, anecdotes and jokes, and solved an endless succession of psychological tests which circulated by e-mail: *The left and the right side of the brain test*, *Draw a pig*, The *Dalai-Lama's personality test*... "You have no idea of the great stuff one can find out there," she would enthuse to Jelena and David whom she supplied with a daily sample of it, and who gently pulled her leg about her obsession. "It's the true modern art of the 21st century, buzzing with new ideas. I, too, would be better off writing a *blog* than a book; everyone reads *blogs*, *blogs* are books of the future."

One of her favourite jokes was *The Automated Answering Service at the Psychiatric Hospital:*

Hello and welcome to the mental health hotline

If obsessive-compulsive, keep pressing 1

If incapable of independent action, get someone to press 2 for you

In case of split personality, press 3, 4, 5, 6...

If you're paranoid, we know who you are and what it is you want. Stay on the line so that we can locate the place you're calling from.

If you suffer from hallucinations, press 7 and your call will be rerouted to the mother ship.

If you're schizophrenic, listen carefully for the voice telling you which number to press.

If you suffer from amnesia, press 8 and quote your number, address, phone number, date of birth, your ID number and your mother's maiden name.

If suffering from post-traumatic syndrome, s-l-o-w-l-y and c-a-r-e-f-u-l-l-y press 000.

If you're bipolar, please leave a message after the bleep, or before the bleep, or after the bleep. Please wait for the bleep.

If you suffer from short-term memory loss, press 9. If you suffer from short-term memory loss, press 9. If you suffer from short-term memory loss, press 9. If you suffer from short-term memory loss, press 9. If you suffer from short-term memory loss, press 9.

If you suffer from short-term memory loss, press 9.

If your self-esteem is low, put the receiver down. All our staff is currently busy and no one is able to answer your call.

If you're menopausal, put the receiver down, turn on the cooling fan, lie down and weep. You won't stay mad forever.

She also sent around a prayer which had to be forwarded to at least five other addresses or *it wouldn't bring one luck. You gone nuts?* Came David's reply. *No, but I'm afraid something bad will happen to me if I don't forward it,* Ana replied.

That mental hospital thing you sent was great, Buba mailed. *Where do you find all this stuff? I'm sending you advice on handling men, for your book:*

1. *Always go for a younger man; they never grow up anyway.*
2. *Don't let your man's mind wander; it's too small to be out on its own.*
3. *Men are all the same, only their faces are different so we can tell them apart*
4. *Remember that having a sense of humour doesn't mean telling jokes but laughing when he tells them.*
5. *Love is blind, but marriage is an eye-opener.*

Watch out for spam, Jelena warned. *Whenever they send you something to forward to other addresses, it is likely to be spam, and that is a punishable offence.*

Ana began suffering from headaches, particularly after long sessions at the computer, but she did not stop.

"Give the computer a rest," Jelena said. "It's doing your head in."

One day, Ana received a strange personal e-mail, signed "Anton":

We don't know each other. I'm sure, however, that we'll meet soon. That's all for the first time, regards, Anton.

The Hand

12th January

TV PROGRAMME *THE EDGE OF SCIENCE*: THE METEORITE THAT MAY HIT EARTH

I missed part of the meteorite story, so my account is incomplete: the most recently discovered meteorite – the name escapes me – worries astronomers more than any previous one. They have worked out it might hit Earth on Friday 13th of don't know which month in 2025 or 2029 – not sure which of the two. The probability of this happening is two and a bit percent. Two percent in astronomical terms means certainty rather than probability, since this kind of outcome is normally expressed in values such as minus to the power of sixth (or to the power of minus six?).

People should have stopped having children. There's still time to do that. Had births ceased in 1950, the youngest people in 2029 would be 79 years old. Quite a suitable age for the End of the World.

The Hand, a Day Later

Everything has been rendered meaningless by the news of the meteorite. Is it possible? Are we and our green planet that insignificant?

So, that means, when we disappear – God will be alone?

Wednesday, 9th November

Jelena stayed in bed on Wednesday while Bruno got ready for work. Later, on the staircase, she met Lola, their neighbour from the floor above. Whenever she saw Lola, Jelena would think: I hope I never become like her. Lola lived alone; she was a widow. "But a merry one," she'd say of herself. In the previous years, various men could be seen leaving her apartment. Of recent male visits had become rarer, but did not stop altogether. To Jelena, seeing Lola on the day she was to meet Pero felt like a warning or even like mockery of fate.

"Hi hun, how are you?" cooed Lola cheerily, already heavily made up and showing a lot of cleavage in a dress of undefined purpose – seemingly a cross between a negligée and a dressing gown, with one side wrapped over the other yukata-style and open to the middle of Lola's fleshy thighs. Her age was hard to guess and could be anything between 50 and 60. She winked lasciviously: "You look gloomy; Bruno must've failed to perform last night?" Two spiral locks of hair had playfully slid out of her untidy bun; she tossed them back coquettishly and her red lips swelled into a pout. "I told you a hundred times, darling: you've got to look after Number One."

"I'm in a hurry, Lola; I'm late for work," said Jelena and ran down the stairs.

When Pero phoned, she said, "I'm sorry, I won't be able to make it. Something has cropped up." He said something but she didn't register all of it. She added, "And it might be more sensible not to." She laughed.

"I'm sorry." Pero seemed not to have heard the unconventional clarification. "Some other time, then."

"Maybe," Jelena said. The receiver in her hand was sweaty again. Not bad, those modern phones, she thought, only they sweat too much.

Rashomon – Friday, perhaps; 11th November

In spite of feeling listless and depressed, tormented by increasingly frequent headaches, Ana had the discipline to finish her book on time; she had always been responsible and mindful of deadlines. The initial enthusiasm generated by David's plan had already left her. She could not make progress; the plot kept eluding her, the characters were wooden, the situations *artificial*. She kept losing the thread, couldn't make up her mind about which of the themes to tackle and, in the absence of true focus, spent her time dreaming up fantastic twists in the plot. But she kept writing, she could not be without writing, although she still believed that her first book was "her story" and that she would never write a better one.

"It doesn't matter," said Jelena. "Let this new one be for the critics, your personal *Rashomon*..."

"What do you mean, *Rashomon*?"

"You know that Kurosawa became famous after *Rashomon*. He'd made great movies before *Rashomon*, to be sure, but the critics didn't get them. Only *Rashomon* was arty enough for their taste. After that, Kurosawa could do whatever he liked, all his stories about medieval samurai knights. I believe he made *Rashomon* in a calculated way: like, they want art – let them have art. But Kurosawa is a great artist, and even his calculated work is good. Only good, however; not great, not a masterpiece. Critics believe *Rashomon* to be a masterpiece to this very day, yet *Rashomon* is a pipsqueak little movie in comparison with *Seven Samurai* and *Throne of Blood*."

"How come you know so much about it?" Ana asked.

"I read his autobiography, and then I saw the movies... You know I'm interested in cultural snobbism. But David, for example, believes that cultural snobbism has its uses, that it can serve as propellant. According to the Law of Large Numbers or whatever, the cultural snobs, while stampeding through the town yelling, 'Quick, quick, must find where stuff is happening!' often manage to advertise the right stuff and pull their followers along. Trend-setters and their followers, that's culture in a nutshell. They pile up culture like furniture..."

"Yeah, and the worst thing is, those intellectual snobs are proud of their tolerance, while in fact they see themselves as higher beings. They are full of concern for garden snails and endangered species or animals bred for fur, but they despise everyone who doesn't belong to their circle. All the lower forms of life, such as Bosniaks, Vlahs, uneducated provincial folk and so on. They only use them for contrast, to make themselves appear even greater. I remember when I was little, a neighbour who had moved from Lika to Zagreb with her family said to my mum, 'It was very hard for us: poor we was, and even worse, we was from Lika..."

"That's why you must write," said Jelena. "In one sentence, you told a story."

"Yeah, and I believe people need to be taught things, because the more we learn, the more we realise we're all the same," said Ana, and Jelena did not feel like asking exactly what she had meant by that.

The Hand

IN MEMORIAM: SUSAN SONTAG (1933 – 2004)

The departure of the most consistent critic of the modern world

... In one of her best writings she called the white race "the cancer of mankind".

Wingbeat – December

The title of Ana's book was *Wingbeat*. "Just listen how good it will sound," David said at the time, "David Antolić: *Wingbeat*."

"I'm a bit uncomfortable about it, to be honest," Ana said. "Still, let it be, now that we started it... Who knows where it'll take us..."

When she consented to David and Jelena's idea about the hoax, Ana could not resist playing with the same idea in the book: she framed the plot by the story of a phony author receiving a literary prize for a book he didn't write. David was delighted with her gimmick ("It's as if you'd given them a riddle to solve," he said) and he was no less impressed by the book as a whole. He said to Jelena, "You told me the book was bad. I think it's great."

"It was bad before. I think it's great too, now. It looks like Ana has made some fundamental changes."

When she quizzed Ana about it, Ana said, "Yes, I struggled with this book for ages; I had no idea where it was leading. David's wave seems to have unmoored me; I knew directly what to do. As if I'd managed to plug into his positive current. Now, even I think it is good... as if it wasn't me who wrote it."

She became disappointed when she read that an elderly writer had written a novel around a similar idea, with the hero of the story entering a novel in an award competition. Jelena and David accused her of vanity. "You're not God, above the flow of time. Your writing, like everyone else's, must be of this time you live in. We are not creators. It's not accidental that today no one writes like Rabelais or Milton."

"I'm not vain, you know I'm not," said Ana, in self-defence.

"In that case you're looking for an excuse to indulge in self-pity," Jelena told her. "Although you know that's not what your book is really about. With you, it's just a gimmick."

Ana's story was unusual. The heroine was a young woman under a life sentence for murder she committed driven by jealousy. At the age of sixteen, she was hurt in a traffic accident and spent several months in bed. From that time on, she kept a diary, not of the usual girly kind but a laconic and dry diary of facts. She'd make note of the most ordinary daily events: at noon I went down the shops but turned back because it was raining. When I got to the shop later, they'd run out of bread so I had to go to another one. On my way there, I met... and so on. In the novel, she reads her diary and tries to rewind her life and comprehend why it had gone the way it did, which signs might have indicated what was going to take place and at what point her life could have taken a different turn, or, rather, what her life would have been like had it not deviated from its preordained course.

The Book Comes Out

When David took the manuscript to *Argus,* they accepted it without reading a single page. "Everything is going according to plan," said David to Ana and Jelena. "Not only did they accept it but said they were pleased I'd gone to them first, blah-de-dah..."

Argus rushed the book out to make both the Christmas sales and the deadlines for the yearly book awards. The book came out on Thursday 15th December, and the public presentation took place the next Thursday, the 22nd, at the Writers' Club.

Even before the presentation, his colleagues from other newspapers kept calling David to arrange interviews and get free copies of the book.

On the evening of the presentation, the Club was packed. Živković, one of *Argus'* editors, gave an inspired address: "A prominent journalist and columnist for *The Herald*, author of the well-known book of essays *Push Harder*, the man best described as..." etc., etc. David smiled, shook his head, ran his fingers through his hair with his usual charm and from time to time winked at Jelena who encouraged him from her front row seat.

Seated next to Jelena, Ana barely dared look at David. "I read in the papers that a woman had published a book anonymously," she whispered. "It just said, Anonymous, instead of her name. The readers only discovered who the author was once the book had become a famous bestseller." Jelena gave her a questioning look.

"I should've done that," Ana whispered. "It definitely can't be against the law."

The photographers kept snapping with their cameras. The uproar was even greater than at David's Journalism Award ceremony.

After the presentation, a queue of fans formed in front David, each clutching a copy of the book in expectation of an autograph. Next, the journalists surrounded him. He gave two statements for the radio and three before the cameras, all three for the national television: for the news programme, for a culture show and for a programme called *Nightlife*. "Why for *Nightlife*?" David asked. "You're interesting material to us," the presenter said, "not just as author, but in other aspects as well..."

Ana stood away from the hubbub and compared it to the modest presentation of her own first book. This is the proof, she thought, that my *real* book's failure is my fault. David sparkled, enjoyed himself and gave relaxed, witty answers to questions. A star.

The reviews started barely a week later, all of them

favourable. The critics praised everything about the book: its style, the originality of its concept, the tension, the subtlety, the convincing characters. A young female critic wrote, *"A good old-fashioned story at last! The author delights in telling it and knows how to step back to give story the pride of place, lavishing his abundant gift of language on its advancement – and not just his gift of language but his love of it. And not just love but awareness of the power of language and the consequent awe of it."*

In just one month the book sold more than 500 copies out of the total run of 2500, which, for Croatia, was a lot. The same period saw the publication of seven reviews of the book and at least as many interviews with the author.

The wave had started.

The Hand

17th January

LIFE: Chinese scientists succeed in growing synthetic brain cells.

Thursday, 20 January

FRONT PAGE: EU threatens to refuse Croatia because of Gotovina

CULTURE: 12 writers in competition for *The Morning Paper* Award: Baretić, Brešan, Dežulović, Gromača, Mićanović, Paljetak, Samardžić, Stojević, Špišić, Tribuson, Vrkljan, Ugrešić.

The author of the best prose book to win 50,000 kuna.

None of the authors was singled out as favourite.

None was singled out as favourite, yet they have the winner of Croatia's five major literary prizes among them!

The Inspector

"Would you please send in..." The Inspector looked down on his paperwork. Stopping just short of a bow, the Sergeant courteously opened the door to a pleasantly curvaceous lady with a beautiful face: she was obviously his favourite. He pulled a chair for her and, when she had sat down, took his own place at the table, secretly checking on the condition of his manly whiskers.

Lola

Jelena feared the prospect of the free, unstructured evening ahead. She was not in the mood for either reading or writing. Bruno had no problems of that nature: he'd use every free moment to slip into the work-bedroom and play PES[103] or Sims[104]. "This is Peter Brackley", the monotonous voice of the virtual commentator would repeat for the thousandth time in exactly the same way while Bruno, immersed in the dynamic football game, gripped the console and shook his legs like Galvani's frog. She was looking forward to a small pile of ironing that awaited her: it saved the evening from being depressingly empty. She was equally pleased when the doorbell rang, although she knew it could only be Lola: she alone always came unannounced.

Lola preferred to drop in for a coffee when Bruno was at home, although she didn't mind chatting just to Jelena. Jelena and Bruno would giggle once she'd left, as she openly flirted with Bruno, always trying to sit opposite him, her thighs crossed high and her bust thrust forward, her fingers twiddling with a thin golden chain, its pendant lost in the deep furrow between her two huge breasts. Lola liked to keep things simple.

"I haven't seen you guys for ages." She threw herself playfully on the sofa and waved to Bruno, having caught glimpse of him through the open door of the bedroom. "How's things?" She winked merrily. "I was worried I might disturb you in the middle of something, but then I thought, they're not silly to let me in if they're in the middle of business."

Bruno said nothing. Jelena thought, he's gone all cool now, and he was all aflutter with Nina sitting opposite.

"Sex is the most important thing in a marriage, y'know,"

---

[103] Pro Evolution Soccer, a computer game from Konami
[104] An avatar-creating computer game from EA

said Lola matter-of-factly, as if discussing a recipe for a cake. Mechanically, she pulled her skirt up a bit. "I told you," she said, turning to Jelena, "what my life with Tomo was like..."

Bruno got up from the desk and muttered, "I hope you don't mind if I shut the door; I've got to finish this tonight..."

Lola waved him off cheerfully. "If you haven't got anything better to do..." Bruno closed the door without a reply. "What was I telling you about..." Lola went on. "Oh, yeah. My Tomo... for him, sex didn't exist. I cried and cried. 'It's not that I want sex,' I'd tell him, 'but how is a woman to know if her husband loves her if he never touches her?' And it's dangerous; it's bad for health to be like that. I've got a friend who stopped sleeping with her husband once their child was born. Fifteen years later, she got breast cancer.... And my Tomo kept making excuses: he was tired, or his life was in a mess or the kids could hear us... Poor sod, he died and he hadn't managed..." she dropped her voice to remain within Jelena's earshot only, "— hadn't managed to fuck his fill, if you'll pardon the expression."

Jelena burst out laughing and said, "I'm sorry, I shouldn't laugh... Can I get you a glass of wine?" she asked.

"Don't mind if I do," said Lola and went on, "I used to threaten him with divorce, told him he'd get home from work one day and I wouldn't be there... But once – twenty years into our marriage it was, I'm not kidding you – I challenged him to tell me why he hadn't touched me for fifteen years. To own up. Did he have another woman, was he gay or what, what was the matter with him that I had to spend my life unloved at his side? And he was like, 'Why is it such a big deal for you? I didn't feel like it, that's all. And you know what? Fuck the happiness that hinges on sex alone.' I never asked him again. I'd made my bed; I had to lie on it."

***

With Lola gone, Bruno re-emerged from the bedroom. "That woman really goes on my nerves," he said. "Next time she comes to bore us, I'll ask her to leave."

"Yeah, like you would!" Jelena retorted readily. "Did we

have anything better to do? You don't like discussing marriage? Is she too hormonal for your taste, perhaps?"

Bruno backed out of the battle he had no wish to fight. Jelena thought of Pero and the drink she didn't have with him – because of fear or for tactical reasons; she wasn't sure which.

**

Waiting for David in the café the following day, Jelena read the column by the prominent Chief editor of a prominent women's magazine: *"...Men don't like smart, confident women. When did you last see a forty-year old man choosing a partner of his own age? Never. They'd all rather have women they can shape according to their own taste."*

"Who are they kidding?" she barked at David as soon as he came in. "Can anyone in their sane mind believe that men choose younger women because they feel threatened by the older ones? It's only their libido they might threaten, nothing else."

"I surrender," said David, holding his hands up.

"Have you heard of the hormone called oxytocin? Nope. Well, oxytocin becomes dominant in women entering the quiet satisfaction phase which follows the initial passionate one. I mean, women enter the quiet phase, and men the boring one."

"There you go again," David sighed, planted his chin in his palms and his elbows on the table and prepared to listen.

"Yeah, but listen: women produce oxytocin during orgasm as well. That means, a woman will produce the same hormone in a quiet relationship and at the peak of sexual enjoyment. Right, bear that in mind and listen; there's more: at the same time, the levels of testosterone, the hormone of sexual desire, drop in men with every new day of their relationship. What do you say to that?"

"Men's unsuitability for lasting relationships is hormonally based, then."

"But that's not the whole story. The same hormone, oxytocin, protects women against breast cancer. This would mean that sexual abstinence leads to breast cancer. That is to say, women, unlike men, cannot live without love. Yesterday I accidentally heard of a real-life example: a woman got *it* – don't want to repeat *its* name – because her husband refused to sleep with her..."

David listened gravely.

"But even if they knew the facts, husbands wouldn't do it with their wives either gladly or frequently. They'd give us their never-ending *unlike you, girls, when we can't, we can't.* You know what is the only possible conclusion to be drawn from this? Fuck the happiness that hinges on sex alone." She told David the story about Lola and Tomo.

If Pero invites her again, she'll accept, she decided.

The Hand

14 January

EVENTS OF THE DAY: 317 unemployed only get 893 kuna per month to feed their families on. Breakfast: just coffee, and a slice of bread and marmalade with tea for the kids; dinner: a small piece of chicken with rice, or sausages with potato; supper: dinner leftovers for the kids, anything still left over for the parents.

LIFE: a restaurant for anorexics and bulimics opens in Berlin.

The Woolly Bear

Most Friday afternoons, Hana would go to David's. They wouldd watch his favourite TV series, *Midsomer Murders*, and then she would stay the night. This Friday was no exception. Having had her fill of sleep, Hana returned home to her mother's around noon, just as Jelena had come round for a coffee. Jelena was fond of Matko and Hana. Resembling David and affectionate like a kitten, Hana often confided in her. Already rehearsing masculine independence, Matko faked lack of enthusiasm for discussions. He was on the point of going out when Jelena arrived.

"Wrap up well, please" Buba shouted.

"Why are you so nervous?" Matko said. "I'm not going to war, am I? Just popping down to Matija's for the drum sticks."

"It's winter outside, wrap up. Don't want you to catch pneumonia for showing off. Of course I'm nervous; I'm tired of constantly asking, got your scarf on, got your hat on, got your gloves, have you put your pullover on..."

"Why do you always think that someone is cold... or that there is something wrong?" Matko asked.

"Why do you have to freeze to be cool? I had no idea I'd given birth to a silly child."

"I'm not trying to be cool; I'm *alternative*," Matko shouted from the hallway, patiently threading shoelaces through the endless row of holes on his Doc Martens.

"Oh, yeah, I forgot," Hana shouted back. "Dad's over the moon that you got into the Rock Academy; he says he'll give you the money for drums but won't have the time to search around for the right ones, it'll be up to you to find them."

"Yesssss! OK, no worries!" Matko said.

"How was it at dad's?" Buba asked Hana.

"How? Minging."

"Hana!"

"You asked me, I'm telling you. Shall I go on? Somehow it seems to me that dad has fallen in love... a woman called him last night..."

Matko halted by the door to hear the rest.

"How do you know he's fallen in love?" asked Buba lightly.

"Well... his forehead kind of spread when he answered the phone, like when someone is happy, and his voice went hoarse like when you talk to someone you care about... He said he had 'other plans for the evening', which must've been me... I felt unwanted."

"Go away, you know how much daddy loves you."

"And I had a stupid day at school. Kiki said in front of the whole class that my bum was like a snowplough and everyone sniggered and I had no idea why they were doing it until Dajna told me..."

"Want me to bust him up?"

"Matko!" Buba said.

"All right then, I'm off," said Matko and ran out.

Hana went on, "Isn't she lucky though, that woman; it's great when someone falls in love with you. Not like me, still nothing happening. I feel like a woolly bear."

"Like what?" Buba and Jelena asked together, laughing.

"Like a woolly bear," Hana repeated gravely. "A woolly bear is an insect whose larva sleeps in its cocoon for thirteen years, waiting to come out. And when it becomes a grown insect and does finally come out, it lives for just two weeks. Imagine, such a long wait for just two weeks!"

"Is that it? Any other problems?" asked Buba laughing and stroked her daughter's hair.

"Don't stroke me like I'm retarded." Hana withdrew from her hand.

"I'm not stroking you as if you were retarded. I'm comforting you with my touch, if you want to know."

"I don't want to know."

"Oh yeah," Jelena said to change the subject, "did you ask your science teacher about the parabens, like I asked you to?"

"I did, but he said he had no idea; he'd never heard of them, but he promised he'd try to find out. He never told me anything though, and I didn't ask again."

"There you go," said Jelena to Buba. "We expect school programmes to start teaching about new scientific discoveries and achievements, about ecology, nutrition and stuff, and the science teacher's never heard of parabens."

"It doesn't surprise me a bit," said Buba. "Yesterday I heard someone say that many teachers didn't know how to switch a computer on."

"You know what the geography teacher told us? You'll love this," Hana said to Jelena. "You know what kind of apple is the most expensive in New York?"

"No, what?"

"The one with a worm in it. And the grocer must open the apple for the customer to see the worm. I remember you telling us when we were little, 'Let's see if we can find our friend the worm in this cherry!' We thought you were a bit wacky. But even the Americans do it now..."

"What happens if they have to open an apple for every customer?" Buba put in.

"Dunno." Hana shrugged her shoulders.

"Americans being Americans, they'll soon start breeding worms to put into apples." Buba laughed.

She poured a glass of wine for herself and for Jelena. "Wow, Golden Plavac," said Jelena, surprised. "How come?"

"I remembered what you told me about our best wines. I should be able to treat myself to a glass of healthy wine a week. Cheers!" said Buba.

The Inspector

"That'll be all for now," the Inspector said. "My colleague will inform you of any further developments in the investigation. Please do not leave the city for the time being."

The Jekylls and the Hydes

"Guess who I saw in town yesterday," Bruno asked over their express dinner: the bean cassoulet that Jelena had brought from her mum's and had warmed up, and pan-fried turkey escalopes. He had even said that the beans were excellent; his chattiness indicated he was in a particularly good mood. Jelena was, with wifely instinct, suspicious of any of his good moods she wasn't the cause of, or the origin of which she did not know. By the same token, "Guess who I saw in town" was Jelena's game and Bruno had learned it from her. It was their good mood game, but they had not played it for a long time. Jelena loved games, quizzes and puzzles. The fact that Bruno was playing her game which he had never found as interesting as she did was a point in her favour. Or did the person he had met in town put him in a good mood? I bore, I burrow, I dissect, thought Jelena.

"A woman?" Had he met a man, Bruno wouldn't be so delighted.

"Yes."

"Young?" Had the woman been old, he wouldn't have even mentioned her.

"Pretty?" As above.

"Yup."

She could hear the beginnings of caution in his *yup*. The woman had to have been young and pretty, then, which meant fanciable, which meant I might have reasons to be jealous. He's expecting me to be pleased for him, because he's had a pleasant encounter, which in turn means it must be either a woman I genuinely like, or it could be a woman we haven't known all that long, so I haven't had the time to become jealous of her?

"Do I like her?"

"You do, a lot."

But I might unlike her if he gets to like her too much, she thought.

"That means, pretty and nice?"

"Yes."

"Have we known her for a long time?"

"No."

"Did I meet her first?"

"Yes."

"Did I introduce you two in King Cross?"

Bruno's jaw dropped. "You always guess right! How?"

"I see it in your eyes," Jelena said mysteriously.

Bruno pretended not to notice the insinuation. "Such a lovely girl," he said. "And the way she came up to me: I'm at the news-stand buying a paper when I feel someone touching my shoulder from behind. I turn round and there she is, laughing. It's early, everyone's sleepy and grumpy and there she is, laughing away..."

There she is, laughing, Jelena grumbled silently to herself. He wants me to share his delight. Or else he'd like me to explain if Nina was being particularly genial for his benefit or is she like that with everyone...

"That reminded me I'd promised to put that subtitling software on CD for her," Bruno said. "So I did, this morning."

"You did? I know of at least ten people queuing up for

software you promised them."

"It happened to be to hand."

"You don't have to apologise for improving," Jelena said. "I feel like Emma Thompson in *Love, Actually*; a proper, majestic, warm, generous wife whose love is boundless, but who is ready for anything at the same time." Why did I think of Emma Thompson just now, she wondered.

"I haven't seen that movie," Bruno said.

On his desk, Jelena spotted a CD-ROM with *For Nina* written on it in black marker. *For Nina* seemed to exude an intimacy which did not include Jelena. There you go, then; I noticed the *For Nina* CD, but he didn't notice Pero's flowers, she thought. "When are you going to give it to her?" She asked.

"We'll have to pop over to her place for me to install it," Bruno said. "We agreed that you and she would arrange that."

But of course, Jelena thought, the pimping wife. *To install it!* A perfect metaphor.

She phoned Nina in the evening to tell her about the software. She didn't want to do it in the office for fear that Nina might tell by the look on her face that she was becoming jealous, which, in all honesty, was not Nina's fault.

She heard a cold, unfamiliar voice. "Hello?"

"Hello, could I speak to Nina, please?"

"It's me." The pleasant, dark, velvety voice and the familiar laughter filled her ear. "Nina speaking."

"It's Jelena. I didn't recognise your voice," said Jelena, still perplexed. The cold voice had taken her by surprise.

"I recognised yours," Nina laughed again.

"I'd never have thought you could produce such a cold *hello*..." Jelena said.

"Yes, I know, I did that on purpose," Nina laughed once more. "I thought it was someone else."

"Like Jekyll and Hyde," Jelena laughed too. "All my friends seem to be Jekylls and Hydes... Bruno's got the software you wanted."

"Already? Fantastic, please thank him for me."

"Is Sunday all right for you?"

"Sunday is fine. I'll have finished reading by then."

"Reading? What?"

"I haven't told you? I've been reading a mountain of entries for the *Uliks* award. For weeks and weeks now."

"You? What have you got to do with *Uliks*?"

"I'm a member of the Translator's Association, aren't I?"

"Yeah? I had no idea," said Jelena, surprised. "That means you'll be voting for the selection?"

"That's right. The problem is, whoever votes must select three books in each category. And there are twelve of those, with at least twenty books per category. Even if you were to read no more than three books from each, you'd end up reading 36 books. And it still doesn't mean you'll pick the best ones."

"Do you know that David's book is competing?" Jelena asked.

"Of course, that's why I particularly wanted to vote in that category," Nina said. "I've read it and I think it's pure genius. I had no idea he was so perceptive. And so talented."

Jelena recalled the sound of the cold *Jekyll-and-Hyde* voice. Nina, she thought, was out to systematically conquer all her men.

Jelena Reads Nina's Book

Jelena borrowed Nina's book from Ana. At the very start she thought of Jekyll and Hyde again: the story was a fast-paced but uncomfortable read, leaving the reader with a lingering nausea. Nina wrote well; raw in places, her style was nevertheless forceful. That critic was right when she said that Nina seemed to communicate in a language she did not fully command, but still managed to express her feelings and ideas to perfection. The book showed its author in a new and unfamiliar light: something dark, dark was hiding behind the calm, beautiful façade.

When she finished the book, she phoned Ana. "I've read Nina's book."

"And?" Ana asked.

"Sick," Jelena said.

"Sick as in good or sick as in sick?"

"Both. She's very talented. The book is interesting, gripping, moving; some bits are so vivid and convincing they make your blood run cold... the junkie couple who are in love, the girl's on the game, she's very beautiful but is slowly ruining herself, and then the boy ODs and dies..."

"Mmm, yeah," muttered Ana vaguely. Jelena thought she might not like her praising Nina's novel. Ana had, however, something completely different on her mind: she had remembered reading in the papers, some five or six years ago, about the death of a young drug addict, apparently of an overdose, but there had been some unusual circumstances about his death... Next morning, she went to the Archive of the National and University Library to research something for her book; she took the opportunity to look up *Nina Ivezić, drug addiction** in the Black Chronicle archive of the dailies from the years 1998, 1999 and 2000.

It took her just over an hour to locate two articles:

The Evening Paper, 20 January 1998. Nikola Marcijuš, 25, a registered addict and a small time criminal, was found dead in the flat of his girlfriend, Nina Ivezić. The autopsy established that the young man died from a heroin overdose. In her statement to the police, Nina Ivezić claimed that her boyfriend had not overdosed accidentally but had in fact committed suicide, telling her not to call the ambulance as there was nothing they could do to save him. Because of the suspicious circumstances, the young woman was arrested and questioned...

The Evening paper, 13 April 1999. Nina Ivezić, suspected of the murder of Nikola Marcijuš, was freed because of the lack of evidence. The court pathologist confirmed that the death was caused by a lethal dose of morphine, most likely a case of overdosing..."

Anton

Next morning, Ana found another mail from Anton, even stranger than the first one:

Ana, guess what? Your book is the best one I've ever read.

I'm not exactly a dilettante in this field; I've been a literary critic since secondary school. I still read a lot and I'm familiar with our country's entire literary production, so you can safely trust my judgement. Reading your book, I felt in the presence of a kindred soul. I believe you have the same effect on all your readers: that of a universal kindred soul. Regards, Anton.

PS: You really look good in the photo on the back cover.

That missive, concerning *The Naked She-Wolf,* meant more to Ana than anything that had to do with her second book. She could not work out if Anton was a lunatic, or an unusual lover of literature, or both, but she didn't care. All that mattered was that he liked the book. She replied at once, trying not to sound too obviously grateful. She did not comment on the remark about her photo, as she thought he had added it out of politeness.

Anton's reply arrived at once; she wondered how he had managed to type it so quickly.

Your book pulses with more life than a thousand hearts. What sort of person are you? I imagine you as full of volcanic emotion. Your book has awakened my curiosity. How did you manage to create such a complete and real world? I read the few published reviews of your book and can safely say that not one of them gives even a remotely true representation of your work.

He had hit Ana's favourite topic. Again, she replied at once:

I wrote about a great number of things simply because they help make up the Whole. I believe a book must be a world in itself, by which I mean that it must be capable of independent life. That means it needs to be a being possessed of everything it needs in order to survive: arms, legs, head, stomach... It must know everything people know in everyday life. I find it hard to explain...

Anton's reply came in minutes.

A few more remarks about your writing: people tend to fall for dry, cerebral stuff. The heavier and murkier the writing, the higher the praise. *Writing is, unfortunately, not a bedsheet to be judged on the merit of its toughness and density alone. Sometimes it needs to be hard; on other occasions, however, it must be transparent and breezy like a thin curtain swayed by the gentlest zephyr, creating ever new patterns and shadows by its swinging motion. Writing is sometimes like a fishing net, capturing the attention of the reader, with many different fish wriggling and flopping around inside it: the smaller fish slip through, while the larger ones remain inside... That's what your book is like. You know what's best in it? The things you didn't say. In bad books, nothing is left unsaid; everything is there in plain view. Such books are boring and rely on the stupidity of the readers. Your book, however, complements the mind of the reader, and vice versa. That's why the reader dives into your book, slots in like a carved piece of wood slots into a log it was carved out from to become one with it once more, keeping just a thin boundary around its form so that they can be separated anew should the need arise... Forgive me for going on a bit, but this is my favourite subject and few people wish to discuss it.*

Your fan, Anton

Ana replied:

Thank you, thank you. Have you read Doris Dörrie? Or Viktorija Tokareva? Reading them, I understood the same point you're making: they're good because of what they didn't write. I'd be proud if the same was true of my work. Actually, the perfect book would be one without any words at all. But that's absurd. Books without words cannot exist, there'd be no story without words... I'm the one that's going on a bit now, but this subject is important to me, too; I, too, have few people to discuss it with...

Anton:

You're "going on" because you sense that I understand you. And I do, but the idea of art that you describe is impossible to translate into reality. In reality, a work of art has material existence, and all bodies give resistance...

She stared at the monitor. The strain of the quick-fire correspondence and the concentration it demanded had worn her out. Her head began to ache. But she thought that Anton had to be one of the endless threads weaving their web around her, and not a single one of them was there by chance. And that she'd been led to Anton, in some mysterious way, by her encounter with Mirta Gluhak. Mirta Gluhak must have been the bearer of some kind of Good News, of a good vibe, as one might put it. Where would Anton's thread eventually take her, will it bring on good things and if it does, will she be aware that they had come to her on Anton's thread? Might it not be a sign that David's scheme with her book was good? Quite simply, an event opens a door and other events begin to flow through it. Ana was now convinced that she had been spending weeks at her computer ardently reading her mail solely for the sake of Anton's e-mail: to be there when it finally arrives.

The Hand

THE CHRONICLE: "By scanning the brain, Dutch scientists have found the key to achieving orgasm. It is all in the mind after all, at least as far as women are concerned. For a woman to achieve orgasm, it is essential that certain sections of her brain be switched off, and in particular the amygdale which regulates the feelings of fear and anxiety. In evolutionary terms, the amygdale is the oldest part of the brain. Under sexual stimulation, its activity drops. Scanning has established, however, that almost all areas of a woman's brain experience a drop in activity during feminine orgasm. This puts women into a trance-like state during orgasm. Their bodily movements become unconscious as their cortex has, for all intents and purposes, stopped working. Therein lies the answer to the question which has been troubling men since times immemorial: do women fake orgasms? When a woman is faking one, all her brain centres are active, the amygdale being the most active of them all.

These discoveries confirm the truth of the perpetual women's claim: that their sexual pleasure, rather than on expert lovemaking or the even less important size of the male member, hinges on being in a relaxed state of mind.

The male brain remains active during orgasm, but the experienced emotions have no impact on the quality of the orgasm. For men, physical contact and activity centred on the genital area remain, after all, the most important aspects of sex."

That is why sex crimes are a male specialty.

Andrej's True Love

Andrej could not keep his mind on work. He was feeling powerful desire; it made his testicles throb with pain. Beads of sweat had broken out on his forehead. Last time he had vowed he would never do it again, but he made for the bedroom just the same. She was still asleep. Slowly and soundlessly, he lay down next to her. She did not move. He inhaled the scent of her hair spread over the pillow; with his breath, he caressed her neck and with his hand, her naked shoulder and her narrow back.

Her breathing changed, no longer deep and slow. She was waking up. That was his favourite moment, when she began waking up under his touch. Only her breathing betrayed her wakefulness, although she knew he knew she was awake. She would go on lying perfectly still. This utter, absolute abandon drove him wild with excitement. His hand caressed one small breast, the soft skin of her belly, the other breast. Almost imperceptibly, she shuddered. His hand travelled down to her thighs and began parting them. Her limp top leg was heavy and motionless; his burrowing hand inched forward bit by bit. He ran his finger along the edge of her underpants and felt her warmth. She remained motionless. He pulled out his hand from between her thighs and reached into her panties, stroking her pubic hair. She shuddered slightly again. His hand spread her slender thighs again, now thrusting his leg under hers. He could not restrain himself any longer. Leaning on his elbow, he tore her panties violently down and rammed his sword-hard member between the two tiny hemispheres. A loud cry escaped him. Filled with love, he stroked her limp hand with gratitude.

At Nina's

Nina's apartment was tiny, tastefully furnished and spotless. She had imagined Nina would be exactly like that: a tidy mistress of a harmonious space. Warm and welcoming, too: in an eyeblink, coffee, biscuits, milk, sugar and a pitcher of elderflower water appeared on the table. "I got it from my auntie, it's home-made," she explained, meaning the elderflower.

Bruno and Jelena sat down on a pretty two-seater sofa upholstered in dark blue cloth with thinly scattered green stars. It reminded Jelena of a two-seater sofa she and Bruno had seen in a shop just after they were married. The sofa had been so pretty and cheerful that Jelena dubbed it "the New Year". They never bought it as they had no money at the time and later, when they did have some, they chose a good quality, practical, expensive leather sofa that was nowhere near as pretty. Nina sat down on a pouffe. Jelena thought that, in her own apartment, Nina looked even more attractive than usual; everything about her fell harmoniously together the way elements of nature did – the way a sunny beach went with the deep blue sea.

Suddenly, like she would sense an inaudible sound, she sensed that Bruno was agitated. Buzzing. Purring. He regarded Nina with roaming eyes unfocussed and off-centre, detached from their base. (Of course, that's why they say, *his eyes popped out*, Jelena thought.) He's not sure what he ought to be looking at, or is struggling not to look, but her face keeps attracting his glance. He's not managing not to look and can't hide his bliss, but he's still trying, because the last vestiges of caution tell him I'll notice. He knows I know him inside out. Whenever he blinks, he's looking for a moment of respite, in which to consolidate his feelings. I'm taking this quite well, considering; Jelena said to herself, for who wouldn't be enchanted by all that charm and vivacity, that... elixir of life. Yes, that's the essence of all enchantment: you're attracted by those who awaken the joy of life within you. That's why everyone wants to be in love. And that's why the capacity to be in love diminishes with age: every soul has a limited body...

He knows I know he likes her. He hides it from me not because he's afraid of me (no, he likes her too much to be afraid; he'd sacrifice me for her if he had to), but because he feels sorry for me, his Jelena, his devoted, vulnerable wife. His used-up wife. The wife he had used up. Nor is Nina inviting him to court her: there is no coquetry in her behaviour, nothing provocative or purposefully feminine. No, attraction is natural to her like gravity is to the Earth. Quite simply, everyone feels good in her presence. She'd try to switch off, douse down, reduce her power of attraction if she knew it was hurting me.

Nina. A fine face, free of make up; large, deep eyes... There was nothing trivial in that face. Suddenly, Jelena knew: if anything were to happen between Bruno and Nina, it would be love. Were he to leave me for her, I couldn't even have the pleasure of saying, "Yup, my husband has gone off with some slag."

She felt as if in a dream. Being at Nina's had no spatial or temporal dimension. It was no longer real. I'm probably exaggerating awfully; I've got to stop, she commanded herself.

Tensely, she took part in the conversation. Bruno ignored her, by nanomicrons, but she felt it just the same. He was interested in what Nina had to say, not what Jelena might have to say. As if he didn't want them to take up any more of Nina's time than they absolutely had to. What did that remind her of? Oh yeah, when they once ran into his new colleague from work, a former beauty queen. She greeted him patronizingly, only stopping short of pinching his cheek whilst completely ignoring Jelena. Instead of introducing them, Bruno ended up muttering something unintelligible. Later, Jelena accused him of being ashamed of her and of thinking her inferior to that long-legged nymphomaniac.

"Why nymphomaniac?" asked Bruno.

"Why are you on her side?" Jelena replied.

She felt much the same way now: he was ashamed of her because she wasn't as perfect as Nina. But that was an expression of closeness. *Ashamed of His Mother*, the saddest story she had read as a child. Cankar?[105] Bruno: *Ashamed of His Wife.*

"Are we boring you?" Nina asked her at one point, with tender concern.

"No," Jelena replied. *Are we boring you? Are we boring you?* The question revolved in her head like a tape on loop. The meaning of the question was: are the two of us, he and I, who are sharing something, boring you who are left out? How did I become the third side of the triangle, Jelena wondered. And yet, Nina had asked her question in all sincerity, genuinely concerned she might have unwittingly left Jelena out. That very same sincere concern, however, meant that she was aware of her power over Bruno. Jelena did not like it when her thoughts took that kind of turn: she always came up with the worst possible scenario. Bruno had launched into a technical explanation, moving his glance between Nina and Jelena. I must be his anchoring point, thought Jelena, but did nothing to make his task harder; she listened with interest, not registering a single word, nodding her head and then repeating the nod in Nina's direction, as if to say, "Haven't I got a clever husband." Nodding, she wondered what it must have felt like, after Nina's lovely young face, to see her own face, older, far less lovely, joyless and twisted with jealousy. She hardly dared look at Bruno as he shifted his glance from Nina to her, to avoid seeing his eyes go dull. She felt ridiculous, smelling strongly of *Deep Red* with its musk note. She hardly ever used perfume; today, she sprayed herself in order to be *competitive*. Now she feared Bruno would notice and realise why she had done it. And with musk, of all things. But she was equally afraid that Bruno might not notice anything.

Nina and Bruno moved to the computer. When was it last, Jelena thought, that a woman other than myself would sit next to Bruno, leaning so intimately towards him that he could feel her breath? Perhaps he, too, had arrived at the age when he

---

[105] Ivan Cankar (1876-1918), Slovenian modernist writer

questioned his attractiveness to women? Jelena planted herself in front of the window, watching tiny people scurry to and fro through the park at the base of Nina's high-rise, and cars on the road alongside the park, moving like images in one of Bruno's video games. When they were leaving, she found that she liked Nina as much as before: it was not her fault. She thanked them warmly and waved to them cheerfully as they got into the lift. Bruno appeared tense, or simply confused, as ever. Jelena remembered the fireflies. Beautiful and cheerful, Nina must have glowed brighter than I, she concluded sadly, and thus won the male. Her mouth was dry. In fact, she felt dry all over, crumpled like a prune.

***

Next morning, after the shrill sound of the alarm clock, hovering between sleep and wakefulness, Jelena *saw* the story of Bruno and Nina. It had come out of nowhere, unwanted and unplanned, and it looked just like a movie. Jelena felt sadness and fear, as she listened to snippets of speech. She heard Bruno say to Nina, "Jelena is jealous of you." She heard Nina ask her, Jelena, seriously: "Are you jealous of me?" and then her own voice, replying, "You're the first woman for whose sake Bruno betrayed me. Not *before* whom he betrayed me – said things about me, although that, too, is treachery – but for *whose sake* he did it." Nina said, "I never wanted any of this; it just happened." What was it she'd never wanted? What had happened? Everyone knew, although no one would say anything.

Next, a dialogue with mum unwound in her head, without any participation of her will, as before: "Hello, is that you, Jelena?" "Yes, mum... how strange you managed to get me." "Why should it be strange?" mum asked, sternly, suspiciously. "Because I'm dead."

On waking up, she forgot the details but remained sad throughout the day. What she had seen seemed unbelievable and at the same time inevitable: did not reason and feeling/intuition unite in the alpha phase, bringing together everything you knew without even being aware of it? What would Bruno say if she told him over coffee: "Look, I know what's going to happen. I saw it in the alpha phase: you'll fall in love with Nina and leave me although you'll feel sorry for me. We'll both be sad..."

In *Apartman*; Meeting Pero Accidentally for the Third Time

It is true, Ana is right: nothing happens by chance; Jelena thought when, on her way to the Contemporary, she spotted Pero on the other side of the street, by the ZKM[106]. If Bruno's got Nina, I've got Pero. What was more, she spotted him just after yet another case of a parked car with a running engine. On her cosmic trajectory, Pero was connected with car exhausts. Romantic it wasn not, but who could know the meaning of that connection? On this occasion, the incident took place on Sava Street, in front of No. 3, next to that weird carpet shop. A red Taunus that seemed to have taken part, a hundred years ago, in the Triglav to Gevgelija[107] rally and had not been washed or serviced since, sat on the kerb. Its engine was on, smoking and stinking. A young man, almost a boy, sat in the driver's seat. Jelena knocked on the car window and when he rolled it down, she said, with all the kindness and gentleness she could muster, "Excuse me, you could well say it's none of my business, but... do you know how badly you're polluting the air, parked here with the engine running? I mean, I know it's possible that you can't turn it off because you won't be able to start it again. If that's what it is..."

The boy gave her a blank look at first, and then, thrown by her gentleness, replied equally gently, "Yeah, I know... I'm just warming the engine a bit..."

Jelena nodded, said goodbye and left. She heard the engine

---

[106] Zagreb Youth Theatre (Zagrebačko Kazalište Mladih)

[107] Another way of saying, "the length of Yugoslavia". But it was an actual rally, from Mt Triglav in Slovenia to the town of Gevgelia in Macedonia.

stop behind her back. She felt proud of herself. One by one, she thought. The lad will definitively remember this weird episode and give it some thought. He might even do what I did next time he sees someone sitting there with an engine running...

She always walked from the office to the Upper Town; that could not have had a special meaning. Everything else, however, could: the fact that she spotted him at all (it had never happened before in their many years of walking the streets of their home town – she would have known if it had); the fact that the day was bright and sunny whilst it should have been cold and gloomy as befitted a day in late autumn; the fact that all morning she had been expecting something good to happen. (Good? Who knows if this is good or bad, she thought. But it's nice.) Firmly convinced that Pero wasn not there just like that, by chance, she crossed to his side of the street, pretending not to see him and to be crossing the street for no particular reason. If he asked, she would tell him where she was going to and then it would look quite natural that she should have crossed the road where she did.

Pero, on the other hand, did not pretend not to have seen her; he genuinely had not. Had she not been preoccupied by good omens, Jelena would have been discouraged by that last fact. But not for long: although he failed to notice her until she was right under his nose, his look of delight was so sincere it sent shivers down her spine. A wave rose and fell in her stomach, like on a carousel.

"Our third encounter means we must have a coffee together," Pero said.

Jelena blushed: he knows how many times we've met! "Er... well... okay," she said, hoping it sounded like indecision. What if he mentions the coffee she cancelled? It was much easier to be direct on the phone. Direct, mysterious and decisive.

"Where shall we go?" Pero asked.

Jelena thought she had seen his eyes flash. She looked around for inspiration. As she was about to say "We could go to *Atrium*", she remembered it was not feminine in a woman to make decisions. To be feminine was to give up control, to totter clumsily on beautiful high heels and to look for support in a man. She remembered how she had read in a women's magazine that women were allegedly genetically programmed to mate with men who were stronger than they, more successful and more mature in their personality and outlook. Such men would often be older than they, too, which is why it was socially acceptable for an older man to have a relationship with a young woman. Men, however, genetically preferred weaker women, less successful than they, and younger. The more successful (older, more independent, with flatter heels) the woman, the harder it was for her to find a partner. High heels were the message: I'm not confident, not independent, I'll depend on you; compared to me, you're strong, a real manly man, let's mate... Jelena was not wearing high heels; as for the rest – why not? She nearly laughed out loud, shaking her head as she wondered at her own thoughts. She saw Pero watching her. Who knows how long since he asked me where I wanted to go, she thought and blushed again. "I don't know," she said. "You decide."

"Shall we go to *Apartman*?" he proposed.

Jelena liked it when a man would choose a quiet place with few people in it; she believed he did so because he was interested in her and her alone.

Apartman, a new cafe/club designed in a seemingly clashing but actually pleasant and comfortable blend of materials and styles, reminded her of a similar place in Paris. The Paris connection enhanced the atmosphere of adventure. *Apartman* consisted of three rooms; Pero and Jelena made for the last of the three, with round tables and dark and light brown leather armchairs. There was even a leather three-seater along the glass panel wall overlooking Preradović Street. They both sat down on the three-seater, Pero to Jelena's right. He'll be looking at my bad profile, a thought crossed Jelena's mind. A large mirror with a quirky bar next to it occupied the far end of the room. The bar seemed to consist of any old bits and pieces that were at hand at the time of its making.

"I can't remember what used to be here before," Jelena said.

"Who's the owner?"

"A young couple, they're both designers. Before, it used to be *Dolce & Banana*..."

Jelena laughed. "A great name for a patisserie, *Dolce & Banana*..."

"The car's all right now?"

"I got it back yesterday," she said.

Pero looked even better than when she had last seen him. As he sat down, he told her, "You look lovely," sounding polite and intimate at the same time.

Take the compliment like a lady, she told herself. "Thank you," she said. You look even lovelier, she thought. Against her will, her glance was drawn to his lips: full and soft. The lower lip had a dimple in the middle which made it look even more sensuous. His mouth is so sexy he should be wearing his y-fronts on his face, she thought stupidly and almost laughed. She averted her eyes and shook her head a bit.

"Is something wrong?" Pero asked.

Not really, Jelena thought. I'm feeling sexual excitement in the presence of a strange man for the first time in my life, that's all. I thought that pure sex didn't exist. And what now? Am I turning into a man as my female hormone level drops? So that's how poor men must be feeling: randy all the time. Is this desire for pure sex brought on by years? Or by years of marriage? Or by years of marriage with Bruno? Perhaps Pero is simply sexy, and I simply normal? Since she had got together with Bruno, not only had she not had sex with anyone else but could not even imagine ever desiring anyone else. Bar falling in love, and one could never exclude that possibility... But that would not be sinful. This, this was sinful.

"You've wondered off... where?" Pero asked, spreading and rippling his handsome lips. Jelena almost felt them on hers and shivered a little.

"I'm very tired," she lied. She was aware she had managed a total of five or six sentences since they had met, a period of at least ten minutes, and even those were merely answers to his questions. "Normally I'm not that quiet," she added.

Thankfully, she remembered: "You tested my perceptive skills. How about testing yours? You're the inspector, after all. Go on, talk."

Pero laughed. "It might be better if you just went on. You were great."

Even that sounded ambiguous to Jelena. "I was always interested in watching people and drawing my conclusions," she said. "My husband always says (Why am I mentioning my husband, she thought; that'll destroy the harmony. Or am I mentioning him to prevent... what, exactly? I don't want to prevent anything!) that I'm a *social observer*. I mean, so do my friends, they tell me I'm always staring at someone... But I'm probably a total amateur, compared to you," she finished clumsily.

"Somehow I don't believe that," said Pero. His eyes shone.

"I'm good at studying women," Jelena said. "I like guessing what their lives are like, if they have a family, if they're divorced..." If they're loved, she added silently. "Let's see how you do it," she said. Ugh! "I mean, how you observe and deduce," she added quickly. "You know, just look at a man and know if he's guilty or not, what's on his mind, where he's been, where he's headed to... I heard that police investigative methods were now incredibly sophisticated; not just DNA matching, but also psychology, non-verbal communication, body language..." Body language, I'd better watch it, she thought and straightened up: she had been inclining towards Pero at a noticeable angle.

"Okay," he said. "Stop me when you've had enough." Jelena nodded. "There, look at that couple by the door. I can see them in the mirror. Take a good look. What do you think they are to one another: colleagues, friends, lovers, husband and wife?"

Jelena glanced at the youngish couple; they may have been between 25 and 30. The girl was pretty and appeared to be listening breathlessly to the man. Slightly hunched, he talked and gesticulated. "Colleagues?" she guessed.

"I think they're at the start of an unworkable relationship. Look: the lad is leaning towards her, which means he cares and is putting in a good effort. He's talking a lot, trying to convince her about something. He keeps touching his nose and mouth, though, and he's coughing from time to time, which means he's not telling the truth. It's not just that he's bragging in order to impress; he's actually lying... His clothes are expensive but in poor taste which, put together with his false gestures, might mean he's making money by illicit means. The girl is modestly dressed and wears no makeup, she looks provincial, a recent arrival. She'd been listening to him raptly for some time, with her face resting between her palms. But then she changed posture: she tilted her head, propping her cheek with her right hand, fingers curled into a fist except for the index finger. In body language terms, that's the posture of assessment. Next, a minimal but significant alteration: she extended all her fingers and rested her face on them, tilting it even more. That's the position of boredom. The boy, I'm afraid, didn't pass muster. Another change: she's been scratching the back of her neck repeatedly, as if saying, 'I don't really agree with you, but...' The boy carries on with his persuasion. She curls her fingers up again and brings them closer to her chin: she's preparing to make a decision. Sensing that, the boy reaches for her other, free hand. She doesn't withdraw it; he is now holding her hand. He's silent now: evidently, he's asked her a question and is waiting for an answer. She's answering now, letting him hold her hand, but her other hand is scratching the back of her neck, revealing a negative or a critical opinion of something, probably of herself. Most likely she's got a practical reason for accepting the young man's courtship – perhaps she hasn't got a place to stay or something..."

Jelena listened to the intoxicatingly sensuous voice, smitten, bewitched, like she used to be when, as a child, she listened to fairy tales. Body language, she thought in a languid, slowed-down kind of way... if someone were watching us now, he'd see we weren't husband and wife, because the way he's looking at me now, it can't be anything other than... the fabulous testosterone gaze... And the inviting mouth, twisted like a lazy snake. "I'm amazed," she said. "I'll always be conscious of my every movement now, whenever I'm with you." Why did everything she said to Pero sound ambiguous? Pero inclined towards her a bit. Again she noticed how intensely blue his eyes were.

"Just act naturally and don't try to lie." As he spoke, only his eyes seemed to smile.

"Tell me more," Jelena said, unconcerned about the clear sound of abandon in her request. Through the glass, she could see a man cross Preradović Street. His jacket was the same as Bruno's. Her thoughts wandered off.

"I'm not that riveting, am I," Pero said.

"It's not you, sorry, I was miles away," said Jelena.

"Where, exactly?" Pero asked.

They sat leaning towards each other, almost touching. One didn't have to know body language in order to understand what was going on.

"I must have bored you half to death with my ramblings?"

Not at all, not at all, not at all, Jelena repeated soundlessly. "I ought to be going," she said. "I've got to finish a text about Dora Maar."

Parting with a handshake, she felt again how large and warm his palm was. "See you," she said.

Pero nodded. He smiled, he was attractive. Jelena, too, felt attractive.

***

She arrived at the Gallery of Modern Art flushed, the way she used to be when she was late home from school, having tarried with another Pero, not daring to look her mum in the eye for fear mum might guess she had been kissing.

Only then she remembered she had forgotten to ask Pero if there was a law against leaving the engine running.

When she got back to the office, it was already dusk. She did not feel like writing. To postpone the inevitable, she phoned Ana. "Where have you been all day?" Ana assailed her at once, irritably and suspiciously.

"In the office and at the Modern," Jelena said.

"I phoned both the office and the Modern," said Ana. "You weren't there."

"You called the Modern? Oh dear. Why?"

"I thought we could meet up for coffee if you had the time."

"I had coffee with Pero," said Jelena, not because she felt like confessing but as an attempt to demystify coffee with Pero in her own eyes and turn it into an everyday, normal event.

"Pero who?"

"The Police Inspector, the one David introduced us to at the presentation..."

"What Inspector?"

"Oh my God, don't you remember? The handsome one that looks like Milan Štrljić in *King's Endgame*," Jelena said frivolously.

"How come you had coffee with him?" Ana asked reproachfully.

"We ran into each other, he invited me, I accepted and it was really nice.... Dangerous, but nice."

"Dangerous, but nice? You were having coffee with him all the time while I was trying to find you? Three whole hours?"

"Why do people always have to exaggerate?" Jelena complained, somewhat exasperated, knowing Ana would be hurt by being included among *people*, yet saying it. On purpose. "I left the office around noon, I got to the Modern before two. I don't know exactly how long the coffee thing took... if it matters."

"You know I know you," said Ana. "I can only say, mind what you're doing!"

"Thank you," said Jelena dryly. "Likewise... I mean, contrarywise," she finished impishly, but almost inaudibly.

"What was that, I didn't catch it?" Ana asked.

"Nothing. I'm off to write my text; I'm full of ideas," said Jelena.

"Have you been drinking?" Ana said.

"No. Speak soon," Jelena said and put the receiver down.

***

She could not write. Having checked that Andrej's office was empty, she called David.

"I hope this romantic adventure will make you kinder and more humane," David said, laughing.

"It reminds me of that movie with Danny de Vito, *Other People's Money,* the one we watched on DVD at mine. De Vito is a ruthless breaker of small businesses. The wife of the owner of a business he's about to shut down comes to see him, offering her own personal money to save it. And de Vito says to his PA, 'Harriet, why do I always bring out the best in people?' So my own mental flirt is going to make me more human, is that it? And the man was simply interested if I'd recovered from the accident," she replied.

"Uhm," said David. "At least our Inspectors are no longer the boorish oafs they used to be."

"That's right. Handsome, smart, brave, sensitive, strong and gentle."

"The key issue here is the state of your body chemistry," David said.

"There's been some recent research that confirms that everything hinges on the arrangement of elements. For example, happiness is not a consequence but a cause..."

"I was thinking of your post-Pero realisations, not of scientific research."

"Let me tell you the rest, it's interesting. Dopamine regulates your willpower; if you haven't got enough dopamine, you don't feel like doing anything... Anyway, I'm sure they'll soon be able to measure all the substances we need in order to be happy, and we'll simply get whatever we're short of from the pharmacy."

"It would be a shame if you couldn't share your thoughts with anyone," he said.

"Yeah, it feels as we haven't had a proper discussion for ages," Jelena said tenderly.

"I was thinking of your readers," David said.

"Thanks ever so much. What are you like! And here I go, believing you're my rock."

"Pero has stirred up your hormones; you need me to hold your legs so that you don't drift up like a balloon."

"Not hormones, not just yet (how I lie!), but, perhaps, my imagination. But you're right, I'm confused. I don't know if he affected my sex centre or my falling-in-love centre. Something like what Nina has done to you." And to Bruno, she thought.

David shook his head. "You know what the difference between men and women is? Men are always looking for adventure, for the Holy Grail, even if only in a video-game. And women... they're always looking for men. Chasing them, sometimes. Like in *Sex and the City...*"

"Fie, macho!" Jelena said.

"I don't mean chasing sex and dicks, I mean looking for love. And when a woman runs away from you rather than chase you, she becomes your adventure, the goal of your game, the reason for your existence..."

"Like the *Angelic Trap* to you."

"That *is* the angelic trap," David confirmed, in the phenomenological rather than the concrete sense. "That's how the Cult of the Adored Woman came into being. The female saint whom you mustn't offend by sinful thoughts was not created by Catholicism but by the male need for adventure and conquest."

"And what about a woman who does it on purpose – seduces and then rejects you in order to be your Grail; what is she? A she-devil?"

"From the male perspective, such a situation doesn't exist. Only other women see it; generally other women who are not themselves adored by anyone."

"Wait a minute, you're saying that women, in effect, don't exist except as a male illusion... at best?"

David did not reply. "At the end of the day," Jelena went on, "the bare fact is, my hands are still shaking." "That's your adrenaline surplus which can be harmful if not used up. Pure chemistry," said David.

"What I'd really like would be to call him and disappear with him for five days somewhere to an Alpine hut... But I'm not going to. I want to be the Grail."

"In the meantime, we could go to the cinema. It's been two months since we've last seen a movie," David said. "They're showing *Crash*, your kind of film."

***

That night, at home in bed, she turned towards Bruno and laid her head on his shoulder. She recalled the conversation about happiness she had with David and laughed quietly.

"How are your chemicals doing?" she asked Bruno.

"What chemicals?"

"Never mind."

He shook his head. Jelena reached down for his groin. Like a well-tuned instrument, Bruno's hand travelled towards her breasts. For a moment she could see Pero's full, dark lower lip, almost indecently sensuous. She wondered if Bruno was thinking of Nina. They might be cheating on each other at this very moment, she thought.

The Hand

23 January

TOMORROW IS THE MOST DEPRESSING DAY OF THE YEAR

25 January

THE FRONT PAGE: The first interview with the greatest Croatian rock legend: Johnny is the same as he was 15 years ago

Johnny Štulić: I was Kurt Cobain's inspiration and *Nirvana* used my music

Asked why he was refusing to return to Croatia, he replied, "Did you know that there's a species of monkey that, before eating it, stuffs a nut up its anus? If it can make it through, the monkey eats it. If not, it doesn't."

26 January

THE NUMBER OF TSUNAMI VICTIMS: 297 THOUSAND

242

Ana Discovers that Andreja is Being Abused – December

The children at her school approached Ana with increasing friendliness. Diminutive, sloppy, always in trousers, trainers and huge t-shirts, she looked like one of them. They readily confided in her, demanded that she joins them in bunking lessons and used her as their advocate when they sought postponement of exams. All the children did, that is, only Andreja Martić did not.

Ana kept a discreet eye on Andreja. The girl was a perennial outsider, a classic example of low self esteem and failure to belong to a group; it did not take an expert to figure out what was going on. Ana approached her slowly and cautiously, as if walking a tightrope. She knew that "Whatever may have happened to you, I can help" would be the wrong thing to say, because it might scare her off and push her over the edge.

She found the school pedagogue's comments in the girl's file: *concentration and memory problems; no notable incidents; a stable family situation; parents are intellectuals with solid incomes; no special comments; no further action required.* He had not spotted anything out of the ordinary. They never spot anything out of the ordinary, Ana thought.

By the end of the half-term, Andreja had eight 'grade ones'[108]. Her attendance was poor. She was sent to the school pedagogue for chats. The Senior Leadership discussed possible strategies. They called the parents in, but only her father came. Her mother, he said, was on tour with the show. The father said he'd noticed that Andreja's behaviour had changed. He'd asked her if something had been troubling her but she said that everything was fine. That made him believe that whatever the problem was, it could not have been anything serious; he thought it boiled down to a teenage hormone storm... he asked the school for advice: should he take his daughter to a good private psychologist, for example? He was prepared to

---

[108] A 'one' is the lowest grade in Croatian schools. It means, 'unsatisfactory', 'fail'. A 'five' is the highest grade. It means 'excellent'.

cooperate in every way, do anything to ensure his daughter's well-being.

Ana noticed that Andreja was losing weight. She was confident in her diagnosis: a sexually abused child. All the symptoms were there: guilty behaviour, withdrawal, the hunched body posture to hide the breasts, an even greater feeling of guilt and even disgust at the arrival of periods... Reporting it would mean being brushed off as someone with a wild imagination and a tendency to exaggerate. She would be able to offer no proof in support of her suspicions as violence of this kind was the hardest to prove. She knew however that she could no longer remain a bystander; she had to take action of some kind. Her careful approach was not yielding any results. Thus, one day, she simply kept Andreja behind after school in her office. It all turned out to be easier than she thought. "I know what's going on," she said, bluntly. "Don't be afraid. It'll all be over and everything will be all right. You'll be free from him, whoever he might be." Andreja responded with a frozen, wide-eyed stare. "It can all be sorted, only you mustn't remain silent. It'll all be fine, trust me. Do you know how I know?"

Andreja glanced up to her as if woken from a dream and shook her head. "How?"

That was a confession. "Because I went through the same nightmare," Ana said softly.

Andreja watched her silently and waited.

"And now it's all right. It's all behind me. No one can hurt me now. I know you're longing to be free again, to be able to go to bed without worries, safe in the knowledge that you'll be able to sleep undisturbed till morning..."

Tears were rolling down Andreja's face, but her head remained straight and her eyes focused.

"Who's doing this to you?" Ana asked gently. "Your parents' friend? A relative?"

Andreja shook her head.

"Your father?" Ana approached the delicate issue with hesitation.

Andreja shook her head resolutely. "A neighbour," she said.

The voice of child psychologist at the Centre for the Care of Children had a no-nonsense, professional ring to it when she answered Ana's call. "What is the problem with the child?" she asked sonorously.

"The child is being sexually abused," Ana said.

"A girl?"

"Yes."

"How old is she?"

"Not quite fifteen."

"Right," the woman said, "come and see me tomorrow at 11."

"Brilliant," said Ana. "I thought one waited for weeks."

"One does," said the woman, "but cases like yours have priority."

Ana liked the way the place was organised, like in American movies. When she handed in Andreja's medical card, she heard a voice behind the counter say, "That girl who's been abused by her father is here."

"Good, call her in at once."

Ana recognised the female voice from the day before. She knocked and said quietly, worried that Andreja might overhear: "Excuse me, the girl was abused by a neighbour, not by her father."

"Really?" The woman seemed to be disappointed. "And when did it start?" she asked.

"Five years ago," said Ana, "when she was ten."

"Right," Dr Bančić said, now quite visibly disappointed. Dr Bančić, Ana remembered later, was the high profile leader of the team at the Centre and hardly a week would pass without her appearing on TV. Sexual abuse of children was her specialty.

Ana felt that Andreja's treatment by Dr Bančić's team had been superficial and routine. The conclusion was that *the amount of harmful influence the exposure to sexual abuse had on the growing process and the personality of the child could not be established and that further outpatient treatment at their clinic was recommended and the possibility of criminal charges against the abuser needed to be considered...* Andreja didn't want to say who the abuser was and begged Ana not to say anything to her parents.

"That doesn't depend on me," Ana said. "The centre will inform your parents and probably call them in for interviews. And even if they didn't, I still couldn't promise not to say anything, because at no point have you told me that the abuse had stopped."

"Ask them to give me more time, please," Andreja said. "I'd like to tell my parents myself."

"All right," said Ana, "I'll try." She got Dr Bančić to agree not to inform the parents immediately as Andreja was afraid of the uproar it might cause, and that all the notifications should be sent to the school, specifically to her as the school psychologist. Dr Bančić exceptionally agreed because she and Ana were colleagues, and also because her interest in the case had somehow lost its edge.

Andreja commented later, astutely: "I have a feeling these guys are disappointed I'm not a complete wreck or something." She was distant and buttoned up with the doctor the way she was with teachers at her school.

"You've got to talk to them," said Ana. "Or else they might send you to hospital for treatment."

"They won't understand, no matter what I say." Andreja looked at Ana with the beginnings of trust in her eyes.

"We recognise each other," said Ana, returning a firm look. "There are many of us, more than you think, and we have to speak out. We mustn't give our abusers another chance, not ever again!"

The last day of school before Christmas Holidays, Ana told Andreja that she was happy to keep taking her to the Centre, although they wouldn't be seeing each other in the school.

"I won't be here, Andreja said. "I'm going skiing with mum. Don't worry about me."

On her way home, Ana saw a youngish man chatting with two girls aged nine or perhaps ten. "Let's go, I've got a sledge in my car," he said. The girls were standing there. Ana thought he was a paedophile, but merely walked past him just the same: what if he wasn't a paedophile; what if he was a dad taking his kids up Mt Sljeme[109]? She tossed the affair in her mind all day. At home in the evening, she did not feel like talking to her mother and went straight to her bedroom.

"You've stopped eating again," her mother squawked. "You're all shrivelled up."

Ana had a headache. Worn out, she fell asleep only towards the morning.

The Hand

6 February

CROATIAN RADIO: *Lonely Planet*, the well-know publisher of travel guides, declared Croatia to be the second most desirable travel destination in the world.

8 February

OF THE SEVEN DEADLY SINS, ONLY GREED SURVIVES

"Wrath, gluttony, sloth, envy, pride and lust are out of date. The new sins for the 21st century, alongside greed which remains, are cruelty, treachery, narrow-mindedness, insincerity, hypocrisy and selfishness.

The research was carried out by the BBC Religious Programme on a sample of 1000 interviewees. The survey discovered that wrath was considered to be number one on the list of the original deadly sins, followed by pride, envy, gluttony, lust, sloth and greed. The original list was compiled by Pope Gregory the Great in the 6th century and represents the vices which stand in opposition to love of God. The list has changed through the centuries and thus there should be no obstacles to modernising it to include behaviours which represent the greatest sins of today – at least according to the Britons that took part in the survey."

---

[109] The highest peak (1035 m) of Mt Medvednica, the mountain just north of Zagreb

Jelena Spots Bruno with Nina

On the morning of the 24th, Jelena did not have to go to work. She took no joy in the holiday and did not feel like doing anything. Bruno had left; he was doing a short day. She dragged herself listlessly to the market. She bought a chicken and some salad, a slab of cooking chocolate, some walnuts and a few eggs, just in case. She did not feel like blowing money on champagne. She halted before an advertising board which proclaimed in large letters, PRICE SLASH! HAKE, FROZEN, HEADLESS 14.97, like something from a horror movie. Back home, she phoned David but he did not answer either his home or his work phone. Ditto his mobile. The recorded message announced, *you've dialled an unrecognised number, you've dialled an unrecognised number...* endlessly. She checked the number in her address book: 0915358628. It was, simply, one of those days when even your best friend's phone number did not exist. She gave it another go. One more time, the same mechanical voice. She thought she might spot David somewhere in the centre, having, perhaps, a beer in *Bulldog*.

She got off the tram at the National Theatre, continuing on foot down Masaryk Street, through the former Balkan Passage to the Flower Market and then to Bogović Street. The crowds irritated her. She put her head through the door of *Bulldog*. It was packed. There was no sign of David: always more visible and audible than anyone else, he would have been easy to spot. Nothing. She walked on along Gaj Street towards Jelačić Square, paused before *Algoritam's* shop-window out of habit but with little interest, and then moved on to the glass front of Dubrovnik Hotel's aperitif bar. She stood there as if in front of a shop-window until she remembered that there were people sitting inside, most likely wondering what that woman outside was doing staring at them through the glass. As she moved off, however, she heard a knock on the glass pane. She leaned towards it – someone inside was waving at her. At last, she thought, I can have a coffee in company. For a moment she hoped it would be Pero but did not dare admit her hope even to herself. But it was not Pero. It was Bruno. She was glad and suddenly full of tenderness, partly masking the guilt about her hope that it might be Pero. But what is Bruno doing here? And who is he with? She went back to the door and entered. Nina was waving at her from the table at the back. Fancy that, she's here too, Jelena thought. Only then did she realise that Nina was sitting next to Bruno whom she could still only see from the back. Jelena forced a smile, aware she had to act normal. She tried to be warm with Nina and "normal" with Bruno. What would count as normal in a situation like this? Jealousy wouldn't be normal. Why couldn't this just be a friendly sojourn over coffee?

"What are you doing here?" she seemed to have heard herself ask. It felt more normal than asking, "What are you two doing here together?" The answer had to be the same anyway.

"We ran into each other," Bruno said.

"We ran into each other," said Nina almost at the same time.

Jelena's thoughts whirled. Anxiety: am I going to join the ranks of the abandoned? Hope: he knocked on the window to get my attention; he didn't have to do that. Suspicion: did he knock because he thought I might have seen him? Hypocrisy: what if it had been Pero knocking? Ah, yes, but to cheat and to be cheated is not one and the same thing. When you cheat, you gain; when you're being cheated, you lose, you lose...

"What are you doing for New Year's Eve?" Nina asked.

"We'll be at home," Jelena said. Bruno didn't answer. He doesn't want to discuss anything involving me, Jelena thought, it isn't sexy. "And you?"

Nina laughed. "Me? In bed, with a hot chocolate and a good book." It sounded mouth-watering. She was almost to be envied her delicious solitude. Jelena imagined how Bruno imagined Nina's New Year's Eve: Nina sipping chocolate, Nina putting her pyjamas on, Nina curling up in bed... yum, yum.

"Hello... Earth to Jelena?" Nina's voice drifted into her thoughts.

"Sorry? I didn't get that," Jelena replied, confused.

"I see," Nina laughed.

Perched on the edge of her armchair, Jelena did not want to order anything. "I ought to be going," she said.

"Me too," Nina chimed in readily. "I've got loads to do..."

They all got up. "I'm going towards the Square," Nina said. "You?" She said goodbye and fluttered away.

Jelena looked at Bruno. "I've left the car on Svačić Place," Bruno said.

"Can I come with you?" Jelena asked.

"What sort of a question is that?"

"I mean, are you going back to work or are you going home?" She sounded neutral, emotionless. She decided not to question him, but did not last beyond the corner of Gaj Street and the Green Wave. "How come you were with Nina?" she asked, looking away.

"I told you, we ran into each other."

"You already said that."

"I told you I already had."

"Do you have coffee with everyone you run into?" Jelena persisted. "No, you don't. So I'm asking, why have coffee with Nina in particular, what is the *differentia specifica*?"

"Nothing; we saw each other, said hello, she asked me things about the software..."

"Who proposed coffee?"

"No idea."

They were silent in the car. Jelena turned the radio on. There was a programme about lost pets on Radio Sljeme: *Golden retriever found on Ban Jelačić Square. Wearing a red collar with the number 1267 on the attached tag...* "Retrievers are so lovely," she said, all soft and gooey at the thought, "It let a perfect stranger check the number on its tag..."

At home, with Bruno ensconced at his computer, she looked for the note with Pero's number in her wallet. She dialled the numbers slowly, without thinking. Before she got to the last number, she put the receiver down.

Venice, After Christmas

As part of her upbringing programme, Buba had planned to

take her children to Venice. She did not ask David to come along, but he proposed it himself. When the departure day began to loom, however, he could not travel because of his work, and Buba asked Ana to come instead, so that the ticket would not go to waste. Ana, of course, did not feel like going. "Why?" Buba said. "Don't be so inert. There won't be any crowds around; Christmas is over. The school is still out, you have no other obligations and it'll help you wait for the *Uliks* nominations."

Ana wanted to stay because of Andreja, but there was nothing she could do outside the school, anyway. "If I could write about travel like Pauletić," she said, "I'd gladly go." She agreed to go in the end and wrote a short piece about her Venetian trip as an exercise. She decided she would show it to Buba in a few years' time, like an old memento.

Buba booked a hotel in Mestre because it cost less and there was a fast bus and rail connection to Venice.

Hana was disappointed. "I'd rather go to Vienna," she said.

Buba said, "You say that because you haven't the first clue of what Venice is."

"Do they have H&M at all?" Hana asked grouchily.

On their first morning in Mestre, Buba enquired about the huge Friday market she had been going on about during the trip down: she used to buy shoes and handbags in Mestre, and sometimes she would buy nice outfits at the market, outfits that made her look "the hottest chick in Zagreb". Hana dictated to her the question for the receptionist: *"Venti anni fa c' e stato un... mercato... venerdi..."* The receptionist nodded knowingly. Of course he knew. He extended his arm and pointed at where they were to cross the street. Just cross and it would be there.

Buba's famous market turned out to be a string of stands, one on each side of the street, with tiny Chinese men and women, along with an occasional Gypsy or a swarthy Italian from the south, selling socks in bundles of ten, scarves, pashminas, polyester tops and faux leather (or, more elegantly put, ecological leather) jackets. "Jesus, what a bunch of peasants you lot used to be," Matko said. Hana didn't even want to look at the stands; she stared straight ahead and managed to mutter through her teeth, "How you humiliated us with the receptionist! We'll have to buy something in an exclusive shop now so that we have a decent bag to carry as we get back in."

The receptionist told them the bus for Venice was to be found around the corner (1 euro per passenger) and that it went directly to Piazzale Roma, from where one could get to Piazza San Marco along the Grand Canal.

"I once stood in San Marco, surrounded by three Italians courting me, and a painter from Sarajevo who gave me a rose," Buba said to Ana. "That's the only thing I can remember from my first trip to Venice. We were going there to see the Biennale. And I remember how jealous David was."

Hana laughed.

"You've pricked your ears up, haven't you," Buba said to her.

Looking for directions, they wandered along the canals and over the bridges. Everything looked deserted; it could have been around three in the afternoon.

"Where are all the people?" Hana asked.

"Must be resting after Christmas," Buba said.

"This Venice isn't much, innit?" Matko said. "A real desert."

When they reached San Marco, the children were visibly disappointed. "Is that it?"

"We didn't prepare ourselves," Ana said. "We should've researched a bit what we were planning to see here. The Doge's Palace, for example... defying the laws of architecture: all airy, lacy structure below, and up there, massive walls... Shylock was tried here... This tower is called the Campanille; it is completely made of brick. It stood here for several centuries and then in 1902, all by itself, it tumbled down and was later rebuilt to be exactly the same as it was before. In the basilica, we ought to see the Pala d'Oro, the Golden Panel..."

"I've had enough," said Hana. "I'm hungry."

"Let's leave the square and find a restaurant," Buba said. "Here on the Piazza everything is terribly expensive."

Hana remembered the way back to the bus by shop-windows, t-shirts, handbags and even earrings she had seen along the way. Matko shook his head scornfully and traced it on the map.

The return to the bus stop was much faster than the trek into town. They got off two stops too soon and in the end, frozen and weary, could not find the hotel. Ana approached a man with a child to ask the way: "*Signore, prego...*" and he just gave her a strange look, pulled the child's hand and walked away from her. Hana laughed and said, "He thought you were begging."

It was already dark. Suddenly, they could hear a cry, then noise and a clamour of voices. Someone shouted, "*Qualcos' è successo? Qualcos' è successo?*" Fearful, they hurried along in silence. When they arrived at the hotel, they felt their courage return and slowed down.

"Didn't you hear someone say, *È già morto!*" Hana said.

"Oh come on, stop making things up," said Matko.

"I heard it, you wally!" Hana said.

Later, in their room, they discussed perfect crime. "I don't understand why no one has thought of it before," Hana said, "but I think that killing someone with a block of ice must be the perfect crime. The ice melts and there's no murder weapon."

"You don't say," Matko retorted at once. "To start with, for a perfect crime, to find no weapon is not enough. There mustn't be a motive, that's essential. And then, the melt water could be analysed and particles of blood would be found in it, and everything would become clear..."

"All right then, I have an even better idea," said Hana. "Someone could take a frozen chicken, take it out of the bag, whack the bloke on the head with it and then defrost the chicken quickly in hot water and roast it and all the evidence would be gone..."

"Stop it!" Buba shouted. "I'm not letting you watch that stupid *CSI* show again. And I'm not taking you to Venice again if that's all it makes you think of!"

A Writer's Truth

Ana sat down to write an e-mail to Anton.

I was listening on the radio to that soldier who'd defended our country in the War of Independence and written six books about it, ending each one with the same sentence: "If someone believes my account not to be true, let him write his own truth, as long as he doesn't allow anyone else to write our truths for us." When you write well, it is as if you're telling the truth and therefore always know what you've said previously and never waffle or trip over yourself. And when you write badly, it is as if someone were constantly lying, not knowing any more what he'd said to whom, and everyone knows he's a liar and no one believes anything he says. That is an important rule that must always be borne in mind. And rule number two: cut everything that can be cut. If you can tell your story in two words, do so...

She neither finished nor sent the e-mail. She could not even remember why she had wanted to write it in the first place.

Mortadella *LeGrand*

In Venice, Buba understood that Venice, like New Year's Eve, made sense only when one was young, beautiful, in love or ready to fall in love. When one was at the age of getting ready to mate, displaying most wonderful ornaments like a peacock in order to find a mate and positively glowing with desire: "Look at me, look at me, love me!" Actually, what went for Venice and New Year's Eve went for life in general.

She phoned David whom she had not seen since the Venice trip.

"Shall I come over?" David asked.

"No, no, I'll come to yours," Buba replied. When she arrived, she mechanically cleared up the stray bits from the side table in the sitting room and put a handful of multicoloured Murano glass beads into a glass bowl: "A prezzie from Hana." She made two instant cappuccinos and sat down.

"And, how was it?" David asked.

"Do you remember that navy suit I used to have, a miniskirt

and a jacket? You adored it but told me that drivers honking at me whenever I was wearing it drove you mad?"

"Of course I remember," David said.

"It was a good label, *LeGrand*, and it was expensive. I bought it at the market in Mestre. The kids laughed at me when I told them: what LeGrand, they'd never heard of that label, and what a rubbish market it was, worse than Hrelić[110]... And then Matko, out of the blue, shouted, 'There's your *LeGrand*!' Delighted, I rushed to take a look – and you know what it turned out to be? A great big *LeGrand*-brand mortadella. I burst into tears, and the kids comforted me, thinking I was crying because my memories of Mestre had been ruined. But that wasn't it. At breakfast that morning, I'd barely managed to squeeze between our table and the neighbouring one, full of skinny Japanese, worse luck, all sitting tucked in close to the table in their disciplined way. I fumed about there being too many tables so that one couldn't even move around. Well, thanks to *LeGrand* mortadella, I understood that the space between tables had not become smaller, but rather that I had traversed the long journey between *LeGrand* mini skirt and *LeGrand* mortadella."

David regarded her with smiling eyes. "Not true, but witty. And the kids?"

"Ah, the kids.... their impressions were pretty subjective, too. When, after a whole day's traipsing around Venice, we got off the bus at Mestre, the kids said, 'City, at last!' Matko said he couldn't live in Venice because it was stuffy and filthy, and Hana said she couldn't either because it was *too unreal.*"

"One simply can't squeeze a proper account out of you guys," David laughed.

"In any case, they quarrelled so much I nearly left them there with Ana and returned to Zagreb." It was nice, moaning to David. His eyes still smiled at her. "They've become pretty horrible, those two," Buba said. "We agreed about who does what at home: Matko makes beds, Hana hoovers bedrooms and

---

[110] Famous flea market on the outskirts of Zagreb

mops the kitchen floor; I cook and wash the dishes. But they hadn't done anything for days. They've got studying to do, or Hana is depressive, or Matko must get together with the girl he met on his summer holiday: she's from Split and in Zagreb for a few days only... This morning I blew my top. I told them I wouldn't come back home until they called me and told me they'd done their chores, even if it meant sleeping at the theatre."

"Clever," David said.

Almost simultaneously, their mobiles rang. Buba was being called by Matko, David by Nina.

"Just so you know," said Matko without as much as a hello, "teenagers are incapable of certain emotions, such as compassion. Experiments were done with little kids and with teenagers; they were shown photos of people feeling various emotions: pain, sadness, anger and what not. You know what they discovered? Little kids understood everything, while teenagers didn't have a clue when they were asked what the people in the pictures felt. Geddit?"

Buba smiled, but her voice was serious when she replied, "And? What do you suggest?"

"Very simply, instead of expecting us to remember our chores or to do them out of pity for you, just give us our tasks, and that's that. If we don't do them, punish us; end of."

"Okay, we'll talk about it at home."

She went on smiling. David had already finished his conversation and was regarding her thoughtfully. Not without pride, Buba related what Matko had said.

Kiddager

Bruno and Jelena spent New Year's Eve at home. They declined Jelena's parents' invitation to dinner and did not invite them over. David was away on business. Ana had to stay with her mother who was not feeling well, and even if that had not been the case, she would have stayed at home as she always did. Buba did not mind welcoming the New Year in an armchair, watching telly. She remembered her colleague Ana Karić saying that for her, New Year's Eve simply meant the chance of an early night, as she would not have to be on stage, there being no performance that night. She felt sorry for Hana, though: no one had invited her so she, too, stayed at home. She and Buba fell asleep on the sofa with a half-empty bottle of *Bollinger 1997*, real champagne David had brought from France long before Davor Butković had written about it. They had been keeping it for a special occasion.

Matko got home in the morning. Buba was already having coffee in the kitchen, reading the paper and waiting for him to arrive with some unease. Hearing the key in the door, she heaved a sigh of relief. "You're late," she said, planting a kiss on his cheek.

"Sorry," said Matko. "The girl was staying the night; I couldn't jolly well leave before her like a sissy, now, could I?"

"Jesus, what's that on your neck!" said Buba in horror. "Did you have a fight? Let me see!"

"It's nothing," said Matko, raising his collar.

"Let me see, I said! What on earth happened?" Buba shouted, folding the collar down again. There was a large purplish-red mark on Matko's neck.

"What are you two yelling about?" Hana called from her bed. "As soon as he gets home, the madhouse starts!"

"What happened?" Buba asked.

Matko laughed. "I'm telling you, nothing."

Only when she saw him laugh did Buba understand she was looking at a *love bite*. "Oh dear, what a vampire that must've been!" she said.

Matko laughed proudly. "You wouldn't have a clue, mum."

Buba looked at him and then she, too, laughed. "Would I not, hm?"

"Yeah, well, I mean, you *would*... but you wouldn't," said Matko.

"How will you go to school on Monday, looking like that?"

Matko shrugged with feigned indifference, but could not hide a proud smile.

"Want to eat something?" Buba asked.

"You bet! I'm starving!"

"Help yourself, then,"

"In that case, I'm not hungry," said Matko.

"And, just so you know," Buba said, "I think I ought to tell you – and you can check it with your dad if you want to – "

"Yeah, what, skip the intro," said Matko, giving her a protective hug.

"I should tell you that those vampire kisses, they're only... you know what they demonstrate? They show you're just playing at sex. They make it obvious that you don't yet know what sex and love are. You still have a childish idea of it all. Real sex is much tenderer. I'm telling you so that you know, so that you're not ashamed of tenderness. You don't need any acrobatics or SM. All you have to do is act as you feel."

"That means I'm still just a kiddager," Matko said good-naturedly and cleverly.

The next morning, David came over to fetch the children for a trip to Samobor, as they traditionally did on the first of January of every year. Buba told him the "kiddager" story. David laughed. He thought how it was never boring with Buba around.

The New Year – the Aftermath

"Happy New Year," Bruno and Jelena called out as the door opened. "How are you?"

"We serve our purpose," Jelena's father said.

Thank God my dad's hale and well, Jelena thought. "Did you have a good time?"

"As good as we could have under the circumstances," dad said. "I didn't even get a chance to test my staggering skills, as Kata had limited my alcohol consumption."

"Would you listen to him, going on and on about himself," mum said. "He sang *Milena, my degeneration*[111], *if only we'd met sooner* all night long..."

---

[111] Jelena's father is phere paraphrasing the lyrics of a popular rock ballad; "Milena, of my generation, if only....etc."

"But before that, I sang *I feeeeel so high; goodbye, o drugs, goodbyyyyyyye...* and she forbade me to."

"Dad, really, you're not the only one who's getting old! Let's have a bit of optimism!" Jelena said.

"Optimism? That's Past Perfect, baby."

"Knock it off," said Kata resolutely. "You always have silly stuff to talk about just before lunch. The table is set, everyone. I've made a *gregada*[112]. How's your mum?" she said, turning to Bruno. "Have you been to see her?"

"We have," Bruno replied. "She's fine and sends her regards."

"Thanks, give her mine, too."

"Mum, we said we weren't going to eat," Jelena said.

"Come on, come on," her father said. "It's a freebie-greebie. Not to be missed."

"Jesus!" mum's voice could be heard from the kitchen. "Looks like it's stuck to the bottom a bit. I hope I haven't burned it."

"You always burn food," dad said. "Because doing three things at the same time is a favourite hobby of yours."

"For shame, how can you talk like that about me! Hobby! Cleaning, doing the laundry, cooking, washing up, those are my hobbies all right. I really have to rush to get round to them all! Right now, for example, I can't wait to get stuck into my favourite hobby, ironing!" Mother was really angry.

The telly was on, as usual: the news, starting with the report about the snowstorm that had engulfed all Croatia. The Winter Services spokesman was saying, "I believe people think that this is the first snow of the year here in Zagreb."

"He didn't say whether *he* thought it was the first snow or not," dad said.

Next, the anchor from Rijeka was reporting from the scene. "Luckily, both drivers were injured but there were no fatalities." Jelena and her father laughed out loud. The previous

---

[112] A simple but delicious Dalmatian dish of fish, potatoes, onions, garlic and olive oil.

year's statistics followed: what Croats had done on New Year's Eve and how much money they'd spent.

"See what great travel deals for pensioners there were to be had," Kata said. "Only, we couldn't go anywhere..."

"Mum, you should've told us you wanted to go; we'd have helped," said Jelena quietly.

"As if! You know your dad, he'd never accept," mum replied just as quietly.

"As if, indeed," said Karlo. "I'm sick of pensioners' deals. The bank sells you a package you then pay back at the rate of 50 kuna per month. For this, they give you a discount on an African safari, and it is a well known fact that Croatian pensioners simply can't be kept away from African safaris. But in exchange for that, you pay two kuna for every flipping cheque you issue, and a big fat charge on every credit card which wears out in a month, so that you don't know the number of your own account unless you've written it down somewhere safe... The fact that these days banks have 'products' says it all. I heard it somewhere the other day: banking products, they said. And what can a banking product be? Can you touch it, wear it, eat it?"

"You always have to be different from everyone else," mum said curtly.

As if starting an argument, Dad asked, "Do you or don't you know how one sows carrots?"

"Ugh, there he goes again," mum snorted.

"No; how?" asked Jelena to defuse the budding argument.

"You make two parallel furrows along the patch and scatter your seeds in, spacing them out by eye. They mustn't be too close together or too far apart. If they're too far apart, they might not grow at all, and if they're too close together, you'll get runty carrots, neither juicy nor sweet..."

"Yeah, and?"

"And do you know which seeds produce the best carrots? The ones that end up a bit away from those in the furrow. Such carrots grow the biggest and strongest of them all, the tastiest and the juiciest, and one of those is worth more than a hundred, no, a thousand of those ordinary, worthless ones..."

Kata snorted contemptuously.

"So you see, Kata," said dad turning to her, "I am that carrot growing on the side."

"You are, are you?" mum said. "So what? Even the biggest carrots get eaten in the end, just like the runty ones."

The Hand

THE CHRONICLE: HUNGER, DISEASE AND ENVIRONMENTAL CATASTROPHE THREATEN THE PLANET

-2 billion people suffer from hunger

-434 million people have no safe drinking water

-Around 42% of carbon emissions come from the burning of oil which produces 37% of energy on Earth

-1000 billion dollars a year is spent on arms

-Every day, between 50 and 100 animal and plant species disappear forever

-The consequences of climate change kill 120,000 people a year

They obviously didn't count the Christmas tsunami victims in.

Ana Makes the *Uliks* Selection

With unanticipated trepidation, Ana opened the paper on the page with the list of nominees for the *Uliks* prize. She felt tension at the back of her neck and a sick feeling in her stomach. Unable to find her name, she felt brief disappointment and then remembered to look for David's. She breathed a sigh of relief. David had made the final selection. An onrush of joy flashed inside her and fled, leaving only tension.

Jelena called her. She could hear displeasure in Ana's voice. "What's the matter?"

"I've just seen the *Uliks* nominees," Ana said.

"That's why I'm calling you! You've seen it, then! Good, eh?"

"Yeah, perfect."

"Eppur si mouove!" Jelena cried, ignoring Ana's gloomy voice. No, really, that girl was...

Ana said nothing. Later, she sat down at her computer and wrote:

Dear Anton,

What would it mean to me, were my book to become a hit or win the Nobel Prize? What would a mad painter gain from a grand retrospective exhibition? Of what use is literary fame and stature to a drunkard? Who needs all that anyway? Ordinary people? Normal people? Not they. They're too busy with the real world to invent new ones. Perhaps because of the children? Yes, perhaps that's it. People are physical beings. And books are dead objects...

Her head ached. Her head always ached when she worked at the computer. This time, she sent the e-mail.

Anton replied:

We spend our lives doing stupid, irrelevant things. Time is really there to be wasted, that is its true purpose. There is no such thing as a great life, but achievements can be great, because they remain. Your book is one of them. How can such a generous, high-spirited artist be such a spiritless woman?

Jelena called her again a bit later. She had an uncomfortable feeling that Ana should not be left alone. "Did you manage to get your head round it yet?" she asked breezily.

Ana sighed. "I'm sorry to be such a bore, but... only normal people can enjoy awards and literary fame, precisely because they're normal. They enjoy them in the same way as they enjoy their children, their home, swimming in the sea, drinking wine. They have to be content in order to enjoy things, and they have to enjoy things in order to be content. Some enjoy, others write, got it?"

"I'm following your argument with difficulty," Jelena said, trying to sound relaxed. "You know what Boris Mutić said when he retired: 'When I can't chop wood any more, I'll write my memoirs. But until that time comes, I'll keep chopping wood, because I enjoy doing it.'"

"There you are," said Ana. "And I'm already writing."

"That reminds me of the last in that series of Tibetan exercises, the one where you don't need sex any more and are consequently redirecting your energy..." Jelena said laughing, and then went on seriously: "You always think you've got all the answers, that's your problem. And you're so hard, exclusive, so... *intransigent*."

"You're right," said Ana. "I'm just a nuisance to you all."

"You know that's not true," said Jelena with a sigh.

The Hand

15 February

ZAGREB: THIS YEAR, THE AIR IS SEVEN TIMES MORE POLUTED: More than 60% of carbon emissions are said to be generated by traffic...

FOUR CHILDREN QUEUE FOR EACH HOSPITAL BED: Last year 55 children were diagnosed with tumour, whilst for years the oncology department at the Children's Hospital has had only 14 beds.

21 February

Zagreb: Soup kitchens serve four times as many people as in 2000

Dolce & Gabanna soon to open their first Zagreb shop

23 February

SCANDALOUS DISCOVERY: 500 foetuses stored illegally in St Peter's Hospital freezer.

A new law banning IVF treatment is being discussed. The Church has raised its voice. A doctor charged with stealing egg cells from his female patients and implanting them into women who came to him for IVF treatment is being tried in court. *I can't see anything wrong with IVF. The only problem is records. Records need to be kept meticulously so that a woman doesn't, for example, receive her husband's sister's egg and ends up carrying a child conceived by a brother and a sister.*

David in Hospital with Pneumonia

One afternoon a few days after his *Uliks* nomination, David got
soaked, caught by a sudden shower while accompanying Nina
to a taxi. He shared Nina's cab up to Lisinski Concert Hall,
from which point he continued on foot. He had given his
umbrella to Nina, but had decided to walk anyway rather than
squeeze into a packed tram. By the evening, he had a runny
nose; the following morning he was coughing badly and
running a high temperature in the afternoon. That evening he
felt quite weak and was feeling his aching chest gingerly over.

She's obviously not good for you, Buba thought when she
heard he had fallen ill.

Whenever he was ill, David would call Buba as if they were
still married. ("He hasn't got a mum, after all, poor chap,"
Hana had said.) That evening, when he phoned, Buba said,
laughing: "Gravely ill again?"

"I can't breathe," David said. "My whole right side is
paralysed, from shoulder to the end of the ribcage... dreadful!"

"Have you got temperature?" Buba asked, practical as ever.

"Yeah," said David wearily, but almost proudly. "38.5."

"You ought to see the doctor, there's viral pneumonia going
round."

"Pneumonia?" David was frightened.

They got to the A&E department of the Hospital for
Contagious Diseases around ten in the evening. The waiting
room was full and the air was thick and malodorous. The
patients were mainly parents with small children. Buba could
practically feel herself chewing bacteria and viruses; she could
almost hear them crunch under her teeth. Exhausted, David
sank onto the only empty chair while Buba queued at the
reception desk. A woman in white hospital trousers and white
clogs, with a warm coat thrown over her hospital top, kept
passing through the waiting room on some kind of errand.
David's eyes followed her every time. When Buba had sat down
next to him, he leant towards her and whispered, "She takes the
patients who are to stay in hospital to their wards."

"How do you know?"

"I've been watching her. She looks like the guide taking people to the Nether World." The woman kept going out and returning with family members and bundles of personal possessions. Whenever there was no one to usher, she would mop the muddy floor in the waiting room, particularly the filthy puddle in front of the desk.

Back from seeing the doctor, David said sadly, "I'm staying. They haven't got anyone to operate the x-ray machine at this time of night."

It was already half past midnight. Buba patted his arm and said, "Don't worry; it's better like this than having to come back in the morning." He cast a timorous glance at the usher who was approaching with a wad of paper in her hands. "Let's go," she said.

Ward One, Room Five resembled a five star hotel rather than a hospital: sparkling clean floor and wall tiles, subdued lighting, a young, pretty and pleasant nurse, an en-suite bathroom with a separate toilet. Only one of the three beds was occupied: a small, grey-haired head peeked from under the blanket.

"Here you are, madam," said the nurse. "the phone numbers for the room, the ward sister and the doctor on duty. And the visiting times. But you can bring whatever your husband needs first thing in the morning..." Buba said goodbye and left, but David took off after her, panting, and caught up with her at the exit. "We haven't said goodbye properly," he said. Buba looked at him, astonished. "They're preparing an IV drip in there," he said.

"So that's why you ran after me," Buba laughed. She went back and told the nurse: "My hus... he got worried that the IV drip was for him."

"It is," said the nurse. David glared in terror. "This way you'll get everything you need inside you," the nurse told him. He nodded meekly. Buba left. By the morning, he had called her five times and dictated the list of his requirements.

Jelena phoned in the morning: "Buba told me you have pneumonia."

"They're still not quite sure," said David anxiously.

"Come, come," said Jelena, "you know what you always say: 'one would need an axe to get rid of me'. But I can't understand how you managed to get pneumonia."

"No idea. Never had one before. It could be because I got wet the other day..." And he related the circumstances of his getting wet to Jelena. She laughed. "I'm sorry," she said. "I know you're in pain, but... I had a feeling Nina would be the crucial element in this story, only I wasn't sure in what way." She continued seriously, "But each cloud has a silver lining: your phone in the office hasn't stopped ringing; everyone wants to personally congratulate you on the nomination."

When Buba arrived, David was just as exhausted as the day before, but looked more cheerful. "Imagine," he said, "they've just done the rounds and the doctor said, 'ah, here's that pneumonia; everything's going swimmingly here!'"

"There you are, then," said Buba. "Happier now?"

"Dunno."

"Go on, you must feel a bit happier," Buba persisted.

"Well, yeah, a bit," he conceded at last.

On top of everything else she had brought him, Buba had to walk to Zvijezda for Vindija blueberry and morello cherry juices, since those were the ones he had ordered. As she was leaving to go to the shops, the little old man in the bed next to David's woke up and pulled himself slightly up on his pillows.

"Can I bring you something from the shops?" Buba asked, raising her voice automatically: a man as old as that had to be hard of hearing.

"No, thanks," the old man said. "Your offer is enough, though, it is a lot." Full of life, his dark little eyes sparkled merrily from under his bushy eyebrows.

When Buba got back and began unloading her shopping bags, the old man said to David: "Lucky you, with your wife spoiling you like that." And when Buba felt David's forehead and said, "You're cool," the old man laughed and said, "And so he should be. That means he needs a woman to keep him warm." He all but winked at her.

Buba offered him chocolate. David said quietly, "He won't take it, he's not eating anything."

The old man gave her a seductive look. "All right then, since you're offering... don't want to refuse you." He took a small piece and placed it on a folded napkin on his bedside cabinet.

David tried to sit up, but ended up clutching his ribs. "Ouch, it hurts," he said.

The old man quickly added, "It mustn't hurt, with a wife like this around."

Buba laughed. When she was leaving, the old man said, "Do come back, we're bored without you."

"You know what's funny?" she said, relating the visit to Jelena. "I, too, started flashing my eyes and laughing seductively once I noticed him coming alive at the sight of me! I mean the old bloke, not David."

When her visits to the ward became regular afternoon routine, the old man took on the role of naughty commentator: he watched what went on and kept warning David: "See your wife off, my friend, since she visits you every day so loyally." "How rude not to hold her coat for her; just look at all the goodies she brought you..." "Go on; take that sour face off, show some spirit when your wife visits you." Buba laughed, David sprang to attention, and the old man offered his excuses: "Please don't take it badly, me saying stuff..."

They never told him they weren't husband and wife any more. Funny, thought Buba, he's happier to see me than David. "And how are you?" she asked him. "Eh, how... I'm old," the old man said ruefully. "Would you like grandpa and me to tell you how we were examined by students, young female ones?" David laughed, in a good mood. Grandpa smiled, too.

"Well, our doctor is a professor and his students are having exams right now in this hospital. Grandpa was one young lady's exam and I another's. They had to look at our charts, examine the symptoms and diagnose us. Grandpa's one asked him which illnesses he'd had. He mulled it over and said, 'Well... I once had typhoid fever.' 'You what?' asked the astonished student.

'Typhoid fever,' grandpa repeated. 'Where on earth did you pick *that* up?" asked the girl, a bit scared. 'On Papuk[113],' grandpa replied. 'Er... when?' 'In '43.' The student shifted her eyes from grandpa to her notepad and back. Should she make a note of that? Or not? The professor struggled to suppress a smile. And she passed the exam."

"You have a lovely wife," grandpa said to David. "A real beauty. And a good woman. Many people would give anything for the privilege of having such a wife."

Buba blushed, pleasantly embarrassed. The next day, she felt that David was seeing her with different eyes; his glance was happier. She was flushed and out of breath after her walk up the hill to the hospital, and David's and grandpa's welcome made her feel good. And beautiful. She became flustered like a very young girl. Her hands were loaded with bags full of juice packs, bottles of water, plastic tubs with food, paper napkins...

When grandpa got discharged, Buba told him, a bit overemotionally: "I'm glad to have met you. I'll always remember you."

"Why?" the old man asked.

"Because... you understand everything," Buba said.

"Like you say, my dear madam; I understand everything. It would be strange if I didn't, at my age." Buba knew that the little old man had understood what no one had told him: that things were not quite right between her and David. Non-lovers and lovers don't have the same feel about them. How strange, thought Buba, such a small matter and yet it changes everything. Everything is the same, only empty, as if you'd arrived at the edge of a precipice: there's nothing ahead, and behind you, there's everything you cannot do without.

"Get well soon," she said.

"Whatever," the old man waved a hand dismissively. "I'm eighty two, dear lady. Even if I don't get well again, it comes to

---

[113] A mountain in the Slavonia region in eastern Croatia, famous for battles between German troops and the Partisans (the Resistance fighters) in WW2.

the same thing."

***

As days went by, David's energy grew. "As soon as I get out, I'm taking you out for dinner." He raised his arms and crossed them at the back of his head, sprawling on the bed and happy in the expectation of freedom outside the hospital. "Another occasion for us to celebrate," he said.

"How wonderful it is to come out of the hospital healthy," said Buba for whom hospital meant the place where her own and David's parents went when gravely ill and where they died.

While David was bursting with appetite for life, she felt as if there was nothing for her to look forward to and expect: home, children, work, food, lots of food; watching telly, here and there a coffee with this friend or that, always the same conversations... She discussed it with Jelena. Jelena said she might be feeling that way – as if there was nothing to look forward to – because she still loved David. Was she sure she no longer loved him?

"I'm not sure," said Buba. "We never got to that stage where love completely disappears, when people begin to bring out the worst in each other... I don't know what I'm feeling, but I can feel what David feels: he's happier like this, free, with all the possibilities open."

"Do you know it has been proved that people who love live longer?" Jelena said. "Which is why men live shorter than women: women simply love more: their husband, their kids, their parents..."

"At least something in our favour," Buba laughed. "Serves them right... But didn't you tell me once that people with friends live longer?"

"That was a different research," Jelena laughed too.

The Hand
Friday, 25 February 2005
FRONT PAGE: THE POPE UNDERGOES EMERGENCY SURGERY

Last night, tracheotomy was performed on the Holy Father to facilitate his breathing.

HE DIDN'T LISTEN TO HIS DOCTORS: The Pope was warned not to meet people and to stay in his palace, but he disregarded the advice.

The Pope has flu, that's all. I know that in an elderly man flu can be harmful, but why panic when the clairvoyants said that the Pope wouldn't die this year?

DEŽULOVIĆ AND HUDELIST WIN *THE MORNING PAPER* AWARD: the best books of 2004: *Christkind* (best fiction) and *Tuđman* (best non-fiction).

TODAY'S EVENTS: Sanader: we have no evidence that Gotovina is in Croatia

Censorship of Spirit and Thought

Back from hospital, David did not want additional sick leave, although he had been advised to rest for a few more weeks. In the office, Dora, Ivana, Dipsy and Piljek gave him a hero's welcome. Andrej was away on business; Nina was not in.

"Welcome and congratulations on your novel," said Dipsy. Everyone joined in.

"It's too soon for congratulations," David said. "Any news?"

"A new WGW advert," Mario retorted readily. "Where it said FUCKING GOOD and ONLY KIDDING, they've now stuck a poster over it saying CENSORSHIP OF SPIRIT AND THOUGHT."

"It's so soothing to find out that nothing has changed," said David, sitting down at his desk with a deep sigh of relief.

Encouraged, Dipsy added, "I'm on my way out, but I've got just enough time for a highly intellectual one, in Latin: *O Antonio, cleanior philthibum lestit pongs*. Ponder upon this, ladies and gentlemen and, once you've cracked it, pardon the pun, let me know. Thank you for your time." He took his jacket off the peg, bowed pompously and left.

David took Jelena to the *Little Café* to celebrate his return. Šime the waiter was engaged in a lively conversation with several patrons at the bar.

"Having a meeting? What about?" said David instead of a greeting.

"Oh, there's you, back from yer winter retreat! Ay 'ear you got cold feet? Were brickin' it, like?"

"You heard right. What's going on here?"

Conscious of his attentive audience at the bar, Šime said self-importantly, "Yous jonalists are de last ter find out about things, innit? That's why yer jonalists."

David didn't question him further, so, after a brief pause, Šime went on: "A swindler is going round cafés cheatin' people an' yous jonalists say nowt."

"How can we write about it, my dear chap?" David said, "Us lot deal with cultural affairs, and that has nothing to do with life."

"Want me ter brin' yous somethin' or wa'?"

"A Coca-Cola for me," David said, turning to Jelena as if to apologise. "I've got heartburn. I've discovered that Coca Cola helps."

"But of course," Jelena said. "It's particularly good for you after pneumonia. It also helps with post-chemo nausea, so it must be good for common heartburn. What's more, it scrapes your entire stomach lining, like cleaning a toilet with a bleach-soaked brush. Not only that, but do you know that..."

Šime, who'd been listening to Jelena's sermon, asked impatiently, "Is dat Coke goin' ahead er not?"

"It is," David said.

Šime snorted ironically and went to fetch the drink without a word.

"Wait, I might actually have the article on me, I printed it out yesterday." Jelena refused to be diverted from the subject. "Here it is..."

"Leave it, please." David pushed her hand back into her bag.

"You're right", Jelena agreed readily. "There are so many things one ought to know about that of late I keep thinking of what Socrates said, *scio me nihil...* Tomatoes, for example, contain lycopene; broccoli and cauliflower contain lutein and wild lettuce lactucin or something... all that health-sustaining goodness. It's impossible to know about all that; one simply has to give up and surrender to chance. I find that frustrating."

Šime, who had arrived with the drinks, hung around to hear all that Jelena had to say. "G'on wi' yous jonalists. Yous think you're so precious dat yous should live forever."

"Haven't you got a fresher joke?" David laughed.

"I've read Nina's book," said Jelena once Šime had gone.

"And?"

"I think it's excellent. You know what I find baffling? She's so incredibly cheerful, jolly, sweet, like a little child, and her book is so dark and bitter. And Ana, who is darkness embodied as a person, writes such light and entertaining prose, unfettered like a child..."

"I've thought of that myself," David said.

"You never told me you'd read it."

"I read it in the hospital. Buba brought it. It's very good, full of the unexpected."

"Is she better than Ana?"

"Totally different but just as good. You're quite right, they are like the positive and the negative of an image. They're each other's opposites to such an extent they almost resemble each other."

"Like those two Greek masks representing theatre: identical in every way, only one has the corners of its mouth pointing down and the other one up."

"That's actually quite extraordinary," said David thoughtfully.

"What is?"

"Writing is like breathing. However well you may have mastered the craft, writing is just the written form of the natural way you express yourself, and self-expression is the natural form of your way of thinking. That's why a writer never really knows when he's being boring, or when his sentences are too long, or when he's rubbish, or even when he's a great writer. He might sort of know how much of what was in his head he'd actually managed to put into words..."

"I know; you want to say that there's nothing hollow about

Ana; she doesn't pretend or lie, and yet her writing is the complete opposite of herself. What's the explanation?"

"You're right," said David. "A split personality, perhaps," he added, laughing.

"Don't joke about it, please," said Jelena and added thoughtfully, "It really *is* strange. Perhaps they both have split personalities. Beware."

"Of whom? Ana or Nina?"

"Nina, of course. She's the one you're seeing, as far as I know."

"I think that's all over," David said.

"That fast? And without passion?" Jelena laughed. "I get it: you got cold feet..."

"No, it's not that. I..."

"She's much of a muchness, even for you. Bruno is *mesmerised*, too."

"I'm sure it's all in your imagination."

"Not at all; I've been troubled by a foreboding feeling from day one. Angelic face, angelic trap... Who could resist her!"

"She's very attractive and beautiful, but..."

"I know; she's the type of woman who seduces with her soul, not her body, and you find that... abhorrent, as if she were luring you into her own world, am I right? A woman's soul, fie, *apage satanas*, you find that as unnatural as sleeping with a man." She laughed.

"Let me answer this quickly while you pause for air: quite simply, I didn't fall in love with her," David finally managed to squeeze in a reply.

Jelena gaped. "You mean, it's possible not to fall in love with her?" she said hopefully. "Why are you looking at me like that? In any case, this goes to show that she uses soul-power: you wanted to fall in love with her, not just sleep with her."

David shook his head and patted her hair. "You got it bad, baby."

The Hand

23 March 2005

EVENTS OF THE DAY: Everyone except HDZ and SDP in favour of complete ban on GM prosducts

Who is everyone? The 0.01% which is Green Action, and the 0.1% covering all other political parties?

Tonči Tadić (HSP): In ten years' time our country will be so contaminated that we'll hardly need the GM-banning law, and Croatia will have lost the historic chance to be a GM-free European country.

24 March

A SHOCKING DISCOVERY: 104 widows of the heroes who defended Croatia in the War of Independence died before reaching forty years of age

Research was allegedly conducted, proving the theory that the cause of their premature death was stress. No one mentions chemical weapons, poisonous projectiles or that mysterious gossamer. Or could it be that an equal proportion of non-war widows die before reaching forty?

Ana's Troubles

After the holidays, Ana continued looking after Andreja, reminding her of the appointments at the Centre, taking her there and waiting for her in the waiting room. On the way back, she would accompany her as far as Jelačić Square where she would take the tram while Andreja would walk on to Novak Street. In the beginning, she would call her home to check if she had arrived safely. If Andreja's mother answered the phone, Ana would pretend to be a classmate. Andreja looked calmer and her mood seemed to have improved. On one occasion, guessing what Ana might like to know, she offered, unprompted: "He's moved... that man who..."

"Thank God," Ana said. "Everything will be all right now."

Within herself, she felt rather good, except for unusually bad headaches which tormented her with increasing frequency. Occasionally she would feel she was losing consciousness for unspecified periods of time while remaining on her feet. And she found her mother's nagging ever harder to bear.

"Is everything all right with you?" Jelena asked her one day.

"Yeah, why do you ask?"

"You look a bit tired."

"Dunno; I'm not sleeping well," Ana said.

Jelena thought this was due to the excitement over the book.

And Anton had been in touch. His latest mail was short and mysterious:

I'm with you all the time... I mean, with your book. Be careful. Someone as sensitive as you might end up taking on a burden no human being can be expected to bear. Why aren't you replying to my mails more regularly?"

The Hand

Wednesday, 3 March

LIFE: HORRENDOUS CHARGES LEAVE JACKSON COLD

Calmly, without emotion, cheek on hand, Michael Jackson listened for three hours to severe charges brought against him.
SANTA MARIA: "The Trial of the Century, as the trial of Michael Jackson for sexual abuse of minors has already been dubbed, began with impassioned opening statements by the Prosecution and the Defence. (...)Thomas Sneddon, the Prosecuting Counsel, told the jury that the pop-star had been plying his victim with vodka and showing him porn movies, while the Defence stated that the victim's mother was simply after Jackson's money..."

O, Antonio

"They've handed out the mobiles," Ivana said.

"Really?" said Mario with lively interest. "I didn't get one."

"You couldn't have. They've only given them to those taller than one meter eighty... just listen to me spouting rubbish..."

Everyone laughed except Jelena who stared at her monitor, scowling.

"... to those with the coefficient upwards of 8.30."

"Ah, so it's not the ones who need it but simply according to pay scale," said Mario. "You weren't that far out, then: they might as well have given them to those taller than one meter eighty, it would've been just as meaningless."

"You must've been given one, then," said Ivana to David.

"I refused," said David with little interest for the subject, leafing through his paper.

"I wouldn't have, if they'd given me one," Mario said.

"You're only allowed to call office numbers and other work mobiles anyway. All other conversations get docked off your pay," Dora told him.

"And you must sign a commitment stating you'll be available all the time, or so I've heard," Ivana said.

"A tether, eh? But it's worth it," said Mario. "What did they say when you refused?"

"I had to write a statement for Fish, and one for the Chairman."

"On top of it all, those mobiles are out-of-date junk," Ivana added.

"Someone's done a good deal again, then," said Mario. "Got rid of junk for a bit of money. Just as when we were given these prehistoric monitors which are only fit for scrap while every PA has a LCD."

"That's not true," David said. "The phones are OK."

"That's right," said Andrej, emerging from behind Dora's back. "It's fascinating how your tongues manage to transform even the best of things into rubbish," he added acidly, darting withering glances at Ivana and Dipsy. He couldn't blame Dora, Jelena and David.

"Oh, you're back?" Dora said.

"Just popped in to get something," said Andrej curtly and went to his office, closing the door. Dora returned to her desk. Before anyone could comment, Andrej left again, nodding vaguely, not expecting anyone to nod back."

"Right, then," said Mario, "have you managed to solve my Latin puzzle, *O Antonio, cleanior philthibum lestit pongs?* Without enthusiasm, his colleagues admitted failure. Mario swiftly picked up a pen and a sheet of paper and wrote the puzzle out, changing spaces between letters to split the words in a different way. "Good, eh?"

Everyone laughed. "Jesus, who thought that one up?" Ivana said.

Jelena felt cast down. At noon, she went to the press conference at the Contemporary Art Gallery. On her way back, she paused before the surreal sign above the door in Radić Street: THE FIRST CITIZENS' ASSOCIATION FOR FABULOUS FUNERALS. She walked back to the *Herald*, slowly, choosing the longest route and buying oranges and bread on the way so that she wouldn't have to do it after work. More sepulchral announcements in Gaj Street: a large advertisement read COOPERATIVE FOR ASSISTANCE AFTER DEATH – NEW MEMBERS ENROLLMENT. I'm noticing things selectively again, she thought. One ought to tell Bandić[114] to break up this concentration of undertakers in Gaj Street, it's getting morbid around here.

She ran into Piljek/Gollum in the reception. "Soldiering on," said Piljek, glaring disapprovingly at her shopping bag. In translation: what are you like, shopping during working hours, whilst I, even though going out, am not on my way home – oh, no, my working day isn't finished, no ma'am: I'm going out on business. Piljek's importance was growing daily. Mocked at first for pushing his illiterate self into the preserve of the super-brains in charge of reorganising the company, he had, a few weeks later, begun to command respect. "That's how it is with people," David said when Jelena commented on Piljek's transformation. "Nothing is set in stone. A semi-literate busybody with a laptop will, by and by, transform into something else, outwardly at first – his status, salary and clothes will change. Internal changes will follow, until we genuinely forget what a ridiculous figure he used to cut and begin meeting him with respect... that's how it goes."

As always with Piljek, Jelena had no idea how to reply to his *soldiering on*. She remembered David's words and began

---

[114] Milan Bandić, Mayor of Zagreb, first elected in 2000

wondering if she had started feeling respect towards the belaptopped idiot. Not yet, she found. She shrugged and said, "'Bye." To make the day even worse, she caught Dipsy giving poor Anđelko the treatment in the reception: "Did you know, Anđelko, that Bosnian television had bought the licence for the Turbo-Kiddie Show? Yup. Only they adapted it to suit their own regional requirements and re-named it Turbo-Wahid Show."

"What's your game, stirring it up?" she could hear Anđelko's indifferent reply.

Helena Phones Buba

When the telephone rang, Buba was stirring chopped onions in a frying pan on the hob; next to the pan, the potatoes were boiling over and in the background Hana and Matko were arguing about whose turn it was to make the beds. "Answer the phone, will you," Buba yelled, exasperated. As usual when arguing with his sister, Matko was the one to give in, perhaps because he was more sensitive to Buba's unrestrained screaming or more sorry to see her nervous, tired and sad than Hana was.

"Yes?" he said into the receiver, his face a question mark. "Just a minute, she needs to wash her hands."

"Who's that?" Buba whispered.

"No idea," Matko replied, shrugging.

It was Helena. "I bet you're surprised that I'm calling you," she said, "but I've been thinking about you a lot, ever since I saw you the other day... I keep having flashbacks of us at school and out and about in the neighbourhood... I must be getting old." She laughed, sounding contrived. "So I thought it would be nice for us to have a coffee together somewhere... at some point... I know you're busier than I am, so if you'd like to, I'll accommodate you."

The onions were burning. Buba was listening distractedly, annoyed that the children were not noticing her signals to take over at the cooker. "Yeah, all right, we could do it.... tomorrow is Sunday, isn't it? We could do it tomorrow morning if you'd like," she said with warmth in her voice, not keen to show how surprised she was. "David will be taking the kids to lunch, so I won't have to cook."

Helena thanked her with exaggerated emotion, obviously moved by her kindness.

The Hand

29 March

THE FRONT PAGE: POWERFUL EARTHQUAKE CLOSE TO SUMATRA

Fears of another tsunami: 50 dead, a wave of refugees

The tsunami was on Christmas Day; now this, on Easter Monday. A coincidence?

THE POPE IS SUFFERING

Images of the Pope's haggard, suffering face were beamed all over the world as he delivered the Easter Blessing from the window of the Apostolic Palace.

GIRL RAPED BY TWO YOUNG MEN IN THEIR CAR

TV NEWS: Ivan Bulj given one of the longest sentences in the history of Croatian justice: 27 years for the murder of 15-year old Anđela Bešlić. The rape of the victim could not be proved. The highest sentence for murder in Croatia is 40 years. The defence will be appealing against the verdict.

31 March

EVENTS OF THE DAY: THE WORLD ORGANISATION FOR FOOD AND AGRICULTURE (FAO): IN 50 YEARS, THERE MIGHT BE NO WATER LEFT ON EARTH

"We can no longer be sure that the future generations will be able to survive on Earth since humans have, in the last 50 years, changed many ecosystems far more radically than in their *entire previous history*. The scientists have come to the conclusion that 60% of the ecosystems providing water and food for mankind and regulating the Earth's climate have been corrupted or exhausted above the acceptable limit. Unless there is immediate action leading to the reversal of the trend, within the next 50 years some of the symptoms already in evidence could become irreversible..."

The Beautiful Helen

Helena was still a beautiful woman, a ripe woman. Her perfect face and her shapely, curvaceous body had only just begun showing the first markings of time.

As she entered *Ban*[115] café on Jelačić Square, all heads turned towards the striking raven-haired woman in a black coat, her ivory scarf bringing out her large, dark eyes. She was aware of the looks which followed her and, unlike those ugly people who stiffen and become paralysed under the eyes of others, tighten their lips and stare fixedly at an imaginary point visible only to themselves, *La belle Hélène* still relished admiring looks which enveloped her like costly perfume or the softest of silks, stretching out before her like a red carpet and making her straighten her shoulders and lift her head high as she glanced around with gleaming eyes. Her make-up was subtle. Her cheeks bore a touch of pink blusher; its colour was refreshing and rejuvenating, making her appear pink with crisp winter air and youth. Save for the mascara on her lashes, her eyes were free of make-up. Her full, sensuous lips, however, were covered with red lipstick. Helena had always marvelled at the ignorance of women of her own age who didn't seem to know that heavy, in-your-face makeup made them look older. Anticipating a similar comment from Buba, Helena was the first to say, "You look great, you haven't aged at all."

"Thanks to Helena Frankenstein[116]," said Buba, laughing.

Talking to Helena turned out to be less uncomfortable than Buba had feared. At times she felt as if they'd gone thirty years back in time.

Laughing, Helena said, "I don't know why, but that

---

[115] Ban was a lordly title (sometimes similar to Viceroy) in several, mainly Slavic states of central and South-Eastern Europe (Wikipedia). Here, it refers to Josip Jelačić of Bužim (1801-1859), Ban of Croatia, Slavonia and Dalmatia within the Austro-Hungarian Empire. Jelačić Square was named after him, and the café after his sculpture on the north side of the square, a popular meeting point and generally referred to as 'Ban'.

[116] A 1970-ies pun on Helena Rubinstein, a brand of make-up

earthquake just popped into my mind, remember, when we all rushed out of the building and waited in the park for hours, because people had said that earthquakes usually came in pairs... You came out with a key hanging around your neck on a chain, clutching half a loaf of bread. Your auntie Anka asked, 'Bubby, why are you holding that bread?' and you laughed and said, 'Well, if I die, I don't want it to be on an empty stomach." You could've been nine or ten. All the neighbours adored you and kept pinching your cheeks. You hated that, I remember..."

"Yes, and particularly that maniac, that disgusting paedophile who used to stare at us through his ground floor window when we were playing. His curtain would always move, and we were scared because we knew he was hiding behind it." Because of the maniac, adult Buba still hated curtains and would not draw them even at night, a bone of contrition between her and Hana who was afraid of the dark behind the window pane. Auntie[117] Marica, the maniac's wife, was an unusual female specimen: coarse, with hair cropped short and always wearing trousers. Fast-witted and motor-mouthed, she'd always come up with original comments on local events. ("Go on then, working class, mend those broken lights in front of the house! Or are you waiting for someone else to do it for you?" Or, "Kids, don't help your mums; they never helped theirs, nor will your kids help you!") She'd tease little children by bringing her face close to theirs, opening her mouth and pushing her lower denture out with her tongue. The children screamed with terror and stayed away from her window. On one occasion, she said to Josip, a seven year old boy from the neighbourhood, "Come to Auntie Marica, and take a look at her old cunt." Poor Josip ran away as fast as he could. Later, he told his older sister what had happened, and she told other girls. Children saw Auntie Marica as a spider waiting in ambush for her prey and constantly supplying her husband with fresh little girls and

---

[117] In Croatia, children refer to all adult women they know as 'Auntie' and all familiar adult men as 'Uncle', so much so that, in child-speak, 'Auntie' and 'Uncle' are mostly synonymous with 'lady' and 'man'.

boys. Helena warned other little girls about the couple on the ground floor and told them to let her know if they as much as brush against them in passing. The interesting thing was that all the children knew about the maniac but none of them said anything to their parents. The adults in the building had no idea of what Marica and her husband were like. Poor Josip wouldn't let anyone kiss him for years, not even his mother and his father, and would say, "You whore!" to anyone behaving a bit more liberally. Buba was shaking off nasty memories. She laughed. "Do you remember how the boys used to sneak around the house in hope to see you come out? And what about the one who was staring at your window while walking and fell into a manhole? He looked like Woody Allen. The whole block remembered him by that stunt. They called him Manhole ever since."

Helena listened, gazing into the distance, then asked quietly, "Have I become very ugly?"

There was so much fear in her question that Buba felt a chill creeping up her back. "You haven't become ugly at all" she said. "You know you're beautiful. You can see how people look at you..."

"I've lost my periods," Helena said. "I have a feeling that everyone can see that..."

"*Welcome to the club[118],*" said Buba dryly.

"What, you too? Already?" said Helena, perking up, comforted.

"Every six months, I bleed so copiously I feel I'm about to die." Buba attempted a joke. "Total hormonal collapse. I'll be going to the barber soon rather than to the hairdresser. And in my makeup cupboard, there's less and less makeup and more and more *substitutes* every day."

Helena didn't laugh. "Everything comes to an end so quickly. We need to let our daughters know. You fly, fly, fly, with the world streaming beneath you, when – wham! You're

---

[118] In the original text, this sentence was in English, quoting a popular phrase..

no longer a bird but a clay pigeon. If a bullet misses you, another one will find you soon. And down you go, down. You know it's no longer what you used to call life, but you can't shorten the agony, you have to fall all the way down to the ground."

"When I get up in the morning," Buba went on with feigned ease, hiding how much Helena's words affected her, "I must first get used to my own face, as every day I discover new signs of degenerative change. Yesterday, for example, I noticed I had a horizontal crease under my nose: that is a future fold. I know that because I used to gaze at that very same fold, the same groove, under my late father's nose."

Helena didn't seem to be listening. "You know, when I see a young couple walking with arms around each other, listening to each other, laughing... I sometimes feel like ripping myself to shreds, tearing my skin off, ripping my throat out, for the sheer desire to be alive like they are, really alive..."

"And when I drop something," Buba went on as if Helena hadn't said anything, "polite men pick it up for me with a kind expression, but they avoid looking at me, lest I should think they'd picked it up because they fancied me."

Helena was silent.

"And before I go out, I always breathe on the mirror and look at myself so that I can preserve that *sfumato*, wrinkle-free, unblemished image of myself in my mind, like Greta Garbo on damaged celluloid tape." Buba laughed.

Seriously and somewhat absently, Helena said, "I'd like to have a friend such as you, the way we used to be when we were little. You're all I've got."

The Hand
4 January

HTV, THE *GOOD MORNING* SHOW: "In animals, ageing begins with the cessation of fertility. The scientists are trying to slow down or stop the ageing process in man. We can imagine, in the near future, a miniature robot not larger than 1 nanometre entering body cells and 'repairing them".

The Anti-Ageing Academy

"I froze right through when she said I was all she had," Buba said to Jelena and Ana when they came round for a coffee. "We hadn't seen each other since her sick leave. When she worked, we hardly exchanged a word. We were only mates as kids. There's something wrong with her."

"She's simply getting old," Jelena said.

"Yes; I have a feeling that she would, in return for eternal youth, sign a contract with any devil, be he ever so vile."

"Who wouldn't? I heard the other day that an Anti-Ageing Academy was to open here in Zagreb..."

Buba laughed again. Everything sounds better if it's an academy: Rock Academy, Wreck Academy..."

"Yeah. Different experts will be brought together in one place to examine people, diagnose any deficiencies and prescribe the right therapy: vitamins, minerals, coenzymes, food, exercises, detox programmes..."

"Not a bad idea," Buba said. "I finally understand why women go for rejuvenation procedures. You know why?"

"To look younger?"

"Yeah, but it's not that simple. No, all those women, all of *us*, believe it to be an opportunity to put our past mistakes right, mistakes that made us grow prematurely old, become fat and droopy, stop looking after ourselves. We feel we deserve a second chance, that we have the right to one... Because in the first part of our lives we sacrifice ourselves to the needs of others. That's why so many women opt for surgery in spite of the pain and the risk involved. And then they promise themselves to use their second chance better and take better care of themselves."

"Yes," said Jelena, "that's true, you're right. I can relate to that. We believe we deserve a second chance."

Ana had until then been leafing through magazines while listening to their discussion without much interest. Now she lifted her head and said: "On the other hand... why should we get one? Biology has its laws. Do you know that, compared to the history of human civilisation, our own age represents just a tiny segment of time?"

"Yeah, and?" Buba said.

"Up until our time, nature has never been as ignored as it is now."

"Yeah, and?"

"We ignore instinct more than anything else; we pretend we don't know what lurks under the thin veneer of civilisation. Why do you think there are so many paedophiles? Because it's instinct: the instinct to have sex with a young, luscious being. But society has proscribed it."

"You're disgusting," said Buba.

"I'm not disgusting. If people spoke openly about it, abused children wouldn't feel like freaks – and every fifth child has been abused. Even children only a few months old get abused. Tell me, how many men do you know whom you'd dare leave alone with your daughter?" Ana asked.

Buba listened thoughtfully. "You're right," she said and added, "How did we get to paedophilia from gerontology?" She laughed and shook herself as if shaking off bad thoughts.

"And do you know what the psychological profile of a typical paedophile is like? Extroverted, pleasant, cheerful, a caring parent, wins children's confidence easily," Ana went on, staying on her favourite topic.

"That's me," Buba put in laughing.

Ana disregarded the interruption. "...hangs out with children, knows their interests and what is bothering them, what they're up to, what fashion they follow, what music they listen to..."

"Ah, and that's me," Jelena put in.

Ana gave them both a stern look. "Have you read recently the confessions of foster-children? It turns out that some professional foster parents take in children as playthings for their sadistic games, as human household pets. And the children weren't even believed when they mustered enough courage to report the abuse, because their foster parents were respectable people."

Buba laughed. Jelena and Ana gave her surprised looks. "I'm

sorry, girls," Buba said. "I just remembered something that... probably... has nothing to do with perverts, but... have you seen the other night in the news the bit about Eva the she-wolf who'd killed two sheep but the farmer had forgiven her because he'd raised her from cub or something, and she'd come back to him... or something like that."

"Yeah, and?"

"The man's name was Adam," Buba laughed. Jelena laughed too. "And the reporter finished with the words, 'And so Eva has come back to her Adam...'"

The Hand

2 April: THE POPE

A programme has been on air now for 48 hours, constantly announcing that the Pope is on his deathbed. They don't seem to want to let the man breathe his last in peace. I still don't believe he'll die, because of the prophecy. Never has the world mourned a man so much.

10 PM, BREAKING NEWS: The Pope died at 21h 37 min

Dear, kind Pope. I'm more sorry about the Pope than glad that the prophecy hasn't come true. (I fear prophecies.)

Tuesday, 19 April

NEW POPE ELECTED: For the first time in 940 years, the Pope is German. Cardinal Joseph Ratzinger has chosen the name of Benedict. Why? After Benedict XV who was Pope during the First World war and is thought to have set up the foundations for the international community. He supported peace and the unity of Europe.

The Pope speaks of the dictatorship of relativism, and I agree. One could even say, the dictatorship of freedom.

The Sinuous Passer-By

Jelena had started forgetting the *incident* with Nina, but her melancholy returned when Nina phoned again. Her own voice sounded harsh and false to her ears. And Nina was sweet and cheerful as ever. She was sorry to be a nuisance again, but something had gone wrong with the software.

When Bruno got home from work, Jelena could feel he was tense. "Nina called," she shouted from the kitchen when she heard him run the tap in the bathroom: he was washing his hands. She'd chosen on purpose the moment when he was out of her sight to tell him the news: she wouldn't have been able to bear seeing the twinkle in his eyes. "We need to see her."

"All right," said Bruno.

She decided she wouldn't ask any questions, but was unable to contain herself. "What do you mean: all right?" Bruno didn't hear her. She asked another one: "Don't you want to know why?"

"I thought you'd already told me and I'd forgotten." Jelena's heart fluttered joyfully: she could be imagining things after all; Bruno's explanation was logical and consistent with his usual confused self.

"Well, aren't you interested to know *now* why we need to see her?"

"I'm not, to be honest. Her software must have crashed or something."

"Do you remember the summer in Crikvenica, our first summer as husband and wife?" she said out of the blue. Bruno gave her a curious look. I can still take him by surprise, Jelena thought. And then: why do I always give such importance to surprising him? Because long ago he told me that he could never live with a boring woman, no matter how pretty she was. That a boring woman simply couldn't be attractive to him. She went on: "We saw a lovely woman pass by *The Promenade*; a sinuous, sensuous, tanned woman, with undyed hair, without makeup, wearing a simple dress which made her stand out even more among all those tarted-up dollies... Remember?"

"I have no idea what you're on about, or why."

"You'd remember if you'd only concentrate. That was the first woman you looked at since we'd got married." Bruno made as if to wave his hand, but didn't quite finish his gesture. "She didn't look striking. I sensed more than saw that you were watching her. I think I even said something, and you said you'd met her once... I don't remember what you said. I thought she was the only woman for whom you might leave me if chance brought you together."

"You found more than one such imaginary case," Bruno said.

Once more, she felt like Emma Thompson in *Love Actually*. "What would you do if you fell in love? She asked.

"Come on, Jelena! What is the point of this discussion?" Whenever he addressed her by her name, he meant business.

"No, seriously, think about it. Would you leave me at once, would you deceive me so that I don't find out, or would you give up your new love? There isn't a fourth option."

Bruno sighed and put down the paper he had picked up. He was evidently not going to read it. "Don't know," he said, "can't get into it. Haven't you got anything better to talk about?"

"Go on, try and concentrate."

"What's the point?"

"I'm interested. After all, we do have such different ideas about marriage, separation, infidelity..."

Bruno breathed out noisily. "If husband and wife could stop loving each other simultaneously, that would be ideal."

"But where's the drama in that?" Jelena said.

"Who needs drama?" said Bruno.

"Your answer is a trifle chilling," she said. "Although it is the healthiest option... Do you remember my colleague who moved to America a few years ago?"

"I haven't a clue."

"Doesn't matter. She used to call me a lot at first, in the throes of nostalgia. She'd ask me all sorts of things; everything interested her. But as soon as I'd start telling her about something – anything – she'd say, 'Right, fuck that, that's not important, this is a transatlantic conversation.' And then she'd ask again, 'How's Dora, still ruling the roost?' I'd start talking, and she'd go, 'Right, fuck that, we've got more important things to talk about, this is an expensive conversation.' And our entire conversation would consist of her *right, fuck thats*."

Bruno could not see the connection.

"Well, you remind me of her. Whatever I say, you go,

'Right, fuck that, it's not important enough for us to discuss it.'" She stopped short of voicing the thought that perhaps their conversation might be transatlantic, too: she did not want to put ideas in his mind.

"You're my crazy wife," said Bruno almost tenderly. Jelena was close to feeling happy: he had said "my", but she knew what was missing: if he'd only touched her, grasped her hand or kissed her, all would have been well. This way, it had remained hollow. There was still tension across the table, the Atlantic.

January; David Gets Notice About the Award

"Hello – we've done it," said David's voice in the receiver.

"We have?" Ana asked.

"I've just received official notification from the Association of Critics: the novel *Wingbeat* has won this year's *Matoš* award."

Ana was silent. She could feel the pulse in her neck. It had started. David was right.

"Say something."

Ana tittered. "Well, congratulations."

"Is that all you can say?" David laughed.

Jelena and David, in a tight embrace, jumped up and down around the office. Jelena tallied it up: "Let's see, that means we've got nominated for *Uliks* and have won *Matoš*. If we carry on like this, we'll end up like Baretić[119]."

Anton Discovers Who Really Wrote *Wingbeat*

Every morning Ana would check her e-mail to see if Anton had written another missive. One morning, he suggested that they should finally meet. Ana became agitated and did not reply for days: if he saw what she looked like, he'd lose all interest in her. She told Jelena of the suitor she'd never met.

"On chat?" Jelena asked suspiciously.

"On mail," Ana said. Jelena continued eyeing her suspiciously, so she added, "He contacted me after reading *The*

---

[119] Renato Baretić (1963-), Croatian author, winner of numerous awards

Naked She-Wolf, he's a fan."

Reassured, Jelena said, "I can see you're all aflutter like a moth next to a light."

"That's exactly how I feel," said Ana. "He wants us to meet, but that's out of the question."

"Why?"

Ana was shaking her head. "I don't want him to see me, and, without bodies, there can't be any kindred souls, at least not in this universe."

"But he's already seen your photo."

"Yeah, the photoshopped one," said Ana darkly. "Did you know it has been scientifically proved how decisive one's appearance is in one's life? That clever man in Rijeka, Dr Turčinović, has done an investigation which proved, for example, that 45% of a candidate's success in an exam depends on looks if the examiner and the candidate are of different sexes. That's a significantly bigger percentage than the one relating to the time spent on study..."

"What's wrong with your looks?" Jelena interrupted.

Ana ignored her. "Even better, they showed court judges a description of a crime and the image of the offender. In one case, the offender was handsome, and in the other ugly. The sentences given by the judges were up to five years longer for the ugly criminal."

"I've no idea what we're talking about right now," Jelena said.

"About why I don't want to meet Anton," said Ana.

Anton was silent for a while, and then an e-mail arrived.

Dear Ana,

A strange thing happened to me. I read the novel Wingbeat, *allegedly written by Davor Antolić. While reading it, I was constantly troubled by a feeling that something in that novel was familiar to me. As soon as I finished, I started reading it for the second time. I'm now sure I know the reason for this familiarity. That story about the real and the false author in the novel helped. Why did you do it?"*

Ana did not reply.

Anton sent another mail:

You break all the rules or else prove that one may have hope of the ideal. I mean to say that, on top of being an interesting writer, you obviously are an interesting person as well, a combination that doesn't occur all that often. Many authors who, at a glance, could never be said to be interesting, had written brilliantly – T. S. Eliot, for example.

Ana was calmer now but still did not reply.

Anton mailed her for the third time:

I recognised you in Wingbeat. *What does that tell you? I recognised your words, your secrets, your themes, your world, that Whole of yours. The Whole is the same, only the story has changed. I'm asking you, what does that tell you? Do you know anyone who could see that? Is there anyone who knows you better than I do?*

Ana:

You guessed right – I am the author of Wingbeat. *David Antolić is my friend. We wanted to break the barrier facing an unknown author whose books don't interest anyone.*

Anton wrote:

Aren't you marvelling at how well I understand you? I read it all in your book. When I asked you if we could meet, you stopped writing back. What would you do if I told you I 'd found out where you live and work, and that you came across me in the street and even looked at me? You even brushed against me once.

Don't be afraid, I'm not crazy, I'm not a maniac, I'm not schizophrenic. But if there is even the slightest possibility that we... give us a chance...

Ana was scared. He is stalking her? A weirdo? She replied cautiously:

A person does not consist of ideas and feelings alone, the parts of a person are innumerable. Were you to meet me, you might end up disappointed. You might not like me at all.

Perhaps it would be better to keep the illusion.

Anton:

I never confuse truth and illusion. You are, I'm certain, exactly as I came to know you, because I translated symbols of illusion into the language of reality and knew you as you are in real life through your image in fiction. I believe you get my meaning. They say, for example, that there is no such thing as perfect murder, don't they? And do you know the origin of that statement? Detective novels and movies. And what inspired detective novels and movies? Like all novels and movies, they were based on special cases, not on the usual and the commonplace. In movies, the rule is that the murderer always gets found out; in everyday life, the very opposite is true: the murderer is never or hardly ever found out. The perfect murder is not only possible but highly likely. That is the difference between reality and fiction. And that is how I know the difference between fictional Ana and the real one, whose soul... no, that's not right, whose entire being I know so well... A.

Ana's reply was short:

Could I ask you not to tell anyone that I am the author of Wingbeat *until David and I make the announcement?*

Anton:

You doubted me? You can count on me. And... remember.

Ana squeezed her temples between her hands. Her headaches were becoming unbearable.

The Hand

Tuesday, 5 April

THE CHRONICLE: 200 thousand Croats suffer from depression. According to the World Health Organisation, by 2020 depression could be world's second most common disease. Among the people who commit suicide, 60% are depressive.

One day an advanced alien civilisation will, judging by the archaeological remains found on Earth, come to the conclusion that humans, having destroyed everything, had no other option

but to become depressive.
DEPRESSIVE GENIUSES
"The connection between creativity and depression was noted already in ancient Greece, and modern researchers have discovered a higher incidence of depression among poets, writers, painters and composers."

Ana Karenina
Buba made Matko and Hana go and see a stage production of *Ana Karenina.* "You haven't read the novel anyway, and who knows if you ever will," she said.

"What novel?" Hane asked.

"Lord in heaven," Buba sighed, "*Ana Karenina*, of course."

"Okay, if dad is coming," Hana said.

Thus all four of them went. Buba remembered seeing David with Nina not so long ago outside *Gavella* Theatre. She had noticed, or rather sensed, they were not seeing each other roughly since David's stay in hospital but she never discussed it with him. She wasn not even interested. Buba was not the one to needlessly complicate her life. By the first intermission, Matko was wriggling in his seat so much that her concentration began to suffer. After the second intermission Hanna, too, began to wriggle. When the performance finished, they were so keen to get out they did not even clap.

"You barely made it through, eh?" said David.

"Ultra-boring," Matko said.

"Boring shows, too, form part of our education and upbringing," said Buba sententiously.

"Yeah? I've actually come to the conclusion that upbringing boils down to breaking of the human will," Matko said.

"To me, the production was great," said Hana in a comically adult sort of way. "I particularly liked it when they made it rain for real on the stage and when they skated on roller-skates, and when Ana and Vronsky seemed to dance around with that piece of linen...

Buba said, "Karenina was a bit old."

Hana said, "I don't get it, that kid was barely three and

everyone called him Sir Joža[120]..."

Buba was gripped by a fit of laughter. "Oh no... haven't you guys heard of the Russian name Seryozha[121]?"

"Why are you laughing?" Hana was hurt.

"I'm sorry," said Buba, unable to stop laughing.

Knowing how quick Hana was to take offence, David said, to get Buba out of a tight spot: "All theatre is good, theatre is a game. That's how one should look at it. A game is played for pleasure; it is there to bring beauty into your life..."

"I know all about games," said Matko. "I'm a professor of gamology. Do you know what the principal difference between games and life is?"

"No, what?"

"In real life, whatever you do, you think of the future; in a game, whatever you do is for the present moment. Instant delight."

"Where did you get this from?" Hana asked in wonderment.

"I read it," Matko said importantly.

"And I've read this," Hana said. "Aim high: that way, even if you miss, you'll end up among the stars."

"What's that got to do with anything?" Matko said.

"You're so arrogant! I always listen to you and don't laugh at you, and you can't wait to make fun of me!" Hana said.

"Actually, dad," Matko said, "I need to show my face at this bash... tomorrow is Saturday. Will you see mum and Hana home?"

"Where's the bash?" Hana asked.

"What the...?" Matko began. Hana elbowed him."At Matija's," he said.

"Can I come?" Hana asked, her face close to his, peering into his eyes.

"All right," said Matko gruffly. He had twigged Hana's supposedly inconspicuous hints: she was forever arranging things so that mum and dad would be left alone together.

---

[120] Croatian nickname for Josip (Joseph).
[121] Pet name for Sergei

"Don't be too long," said Buba. When she and David got home, she brought out the remainder of the Golden Plavac she had opened with Jelena and poured a glass for herself and one for David. It had been long since they had spent a Friday night together.

"Shall we order a pizza, what do you think?" David asked. Another thing they had not done together for a while.

The wine and the ordering of pizza once used to mean that they were pausing and taking time out just for themselves; a secret, intimate signal only they understood. It used to be their regular evening ritual when their still very young children would go to bed early, when David did not have to attend a first night or a promotion, when Buba wanted to take a break from cooking and be a desirable lover. She blushed.

While David collected the pizza from the delivery boy at the door, she glanced furtively at the mirror in the entrance hall.

What is a Man Without a...

Jagoda Franjić, the prominent critic, stood next to Ana applauding noisily as David mounted the podium to receive the award. To Ana, the sight was a familiar one: the hall of the National and University Library echoed with admiration and affection for the handsome author. David waved to a few acquaintances and winked discreetly at Ana who was standing behind the back row of seats, next to the door, as if guarding the exit. *La Franjić*, mildly whiffing of wine, nudged Ana's arm gently and said, "I voted for him. Do you know why?"

Ana shook her head.

"Because it's the only novel in the whole of this year's crop – and I've read absolutely everything that has been published, that's my job – the only novel that's neither girly tattle nor male... you know the usual name for that sexual activity men engage in with themselves, starting with *w*? Well, that particular activity has become the emblem of male writing. I've done a bit of research: this year; five novels written by men were published. Out of the five, only two don't mention the said activity. The remaining three mention it exactly 29 times.

Long live emancipation. My fellow critics – ladies included – have taken note of the fact that women have achieved emancipation. Like, there's general fiction and women's fiction. Women's fiction on one side, as an exception, and then the mainstream fiction, all produced by men. If I can only be bothered, I'll write an essay about male fiction and support it with my wanking stats. Plus a chart of top wank-scenes in modern Croatian novels. Next, an anthology is in order. Then I'd sort the wanks according to function: wanking as theme, wanking as background, proper sexual wanking, hygienic wanking (in the shower), wanking on account of unrequited love, bored wanking, warming wanking (because the central heating is broken down)... But the most recent arrival on the scene and the most dangerous type by far is the so-called creative or *fine artistic* wanking... You know what title of the essay would be? *What is a Man without a Wank.* No offence to Tomić[122], but he does lend himself to paraphrasing."

Ana laughed. Not bad: women's writing, men's wanking.

"You find that funny?" the lady critic looked at Ana, as if offended by her failure to recognise the magnitude of her discovery. "You know," the critic went on, "I can tell after the first page of any book not only who the author is but which clan he belongs to and which paper supports him. It's like having x-ray vision and seeing a skeleton instead of a person..." Ana laughed again. "But this I don't get at all. It doesn't belong anywhere. I wouldn't have been able to guess the sex of the author had I not seen the name. It doesn't belong to any strain, it's not trendy. Actually, I don't understand how it managed to win the award at all, bearing in mind that awards are handed out by robots and won by clones..."

Ana laughed once more.

Ms Franjić glared at Ana's face and said, "Everything's funny to you, isn't it?" She turned contemptuously away and applauded.

---

[122] *What is a Man Without a Moustache* is a novel by Croatian author Ante Tomić

Ana looked for Buba and Jelena: they were in the front row. They were not clapping. With a cramped stomach, she let her eyes glide over the venerable writerly, critical, editorial and publishing heads. They were all there: members of both the Authors' Association and the Association of Writers, clans around rival publishing houses, critics attached to warring clans, their backhander-taking tame journalists, those who came for a chance to see themselves on telly if cameras happened to pick them up, an occasional drunken marginal who did not belong to any clan as none were interested in him while he believed it was because he did not want to belong, because he was better and greater than others, only chronically misunderstood...

"...and so, as this year there was no doubt as to who should be the winner, our panel of judges decided unanimously..." Ana was roused from her thoughts by the voice of the perennially unshaven and untidy Tihomir Mirić, Chairman of the Critics' Association who had, probably in honour of the grand National and University Library building and its majesty, put on a thin, frayed tie which spiralled down into his blazer. His short hair, neatly cropped, carefully brushed back and most likely kept in place by hairspray, stood out from his untidy figure.

The audience applauded. David waved to them and bowed slightly. The applause became louder. David smiled. Ana was cramped up and tense. Ms Franjić was clapping, hands raised above her head. Her handbag swung on her shoulder to the beat of her applause. Jelena was looking around, searching for Ana.

"...much has already been written about this novel, so I'll keep it short. The profession was unanimous in their opinion that we were looking at a unique work which stood out from the entire literary production of recent years – or dare I say recent decades, both mainstream and fringe. To say that the book is refreshing would hardly be enough: everyone who has read it will agree with me when I say that what we have here is a work pushing the boundaries of literary expression so strongly that I dare predict it will speed up the progress of literary history. In fact, the official statement by the judging panel – the one you received with your invitation to this ceremony – contains a formulation along similar lines. And so I propose to cut the long story short and hand over to the author..." There was more applause as David waved again, both in acknowledgement and in dismissal of the applause. "...to whom I express once more my most sincere congratulations." Mirić shook David's hand firmly and kept shaking it for a long time.

David laughed and moved closer to the microphone. "You've all heard it, haven't you: the book that'll speed up the progress of literary history..." Some faces showed confusion: how could David be so immodest? Here and there, a solitary burst of laughter: David sounded as if he was joking at his own expense. Everyone, however, liked him. He continued in a more serious mode. "This is an example of a masculine book... isn't it?" He swept the auditorium with his glance. Ms Franjić was all ears, craning her neck towards him. "You're all aware of modern classifications: women's fiction, *chick-lit*, reality fiction, *strip-tease* fiction... Like all classifications, they represent accepted conventions critics and academics need for orientation. Still, what is it those categories have in common? They're popular and they're underrated." He paused again and looked towards the nearest rows. "Don't worry, I won't be long... And how do we know they're popular? Because they sell well. Why are they underrated? Because they're entertaining and easy to read, and probably because they sell well. So male writers did whatever they could to place them where they belong: among trivial literature. Why am I, a male writer, award-winning and therefore held in high public esteem, telling you this? Not only to put the injustice towards women writers right, but also because I am a literary critic, not just an author, and it is part of my job description to spot certain phenomena as they emerge. In short, having done necrophilia, genre, literary fiction and whatever else might belong under the male fiction label – which doesn't sell all that well – men launched into women's fiction, I being no exception. And we're doing very well, thank you... But why did men start writing like women?"

The Franjić woman was all agog; motionless and leaning forward, she listened to his every word. In the pause following David's rhetorical question, she turned to Ana: "Man, he's right! I know exactly what he's talking about! What a guy!"

"Well, why?" David repeated. A weak murmur soughed through the hall. "I, for one, don't know. Maybe because we, too, wanted to see twenty editions of our work, to tour like pop-folk stars and to pocket ten thousand kuna a month. Or maybe we, too, got liberated at last. Perhaps we grew up and realised it wasn't true that boys never cried. They cry, they do cry – how could they not cry? And they fall in love, they love, they suffer, they keep diaries and sometimes feel like writing women's fiction in order to be able to put on paper what really interests them, and that needn't be monsters, graveyards, war, chopped-off limbs and boozing a trail through Europe's bars. Men, too, have started writing about reality. A young lad has recently written a novel called *Love is All...* A new trend is upon us."

Ms Franjić applauded, the rest of the audience followed suit. "Hear, hear!" she shouted loudly, "We've had enough of wanker tyranny!" A few people looked at her with consternation.

David heard the comment and laughed. "Thank you," he said. "Well, that's that, then..." He bowed and stepped away from the microphone. The sloppy Chairman of the Critics' Association spoke into it but no one was listening. The applause grew ever louder, *La Franjić* leading.

Someone tapped Ana's shoulder. "Ana, what are you doing here?" It was Branko, also a critic, with a regular column in *The Garland*. They knew each other from secondary school.

"David is a friend," Ana said. "You?"

"Line of duty. But I've read the book and I must admit it's excellent. Have you read it?"

"Yes. It's okay," Ana said.

"An incredibly good story, no fancy cheap thrills, sensitive... he's really earned the award," Branko said. "And what about your book?" he asked. "I heard about it, *The Hungry She-Wolf...*"

"*The Naked She-Wolf,*" Ana corrected him. "You haven't read it?"

"I haven't had the time."

"Read it. I'd love to hear your comments. You don't have to write a review," said Ana.

"I will, but I can't promise to do it soon. You know when I last read a book I didn't have to review?" Branko asked. Ana shook her head. "I can't remember!"

"Are you saying you never read for pleasure?" Ana asked.

"Pleasure, my foot! Even if I had the time, I wouldn't be able to read like a normal person any more."

"Why do you do this job, then? You chose it because you loved reading..."

"One must do something," said Branko and shrugged.

Having said goodbye to Branko, Ana went looking for Jelena and Buba. They were already with David. "Congratulations," said Ana.

"I feel as if I've really won the award," David said.

"Everything's going according to plan," said Jelena.

The Hand
31 March
CHRONICLE: Genes responsible for cancer are being mapped
TV MAIN EVENING NEWS: Two children under five were diagnosed with skin cancer in Zagreb.
TV NEWS: 13 thousand Croats die of cancer every year

A strange coincidence in the choice of news, unless it is some sort of an international cancer day today. As far as I know, March the 31st is World Theatre Day.

Ana's Mum is Ill
Ana had one of her horrendous headaches again. She could barely take in what the doctor was saying. Cold shivers crawled up her back. Mum is ill. Cancer. Why didn't I believe she was

ill?

"Who's going to tell her? I?" she asked Dr Zmajević.

"We'll tell her," the doctor said. (A dragon, belching fire.[123]) "As far as you're concerned, just stay with her. That's what she needs most now."

"So, patients get told. I've always wondered..." Ana said.

"We tell them everything," the doctor said firmly. "Helps them mobilise for the battle ahead."

My mum won't mobilise, Ana thought. She'll grab onto me like the dead arms of a corpse reaching out of the grave. She shuddered. Finally she mustered enough courage to ask what mum's chances were.

"We'll talk about that when we have all the results," the doctor said.

She felt shame, but could not immediately identify the cause. She examined the immediate past moment by moment. What were her first feelings when they told her mum was mortally ill? Fear? Yes. Sadness? Yes. But underneath all that? Relief that she, Ana, wasn't ill. First the relief, then the sense of guilt for the selfishness of it. Next, readiness to devote herself selflessly to her sick mum, because the selfish need to score one up on her was satisfied: she'll die and I'll live on... A sentence she had read in Andrea Zlatar's column in *The Garland* floated into her mind. Of all the sentences she had read, she had memorised that one, word for word, letter by letter, God knows why: *Not even the sunniest day can make a cancer diagnosis go away. Not even the sunniest day can make a cancer diagnosis go away. Not even the sunniest day can make a cancer diagnosis...*

Not even the sunniest day can make...

Not even the sunniest day...

But the diagnosis is not mine, not mine. Not mine. It won't cancel out my lovely, sunny day. *Today is Such a Lovely Sunny Day*, Jelena's favourite song, a crazily merry song.

"She didn't have any symptoms," Jelena said. "Cancer is really so..."

---

[123] 'Zmaj' means dragon in Croatian.

"Cancer is not a silent killer. It does have symptoms, only people take no notice of them."

"That's true, you're right... Have you spoken to the doctor? What's the prognosis?"

"Not good, I'm afraid. They haven't said anything concrete, though. I asked Dr Kristić, you know, Auntie Klaudija, that old neighbour of mine for whom I sometimes do a bit of shopping... She retired ages ago, but she used to be a surgeon. Judging by the size of the tumour and the lymphatic nodes, she says mum could live another year. With modern medicines, perhaps even longer..."

"I read about a very surprising fact somewhere," Jelena said. "The survival rate with lung cancer seems to be quite high, much higher than people generally believe. I can't remember the exact figure, but it's definitely higher than 50%."

"Yeah, but do you know what the medical profession and the data analysts mean by survival? It's not, as you might imagine, surviving cancer and then dying naturally of old age in bed or getting run over by a car. For them, survival is if you make it through five years after the initial diagnosis. If you die after five years and a day, you'll have – statistically – survived. I expect they don't even consider the secondary cancer, the one that develops from the metastases of the original one, to be the same illness. Mum might die in two years' time from a brain tumour brought about by metastases, but in the lung cancer stats she'll be recorded as survivor because there will be no end outcome to the initial lung cancer input: she will not have died of lung cancer but of brain tumour. To the analysts, throat cancer mortality runs around 30%, breast cancer 40%, prostate ten... And so one wonders which idiot had made it up that cancer was a mortal illness."

"What are you going to do?" Jelena asked thoughtfully. "Your mum wasn't easy to deal with even while she was healthy, and now... You must talk to her, tell her what a beautiful, fulfilled life she's had. I've read somewhere that there are psychologists specially trained to do that sort of thing..."

"No, that wouldn't help," said Ana. "I have a better idea: I'll tell her, 'You know, mum, by a strange coincidence I, too, happen to be seriously ill, only I didn't want to tell you before because you'd have worried. It's my stomach. I'm going to the hospital tomorrow. When they open me up, they'll see how far it has spread. While you're in here, I'll be at Rebro[124].' She'll say, 'If only it were just me who was ill! All I wish is for you to be well, and as for me, I'll manage...' And she'll fight for her life to the last ounce of her strength but she won't moan, because it won't do for her to moan about herself while her child is ill..."

"You're nuts," said Jelena.

"What's wrong with that?" Ana asked.

"What makes you think she'd believe you? She can see you're well."

"She'll stay in hospital at least ten days after her operation, and the surgery is not due till next Monday. I'll have enough time to 'recover' from my operation..."

"What on earth are you saying?"

"Well, if that's not possible," said Ana calmly, "then I can think of only one other way of saving her form fear... a whack on the head with a mallet."

Jelena looked at her as if seeing a spectre.

Ana laughed, but her eyes remained sombre. "Why are you looking at me like that? Our society is hypocritical towards old people," she went on calmly. "All future social systems will have a humane way of getting rid of the old and the weak. Old people have no consideration for others and it doesn't occur to them it might be time to... instead, they keep on fighting to the last... they *cling* to life and cosset their sick bodies, all because the human brain ages slower than the body; it starts once you're over eighty..."

"There's a science fiction film where the society has organised it so that old people are killed when..." Ana gave her a bored look. "Your mum is not old," Jelena said.

"But she *is* ill." Ana was implacable.

"If that were so," Jelena said, no longer hiding her

---

[124] The largest teaching hospital in Zagreb

revulsion, "people should, as soon as they grow up, perhaps as soon as they're born, simply sit down and expect death. Then there'd be no point to anything."

Ana shrugged. "What makes you think there is a point?"

"The fact that we exist," Jelena said.

"Don't look so flabbergasted," Ana said.

Jelena felt nauseous after the discussion.

***

Ana went to see her mother and sat on her bed, by her feet. Mother said, "It's all up with me, my Ana."

Like in a soap opera, Ana thought. "Mum, don't," she said.

Her mum's eyes were black and hollow with fear. Her mouth was pursed tight, her jaw clenched, giving her face a hard look. Ana moved closer, lifted her mother's thin body up a bit, took it into her arms and rocked her mum gently for a long, long time. "Everything will be fine, everything will be fine," she repeated softly and monotonously. Reclining on Ana's shoulder, her mother trembled, small and light as a child. She exuded a feeling of mortal fear. If mum had a sense of humour, Ana thought, I'd tell her that, on the bright side, she won't be around when the world ends in 2012. She remembered how her mother chided before her Venice trip. "How can you enjoy a trip you paid for with your credit card! I wouldn't pay interest to the banks on principle; don't you know that's how they make their money? I never spent any money I hadn't earned."

"It's not that expensive, mum," Ana had replied dutifully as she always did. "They gave us a discount for booking online..." Had she dared, she'd have also said, "Life is short and valueless When the reckoning time comes, we won't remember the interest we paid to banks, but we just might remember Venice. We might. Or we won't remember anything, so it won't matter anyway."

The woman on the bed next to her mum's was probably just as ill, but was of a better disposition. She was younger than Ana's mother. Her family visited every day: her skinny, runty, sad-faced husband and her three devoted teenage sons. The youngest could have been fifteen and the oldest around nineteen years old.

"How can you say your end has come, my dear lady," the woman said. "Only our dear Lord knows such things."

Ana regarded her approvingly. She had heard that the woman had refused chemo after her surgery. Instead, she had started a self-prescribed starvation cure. The doctors disapproved, but the woman told Ana conspiratorially, "I'll starve the beast, and then we'll see who wins in the end."

The woman on Ana's mother's right, on the bed by the window, was to go home. Mum whispered into Ana's ear, far too loudly: "She's gravely ill. They're discharging her because there's nothing they can do. She's done for." The woman was putting on makeup: she applied mascara, green eye-shadow, red lipstick and a strong brick-red blusher. She turned towards the window, took off her turban and put on the wig she had been keeping in a plastic bag.

"Why tart yourself up like that when you'll be taken home by ambulance?" mum asked.

"So what," said the woman. "I won't give them the pleasure!"

"Me, I'll be joining my Marta," said mum in a voice full of pathos. Her best friend Marta had been ill with cancer for a number of years. Around the time she lay dying, mum asked Ana to copy addresses and telephone numbers from their old address book into a new one. Ana found Marta's number and asked, "Shall I copy Auntie Marta's number, too?" Mum said she didn't need to. Ana thought about it frequently afterwards: that was precisely what was so tough for mortally ill people; they no longer belonged to the world of the living but were not yet dead. The phone number of a mortally ill woman would have been like a dangerous germ among the numbers of healthy people: it could spread. And it would have been useless, too: there were no phones in heaven.

The Hand
Friday, 22 April

FRONT PAGE: Acting on their Director's orders, the staff at Zagreb Zoo killed a sick camel using clubs and axes. Drenched in blood and howling piteously under their blows, the camel took two hours to die.

THE DAY'S EVENTS: THE PROTEST MEETING OF THE MONGOOSE ON ST MARK'S SQUARE

"Sixty explosive technicians from AKD Mungos[125] staged a meeting yesterday at noon on St Mark's place, in protest against the redundancies at Mungos, a company that has gone into receivership last week. The technicians demanded that alternative work be found for the company's employees."

Where have I put that stuff about the areas which still haven't been cleared of landmines?
June 29th

TV NEWS: Dr. Plavšić, toxicologist, warns of the fact that Croatia still has no law regulating the production and the use of toxic chemicals. The existing law, regulating the transport but not the production of hazardous chemicals, has been passed without debate two years ago. Without any reference to health and safety issues, it only regulates the medical treatment of people once they have been poisoned, and how to deal with the consequences in such cases. That means that Croatian companies producing hazardous chemicals can do as they please. If an error occurs during their production, some chemicals can kill any person after a single inhalation within the radius of 350 metres. This threat is not limited to the facility in Kutina[126].

CHRONICLE: Unfriendly people suffer more heart attacks.

---

[125] AKD Mungos d.o.o. ('mungos' meaning 'mongoose') is a Croatian company specialising in landmine clearance, employing a large number of experts for handling explosives.
[126] A petrochemical plant in Kutina

Mother's Revelation

Every afternoon after work, Ana would visit her mother in hospital. Almost daily, she would stop by Aunt Klaudija's, describe the latest developments in her mother's condition and ask the old surgeon what it meant.

The hospital was situated at the far end of the town, a large green building. Although she did her best to avoid the rush hour, it took Ana nearly an hour to get there. Mum was always full of requests. "The doctor said I have to drink a lot, at least two litres a day. Get me some fruit juice!" More, more, more, she always wanted one more thing. And she kept demanding stewed vegetables. "All I need is some stewed veg, nothing else." Just the veg, stewed! It's easy to say just the veg, Ana thought. To make the stewed veg happen, someone had to go to the market, buy the veg, prepare it and cook the stew. One had to put it into containers, put those into plastic bags to avoid spillage, remember to pack the fork and the spoon... Then arrange it all on mum's bedside cabinet already crammed with objects, in the narrow space between two beds. Later, pack the dirty dishes away while asking, "Was it nice, mum?"

"Too salty, but still better than hospital food."

Mum, oh mum. No chance of gratitude here. There's not a contented bone in her. Perhaps that's why she became ill in the first place. But then again, at her age, one is expected to be ill rather than healthy. Perhaps her greed has kept her in good health until now.

"How are you, mum?" Ana sked, thinking how mum had never once asked her the same question. She had actually never in her whole life asked: "How are you, Ana?" Mum just waved her hand and raised her eyes heavenwards.

Ana said, "And I, I'm tired, terribly tired."

"I know," mum said, meaning to sound sympathetic. "I know; you're not up to it."

"Not up to what?"

"It's all too much for you," mum explained.

"What's too much for me?"

"You're not used to having to do everything yourself... I've had enough, put it away!" Mum pushed the bowl away.

Ana asked no more questions. Silent, she picked up mum's bowl, placed the used spoon and the left-over bits of crust into it, put the plastic cover on and put the bowl into a bag.

"Would you like some fruit juice?" she asked.

"Later," said mum and sighed.

"I've got to go," Ana said abruptly.

"Already?" mum said. "I wanted you to rub me down a bit with a towel..."

"I will, I will," said Ana. "I forgot."

After the wash, Ana plumped up the pillows and pulled her mother up into a semi-sitting position. "Feeling better now?" she asked, trying to sound warm.

"Sit down now, I need to tell you something," mum said, glancing at her roommate who was asleep and breathing heavily.

"What?"

"I'm gravely ill..." Ana tried to interrupt her but mother silenced her with a commanding gesture of her hand and continued: "From what I've seen here, these things can move fast: you can lose consciousness just like that, in an instant. That's why I've got to tell you a few things, while my mind is still clear..." Mother's face was hard. "To begin with, I've made a certified Power of Attorney for you to be able to draw money from my accounts. Just so you know. You'll collect this together with my Last Will from my solicitor – you'll find the address at home among my papers – when you show him my Death Certificate. That's in case I die before I manage to sort it all myself with the bank. I'm better at that sort of thing than you; you always get confused with money..."

Ana shrugged; she had thought it would be something of greater importance.

"Next thing, listen carefully... regarding your father..."

Good riddance, may the Lord forgive me, Ana could hear the rest of the sentence in her head.

"...he didn't die when you were five. I won't beat around the bush. He's still alive. It would've been better if he wasn't, but he is. You know him, but you don't know he's your father. And he doesn't know you're his daughter either."

Listening to her mother's panting, hoarse voice, Ana was trying to connect her seemingly unconnected words into a whole that would make sense. It seemed to her that they could be arranged in several different ways among which she could, if she only made herself concentrate, pick out the one that suited her most: he's still alive, he didn't die, good riddance, may the Lord forgive me, he didn't die. Then she finally understood: my father is alive, I can find him... Having had grasped the information, she worried about where to file it, as if the most important thing were to find the right place for it, a place where it won't get lost – like in *My Documents* folder, for example.

"It's up to you what you do... but don't expect anything," Ana could hear her mother's voice. "Bear in mind that he's a cad and a piece of shit and that it's a crying shame you carry too many of his genes. He ruined me; my father renounced me because of him. I lost my family because of him, I lost everything."

And got me, Ana thought. So what am I to do about it? What's the use of having a father like that? "Why do I have to find out about it now when I didn't have to know about it before?" she asked, hoping feebly that she could still escape the full impact of mum's revelation.

"Because it's proper, and humane. You're his blood after all. He could have had a son whom you could have married without knowing he was your brother. People need to know who they issue from."

"All right," said Ana. "Who do I issue from?" She tried to sound calm and cool; perhaps mum would stop then; she might be saying stuff just because she enjoyed torturing her.

"Your father is Andrej Martić," mum said and pursed her lips together very hard.

Instantaneously, Ana's headache returned, even before her mother's words reached her. Andrej Martić? Could her mother, behind her pursed lips and firmly closed eyes, be enjoying herself just a bit: such tremendous, shocking news! Ana could not think of anything to say that would sound cold and disinterested. "Andrej Martić? From *The Herald?*" She sounded calm; she was doing well.

"Yes, yes," mum confirmed triumphantly, as if disappointed with Ana's lukewarm reaction: she could never understand that child.

"But he doesn't have a big nose at all," Ana said.

"Did you understand what I said?"

"I did," Ana said. "I have a father, he's alive, he's Andrej Martić." *Good riddance, may the Lord forgive me.* "And I'm not to expect anything because he's a cad and a piece of shit... a cad and a piece of shit, and I've got his genes." Woman, why did you get involved with all those cads, she thought.

Mother looked at her silently, without sympathy. That was fortunate: had she shown any, Ana would have cried and cried and would never have stopped.

"Is that all? In that case, I have something to say to you too," said Ana calmly. "You're always upset for being the last one to find out about things I do, so I'll give you some fresh news: I've finished my second book and it's been published..." Let her think the book matters to me as much as her news about my father.

"Published? When?" her mother schreeched.

How she screeches, Ana thought. She's really hurt I haven't told her sooner. And that she hasn't managed to shock the hell out of me. She laughed.

"What's funny?" Mum eyed her suspiciously.

"The book was published under David's name, not mine. It's already won a prize."

"I'm speechless," her mother screechled. "You're old enough to know what's what, but you go on doing stupid things like that."

"The award ceremony is tomorrow."

"A fine affair," mum said. "You'll end up having to prove in court you're the author."

"I won't have to," Ana said.

She only thought of Andreja the following day when she saw her at the school. Sister. Who knows why God has given her a sister, she thought. And why he has given her to Andreja as sister. She searched the filing cabinet again for Andreja's records. Father: Andrej Martić, 9th October 1950, Zagreb, journalist. Address: 48b Novak Street. Marital status: married.

Ana Gets the Sack

The first few days after her mother's revelation, Ana avoided Andreja at the school as much as she could without letting the girl notice. She needed time to get herself together. She had vague hopes that Andreja might eventually benefit from having a sister. For the time being, she surprised herself by managing to put Andrej Martić out of her mind. In any case, the revelation had not changed her life at all, not even a bit.

Ana's headaches got worse. A week after mum's revelation, she unexpectedly lost her job. This is how it happened: she got to work in a relatively good mood, determined to stay positive. The pupils were talking noisily when she entered the classroom; she waved a greeting and gave them a sign to settle down. At a desk in the first row, Ana-Marija, a pretty and well-developed girl who was usually reticent and quiet, chose on this occasion to sit sprawling on her chair, with hands folded over her protruding belly. Its bulge was reinforced by the low cut and the tight fit of her jeans. Sitting motionlessly, the girl did not straighten up even when Ana had sat down. "Ana-Marija," Ana said, "I had no idea you were pregnant!" The classroom roared with laughter.

"What's wrong with you, Miss," said the girl, "I'm not sixteen yet!"

The class roared again. That made Ana realise she had made a mistake. Naively, perhaps, she had thought that private schools, unlike the state supported ones, were open to pregnant students. Ana-Marija's parents came to the school to demand that justice be done. A few days later, the Head handed Ana a letter of Exceptional Dismissal. "I'm really sorry, Ms Marton, but there's no way I can justify your imprudence. The kids have told their parents; everyone is appalled. Your being the school psychologist makes it even worse." Ana said nothing. She had nothing to say. Her autism, Jelena's term for her detachment from the outside world, had its price.

Before she left, she looked for the girl with the belly. "I'm sorry," she said. "It was silly of me. You were sitting... you know, as if guarding your tummy... and I thought that was why you were in a private school... I'm sorry." She was truly sorry, because the girl was one of those children that do not quite fit in. She did not stand out and did not look contented.

"It's all right," Ana-Marija said. "I know you didn't do it on purpose..." Turning to leave, she halted. "Can I ask you something?"

"You can ask me anything you like," Ana said.

"Is my stomach really so big that I look pregnant?"

"No. I already told you: you were sitting in such a way that it appeared you'd stuck out your tummy on purpose, as if to relieve pressure, and you even folded your arms over it... it really looked like it. God knows what came over me; someone else in my place would probably never have thought you were pregnant..." She knew she did not sound convincing. She placed her hands on the girl's shoulders and said: "You know what, when I was fifteen, we were about to move to another part of the town and I cried terribly, not because I had to leave any friends I loved at the old address; no, I never used to hang out with anyone and no one wanted to hang out with me; as soon as I'd get out, the other kids would disperse as if I was a leper. Do you know why I cried? Because I thought it was my task to live my life in such a way that as few people as possible get to meet me, a monster... that as few people as possible have contact with my ugliness and... my misery... as if I was some kind of germ, spreading TB or something... and must save mankind from myself."

Ana Marija looked at her with serious eyes. Ana embraced her. "Forgive me," she said. "I only wanted you to know that you're a wonderful, beautiful and smart young lady and that there is nothing wrong with your tummy... more likely, with my head..."

"Is that why you've become a psychologist?" asked the girl cleverly. They both laughed.

The Hand
Monday, 25 April

FRONT PAGE: A US paedophile gets 21 years; a paedophile from Rijeka gets 8 months' suspended sentence

"On Thursday, the US federal Court sent Tony Guerriera to prison for 21 years and 10 months for possession of 2000 pornographic photographs and 90 pornographic films of children. In September of 2003, the offender from Rijeka had ten times more "material" but Croatian law is far less hard on paedophiles (...) The international legal community had already issued a severe warning to Croatia for not explicitly including the internet and the new media in her Criminal Law."

Anton Knows
Andreja burst into tears when Ana came to say goodbye.

"It's all right," Ana said comforting her, "it's all right. Everything will be fine. We can see each other outside the school; you can come to see me whenever you like. I'll still go to the Centre with you..."

"Who will they send their information to now?" Andreja asked.

"It might be the time to tell your parents," said Ana. Parents... our father. Oh my God.

"No, please, not yet, Miss," Andreja said.

"I'm not your teacher any more; you can say 'thou' to me now."

Andreja gave her a shy nod. She was crying.

"Are you OK?" Ana asked, concerned.

"He's back," said Andreja, staring at the floor.

"You *must* tell your parents," Ana said.

"No," the girl cried, horrified. "Not them. He would..."

Ana felt a sharp stab of pain in her head.

When she got home, she was not surprised to find Anton's

e-mail on her computer. She had been expecting it in a way. Anton always sensed that something was going on. The content of the mail upset and confused her.

Dear Ana, I'm sorry you lost your job. Never mind, though. You have other, more important work to do. You have a sister who needs looking after. You're already beginning to guess who Andreja's molester might be, I know, and I want to confirm your doubts..."

What is it I'm beginning to guess, she wondered. What is he on about? I have no doubts. How can I possibly know who that man is?

The Hand
28 April

TV MAIN DAILY NEWS: Sexual and other abuse of inmates of the Children's Home in Brezovica comes to light.
9th May

The construction of the Mediterranean Institute for Life Research is finally complete. *Well done, Academic Radman! Oops, they say he's not an Academic in our sense, that the French Academy doesn't compare with ours. All right, then: well done, Dr Radman!*
10th May

Three members of family Gomelt died in a horrendous car accident: Paulina, Ivan and their 10-year old son. The family's tragic destiny has thus come to its conclusion: a few years ago, their eldest son drowned in Kupa River.

What kind of a monstrous jackpot did that family win? Could the introduction of a minimal difference have saved them?

The Truman Show

"We need to talk," said Helena to Andrej one evening when he got home earlier than usual. She had managed to grab him before he vanished into the bathroom, as he would normally undress and go to bed immediately after his bath.

"Talk about what?" He gave her an irritated look.

"I feel like I'm on The Truman Show," Helena said abruptly and clumsily.

Andrej sniggered cruelly. "You're crazy," he said, pushed her aside slightly and disappeared into the bathroom, slamming the door.

Helena remained outside, facing the door. She had prepared what she wanted to say but was suddenly no longer convinced that a discussion would change anything. It was however necessary to clear things up while she still had enough time for some sort of a new start. Squeezing her mouth between the doorpost and the door so that Andrej could hear her, she said, "I don't know why you asked me to marry you and why you chose to turn my life into a farce while I believed I was living a life, but..."

"You're crazy," Andrej repeated from the bathroom.

"I know you know what I mean. I'm off to Osijek tomorrow for a performance," she shouted. "I'll be back the day after tomorrow. We'll talk when I return; don't imagine you can wriggle out of it. And Andreja is on the morning timetable, just so you know, because of her meals."

She got back from Osijek the following afternoon: the show was cancelled because of the lead actor's illness. When she tried to unlock the door, she could not insert the key into the keyhole: another key was already in it. She rang the doorbell but no one came to open the door. She tried to unlock the door again, without success. She rang the doorbell for a long time and finally called the home number on her mobile. It took a while for Andrej to reply.

"I'm outside the door," Helena said. "Didn't you hear the doorbell?"

"No," said Andrej and put the receiver down.

Helena heard the creaking of the bedroom door and Andrej's footsteps in the corridor. He opened without a word; his face wore a dark expression. Helena put her luggage down, took her coat off in the corridor and made for the bedroom. "Where is Andreja?" she asked. She opened the bedroom door and saw the unmade bed, scattered cushions and crumpled sheets. Andreja was there, by the window, looking out. She did not turn her head when the door opened. Could her hearing be getting worse? Helena thought. "Andreja, it's me," she said. Andreja did not react. Helena went up to her and turned her round face to face. The girl's face was wet, her eyes were red and her blouse unbuttoned. She turned her face away. "What's happened?" Helena asked, her voice breaking with fear. Suddenly, she heard Andrej's voice in her head: "Are you trying to kill my Andreja? Are you trying to kill my Andreja?" That was what he said when Andreja had meningitis. He did not say my child, my daughter, he said *Andreja*. Aghast, she held Andreja in a tight embrace. Andreja sighed once, as if waking up from a trance. Helena hugged her and kissed her, trying to button up her blouse. The girl just stood there, motionless. Helena pulled her closer feeling the rigidity of her body. She forced her daughter's head down to rest on her shoulder as if manipulating a doll. At that point, Andreja sunk limply down onto her mother's body. Helena swayed under her unbalanced weight; her own legs felt soft, as if made of dough. Her glance searched for a place to sit down, but she looked away to avoid seeing the crumpled bedding on the unmade bed. Helena led her daughter slowly to the sitting room and sat her down on the settee. She could hear sobs echoing through the air and rebounding against the walls, unaware that they were her own. "Mummy's little darling, mummy's little darling, mummy's little darling," she wailed mournfully. Everything spun fast around her, the sound, the room, the furniture. Suddenly she spotted Andrej taking his jacket off the clothes hanger. She leaned her daughter gently against the back of the settee, sprung to her feet and darted into the corridor, her arms stretched out before her as if she were blind. "You monster!" she screamed. "Monster! Monster! Monster! You beast!" She screamed and screamed and screamed until her throat hurt, and then she growled. She thrust both her fists into Andrej's face, her fingers curled into claws. He pushed her away with disgust and left. She just stood there; her legs refused to move. As if welded to the spot, her back turned to Andreja, she spoke hoarsely, struggling for breath: "What have I done, what have I done! What have I done! My darling child, my sweetie, my darling baby! It'll all be fine, my darling." She didn't understand her own words any more, they flowed continuously out of her like a rosary; all she knew was she had to go on speaking no matter what...

Soulmates

By a stroke of luck, the *Men and Women* magazine, with offices one floor above those of *The Herald*, needed someone for their Agony Aunt column, *Soulmates*. The position was freelance and not particularly well paid, but tailor-made for Ana who got it on Jelena's recommendation. She was to start at once. Jelena was pleased about that. "You'll be able to get out of your own head a bit," she said to Ana.

And I'll be closer to my father, thought Ana with irony.

Most of the readers' letters came by e-mail. Ana composed her replies mainly at home, visiting the office several times a week to pick up the letters that had arrived by surface mail and to attend meetings. The downside was that most of the letters were about love troubles, a topic that went on Ana's nerves as she could not muster any interest in it. *My wife loves sex but doesn't like kissing. I miss kissing. What might be her problem?* Or: *My boyfriend loves me, but I feel that for us to have sex at this stage would be too soon. Am I right?* Or: *I'm pretty, desirable and happy by nature, but I've found out that my husband is cheating on me with my best friend...*

Now that she came regularly to the office, David and Jelena kept an eye on Ana, aware of the challenging period she was going through: her book, her mother, a new job. From time to time, they got her to join them in the *Little Café*.

Ana and Nina

Nina took particular interest in Ana who kept her at a distance in a way that was not particularly subtle, because she thought that Nina was being condescendingly kind to her. One day they found themselves alone together at the table in the *Little Café*. Jelena had not arrived yet and David was at the bar, talking to someone.

"How does it feel to be liked by everyone?" Ana asked Nina somewhat brutally, with an intention to chase her away rather than start a conversation.

Nina was surprised but did not look embarrassed. Her laughter was relaxed and genuine. "What do you mean?" She laughed once more. "Where did you get the idea that everyone likes me?"

"Because everyone does," said Ana, looking straight into her eyes, unsmiling and serious. "Is it possible you haven't noticed?"

"I never really thought about it," Nina said.

"I don't believe you," said Ana. "Perhaps you're so used to it you really no longer notice."

Nina laughed as if brushing the comment away.

"So tell me, then, how does it feel?" Ana demanded once more. "It is the one thing I can't imagine."

"Ah, you're asking me that as a writer," said Nina.

"Why do you say that?"

"Because I do the same. Although perhaps you don't like what I write."

"Oh no, I like it. Only, I find there's perhaps too much... plot in your book, like in a Hollywood movie."

Nina smiled. "You find it hard to believe that all those things could happen to my characters, while in fact... Would you believe me if I told you every word was true?"

"I know that something like that really happened to you," said Ana.

"We'll talk about it another time."

"All right," Ana agreed. "And you probably found my book boring."

"Not at all. I already told you I liked it. I'd read it before I knew you were the author," Nina said. "It's entertaining, it takes you by surprise, it's cheerful... It struck me that all your characters are beautiful and exceptional people."

"Writing is a substitute," Ana said. "Since I have the opportunity to create people exactly as I want them to be, the least I can do is make them worthy of existence."

Nina listened carefully while remaining relaxed. Ana was envious. Always tense like a coiled spring, she did not even know what it was like to be relaxed. "Please don't think me envious or mean," she said, "but you must be aware of the fact that your book is doing better than mine because you're prettier than me? I'm not envious of you, but can't help noticing..."

Nina regarded her without discomfort. "No, I'm not aware of it. But I do believe you when you tell me that that is your perception."

Ana looked at Nina's beautiful face. "I wonder what it's like to hold all the trumps."

Nina nodded, sunk in thought. "All the trumps..." She shook her head absently.

"I know, beauty is relative, it is in the eye of the beholder, de gustibus... and so on. But I'm not speaking strictly of beauty. And besides, one values most what one doesn't have," Ana replied.

"Perhaps you think you're not pretty because you weren't loved enough?"

"Or I wasn't loved enough... because I'm not pretty enough." Ana laughed.

Nina placed her hand on top of Ana's. Ana withdrew her hand. Nina said, "Perhaps I wasn't loved enough, too. We might have more in common than you think... I've got to go, my mother is alone at home and she's not well."

"Yours too?" Ana smiled. "I'm sorry. That's something else... we have in common. Is it serious?"

"Depression. There are days when she hardly budges from the spot. Yours?"

"Cancer."

"I'm sorry," said Nina.

Ana shrugged.

The Hand

6th June

EVENTS OF THE DAY: D.V. (57), the university professor who was arrested last week on suspicion of filming child pornography and engaging in lewd sexual behaviour in the presence of minors, is under suspicion of having sexually abused children he took from the Lug Children's Home into his own personal care during the winter.

(In the box:) "Sexual activity in the presence of a child or a minor is punishable by a custodial sentence from three months to up to three years.

For sexual intercourse with a disabled person according to the Article 189 of the Criminal Law, a custodial sentence from six months to up to five years can be given. This relates to a situation where inability to offer resistance due to mental illness or disturbance or to insufficient mental development is exploited by the offender to obtain sexual satisfaction.

If the same offence is committed in a particularly brutal or humiliating way, or if the victim has been subject to more than one intercourse by several perpetrators, a custodial sentence of between one and ten years can be given."

20 June

A TV PROGRAMME ON PAEDOPHILIA

The Sunja case: A child of four and a child of six were abused by their own father and mother, who, together with the children's godparents and uncle, used the children in their sexual orgies.

The cook's diary: The cook at Brezovica Children's Home kept a diary where he described in detail his sexual activities involving female inmates. Having had read the diary, the Manageress gave him a severe verbal reprimand and dismissed him, but did not report him.

Paedophilia is a fashionable subject.

23 June

FRONT PAGE: The Brezovica Scandal; Court Expert Kept Sexual Abuse Secret.

A three-year old child told about "drinking from daddy's

willy that was stinky and hard". The father was freed last week because the expert, a psychologist, "forgot" to quote that particular part of the child's statement. The same psychologist acted as expert in the case of abused children from Sunja, and she is also responsible for the cover-up of the Brezovica scandal.

The Brezovica Childrens' Home is owned by the Church, whose representatives claim that the media have blown the scandal out of proportion in order to attack the Church. It is true that the representatives appear to care more for the Church's reputation than for the fate of the abused children ("if they have been abused" they hasten to add), but I'd like to ask all those who get so worked up about paedophile priests: is this crime less serious if the paedophiles belong to a different profession?

Anton's Second Discovery

Walking through the city, Ana looked at people's faces, wondering if Anton was among them. She felt he was around, and that he knew everything. This time he even mailed her at her work address:

Dear Ana, I've noticed you've got a new job. You do it brilliantly, but then you do everything brilliantly, although I know how much you've suffered recently. It is well that you've managed to put Andrej Martić out of your mind for the moment. It is not yet time to turn your attention to him, although he deserves hell because he destroyed three wives and three daughters. It's interesting: you know both your sisters and are, in a way, the link that connects them. You'll help them.

How does he know about Martić? What does he mean, three daughters? He's mad.

You're wrong, she replied, *there's only two of us. And how is it possible for you to know all about me? Who are you?*

Anton did not reply.

Ana's head was splitting with pain. The last she remembered was walking along the street. And now she was at her desk, in front of the computer. That had happened several times recently. She was not too concerned: she had always been prone to moments of absence. And madness was the one illness she did not fear.

Nina

Nina slowly opened the door of her mother's old workshop. Ever since she was little she would enter the once genteel, now dilapidated two-storey building at the top end of Radić Street through the workshop, avoiding the main entrance. The machines were still in the workshop and mother worked there rather than at the large new premises which had been standing empty ever since she'd had to let her two seamstresses go. The only one left was Auntie Mira who had no income and nothing to live on so she helped Nina's mother and in return shared her meals and heating. They both survived on Nina's handouts and the income from rent: mother had rented out most of the building, for small money, since the house was in poor condition. Wearing her old velvet dressing gown, in places worn down to its brownish weft, mother sat facing the window. Her hair was gathered into a loose bun. When she slowly turned around, Nina could see her nightie under the gown although it was late afternoon. Mother was undergoing treatment for depression.

"It's you," mum said tenderly.

"Are you alone, mum? Still not dressed? Where's Auntie Mira?"

"I'll get dressed directly." Mother wrapped the gown tighter around her body. "Auntie Mira had to go to the dentist; she'll be back soon."

Nina put her arm around her mother's shoulders. "You'll get dressed now, and then we'll quickly make something for lunch." She spoke calmly and seriously, without false cheer, careful not to treat her mother like a helpless child: she would never humiliate her like that.

"My lovely girl," said mother and stroked Nina's hair.

Nina could see the open envelope with the bank's logo on

the window sill. Another notice. She took the letter out: *If by... you do not... seizure of assets...* She folded the paper and put it back into the envelope. Before the war, mother had borrowed money from the bank to buy new machines and modernize the workshop. The new machines now stood idle and would be worth next to nothing if sold. Mother had managed to keep up with her payments for a few years by skimping on herself, but during the war the business declined further and soon there was no money for supplies, and barely enough for her seamstresses' wages. Worst of all, she noticed that valuable objects had gone missing from the house, and money too, when there was some around. She adored her daughter and only understood what was going on when it was already too late. She put Nina's rudeness and talking back to teenage rebellion and growing up without a father. When she discovered that Nina was taking drugs, the girl left home. It took Magda a long time to find out where she was, and then she read in the papers that *the body of a 25-year old man was found in Nina Ivezić's flat...* Following the police investigation, Nina was sent to Vinogradska Hospital for treatment. Magda went to visit her every day, crying. Nina's doctor seemed casual and indifferent. "How come you never noticed anything before, madam?" he said flatly. "There's little we can do now, it's too late. Cases like hers seldom make it." But Magda kept coming. She'd sit with Nina or, when Nina didn't want to see her, in the corridor. She prayed for a miracle and a miracle happened: Nina pulled through. "Only in one of a thousand cases," the doctor said, pleased and proud as if it had happened thanks to his efforts. Much later, Nina filled Magda in on the missing bits of the story: Mladen had been a heavy user and had got Nina, whom he genuinely loved, into drugs. Knowing that he himself was beyond help, he tried to save Nina while there was still time. Nina knew he would die unless he got himself off drugs with medical help. She decided to ask her father to help them. Her father was Andrej Martić, a prominent journalist of high renown and with a good income. She knew where he lived; she followed him and intercepted him at the entrance to *The Herald's* office building. "I never asked you for anything before," she said. "I'm asking you now to help us get well again. We need money for rehab. If we don't get off the drugs, we're finished." She was thin and pale. A web of capillaries covered the whites of her huge eyes. Her nose was running and she was shivering with cold. Andrej regarded her with disgust; he seemed ready to push her away. He produced a wallet from his pocket, took out a neatly folded hundred kuna note[127], thrust it into Nina's clenched fist, spun around and entered the building. A few weeks later, Mladen overdosed on purpose. "Go back to your mum," he said. "You can still make it."

Her mother indifferently gulped down huge mouthfuls of food: she had no appetite and did not care what she was shovelling down her throat. "Would you like me to stay with you for a few days?" Nina asked her.

"No, no, please don't worry. I'll be fine. Auntie Mira sleeps here now; in the morning she does the bits that need doing in the workshop and still has the time to make lunch... Everything's fine. It's just that today, I'm a bit... y'know..." A few years ago, mother had made Nina move away, fearing that the unhealthy atmosphere and her depression might push her back into drugs, and would not let her hang around the house in Radić Street for long.

"You've had a new warning?" Nina said.

"Don't you worry about it, I'll see to that," said mum.

"I'm going to do it," said Nina after lunch.

"Do what?" mum asked.

"I'm going to ask him to help us."

"Leave him alone, we'll sort something out. I've got that life policy..."

"Which is worth a lot less if you cash it in early, and is small enough as it is," said Nina. And is not valid in the case of suicide, she wanted to say but did not dare to.

She went back to the *Herald*, knowing Andrej would be there. Everyone knew he hung around the office because he did

---

[127] £11.17

not like being at home. In the afternoon, however, no one was allowed to disturb him without previous appointment. When Nina entered his inner sanctum, he nearly shouted at her, but something in the expression on her face stopped him.

"What do you want?" he asked.

"I told you already: the bank will take mother's home and her workshop if she doesn't pay off at least part of the mortgage. She'll lose everything. We need twenty thousand euros to save the workshop."

"I told you I haven't got that sort of money," Andrej barked. "I gave you a job, I found you another one at the Television: what more do you want?"

"You'd be the last one I'd ask if we had any other way out. And I'd never ask you if it was just me. But I fear for mum."

"I told you I haven't got the money," Andrej repeated.

Nina regarded him with disgust but also with the curiosity of an explorer watching a rare animal from a safe distance. "Don't you feel the need to do at least something in the end?"

Seemingly calm, Andrej was shuffling through the papers on his desk. "I told you I haven't got the money," he repeated unflinchingly.

"You know why I managed to save myself?" Nina asked. "To make you pay for those hundred kuna one day."

"Why should I rescue Zagreb's junkies?" Andrej said impatiently, with contempt.

"Because your daughter used to be one of them. You never loved mum either, am I right? Did you really marry her just to be registered at a posh address?"

Andrej's eyes were hard. "All of you..." he started, and stopped.

"All of us?" Nina was trying to sound cold. "All of us you conceived, or all you married and then sucked dry like a vampire? Have you been keeping records? Do you even know how many of *us* there are?" She tried to look into his eyes, but they were aimed at a spot above her head, appearing bored. "But you know what's best of all, eh? *All of us* are your legal heirs. Whatever you don't give us now, you'll hand over when you die. And you know what's worst of all? You bring out the worst in people, which means..." She brought her face close to his; he backed away as if fearing human closeness. "...we might try and make it happen sooner than you think!" She left the room, leaving the door wide open in her wake. Her steps echoed down the corridor.

Andrej got up, took off his blazer and went to the toilet. He splashed his face with cold water and smoothed down his hair with wet hands. He stood leaning on the wash basin and regarded the weary face of an old man in the mirror.

***

On his way back to the office, he heard David talking to someone whose voice he couldn't recognise.

David was talking to Ana: "Here, sit down at my desk and read the explanation."

"Frankly," said Ana, "I'm tired and I'm going home. And I've first got to stop by the hospital to see mum... A book award is the last thing on my mind now, to be honest, however much I may want one."

"If you carry on being such a miseryguts, I'll reveal that you're the author of *Wingbeat* before the award is given, so when you don't get it, you'll be sorry," David teased, somewhat childishly.

Surprised, Andrej raised his eyebrows. He waited for the voices to quieten down before entering the office, like in vaudeville. Ana and David gave him wide, surprised looks. Thanks to their intriguing revelation, he managed to forget the unpleasant conversation with Nina faster. David waved casually, but Ana looked petrified: a bad omen. With an almost imperceptible nod, Andrej made his way through to his office without a word of greeting and closed the door behind him.

The Dead Leaf

Every morning Jelena would watch from her bed a single remaining dead leaf in the bare crown of a strange-looking tree outside her window. Her eyes would search for it the moment she would wake up. A hanger-on, she thought each time, the only one of his family to reach such a ripe old age. Although it was brown and dry, while watching it, she seemed to partake of its vitality which had kept it hanging on its branch, the sole survivor.

That morning, for the first time ever, she took a closer look. She was disappointed: the leaf was not attached to the branch by the stalk; no; it had dropped off a higher branch and had been merely arrested in its fall, spiked through by a twiglet, captured, half-rotted away, doomed to some ghastly kind of leaf-death. The bare black branches with a single leaf on them now took on a ghostly and menacing appearance. Leave it, forget the leaf, she tried to control her swirling thoughts. Is today going to be yet another bad thought day, she wondered.

Remembering her row with Bruno the night before, she felt numb with fear. It was one of those massive rows that started with something small. She couldn't even remember what had triggered that one off.

"I can't stand your constant nagging any more," Bruno had said.

"You can't stand anything I say or do to you because you no longer love me."

Although Bruno stayed silent, she could hear him in her head as he replied, "That's right. I don't love you any more. It would be best if we separated."

She was certain she had had a telepathic experience. Feeling ice-cold inside, she looked at Bruno and waited for him to say aloud the words she had already heard. He opened his mouth to say something – and did not. The icy moment had passed. She asked him nothing more, and he did not speak. But they both had the look of people who have just come back from the edge of the abyss, exhausted and relieved.

After the row, Jelena went to see her mum and dad. She craved their company, she needed their protection. Dad was alone at home: mum was at the church. Rather gently – unusual behaviour in his case – he asked her if she'd like a coffee and complained of his bones which hurt him when he lay in bed, so much that he spent the whole night half-awake, tossing around. He felt his thigh and flapped the largely empty trouser leg: "Bare bones, no flesh, no circulation; I'm lying on my veins." Indeed, thought Jelena, when did his legs become so thin? She had not noticed; her dad always used to have firm, strong legs.

She had consoled herself that everything would look brighter in the morning, but the morning had started with the rotten leaf. She tried to disperse bad thoughts. I must chase them away, sweep them away with the largest broom I can imagine, but I haven't got a single good thought to catch and keep to use against all the bad ones. Bruno had already gone to work. She got up and phoned mum and dad to hear how they were, hoping to shrink her worry zone. Mother answered the phone. "How's dad?" Jelena asked.

"Fine, why? We've just got back from the market... He managed to embarrass me again. He keeps talking rubbish. He asked the lady from whom I always buy chicken, 'Madam, did this chicken of yours die after a long and serious illness, seeing it's so skinny and blue?' Just imagine!"

Jelena laughed. "Let him! I'm happy he's still spewing blarney."

All will be well, she thought. Now there's a thought to catch. It's a bit facile, but it's positive. She fell asleep, repeating to herself: I need good thoughts to catch, good thoughts to catch...

***

"Garbage in, garbage out", said David and laughed for a long time. His teeth glittered as if fluorescent. But it wasn't David, it was Dipsy. Jelena felt pangs of pain similar to the period ones. She went to the toilet and saw she was bleeding. She trembled with fear. Then she found herself in bed next to Bruno. Awake, he was watching her calmly. She told him he had to drive her to the hospital.

"Your baby is dead," the doctor said.

"It's good that it's dead; it was brought to me by the Angelic Trap that is, in fact, the Devil, and you're the Devil and you kill babies," said Jelena and burst into tears.

Bruno was sitting next to her. He said, "They didn't tell you that the foetus was deformed."

"Why are you so pleased?" Jelena asked.

"Well, as it was deformed, it was best that it..."

"Ah, so you're saying that the Angel is a real Angel, doing good? That means you love her?" Jelena rattled on. "You're saying, if I hadn't seen you with her, I'd have given birth to a deformed child?" She couldn't stop crying. Her shoulders shook.

Bruno was sitting next to her, gently shaking her shoulder. "You've had a bad dream," he said.

Helena is Scared

"Hello, it's Helena."

Buba sighed wearily. Helena. She was not in the mood for Helena. "I'm sorry, must dash," she said. "I've got a meeting, I was just at the door."

"I'm not going to keep you," said Helena, "only... I haven't got anyone to talk to."

"What's happened?" Buba asked.

Helena's voice sounded strange. "Andrej was here just now."

"What do you mean, was? Isn't he normally there? I don't understand."

"No, no, he left. But he was here just now. I can't stop him... I think he's going to kill me," she said.

"Why would he kill you?" Buba suppressed a shudder, only just.

"To get rid of me."

"He doesn't have to kill you to do that. You can simply separate."

"I found him out," Helena whispered.

"In what?"

"Can't tell you. Something horrible..." Helena fell silent. Only her breathing could be heard.

"Hello?" said Buba.

"I'm afraid of what Kalida said. That I'd change if I left the tall man and that I'd never be what I was before. I can feel a change coming."

"I don't understand, what do you mean?" Buba asked, trying to control her panic.

Helena continued with unnatural calm: "I don't care about myself, that's clear to you. But what about Andreja? I must save her..." She fell silent, and then Buba heard the receiver come down. She immediately dialled Helena's number, but there was no reply.

Stressed

After her bad dream, Jelena did not mention Nina to Bruno again, and Pero felt like a distant memory to her, like a story from a happier time. She kept swallowing Seroxat and stuffed herself with sweets: she had obviously entered a phase of self-destruction. In a single afternoon she managed to put away ten small Bobis mandorlato[128] bars. Bruno told her she was wolfing them down like the madmen in Vrapče Mental Hospital do when their family brings them sweets. Their row was over; they made up but there was no closeness between them.

"Hmm, interesting," Jelena said. "You know what sweets are? Desserts. And what happens when we read desserts backwards? Here, look!" Triumphantly, she scribbled with a pencil DESSERTS/STRESSED.

"Yet another trick you found on the web," said Bruno, but she danced off to the bathroom, singing, "It's springtime, I'm restless within..." She wanted to say: when I go around with no knickers on, you see me as an exhibitionist, when I eat mandorlato bars, you see me as a madwoman – the situation is clear. But she said nothing. One doesn't always have to say everything. She returned from the bathroom, sneaked up to Bruno from behind and said, "Boo!" Bruno laughed.

***

Then next day they were to have lunch with Mum Dubravka.

---

[128] Venetian white honey and almond nougat

In Vlaška Street, on their way to the restaurant, the three of them almost bumped into Pero. Pero stopped and offered his hand to Jelena, smiling. He seemed not to have noticed at first that Jelena was not alone. Jelena introduced him to Mum Dubravka, and then said to Bruno, "This is Inspector Pero Kovačić, you remember him; we met him at David's award ceremony." With a spark of malice in her eyes, she watched the blank look on Bruno's face: she knew he won't have a clue they'd ever met Pero... Serves him right for not having normal *husbandy* feelings, such as jealousy... How funny, there they are, Pero and Bruno side by side, and I'm not thinking about Pero but about good old Bruno. She shook her head. She realised everyone was silent. An awkward situation: if no one has anything to say, why did we all stop? If we stopped and no one is saying anything, the whole thing looks suspicious. She felt she had been found out, but she did not feel guilty, not any longer.

"How's work?" she asked.

Pero nodded and smiled. "How's David? I heard he was in hospital."

"He's fine now," Jelena said.

They took leave of each other clumsily. "See you," said Jelena, but did not offer him her hand. He really is handsome, she thought. And so what, she thought next.

Mum Dubravka shifted her penetrating eyes from Pero to Jelena and back. When they said goodbuye and parted, she said, with the nod of a connoisseur: "A handsome lad." Jelena almost laughed: the old mare was still kicking.

At home, Bruno asked, "If we met him together, how come I don't remember him while you greet him like an old friend?"

Hello, Jelena thought, what's this? Did he acquire a chip for emotions? "That's because he's my ex-future lover," she laughed.

"You mean, it's like, you tell a truth you know everyone will take for a lie?" Bruno asked.

Wow, Jelena thought again, is that still the same husband? There, that's Pero's beneficial influence.

But the Pero magic had vanished. Because the fear of losing Bruno had grown like a Pilates ball and had squeezed everything else out, even Pero. So much for my affair: it's finished before it has even started. Ana was right, one needs to know how to interpret omens: didn't I always meet Pero after car trouble? And cars are, after all, consumables. Shame on you, Jelena.

Ana's Mum Dies

Mum was already skin and bone; her nose had become pointed, her eyes were sunken and her skin tone had turned grey. Her thin hands on the white duvet cover gave Ana the creeps. She made herself sit with mum even when there was nothing to do – neither massage her, nor give her oxygen or moisten her lips with a wet gauze cloth. At times, she would be overwhelmed by tenderness. She tried to prolong such moments and make them more frequent. Mother had water in her lungs and breathed as if suffocating. She already wore morphine patches. She did not know what they were, but kept asking for "something stronger for pain". Then they sent her home.

While waiting in the treatment room for the sister to bring her mother's test results, Ana spotted some bottles with rubber seal tops in a glass cabinet, all labelled *Plivacilline*. She pushed the door left open by the sister and took a bottle from the cabinet. On the lower shelf, there were some ampoules with sterile water for injections. She took two to be on the safe side and stuffed everything quickly into her handbag. When the sister returned, Ana was sitting and waiting calmly, her handbag on her lap.

That same day, once she had settled her mother down in bed, she got Auntie Klaudija to sit with her a bit while she popped down to the pharmacy at Savica. She needed more than just penicillin for what she planned to do.

"Have you got any ether?" she asked.

"Ether?" the pharmacist repeated. "What do you need it for?"

"I don't need ether," said Ana. "I just need information

where one can get it. It's for a book, you know." She smiled as sweetly as she could, but evidently not sweetly enough, as the pharmacist kept eyeing her with suspicion and dislike. "Ether is no longer used in medicine," she said sternly, "except, perhaps, as solvent in labs."

"And does the one they use as solvent stun as well as the other one?"

"Of course it does," said the pharmacist and moved away a step.

"Just one more question, if you'd be so kind." Ana would not budge. "Where do the labs get it?"

The pharmacist seemed just about ready to press the panic button behind the counter. "I'm sorry, madam, I haven't got the time; the customers are waiting..."

As Ana exited, a tiny old lady, her back bent almost double, spoke to her. "You could find ether in vets' surgeries, miss. Once, when we took our Lara... that's our setter bitch... she's dead now... to the vet to have a tooth out, they put her to sleep with ether. Admittedly, that was long ago..."

"Thank you, I'll ask," said Ana and went out.

The chance (the omen!) had it that the very next day Auntie Klaudija asked her to pop over for a minute and get her potassium permanganate off the top shelf because her haemorrhoid inflammation had returned. Ana mounted a chair and, at the bottom of the shelf, saw a bottle with an aluminium seal over its cork. It was labelled *Ether*. She put it carefully in her pocket. Back in her own flat, she placed the penicillin, the ampoules with sterile water and the ether at the bottom of her wardrobe and concealed her hoard with neatly folded towels.

At night, she slept next to her mother's bed, afraid that mum might die in her sleep without her noticing.

Mum's face got darker and darker, her expression ever more malicious and her eyes became murky like openings leading to a black cave, and somehow extinguished. Sometimes they followed Ana like a caged beast's eyes follow passers-by: reproachfully. From time to time she would move her thin arms feebly, as if raising them to grab Ana. Ana knew a few things about what was happening to her mother: in the final phase, the metastases attack the nerve endings and the personality of the sufferer changes, becoming twisted. And mum had not been exactly tender even while still in good health.

"You know what the worst thing about cancer is?" she said to Jelena. "The dying process is so painful and hard that you stop being yourself. Your nearest and dearest can no longer recognise you and stop loving you before you die. And you have enough presence of mind left to be conscious of the fact that they don't love you any more. You might long for death at that stage, but you spitefully enjoy being a burden and a pain: they deserve to be tortured because they don't love you... I can see that in mum's eyes."

"The Tumour Institute is opening a centre for dying with dignity," Jelena said. "Dying patients will be brought there. Their families will be able to visit, and the hospital will provide complete care. Actually... it is a centre for dignified family life, among other things."

There's just this tiny problem, though, Ana thought: dying alone among strangers is terrible. She was so sure about that as if she had experienced it herself. In spite of that, she longed to get away from this unfamiliar, terrifying woman. Later, however – she knew that, too – she would regret the time she had lost.

When mother died, Ana felt cold as if transported by a time machine to the desolation of the Ice Age. Sobs poured out of her with tremendous force, as if someone had lifted a dam that had been holding them back. They came not from her throat but from somewhere deep within her chest as if they'd been waiting there in readiness. She couldn't stop. "I always thought," she said to Jelena, "that, when mum died, I'd first of all feel free. That I'd be able to say aloud all those things I'd thought about her but had never dared to voice them. And now I can't even remember a single bad thing about her. All I feel is terrible loneliness."

Ana had understood long ago that people could not bear the thought of dying not because they were losing the world but because the world was losing them. That was particularly true for her mother. She tried to fill the unbearable emptiness with that thought. A week later, she noticed the plastic bags her mum used to keep had run out: she had nothing to put the rubbish in. That was the difference between life with mum and life without her.

Becoming Close

Jelena's birthday fell on Women's day. That had always annoyed her and she was pleased when the new Croatian state deemphasised its importance (no disrespect to Woman's Day). She did not feel like getting up and phoned the office saying she wasn't feeling well. Bruno left early, with no mention of her birthday. Her mother was the first to wish her a happy birthday, and then her father took over the receiver:

"Well, happy fortieth, then."

"Don't rush ahead, dad – I'm not forty yet. I'm thirty nine."

"Ah, well, one year more or one year less, what's the difference?"

"Thirty nine is quite enough for me, thank you."

"Come, come, that's nothing; there are worse things to worry about."

"You wish me a happy birthday as if I had flu and you were trying to make me feel better by telling me it'll go away."

"Hmm... only this one won't go away."

"Thanks a bunch, dad." I worry about him, and that's how he repays me, she thought.

"Come on," dad laughed and added with unusual tenderness: "You know I wouldn't joke about something that was incurable."

Jelena laughed in a somewhat forced manner, but she was moved.

Stocktake: even though nothing new had happened, ever since her nightmarish experience in alpha state Jelena considered the Bruno and Nina affair an accomplished fact, more or less: Bruno would fall in love (had fallen in love) so seriously that he will leave her. The fact that David did not fall

335

in love with Nina proved nothing; David was, after all, a special case.

Nina had no idea of what was going on in Jelena's mind. In all innocence, she called, on Women's Day of all days, to remind Jelena of the software. "They said you'd phoned in sick. You're not seriously ill, I hope?" she said warmly.

"Not at all; it's simply my birthday," Jelena said. "Why didn't you call sooner, he's completely forgotten about the software. Me too."

"I heard of a new one in the meantime, an even better one. All the translators for television are already using it... it's called PNS Editor..."

"PMS?" Jelena laughed.

"PNS," Nina laughed too. "This is the last time ever, cross my heart. He must be sick at the mention of me and my software."

I wish, Jelena thought. Aloud, she said, "Why do you apologise; he loves fiddling with those things. Only write it down correctly for me, you know I'm analphabetic when it comes to IT." Hm, anALPHAbetic. "I'll call him straight away and then I'll call you back. Perhaps we can meet you this evening in *Friends* and give it to you."

Bruno took the order without grumbling. Jelena was resigned rather than worried: if it must be, let it be. She felt like Bruno and Nina's alibi.

Late in the afternoon, Bruno phoned from work with the news that he would be late because something at HT needed urgent sorting: would she postpone their rendezvous with Nina. At first, Jelena felt relieved Bruno and Nina would not see each other than night, immediately followed by a sting / lump in the stomach when she realised that her muddleheaded Bruno had actually managed to remember they were to meet Nina.

"Fancy coming down to meet me? We could go somewhere for cakes. I've got this sudden craving for *kremšnite*[129]," she

---

[129] Custard and cream cake

heard Bruno say. "You could give her the software at work..." The lump in her stomach withdrew before a small wave of happiness.

Calm and content, she phoned Nina.

"All right, never mind," said Nina. A bit too fast, perhaps, as if not wanting to sound disappointed? "We can get together without Bruno," she added.

"Not today," said Jelena. A bit too cold, maybe? "I'm meeting Bruno in town when he finishes work." He's mine after all, my husband, my beloved, my close one, my true one. Mine! Proudly, she savoured the fact that she can be with Bruno that evening while Nina cannot... Ashamed of her two-facedness, she added warmly, "I'll bring you the software tomorrow to the office."

***

They had their cakes at *Vincek's*, in Ilica, eating greedily in silence because the place was packed as usual. When they got out, Jelena threaded her arm through Bruno's but he extracted his arm and took her hand instead: he never liked to walk arm in arm, but it had been a long time since they had last walked holding hands. Encouraged, she said, "Shall we go to *Old Pharmacy* for tea with milk?" Bruno nodded and turned at once into Margaret Street. They found a window table in the front room and were served by the owner in person. He recommended Lady Grey to Jelena, and Bruno had a glass of Babić[130]. "Tsk, tsk, tsk" she shook her head disapprovingly. "What unsophisticated palate you've got, following *kremšnite* with Babić!"

"I've got to tell you something," Bruno said.

Jelena felt a shudder run through her. Divorce? She didn't dare speak lest her voice should tremble and give her fear away, and she put her cup of tea down to hide the trembling of her hand.

"I've been thinking a lot recently..."

---

[130] A Dalmatian red wine

Jelena felt a ball of wool wedge itself in her throat.

"...but I wouldn't like to decide without you..."

"Yes?" said Jelena to hurry him up, unable to wait any longer.

"I've decided to start a private IT business," Bruno said.

At first, Jelena couldn't understand the meaning of what he hed said; she just felt the rush of air into her lungs: the ball of wool had vanished.

"Yeah?" she said vaguely.

"You're not surprised?"

Jelena tried to understand what he was saying; it wasn't divorce, it was something much better, something nice...

"You have my support," she said stupidly.

Bruno was explaining: the situation at HT was uncertain and the same was the case with all large firms: they needed fewer and fewer people. He loves his work and knows enough about computers to tackle anything on his own; one didn't need a large initial investment; although private IT firms were numerous, there was room in the market for everyone and all were doing well; it was still a profession with a future...

Jelena could barely listen for joy. She just kept nodding her head in agreement. She realised how much she loved him.

When they got home, Bruno switched on the lights and turned on the telly as he entered, taking off his shoes and remaining in his socks. He unbuttoned his shirtsleeves and rolled them up to his elbows. Jelena watched him, thinking how handsome he was. She went to the bathroom to wash her hands. Bruno came up to her and embraced her from behind, smiling. She felt too embarrassed to look at the image in the mirror above the sink. Shyly and clumsily, she extracted herself from his embrace and went to the kitchen to prepare tomorrow's dinner. While Bruno was in the shower, she chopped up the onions and put the beef on.

Bruno followed her into the kitchen. "I simply can't stay away from you... when you're cooking. This smells good already!" He did not mind the smell of frying onions in his hair.

"Shall we open that Blatina[131] we got from dad?" said Jelena merrily. Don't forget, it's the little things that matter, she reminded herself.

She felt calm and almost happy, like after a breast check-up.

He kissed her hair. "Do you know why I postponed seeing Nina and asked you to come to town?"

"Because you love only me?"

"Yes. Because you're my one and only, and my beloved," said Bruno, as if telling a funny story to a child. From behind his back, he produced a beautiful red rose. "And a happy birthday to you!"

"You remembered," said Jelena, too excited to smile and closer to crying.

"And please don't ever imagine that I could prefer any other woman, no matter how lovely, to you."

Jelena gaped with amazement. So he knew, she thought. He knew what I was afraid of. He always understands everything although he always looks as if he hasn't noticed anything. If that is so, why did he let me suffer, why didn't he dispel my doubts? Why didn't he simply say, "Forget all that crap! I love you, and that's that!" I'd have said it in his place...

"When I saw you with that inspector, I could sense from the way you were that..."

Pero? Was it that simple? Jelena almost laughed. David was right: men *were* very simple; one just needed to make them jealous. Jealousy woke even the dullest up. Not the dullest, that is, she corrected herself in her new mellow mood, the most *restrained*.

"...you could potentially like him. And I realised I could not live without you."

Whatever his reasons might have been, Jelena was happy. Later, undressing, for the first time in a long while, she did not feel self-conscious about Bruno seeing her in her underwear and noticing that she was not as round and as firm as she used to be: she was feeling beautiful. She lay down beside Bruno. His

---

[131] Red wine from Herzegovina

hand stroked her gently, gliding lightly over her shoulders, between her breasts, then down towards her belly and her hips... Jelena pressed her body close to his excitedly; she could feel her pulse against the surface of the pillow. Bruno's hot hand burnbed on her skin. They kissed long and hard. Jelena thought she wouldn't be able to stand Pero kissing her like that. And that the time for that final Tibetan exercise hadn't come yet. She was so happy she wanted to cry. She opened her eyes. Bruno was there, beautiful like a fair-haired God, powerful and gentle at the same time. His body arched above her. She liked to be completely under its cover, as if in the shade of a mighty tree. Bruno would always ask, "Am I not too heavy?" and she'd always hurriedly wave his worries off: "You're not, not at all, squeeze me, squeeze me!" She passed her hand over his lips and brought his face closer to hers. She was afraid she might weep with joy: that wouldn't be sexy. Bruno kissed and kissed and kissed her as if she were all new, fresh and juicy. She felt desirable enough to relax and enjoy herself...

Later, she lay with her head on his shoulder. "I thought that..." she began, but Bruno stopped her with a gesture. She grabbed his hand and said very quickly, "Ithoughtitdneverbeasg oodforusasbeforeandevenbetter."

"Shut up," said Bruno and embraced her harder.

Once more she prevented his hand from stopping her mouth.

"IadoreyouandImhappyyouremyhusbandnowIknowyoulove meandIwassoafraidyouwould..." She fell silent. Bruno was right, it was better she didn't speak. She drew even closer to him. He embraced her. It's impossible I imagined all that with Nina, though, she thought. Perhaps he's simply come back to me? I don't understand anything. But... why should I understand? Why should one understand anything? I don't give a fig about what happened. The main thing is, it's all right now. In any case, it is the only fairy tale in this story: that a husband can be in love with his wife. All fairy tales are about love being possible... But her resolve didn't last long, and in any case she felt beautiful and loved enough to dare ask, "And Nina?"

"What about Nina?"

"Come off it! Don't tell me you don't like her."

"Nina? A sweet girl."

"Haven't you fallen half in love with her? Three quarters in love? Wholly in love?"

Bruno regarded her smiling, with raised eyebrows. "So that's what's been eating you?"

"And what's been eating you?"

"This own business thing; I didn't want to talk about it until I got it all sorted in my head..."

Jelena, you moron, you who always know everything – how come you didn't realise that men, unlike women, care about work enough to change their behaviour. And besides, in this country employment is a far more painful issue than divorce; here, it's not those who work who survive; it's those who steal and rob. Small wonder Bruno took so long to make his mind up... Of course, that's the answer. And even if it wasn't – I couldn't give a toss. How we are now is the only thing that matters. "And it's okay if sometimes you can't really feel something," she said aloud. "I'll treat you like an alien and teach you human emotions."

Bruno's laughter rang through the bedroom. Jelena laughed too. "This Blatina is not good enough for this momentous occasion." I feel like a plus-human being now, she thought. Bruno is plus too, because he's making me happy. She did not say it aloud lest she confuse Bruno. She got up and fetched a bottle of precious Macedonian wine, *Fillip Ftori*, with a big red heart on the label, as well as two slender crystal glasses they had bought in a sale, together with *Calgonite* dishwasher tablets. The heart picture was meant to convey the message that wine was good for heart patients, but a heart was a heart just the same, she thought. She raised her glass for a toast. "May we be happy together," she said.

She was happy. She stretched contentedly: I'm full of oxytocin.

Normal People

A few days after the funeral and all the other things she had to endure, Ana was dragged out almost physically by Jelena. She was not any gloomier than usual, but, strangely, much chattier. She hardly stopped talking. Jelena thought it was better for her than silence.

"Yesterday on the telly I saw an incredibly clever psychiatrist who is also a psychotherapist. A Freudian, Dr Klein. Did you watch him?" Ana asked, running her finger over the dewy surface of her glass of iced tonic water.

"Nope," said Jelena.

"Shame. He was asked if any man could be a murderer. He could be, he said, but didn't have to be. And the journalist was surprised in a dense sort of way: how come? Why's that? How come we don't kill each other in the street then? Because we have laws, the psychiatrist said. But all laws are merely a thin crust of civilisation on the boiling sea of instinct. And one of our strongest instincts is the one for destruction." Ana glanced at Jelena to check if she was listening attentively enough. Jelena nodded.

"And the strongest motive for releasing the destructive instinct is revenge." She went on, stressing each word: "Above all, it is the revenge against the innocent, because the culprit usually gets away or is too strong for the avenger to defeat. Or is no longer alive. The child of an abusing father, for example, will avenge herself on innocent people, and even on her own child, the most innocent victim of them all..."

"That's true," Jelena said.

"One could say that we should ideally be looking to direct our revenge at the real culprit, since we crave revenge so much."

"Is that what the psychiatrist said?" Jelena asked, surprised.

"No, I said that." Ana smiled. "But he's really terribly clever. They asked him, for example, what he thought about letting Vrapče patients home over the weekend, if it didn't put the public at risk, and he said that the patients got re-socialised that way; and as far as threat to the public was concerned, murderers were much more often to be found among people who were not under any medical treatment, the so-called *normal* people. As we're all normal people, you can draw your own conclusions... By the way, I might be reinventing the wheel, but it appears that only the not-normal are normal, as the normal ones are so few that they're no longer the norm."

"Yeah, reinventing the wheel," said Jelena. "And you remember all that from the programme?"

"I was interested; the guy is really so clever. He also spoke about sexual perversions, about paedophilia. He said he left such cases alone, since he could choose what to work on. He said he wouldn't know what to do with a paedophile. Sexual perversions were hard to treat, he said, because there's no proper motive, it's a disorder of instinct..."

"I've got to go," Jelena said.

"Oh yeah, I found an article on *Seroxat* on the internet," Anna said. "Something we didn't know: that it is currently the world's best selling antidepressant but that the manufacturer is hiding its dark side: it is highly addictive and withdrawal symptoms are severe: allegedly, in some cases, it can end in suicide... I'll send it to you."

"What should I do, then?" Jelena asked. "Should I start taking myself off it?"

"What should I do?" she asked David.

"Drink more wine," he said.

Ana Gets the Sack Again

"What the hell is this? What sort of deranged crap do you call this? Where's Martić?" The Chief Editor burst into the office bawling, clutching *The Review*, the Friday edition of *The Herald*, opened on the *Soulmates* page. He read the column aloud: *Dear reader, if your wife no longer excites you but you nevertheless do not wish to leave her, you have a number of options open to you: ask her if she'd consider abstinence; suggest that she finds a lover; ask yourself what it is that does turn you on: a very young woman, perhaps? A little girl? A little boy? Perhaps your instincts were simply not made to be contained within the boundaries of civilisation...*" The Chief Editor lost his breath for sheer intensity of his annoyance and upset. "The man's written a letter of complaint to the Journalist's Association... luckily unsigned for now, but... Where's the author of this sick text? Send her at once to the HR to sign the cancellation of her contract! And send me Martić when he turns up!" he yelled and slammed the door behind him.

The Hand

14th June

THE FRONT PAGE: Michael Jackson innocent of all charges

TV NEWS: Another man was arrested on suspicion of sexual molestation of children. He is 59-year old M.D., janitor and carpenter at Brezovica Children's Home.

TV: discussion about paedophilia.

"The experts say: Paedophilia is a medical term. In legal terminology, a paedophile is one who has "committed a sexual offence on a child." Paedophilia is difficult to prove both clinically and legally. For example, right now a man is freely roaming Međimurje[132], in spite of having a criminal record and being known for luring little girls to solitary places and then putting his hand into their knickers. He has never been arrested because there is not "enough evidence" to do so. Of all the reported cases, only 14% were actually diagnosed as paedophilia and even those only "conditionally".

People wrongly think that sexual abuse of children as a rule includes physical violence, making it even harder to diagnose cases correctly. In 87% of cases, the paedophile is someone close to the child, often a parent or a close relative, thus combining paedophilia with incest. The paedophiles entice children into their clutches and establish relationships of confidence, mostly without any physical harm to their victims.

---

[132] Međimurje is a historical and geographical region in northern Croatia, bordering with Slovenia and Hungary

In 1996, 75 cases of "sexual offence on a child" were recorded, while in 2004 there were 348. The opinion is that the larger number of cases does not indicate a rise in the number of crimes committed but rather in the level of awareness and the availability of information, as well as better coordination of the public services involved.

It is estimated that only 10 percent of the total number of cases get reported. Of those ten percent, only 5 percent reach court, and of those 5 percent, only 2 percent receive a sentence.

Having served a custodial sentence (usually less than a year), the paedophile reoffends in 40 to 80 percent of cases. Among those who undergo treatment while in custody, only 7 percent reoffend. Sexually abused children suffer from depression four times more often. The majority of them will at some point consider suicide with the intention to die, not as a call for help. Such suicides are most frequent following their abuser's acquittal. But even among those who do not attempt suicide, the majority gives up on life."

Andreja Comes to Stay With Ana

Dipsy was spreading rumours that Fish's wife had completely gone off her trolley. After her last conversation with Helena, Buba had been trying to call her but there was no answer. This time, the phone had only rung once before Helena picked up.

"You remembered me," she said tenderly, melting with emotion.

""I did. We can talk in peace and quiet now, the kids are out..."

"...so you and your husband can have yourselves a nice fuck," Helena said.

"Pardon?" Buba tried to laugh.

"Yeah, why are you laughing? At least you've got someone, and I'm alone..."

"I'm alone too," Buba said. "I'm divorced, have you forgotten? How are you?"

"I'm fine," said Helena cheerfully, in a strong voice.

"Want to come out for a coffee?" Buba asked.

"I'd rather not if you don't mind," said Helena. "I'm not exactly on form. I'll call you." She hung up.

***

A few days later Andreja phoned Ana. "I heard your mum died," she said. "I'm sorry.

"How are you?" Ana asked.

"My mum's not well. She was taken to the hospital this morning."

"To the hospital?"

"To a mental one. Not for the first time." Andreja's voice trembled.

"And you?" Ana asked.

"Can I come over?" Andreja asked. Ana gave her the address. Half an hour later, she arrived with a rucksack. "I'll tell you everything..." she began. "Only promise you won't ask me any questions."

"I promise," said Ana.

"It wasn't a neighbour back then."

"Who was it, then?"

"My dad." Andreja sobbed convulsively. Ana shuddered. Why didn't I do anything? I could have done, I knew, even back then.

"I told him I'd report him if he tries to take me back home. That I already have a file in the Centre... Don't worry; he doesn't know I'm here."

Ana held her, rocking her gently. She asked no questions. She almost said, "I've got something to tell you too," but realised the time was not yet right. She'd tell her when all was over.

The Spring Crop of Awards

Following the Critics Association's Award, *Wingbeat* raked in two more prominent literary awards by the end of February: *A.B. Šimić*, the Writers' Association Award, and *Tin Ujević*, the Authors' Association Award. Had it been part of a plot in a novel, it wouldn't have been very convincing; in reality; it was however, the outcome everyone expected. What could be more normal than David the lucky one, everyone's favourite, winning all the best prizes?

"It's beginning to be boring, isn't it?" he said to Ana.

"Yes, to you," said Ana.

"It'll soon be the same for you," said David. "That is the object of the exercise."

At the beginning of April, the winners of the Uliks award were announced. David had won it for two categories: for *Push Harder* (best journalistic non-fiction) and for *Wingbeat* (best novel). The Awards Ceremony was to be held on April 15[133], at the Velesajam[133] Congress Centre.

Helena Phones from the Loony Bin

Buba took a few days' holiday again, to tidy up the flat in between the former and the potential future tenants. She had unused holidays carried over from last year. She kept away from the theatre and no fresh gossip reached her from David's direction, thus she had no idea of what had happened until Helena phoned again.

"Hello," she said in a hoarse, rough voice.

"Hello?" said Buba, feigning good cheer but genuinely relieved to hear her voice. "It's been a while, hasn't it? Where have you been?"

"I'm right here, in the loony bin," Helena said.

Buba shuddered.

"They bunged me up in the loony bin as if I was mad," Helena said. "But I'm not really mad, I'm just a bit mad."

"Why did they put you in the loony bin?"

"Eh, why! It suited them. I'm in their way. All sorts of things happened. The police robbed me; they took away my diary and my address book..."

---

[133] Velesajam ("Grand Fair") is a large exhibition area in Zagreb, on the south side of the Sava River, where twice yearly an international general exhibition used to take place in a number of "pavilions", and where now exhibitions and other events are held throughout the year.

"The police? Why the police?"

"They were the ones who took me to the loony bin. I danced on the stage a bit..."

"You danced on the stage?"

"I did," said Helena defiantly. "It's my stage. That was my role; they were going to take it away from me just like that, without a by-your-leave. So I danced, to show them how it's done. And they called the police, and the police took me off the stage..."

Buba was sweating, but her voice sounded calm. "When are you coming out?"

"Don't know; they don't tell me anything."

"Do you need something? Where are you? Would you like me to come and see you?"

"I don't need anything, I only wanted to hear you. You always tell me something nice."

"Where are you though?"

"Jankomir. They promised to let me go home for the weekend. Did I call or did you?"

"You called."

"Then I must hang up to save money," she said and hung up.

"I'll call you at the weekend," Buba managed to say before the receiver hit the slot.

Sadness

She phoned as promised. "When do you have to be back?" she asked.

"They gave me till Monday," Helena said. "Socialisation."

"What socialisation?"

"That's the programme: they let us out for socialisation." She sighed. "You know, when the police took me away, I didn't understand why they were doing it, but it was crystal clear to me I'd always remember that moment, because in that moment my life changed forever..." Immersed in thought, she added, "No one knows what sadness is; real, terrible sadness. It is as if someone has stuffed a rag into your mouth and won't let you take it out." She cried. "I don't want to live like this any longer. But I'm not going to kill myself, I'm not the type. I could if I wanted to: it's full of tablets, my home is... Thank you for phoning me," she said. "I need someone to whom I can tell everything. I can't stay silent any more..."

"Talk away if it makes you feel better," said Buba.

"Much better," Helena said. "Forgive me for boring you. And for crying. I'm actually much better, only my memory's playing up. I sometimes get back from lunch asking when's lunch. And sometimes I know at once when I'm talking nonsense, while at another time it takes longer. My memory and forgetfulness seem to have been arranged the wrong way round. Or it might be *them*, pulling me... I was always special. Everyone used to say, how pretty she is, how smart. I think differently and must quickly translate in my head into their way of thinking. I have no one to talk to. I can tell you, you're a clever girl. And you know I'm not making it up. You know how many men adored me. Do you know who Scheherazade was? It was me, only no one was to know. And Cleopatra. Now they're trying to put it around that she wasn't beautiful, only smart. Fuck them. People are mean, just like our lot at the theatre. But truth will come out. I should know. If you knew how Mark Antony and I fucked, like lunatics! He ate out of my hand. I'll tell you all about it tomorrow. And how I danced! My dance entranced anyone watching. Women would tie scarves over their husbands' eyes so that they couldn't see. Whenever I appeared on stage, not a soul could be heard breathing. People used to say that I was bathed in blazing light, like stage lights, but there were no stage lights."

She ran out of breath and fell silent. Buba waited.

"They had it in for me because I'm special, but normal-special, faultless. That Petra that was caught fucking Palić underneath a pile of props... now, she's a woman with a genetic fault. Have you heard of people like that?"

"No."

"You haven't heard of people with a genetic fault? You must have. They're people with three orifices down there... how can

I explain it... Haven't you ever seen it?"

"I haven't."

"You haven't?" Helena suddenly sounded suspicious. "I'm sorry to have taken so much of your time..."

"Not at all. I'm glad if it makes you feel better. But, you know, you don' have to tell everyone..."

"Why?" Helena asked suspiciously.

"Well... the fewer people know about it the better. Your goal should be to get out of the loony bin as quickly as possible."

"I'll get out anyway," Helena said with determination

"You can tell your close friends, but not everyone..."

"Why?" She was suspicious again.

"You know what people are like," said Buba vaguely.

But Helena was satisfied with her reply. "Are you in awe of me?" she asked finally, as if overcome by her own greatness.

"I am," said Buba.

***

On Sunday, she visited her. Helena had put on weight and had become limp and flabby. In the hour that Buba spent with her, she finished two whole cartons of fruit juice. Every surface in her room – the dresser, the bed, the armchairs – was buried under piles of scattered sheets of paper, stage scripts, photos...

"I hope I haven't revealed any secrets to you last time on the phone?" Helena said. Her expression was firm. "I couldn't have done; they know all that anyway. I'm being careful not to tell what I'm not supposed to..." She waved a hand and laughed. "I know so much you'd be amazed." She leaned towards Buba confidentially. "I created theatre, too; did you know?" She continued, more quietly: "They've been testing me in all sorts of ways to see how my brain worked, ever since I was little. My brain works from left to right..." She sat back, smiled and said in a louder voice, "Thank you so much for coming. I've known for a long time you're all I've got. Haven't I told you that straight away? You know me the way I used to be, I can't hide from you how different I am. And now I haven't got anyone.

The others don't know me. If I were to tell them all this, they'd really think I was mad. And I feel I need to talk, perhaps because of all the medicines they give me. I'm opening up under the influence of those medicines. You know I'm not a chatterbox; I'm a secretive woman, a mysterious woman. But it's okay, I'm only telling this to you. Forgive me for going on like this, I'm all alone..."

"Where's your daughter?" Buba asked. She would have been embarrassed to ask about Helena's husband.

"Andreja will be with my sister until all this is over... and he..." Her face darkened. "...I don't know where he is, the beast."

"Would you like to go for a walk?" Buba asked bravely.

"Don't know," Helena hesitated. "What do you think?"

"It might do you good," said Buba, angry with herself for keeping her fingers crossed that Helena might refuse.

"Yeah? You reckon? You're so kind," Helena said. Her face brightened up. She got up fairly quickly and said in the small, coquettish voice of a little girl, "I need to tidy myself up a bit. Wait for me?" She went to the other room but came back almost immediately and sat down again. "I haven't told you the most important thing... I hope I can; it'll be common knowledge soon anyway..." She stopped talking and looked straight into Buba's eyes meaningfully. "Have you ever asked yourself, Helena = Helen?"

Buba returned a perplexed look. "What do you mean, Helena = Helen?"

"You're confused, I know. That's to be expected," Helena said, pleased. "Helen... of Troy; what do you think? ... It hasn't even crossed your mind, has it? It's me." She was suddenly on the verge of tears. "They used me, my beauty and my intelligence, and look at me now..."

Buba was afraid she might start crying, so she asked her questions about Helen of Troy until she brightened up again. "I'm feeling happier now; I'd really love us to sit down somewhere and have a coffee, eh, what do you think?" Buba remembered she had read how psychoses took account of social and technological developments. Those with delusions of grandeur no longer claimed to be Napoleon or Alexander the Great but identified instead with more recent characters. Helena's idea of grandeur, however, included the whole world and all the historical epochs.

They entered a half-empty café at Ribnjak. Helena sat down with knees spread apart. She sat like women with huge bellies or simply careless women sit, but the expression on her face was seductive. They were served by a stone-faced waiter. Provocatively dressed and made up, bedecked by jewellery, Helena attracted many looks. She twisted her neck to return a pleased, flattered look to every gaping passer-by.

The Hand

23rd June

THE BACK PAGE: Roberto Calderoli, the Italian Minister for Social Reform, advocates sterilisation of rapists and paedophiles.

This problem could be solved by a "skilful snip of the scissors," he said in Pontida on Monday. A day later, he softened his statement a bit, proposing chemical castration: using chemicals that cause impotence. "Why does everyone look so shocked?" he said. "After all, I wasn't proposing that we cut off the hands of thieves! Chemical castration is already in use in Denmark, Sweden, Germany and France, and also in some states in the US, yet no one's shocked there. Although it's true that physical castration –with a knife, albeit a surgical one," he said humorously, "would be more effective as prevention."

Just as amputation of fingers would be, or perhaps the amputation of whole hands – even better, of entire lower arms. One could consider cutting the tongue out, too, while one is at it, and, just to be on the safe side, extracting all the teeth.

Ana's Makeover

Jelena and Buba had a job persuading Ana to let them tart her up for the awards ceremony at which David would reveal the true name of the author.

"You must win them over by your looks as well," Jelena said. "You won't be in the background this time. You'll be central to the event and you simply must look perfect." She laughed. Ana shuddered.

It was early afternoon when Buba and Jelena rang Ana's doorbell, each with a sizeable bag full of all manner of equipment, clothes and shoes. "The makeover team has arrived," said Buba.

Ana stood aside to let them in, without enthusiasm. Jelena was surprised by the stale odour she could smell as soon as she entered the corridor. "Why don't you let a bit of air in? It's terribly stuffy in here."

"Is it really?" Ana asked. "You know how sensitive I am to the cold."

Without asking for permission, Jelena opened the window in the sitting room a bit and switched on the light. Buba laid out whatever she had brought on the low coffee table: tiny bottles and boxes, creams, blushers, eye shadows. "While you're making coffee," she said, "I'll mix you a facial mask."

Ana examined the objects on the table. Tiny droplets of sweat had broken out on her nose and above her upper lip. "We've also got stuff to calm you down," Jelena said. "Magnolia bark extract against stress, and *Persen Plus*, and..." Triumphantly, she produced a bottle of *Aleatico*, "... and there'll be a glass of fine, mellow, sweet wine that cheers one up for all of us."

"Yes, please," said Buba, mixing a mask of eggs, lemon juice and honey. "You'll see," she said to Ana, "you won't be able to recognise yourself. I watched Oprah yesterday on the subject. It's absolutely wonderful, women get pampered for days on end, whole teams of professionals work on them. And when you compare before and after, the difference is enormous. But the greatest difference is in the way they feel about themselves: after the treatment, they feel beautiful, they're happy and smiling, oozing contentment, whilst before they had a worried, sour expression. Most of them end up weeping with joy. Oprah asked one of them how she felt now, and the woman said, 'I feel like myself.' Do you remember, Jelena, when I told you that most women who opt for plastic surgery do so because they believe they have the right to beauty which they unfairly lost? That's what they mean when they say, 'I feel like myself...'"

Ana listened without curiosity. "While you're preparing your witches' potions, I'll have another shower," she said. "I'm all sweaty because of nerves."

"Strange, she really isn't interested," said Buba, shaking her head. Before she could say anything else, Ana came out of the bathroom, pale and with the look of fear on her face.

"What's the matter, what's happened?" Jelena and Buba asked together. "Are you unwell?"

Without a word, Ana opened her palm and showed them the two halves of the Luxor ring, now broken. She had not taken it off her finger for months. It had become scratched and deformed, and copper was showing underneath its nickel-plated surface. Buba gave her a questioning look, but Jelena understood at once: she knew how strongly Ana believed in the power of the ring. She brought Buba up to speed.

Buba shrugged. "Yeah, and?"

"It broke just like that, for no reason," said Ana. "That means even the ring cannot help me any more."

"Rubbish," Buba laughed. "I wouldn't look at it that way. Quite simply, it's fulfilled its task and you don't need its help any more."

"That's right," Jelena agreed, amazed at Buba's positive attitude. Honestly, why does she need Seroxat, she wondered. "That's it, the ring's purpose has been achieved," she said firmly.

Ana shrugged. "What should I do with the pieces? Perhaps I ought to keep them on me?"

"It doesn't matter; chuck them or put them in your wallet, it doesn't matter," said Buba. "But let's get down to business or we'll be late."

The Luxor ring spoiled everyone's mood. They had a glass of wine each, in silence, to wash bad thoughts away.

At four sharp, when the *Mrs Marple* signature tune started on the telly, Ana was finally done. Buba and Jelena didn't let her have a look at herself in the mirror until every last bit was finished.

"Let it be like a real makeover," Buba said.

Dried on large curlers, Ana's hair was glossy and wavy. Under a layer of almost transparent liquid powder foundation, her complexion was perfect, without a single spot. Her cheeks were gently brushed with blusher, her lips covered with gloss. In charge of Ana's eye make-up, Jelena had made her beautiful hazel eyes large and gleaming. Ana was wearing Jelena's red silk dress with tiny black-and-green flower print, and her own black blazer over it. Jelena's girly black kitten heels were on her feet. She wore no jewellery other than Hana's brass earrings with stones the colour of ruby.

When she was finally allowed a mirror, Ana said, "I don't feel like myself; I look a lot better than myself." Her expression showed no joy.

"We can now see what an excellent job we've done. You need to relax now, keep your eyes closed if possible and meditate – that's what's most important for calm and beauty," Buba said. "You've still got loads of time."

"No, I don't want to relax," sad Ana. "I've got a small errand to do now, and you're going to let me do it. Since I'm, after all, an adult and of sane mind, you're not going to ask me what I'm up to. I can tell you, though, that it is something positive and constructive. See you at Velesajam at half past eight."

While Jelena and Buba looked on, perplexed, Ana phoned for a cab. It took her to Trešnjevka Market Square where she hung around looking at *Pitarello's* shop window. Then she took another cab to Gaj Street. She went to the Central Pharmacy, convinced she'd be less conspicuous there and would not be remembered. Even if the police questioned people, no one will ever recognise me, all blinged up and totally changed as I am, she concluded, satisfied. Her turn came quickly. "A hypodermic syringe, please," she said. It seemed to her that the pharmacist was giving her a suspicious look, but she resisted the impulse to add an explanation: that would have been even more suspicious.

"Volume?" asked the pharmacist dryly.

"Twenty cubic centimetres," said Ana. It might have been better to have said 'cubics', she thought, but then she might have come across as someone in the habit of buying hypodermics, which would have been suspicious too. She was pleased at the thought of the volume: 20 cubics, not bad. She was worried that the pharmacist might read her thoughts. "And a needle, please."

"Thickness?"

In panic, Ana searched for the right answer. "Well... dunno... whatever I need for washing a wound... my mum's sick, you know..." It was good that she hadn't used up her explanation sooner.

"One?"

Ana nodded.

"Right," said the pharmacist and went to the back of the shop to look for a needle.

She paid four kuna for the lot. Only four kuna, she marvelled, for such an important piece of equipment! She returned home by cab, having picked one up at the rank by the Cathedral. Without looking, she felt for and found what she needed at the back of her wardrobe: the ampoules of sterilised water, the bottle with penicillin, and ether. She mounted the needle onto the syringe, broke open a water ampoule and, using the needle, filled the syringe with water. Next, she pushed the needle through the rubber seal on the penicillin bottle and emptied the syringe into the bottle. She shook it to mix the penicillin powder with water and then drew the cloudy liquid back into the syringe. She placed the prepared hypodermic into her old pencil case, closed the case and placed it at the bottom of her handbag. Picking up the bottle with ether, she located the small metal tongue on the lid, the tongue one had to pull to free the lid from the seal. She practised finding it by touch alone, without looking at the bottle. She put the bottle into her handbag in upright position, in the mobile phone compartment. It was a snug fit. Next to the bottle, she wedged a piece of gauze, folded small. She added a wound-up length of green nylon string, thin but strong. Her mother used to bind plants in the garden with it. She looked around as if checking if she'd left everything tidy and in order, smoothed down her dress and exited.

The Hand

30th June

ON THE Edge OF SCIENCE PROGRAMME: THE INDIGO CHILDREN

"The indigo children represent a new stage in human evolution. It is said that they were sent to warn us of changes. They chose their earthly parents themselves. They are already adjusted to the coming changes and will show us how to live in changed circumstances. Everyone agrees that in the next few years, Earth is to undergo huge changes. In a few years' time, for example, large parts of Europe will be under water. The indigo children have indigo auras indicating high mental activity, intuition and intelligence. Normal people have an indigo aura only at brain level; above it, they have a higher frequency lighter one. Lower down the body their aura is darker, and at leg level it is low-frequency and brown. Because of their high frequency auras, the indigo children appear to be living at a higher speed than the rest of the world, which is why they're often thought to be hyperactive and given medication. The first indigo children were born in 1958. The second generation was born in the seventies, the third in the eighties, the fourth in the nineties and the fifth at the start of the millennium.

An even more advanced subspecies is now emerging: crystal children, who are far more resilient to the current living conditions on Earth."

The Afternoon of the Awards Day

In the afternoon of the Awards Ceremony day, all spruced up for the occasion, David decided to return to the office to finish a text he had to hand in the following morning, steeling himself for the endless calls from journalists he expected to get that day from the word go. As soon as he sat down, he heard the door to Andrej's room open. He was surprised to see Andrej. "You're here too?" he asked.

"Listen," said Andrej, "what the hell are you up to?"

"What are you on about?" David gave him a surprised look.

"About the novel and the award."

"Tonight's award?"

"All the awards *Wingbeat*, the novel you didn't write, won. I was on the Committee, there'll be a scandal..."

"When did you find out?" David asked. "And why did you wait till the last day?"

"That's not important. What you're doing is ridiculous and I'll ask that you be thrown out of the Journalists' Association. The rest will be for the Prosecutor. You've got two hours to think it over," said Andrej.

"Do whatever you like," said David and turned back to his computer.

"What do you take yourself for, a Robin Hood, a Samaritan, some sort of a social moderator?" Andrej sounded as cold as ever.

"And I haven't got the right to be one, eh? Bearing in mind my nose isn't clean either, is that what you're trying to say?"

"Oh, I get it," Andrej muttered in a sneering tone. "*Atonement.*"

"Interesting – what you said just now had more feeling to it than anything I've ever heard form you before," David said, turning to look at him. "It sounded almost human."

Andrej went back to his room and slammed the door. Like in a vaudeville play, another door opened the very instant. It was Ana, but David didn't recognise her at first. When he did, he whistled through his teeth. "Ana, is that you? Man, you're a superbabe! How did you manage to hide all this glory before?" Ana smiled bleakly. "You're carrying on like a tragic heroine, and you look good enough to eat," David added. "What are you doing here at this hour?"

"Andrej asked me to come, didn't say why. Maybe he'll give me my job back."

David nodded. "Listen, don't let him get to you, no matter what he says. Just remember, tonight is the Awards Ceremony!"

"It's not my ceremony anyway," Ana shrugged but managed a faint smile.

"Yeah, well, we don't know about that yet. Anything could happen," said David.

"And why should I get nervous, anyway? I have no reason to."

She knocked on Andrej's door. From within, one could hear, "Yeees?"

She came in and closed the door. Andrej's desk was at right angles to the door and Andrej was sitting with his face turned to the window. One could see his striking profile from the door. When the door opened, he turned to see who it was. Surprised, he said, "Who... What can I do for you?"

"I don't believe you recognise me. I'm Ana Marton."

"Ah, yes indeed, I didn't recognise you. Is there a problem?"

Ana approached without reply. Not attempting to hide his irritation, he asked, "You're no longer on my editorial team. How did you know I was still here?"

"True, I'm not on your editorial team." Ana was standing near the door, closer to Andrej's chair than to the desk; this meant he had to turn his head in order to see her. She moved a step closer, rummaging through the handbag that hung over her shoulder. Andrej looked at her inquisitively. It seemed that she was looking for something she wanted to show him. Clearly unable to find it, she had pulled her bag round to the front, onto her stomach, without taking it off the shoulder. Both her hands were now in the bag, digging away.

"We can say 'thou' to each other, actually," she said.

Andrej raised his eyebrows. There was something strange about Ana's behaviour. With pointed hesitation, he said, "It is not my custom to..."

"I know; it's not your custom to be on intimate terms with people you work with, particularly your subordinates. This will be an exception, though... and a brief one." Inside the bag, invisible to him, she skilfully tore the aluminium lid off the bottle containing ether and, holding the bottle with her left hand, lifted the cork stopper. Her right hand was already clutching the folded gauze.

Andrej was sure now that something was amiss but before he could say anything, before he could even smell ether, Ana pulled the ether-soaked gauze quickly out of her bag and pressed it firmly over his nose and mouth with both hands. Taken by surprise, he could offer no resistance; by the time he'd realised what was going on, he was already woozy. Abruptly, he slumped in his chair. His head dropped onto his chest. Ana reached again into her bag, produced the string and made a noose. She brought Andrej's limp hands together behind the back of the chair, wound the noose around them and tied them firmly to the chair. She tied his legs together too. When he opened his eyes again, he was bound so tightly that his head was the only part of his body he could move. Ana laughed. He stared, uncomprehending.

"Let's make a deal first: if you try screaming, you're done for," said Ana, flashing a large knife with a narrow blade she had in her bag in front of his face. "If you stay quiet, we'll finish our business quickly."

Andrej nodded obediently, but his eyes were narrow slits full of anger and contempt.

"Let's see, now... do you remember your first wife?" Ana asked.

Andrej was silent.

"You say nothing? It was a rhetorical question anyway. She died not so long ago," Ana said. "You can't remember your first daughter. Perhaps you don't even know what name you gave her."

Andrej frowned. "You? Ana?"

"I. You barely managed to remember, eh? Ana, yes, Ana. It is I." She regarded him, grinning. "And, how do I look to you? Mother used to say I'd *drawn your genes*. Are you disappointed? You can't be proud of me, that I know." Still speaking, she reached into her bag, watching Andrej whose eyes followed her movements. She produced the pencil case and placed it on the desk in front of Andrej.

"Speaking of genes... do you know what I feel right now?"

Andrej did not react.

She drew closer, threatening. "I'm listening. Well? Can you guess?"

He shook his head.

"Try," she said and drew even closer.

"Hatred?" he muttered, clearing his dry throat.

"Oh no," Ana laughed. "Don't flatter yourself. I feel *revulsion*. And do you know why?" Andrej looked at her as if she were a raving lunatic.

"Because all my life I've been wondering what genes I was made of. I imagined I had, perhaps, some nice, healthy genes. And then I found out who my father was." She looked at him as if about to spit in his face. He moved his head away a bit when Ana brought her face close to his. "Imagine what it's like to find out you're carrying sick genes... that I'm full of your unhealthy, deranged genes!"

She opened the pencil case. Andrej stared at the hypodermic. "Have you had your tonsils out since you left my mum?" Ana asked. Andrej shook his head. His eyes widened and filled with fear. "You're not stupid, are you? You're getting it, eh? We may be many things, but stupid we're not... When was the last time you had tonsilits?" Andrej stared at the hypodermic with horror. "I've had it many times. Genes are genes, you know. Mum used to say that she'd had it with us and our tonislites. I'm allergic to penicillin too, just like you," Ana said smiling. "Daddy's little girl, a chip of the old block."

Pale and sweating, Andrej said nothing. "Mum said you'd survived anaphylactic shock once, you barely pulled through... Scared, are you?" She looked at him and laughed. "One always injects penicillin into the buttocks; that's where the large muscles are," she said. "Your butties are not large at all, though. You exercise, don't you? Perhaps you play tennis? Or go to the gym?" Andrej was silent. Sweat poured down his temples from his forehead. "Cat got your tongue?" Ana asked in a little-girl voice.

"You're crazy," he said, apparently horrified by the realisation more than by her threat.

"Is that so? And you aren't?" Ana drawled lazily. Slowly, she picked up the hypodermic, ejected the air expertly and, holding the syringe between her fingers, with the other hand on her hip, leaned towards Andrej. "I want to remember your fear; that'll keep me happy for the rest of my life." She made a move as if about to administer the injection. Andrej flinched. "Oh yeah," she said as if she'd just remembered something, is it true you've got three daughters?"

Andrej was silent. Ana brought the tip of the needle closer to his skin. "It's true," he said.

"I know of Andreja..." Andrej gave her a fearful look. "I know everything," she said. "Now, who's the third one?"

Andrej was silent.

"Tell me! Now, when you're no more, the three of us will need to stick together." She brought the needle a hair's breadth closer.

"Nina," he muttered.

"Who?"

"Nina Ivezić."

Ana became still, thinking. "I knew it," she said slowly. "So that's it, then. Nina... the beautiful sister... you abandoned even her." She shook her head as if shaking off unnecessary thoughts. "It doesn't matter now. You're leaving three happy orphans behind." She laughed, then became thoughtful again. "It's interesting, this good and evil lark... One man can do much evil but little good. One must hand it to you, mate: you've been productive. You've made something of all of us..."

"Why are you doing this?" Andrej managed to say. "What do you want?"

"... You've created junkies, depressives, madwomen... murderers." She whispered the last word more to herself. She turned on the radio by the door. Soft music filled the room. Ana turned the volume up. "Background music," she said.

"What was your question? What is it I want? I don't want anything, particularly not from you. What I got from you is already too much. And the answer to your first question... hm. It's not that simple." She laughed. "Or it is. Yes, it is, quite simple. Why beat around the bush, it doesn't matter to you any more anyway... Let's say I believe that it is my task to free the world of a villain... Nothing personal... Right, that's enough! We've said more to each other now than we'd done in our whole life." She bent down behind Andrej's back. He thrashed madly but could not escape the needle. Ana emptied the syringe into his buttock, leaving the whole hypodermic stuck in the flesh in the hurry to see the expression on Andrej's face. She leaned towards him again. "I don't want to miss this. I must remember you dying, to be sure that you..."

When convulsions and suffocation started, Andrej's face turned grey and his lips became blue. "That's good," said Ana. "Cyanosis has already begun; it'll all be over in no time."

As he died, he fell forward, his face hitting the desk. His arms hung down. The hypodermic stuck comically out of his body. Ana left the room, leaving the door ajar.

David looked at her inquisitively. "And?"

"He offered me a silly little job, nothing important," Ana replied nonchalantly. Her dress swayed because, inside it, her body was shaking, but David couldn't notice anything.

"Great," said he, a bit nonplussed. "Didn't he mention tonight's Awards Ceremony?"

"No, why?" Ana said. "Must dash, I'm meeting Buba and Jelena to go to Velesajam together."

"Wait for me, I'll be five minutes."

"I'd rather have a stroll alone," said Ana.

"Okay," said David. "See you there."

"See you," said Ana. "Oh yeah, have you got Nina's number?" she asked.

"I've got it," said David and flipped out his mobile to find it in the contacts.

Once out of the building, Ana phoned Nina's number. "It's Ana Marton" she said.

"Hi, how come you're calling me?" Nina sounded very friendly.

"I've just found out I'm your sister," said Ana looking around, wary of being overheard. Nina said nothing at first; all Ana could hear was her rapid breathing. "And we've just lost our father. It's finished," she said. "I've got to go now, I'm in a rush..."

"Wait, wait," Nina cried. "Where are you... where is...?"

"The body is in the office," said Ana and ended the call.

In the office, David turned off his computer with a sigh. Writing was obviously out of the question. He decided to go for a drink before the Ceremony. He shouted goodbye to Andrej through the door that Ana had left ajar. There was no answer, which was hardly surprising: Andrej seldom returned any goodbyes. Passing through the reception, he waved to Anđelko. "What is it with you people today," Anđelko said, "are you doing an extra shift?" David laughed and left the building.

It was getting dark when Nina got to *The Herald*. "Anyone up there?" she asked Anđelko, breathlessly. He shook his head. "Where's the fire? Everyone's rushing around today."

Nina darted past. The office was dark. Andrej's door was half open. When she entered his room, she nearly screamed although she knew what to expect. She went up to him and felt the body. Andrej's eyes were open; he wasn't breathing. The stiffness had not yet set in. His forehead was still gleaming with sweat. Expressionless, Nina stood there and regarded the body. "Too late," she said quietly. "This could've been a job for me to do." She placed her handbag on the desk and, frowning with disgust, tried to untie the string, without success. She went to the main office, found the scissors in the pencil box on her desk and brought them around. Only as she cut the string around Andrej's hands and feet did she noticed the hypodermic, still planted in his buttock. She extracted it and stuffed it into her handbag together with the string. She felt Andrej's trouser pockets, and then the pockets of the jacket hanging off the back of the chair in which he'd been sitting. She found a wallet in one of the inner pockets, containing a few notes of, twenty, fifty and hundred kuna. She took the money out, put it on the desk and searched through the rest of the wallet. In the cards pockets, she found an American Express Gold card, a Diners card, a Mastercard and a Visa. Having laid them all out on the desk, she put the wallet back into the jacket. Remembering something, however, she took it out again and wiped it outside and inside with the hem of her skirt. Then, using her skirt to hold it, she replaced the wallet again. She put the money and the cards into her handbag.

The *Uliks* Award ceremony

Ana was pale, wiping tiny droplets of sweat off her nose and the upper lip with swift strokes of her index finger.

"You look gorgeous," said Jelena. "The sexy author. They'll regret not giving you the award while they had the chance."

"It's still cheating," said Ana gruffly.

"In a good cause."

"Hum, yeah. We actually cannot tell good from bad any more. That must be the relativism that the new Pope is talking about."

"Forget that now. Just remember what it feels like to be invisible no matter what you do."

"Yeah, you're right. My mum would be pleased now," Ana said.

A makeshift stage had been erected in the central area of Pavilion 8 at Velesajam. The foldable screen behind the long table was lavishly plastered with Award posters and enlarged covers of the winning books. The first two rows of chairs all had "Reserved" notices on their seats. The critics, the authors and those with invitations were all on their feet; only the ordinary public and the culture vultures were already seated. Friends and relatives flocked around the winners. The building's poor acoustics made the hum of many voices and the laughter that rose from the gathering sound unpleasantly loud.

The Ceremony was to start at eight. At ten past, Jagoda Franjić, followed by the *representatives of the Associations*: those of translators, of literary critics, of authors; then of

Matica Hrvatska, of the Croatian Academy and so on approached the long table on the stage. They all sat down; meanwhile, all the empty seats in the auditorium filled with people. Jagoda tested the microphone, coughed and stood up. "Good evening, ladies and gentlemen. I welcome you on behalf of the Committee of the *Uliks* Award and its President, Andrej Martić, who unfortunately couldn't be present here tonight. I suggest that this is all we need by way of introduction and propose we move on to the Awards forthwith..."

The audience fell silent. Ana was trying to swallow, but her throat was dry and she had no saliva to moisten it. She grabbed Jelena's hand.

David rushed into the hall the very moment Jagoda Franjić called "David Antolić" for the first time as "the winner of the Award for the best Croatian nonfiction book of 2004." The cameras began clicking and the lighting technicians turned their spotlights on him. It was a sight recorded many times before: handsome and smiling, David headed for the stage, running his fingers through his hair to smoothe it out and waving to those who said hello as he went past. He received the award and the congratulations, waved at the audience and took a seat in the first row. Buba had made room for him between her and Ana.

The ceremony swiftly moved on through the categories. The Best Novel Award came last. Jagoda Franjić explained the reasons behind the judges' choice: "Even though *Wingbeat* is a first novel, it seemed to us that, having won three important literary awards, it hardly belonged to that category, if for no other reason then because it wouldn't be fair towards all the other first novel entries for 2004. One could in fact say that *Wingbeat* has, in just one season, grown from first novel into – there's no other word for it – a classic. For the second time tonight, I'm calling David Antolić to the stage..."

Her words were drowned by the applause. Smiling and bowing discreetly, David took the microphone. "I feel a bit like those American preachers in sequinned suits who lure the credulous with honeyed words, because at each awards ceremony I end up preaching something I personally believe about our contemporary literature... And I'll do the same on this occasion, too." Laughter could be heard. "Everyone in this hall, except perhaps the mums and the dads and the kids and other relatives of the winning authors, follows literary and other cultural events and is aware of the underlying trends and fashions. You all know that. But do you know that you hold the fate of writers and literature in your hands? You're the audience in the arena. Your thumb decides the outcome. People are usually unaware of their own personal responsibility when they're part of a mass; they underestimate their power and believe it's useless to say anything that differs from the majority opinion because no one will notice anyway. But you're wrong; it will be noticed. Someone always notices. Whenever something needs to be heard, the way will be found. And every one of us is equally important. Never agree to become an intellectual robot repeating whatever has been fed into its memory. A friend of mine has her own term for such people: *cultural shopaholics*. An excellent term. It makes one think of a crowd of people frantically rushing around shelves with cultural products, afraid they might miss out on something. I call those people *mercenaries of the cultural establishment*. Don't be *cultural mercenaries*, because culture doesn't pay very well. Always ask yourselves what it is you really think about something. If you don't have your own opinion, keep your mouth shut. Don't hit the buzzcock, as Tarik[134] would say in *Who Wants to be a Millionaire*. Don't repeat what the others say, there's nothing in it for anyone."

The hall had gone quiet. Bent forward, Ms Franjić listened intently, most probably thinking, oh that Antolić, one never knows what he'll come up with next.

"I really think that *Wingbeat* is an excellent book and that the judges have chosen well on this occasion," he said with a broad smile. He paused and swept the hall with his glance, row

---

[134] Tarik Filipović. He hosted the Croatian version of "Who Wants to be a Millionnaire" until 2009

by row, on both sides of the aisle. There was laughter. "You know, it's not easy to be a writer, a good writer. To be a scribbler is another matter, but to be a real, good writer is very hard indeed. Why? Simply, because a writer must be cleverer than his cleverest character, more imaginative than the most imaginative one, wittier than the wittiest, crazier than the craziest, happier than the happiest, more stupid than the thickest, funnier than the funniest, sadder than the saddest. When, in Mamet's movie *The Heist,* someone asks Gene Hackman how he managed to think up such a clever thing, he replies, 'I imagined someone much smarter than me and asked myself what he'd do in my place.' That's similar to how a writer works. A writer is creative, and a *creator.* This book is the best example." No one laughed at what was, even for David, extraordinary conceit. "And I'm not being brazenly conceited," David said at the right moment and paused to give the audience time to catch up with him. "Although I would be if I was the author of the book." Pause. "But I'm not." Pause. A quiet, very quiet murmur began to rise from the audience. "I'm not the author of *Wingbeat,*" he reiterated. The audience was now completely silent; then, like the sound of an oncoming train a loud "Huuu!" could be heard, as if everyone had breathed out loudly at the same time.

Ana felt something like an electric shock, but the current didn't leave her; it stayed inside, shaking her from her very centre: her stomach cramped up first, then her throat, then the back of her head, finally reaching her arms and legs. Like a doll screwed down to the ground, she could not move. She saw David's arm and hand, extended towards her like God's finger towards Adam on the ceiling of the Sistine Chapel, and all the white blobs that were faces turned towards her, aiming at her. Her ears buzzed.

She couldn't even hear David say: "The book was written by Ana Marton, a very good friend of mine. Why did she publish it under my name? She had, as it were, sacrificed herself to the book, believing that the book would become a hit and win awards if people thought I'd written it. It wasn't however, her idea: it was mine. It was an experiment with an expected outcome. You could say that the novel would have probably won the award even if it had been published under Ana's name. I say it would not. Ana Marton is the author of a fascinating novel, *The Naked She-Wolf.* I know this is not normal procedure for an awards ceremony, but this evening everything is off the normal scale – who among you has read *The Naked She-Wolf?*"

A few hands went up: Jelena's, Buba's and two or three more, perhaps.

"And how many among you have heard of that book?"

Only a few more hands went up.

"You see?" David said. "Now, that's bad. It's not unusual, it's not unexpected, I'm not at all surprised – but it's bad. And do you know why it's bad?" A murmur could be heard from the audience. "Because it is a great novel. A masterpiece, I daresay. I will even dare to say that it is the best work of Croatian fiction published in the last ten years." The audience was silent. Ana's hearing had returned, and her soul had re-entered her petrified body, but she was still shaking. "And why have only five of the two hundred people gathered in this room read that book? Because Ana Marton is not important, she doesn't belong to any clan, she is not famous, not powerful. Why should anyone read a book by an insignificant author! And even if one does read it and happens to enjoy it, he might say: the fact that I like this book doesn't prove anything; it still might be common pulp, so I'd better not tell anyone I liked it or I might make a fool of myself; after all, if it was any good, wouldn't someone have written about it, noticed it, given it an award..?" The audience was muttering, surprised, or even offended. "You all know I'm right although few of you would be prepared to admit it," David went on. "But *The Naked She-Wolf* didn't win a single award, was not on any 'best book' list, didn't even make the selection for most of the awards..." David paused dramatically. "Whilst *Wingbeat*... *Wingbeat* won the Critics' Association Award, which is one of the most important literary awards in the country; the Writers' Association Award and the

Authors' Association Award. And now, it has won *Uliks*, the most inclusive and the most democratic literary award in the country. You might say it was because *Wingbeat* is the second book by the same author, and the second book is always better and more mature. That may be so. But I'm telling you – Ana will not be hurt by this as she knows it is true – that *Wingbeat* is not as good as *The Naked She-Wolf.* It is an excellent novel, imaginative, interesting, with an unusual structure, but, compared to the *She-Wolf,* it is just an interesting book among many... I'm not sure I'll ever be forgiven this little prank. Perhaps I'll never win another award. People tend not to forgive you if you show them up. But if they are shamed, it means they've understood. And if that is the case, our mission has achieved its objective."

The silence was total. It ended when Ms Franjić got up dramatically, stood there for a quiet moment while seemingly making up her mind on what to say and then, saying nothing at all, applauded with hands raised high. Several representatives followed suit. Buba and Jelena were next, and then everyone, little by little, joined in.

While the applause slowly gained ground in the hall, David approached the mike again. "There's one more thing I'd like to do: bring the real author before you, so that you remember her. Ana, please, come up..." Ana shook her head. "Come up here, please, come," said David. His smile was wide and relaxed. Ana set off towards him and, on wobbly feet, climbed the two steps that lead to the stage. She looked beautiful and delicate. David reached out and literally pulled her over in his direction, helping her make those last few steps. He handed her the microphone.

Ana took the microphone and regarded the audience for a few seconds in silence. Those in the rows close to the stage could see tears streaming down her cheeks. "Writing is the most important thing in the world for me," she finally said. "I'm glad that you liked *Wingbeat.* I don't really mind if you liked it because you thought it was written by David Antolić. What matters is that you've read it. I'm not afraid of people not liking my book when they've read it. I only fear they might not read it. I know what happened here today is a scandal. But if that scandal will make you read *The Naked She-Wolf*, I'm prepared to bear the consequence... I'm taking full responsibility... for everything. I'd do it all over again. And a huge thanks to my friend David for lending his good reputation to my book..."

She handed the microphone back to David who placed it into the hands of happily excited Jagoda Franjić. She kept opening and closing her mouth. It was not clear if she was trying to say something or simply gasping for air. David threw an arm over Ana's shoulder and guided her to the empty seats next to Jelena and Buba, to the sound of thunderous applause. Before she'd reached the first row of seats, Ana wriggled from under David's arm and returned to the stage. Looking neither left nor right, she went up to baffled Ms Franjić and, without looking at her, took the microphone from her hand. She moved to centre stage and spoke into the mike: "I've got something else to say... who knows when I'll get a chance to speak again, and it's important. I realised two important things. When I tell you about them, you might find them insignificant, or self-evident, or too generalised, but I'll tell you anyway: when you write, it is crucial that you write about what concerns and excites you. If it matters to you and if you find it exciting, your readers will feel the same. In more technical terms, you need to have a universal theme and a wide range of emotions. Remember this, even if it seems so obvious it hardly needs pointing out. That is why the best stories are one's own stories, stories about oneself. I believe... I *know* that every individual has one story, their story, the only story worth telling. Why? Because that is the only story that really concerns them and excites them. *Wingbeat* is literature, it is fiction, a construct. It might be skilfully written, it might be interesting, but it is bloodless, it isn't alive. *The Naked She-Wolf* is my story. It lives; blood, the elixir of life, flows through it. It can excite you, make you laugh or cry, frighten you and give you courage, because I lived it like that, as you read it... It doesn't matter if I lived it in reality or in my head... remember this, too: it is important to live, whether in a dream, in one's imagination or in reality. It took me ages to understand this; for a long time I thought my life to be subordinate to... don't know what, exactly... to art, to creativity... And life is the only alchemist; a writer is merely the narrator. *The Naked She-Wolf* might be structurally awkward; some parts might need to be removed, other parts should perhaps be added to it. But that's not important; what is important is that *The Naked She-Wolf* is a living story; you empathise with the Naked She-wolf because she is a real, imperfect, living character. In the jargon of the critics, the reader identifies with her. I'm not being patronising here; I'm saying all this because no one ever teaches us to appreciate obvious and simple things such as laughter or tears, rather than *cleverness*. And that is why my friends and I did what we did."

She spun around, handed the microphone to Ms Franjić and slowly, as if in a trance, started towards the audience. The hall was completely silent.

The Investigation

His colleagues the journalists have gone too far now, David thought when he was woken by the telephone the following morning. But it was Dora. "Please come to the office, the police is here. Andrej has been murdered," she said in a weepy voice.

"Pardon? What? Murdered? I don't understand. Is this a windup?"

He rushed in, half-dressed. Jelena, Nina, Dipsy, Ivana, Dora and Anđelko were already there. Ivana and Dipsy were standing as there weren't enough chairs for everyone. Piljek was not around.

"Where's Pilkie," Dipsy asked flippantly. "Is he not a suspect?"

"Don't you know?" said Dora, still tearful. "He's in hospital. His son has telephoned. He got ill before all *this* happened..." At the word *this*, she cast a disgusted look at her colleagues, as if it was their fault she got entangled in this mire.

"What happened to him?" Ivana asked.

"Heart," said Dora in the same accusing tone.

"Be quiet, please!" said the middle-aged policeman standing beside Inspector Pero Kovačić. The Inspector was sitting at Nina's desk. His face was barely discernible against the daylight coming through the window. The portly older policeman, his Sergeant, was the old-fashioned law-and-order type, with the weary, self-important expression of one about to enter a well-deserved retirement and take with him all that was good about the police: the people, the methodology, everything.

David reached the centre of the room, halted, greeted everyone, then went over to Pero and offered him his hand. "Who would've thought we'd meet under such circumstances."

The Inspector nodded a greeting and said, "I need you to tell me exactly what happened here yesterday. Who wants to kick off?"

David glanced at the others, obviously intending to say something. Nina was faster. "I might be the last one of the editorial staff to have seen him alive," she said. "I got here late last evening; everyone else had already left..." Anđelko nodded, confirming.

After the questioning, the Inspector told the Sergeant he could go and dismissed everyone else too, except David and Jelena. "This is unofficial now," he said. "Have you got time for a coffee?"

"Sure," said David. Jelena just nodded.

Leaving, Dipsy asked David, "Who's to get his job? You?"

David shrugged.

Everyone in the Little Café already knew of Andrej's murder. Šime merely nodded at them and said, "I've 'erd all about it, fuck his sunshine!"

"How well do you know Ana Marton?" Pero asked.

"She's a close friend of ours," Jelena said.

"Did you know she is Andrej Martić's daughter?"

"Ana!" Jelena was astonished. "I had no idea... Jesus... Ana is Fish's daughter..." She shook her head, not comprehending. "Wait a minute... did she know?"

"She may have found out recently."

"You think she killed him?" David asked.

Pero nodded. "It is a possibility." He asked them what Ana and Andrej's relationship was like: if they had noticed anything out of the ordinary, how Ana had behaved the day before, if she had been agitated or more tense than usual..."

"She was excited and tense because of *Uliks*," Jelena said.

"Oh yeah, I heard about the last night's scandal," said Pero. "You revealed that you weren't the author of *Wingbeat*..."

"Is that against the law?" David asked.

"No idea, I don't do author's rights. But it doesn't sound good."

"And Andrej was supposed to be there as the Critics' Association representative... but wasn't," said Jelena redundantly.

"He'd found out about the hoax; that afternoon he was threatening to reveal everything," David said. "But I wouldn't kill him for that," he added. "I actually thought he'd told Ana to come for the same reason, but it wasn't that, it was about a job."

"Yeah?" Pero said.

"That's what she said when she came out of his office."

"Any idea where she might be?" Pero asked. David and Jelena looked at each other and shook their heads. "We parted last night after the Ceremony," Jelena said. "We all went our own ways..." She paused briefly. "We didn't go out to celebrate because Ana said that she had yet to decant it all and that the day had felt more like a century to her..."

"Perhaps you didn't know that Nina Ivezić was his daughter too?" Pero asked.

"Jesus," Jelena muttered.

"Surreal," David said.

When they left Pero, Jelena phoned Ana but there was no answer. She kept phoning the whole evening but she was not at home. Her mobile was switched off.

***

When Inspector Kovačić rang the doorbell with name *Šoljan* –

Martić on it, a woman in extravagant finery, whom he suspected to be Helena, opened the door. Had she not been made up so heavily, with her hair in a beehive, and had she not been wearing a low-cut evening dress, Pero would have seen nothing strange in her behaviour. She was calm and the tone of her pleasantly deep voice was measured as she spoke. "I didn't kill him, although I know I am the prime suspect," she said theatrically, as if on stage. "I'd love to have killed him, though," she added with a charming smile. "But that's not important now; the main thing is that he is dead." She clasped her hands together in her lap as if to emphasise the finality of her statement with a gesture. "And now you'll ask me where I was yesterday afternoon, won't you?" she said coquettishly, raising a hand to adjust an escaped wisp of hair. Discreetly, she pulled the hem of her dress up an inch or two to reveal her knees. "I was here, alone. I am on sick leave. You probably know I'm currently recovering from... the consequences of an exhausting medical treatment. My daughter is at my sister's. You said he was murdered sometime in the afternoon?"

Kovačić realised she was trying to play a role. "Why did you say that you'd loved to have killed him," he asked, "when you know such statements can be used against you?"

"How sweet, that you should care about me," said Helena adjusting her hairdo again and smiling seductively.

"Why would you have killed him?" the Inspector insisted.

Helena's face darkened. "I don't want to talk about it," she said. "If that's all, then... if you please... I'm very tired right now."

Exiting, the Inspector glanced back at the house and saw Helena in the window: she was smiling and waving seductively.

***

"My God, what'll become of young Andreja now? Her father murdered, her mum a schizophrenic, she herself only seventeen, a minor," Buba was saying to Jelena as they drove to Ana's. She had not been answering her phone, and they were well into the second day since the murder.

"I don't know," said Jelena. "It would be best if the system forgot all about her so that she doesn't get dragged round all the social services. You have seen what goes on in children's homes. Does Helena have a brother or a sister?"

"An older sister. I don't remember her all that well; she left home young. I don't know where she's living now... Yes, of course, Andreja can stay with her..."

They rang Ana's doorbell, but no sound could be heard inside the flat. They peered through the windows. Protected by a grating, the bathroom window was slightly open as always, because Ana was afraid her gas boiler might leak. Everything appeared to be normal. They wrote a note and pushed it through the door: *Get in touch at once, Jelena and Buba.*

An elderly lady whom Jelena recognised as Auntie Klaudija waved at them from her window. When they approached, she asked, "Excuse me, what's going on? Where's Annie?"

"We were about to ask you if you've seen her today or yesterday," Jelena said.

"No," said the old lady, "and that's weird, you know... Normally she says hello to me almost every day. I think I last saw her... it could've been last week. She had a young lassie with her..."

"Lassie?" Jelena repeated.

"Yes, yes... they went in together. I was going to ask Ana to give me a hand with something but I didn't want to disturb her when she had a guest... That's right, I remember now, it was Monday; I wanted her to read my electric meter."

***

After Helena, Inspector Kovačić went to see Nina.

"You found out he was my father, then?" Nina asked calmly.

"It wasn't hard: it's in your official documents. And in his," the Inspector said.

"Yes, I know," said Nina. "Would you like a coffee? Or something else?"

Pero shook his head. "Why did you go to *The Herald* that afternoon?"

"I went to ask him to help us, mum and me... Mum was in debt; she'd taken out a loan to buy new machinery. It was a big loan, seventy thousand euros, with monthly payments of seven thousand kuna, and her business was not doing well. She's being treated for depression; she's suicidal. I asked him to lend us twenty thousand euros. He said he didn't have the money..."

"You know that Ana Marton was his daughter, too?"

For a moment, Nina didn't know what to say. The fluttering of her eyelashes made the Inspector think, correctly, that she was thinking of a lie. "I know; I found out recently."

"How?"

"I searched, I dug through the archives. I've got a friend in Petrinja Street[135]."

"Why?"

"Why I searched? I wanted to know who my father was. Isn't that natural? I wanted to find out who my granny and granddad were and if I had any family. And so I found out I had two sisters."

As he was about to leave, the Inspector added: "He had a number of credit cards on him. They've all disappeared. Did you know that?"

"No, how could I?" said Nina without batting an eye. "What did he die from?" she added quickly.

"From anaphylactic shock," the Inspector said.

"Of course," said Nina, "that's why he was so grey." As soon as she said that, she bit her lip.

"How do you know he was grey?" asked the Inspector.

"Well... people said," said Nina, trying to sound calm.

When Pero left, she picked up her mobile and texted: "I had oleander leaves[136] in mind. This is better. Are you OK?"

---

[135] The Police-run Public Records Office which issues personal documents such as Passports and ID cards is in Petrinja Street.

[136] Oleander (nerium oleander) is a widely grown decorative shrub widely believed to be lethally poisonous. While it is indeed poisonous in all its parts, it is however in reality almost impossible to kill anyone using oleander. On the contrary, it is used for medicinal purposes, in particular in treating cancer.

The reply came at once: "I'm fine. Everything will be fine now."

As soon as she had read the text, Nina deleted the messages, the one she had sent and the reply she had received.

***

Although the Zagreb – Rovinj coach lacked no comfort including air-conditioning and a toilet, the passengers protested when the driver announced that he would not be stopping before Rovinj. At the request of senior passengers who were the loudest in demanding to be given at least a chance to stretch their legs, the coach turned into Pula's new Coach Station. "Ten minutes only," the driver said unpleasantly, tucked his shirt into his trousers and waddled towards the coffee machine with his stiff driver's gait.

Ana tried calling the number Andreja had given her, Aunt Laura's number in Rovinj, but discovered that the phone's battery was flat. "I'll try calling from the phone box. Coming?" she said to Andreja who was sitting next to her, completely relaxed, her head resting intimately on Ana's shoulder.

Andreja shook her head. "Nah; I'm, like, totally sleepy."

"Want me to get you something?"

"Not really," Andreja said.

"Something to read?"

Andreja waved it off at first, but then said, "Dunno... okay... *Teen,* haven't read it for ages..." She smiled. "And *Okej.*" Ana smiled, too. "And *Bravo,* if you've got enough money," Andreja added with a broad smile.

"I've got enough," said Ana and set off.

"And *Kviki* peanuts and lemon drops," Andreja shouted after her. "And a Pepsi would be nice." She was laughing now. "Bring anything you can think of," she laughed again.

Ana was content. She was confident now that everything would indeed be all right.

***

On the second day of the investigation, the Inspector and his

Sergeant returned to *The Herald*. Everyone except Jelena was already at work. "Jelena and Buba are still trying to trace Ana," David said to Pero.

Pero nodded. "So are we."

Waiting for the questioning to start, Dipsy leaned towards Ivana and whispered, "You know what the difference is between a paedophile and a paediatrician?" Ivana shook her head. "A paedophile really loves kids," Dipsy said. "A good one, innit?" Dora shot him a reproachful look.

Jelena entered and stood by the door. She looked tired and worried. "No one has seen her anywhere."

Pero's mobile rang. He took the call, listened and said, "All right, thanks." He turned to Jelena. "We found her."

"Is she all right?" asked Jelena fearfully.

Pero nodded. "She gave herself up as Andrej Martić's murderer. She hadn't done it sooner because she was taking his daughter... her sister... by coach to Rovinj, to her aunt's."

Nina rose from her chair before he finished speaking. "She didn't kill him. I did."

***

The investigation lasted several months, with Nina Ivezić and Ana Marton as suspects. They both had equally strong motives and equally good chances. The fact that they both claimed to be Andrej Martić's murderers made the investigation more difficult. It was, in fact, about to be suspended when Inspector Pero Kovačić received an e-mail from an unknown sender, signed Anton. The attachment contained the correspondence between the said Anton and Ana Marton. In her last e-mail to Anton, Ana had written, *Thank you for the information you gave me and for your support. This evening all will be over. In other, more melodramatic words, the three sisters will be avenged. Or: three flies with one blow! A.* The police tried to identify the sender. It didn't take them long to establish that Ana's and Anton's mails had been sent from the same computer. The psychologists found that everything was written by the same person. Ana Marton was sent for specialist psychiatric examination. She was proclaimed mentally incompetent at the time of the murder and was freed from charge, with the instruction that she must undertake treatment. The awards won by *Wingbeat* were not taken away from her.

Epilogue

"There you are, Inspector, that's everything," said Ana, passing a hand over her forehead as if drawing aside the curtain on a window that hadn't been opened for a very long time.

"I'm not the Inspector," said Dr Novosel.

"You're not the Inspector?" Ana regarded him with a puzzled expression. "Who are you, then?"

"I'm your doctor."

"What are you doing here in the police station?"

"This is not a police station. This is a hospital, the Green Peak Psychiatric Clinic."

"Psychiatric Clinic?" Ana frowned. "You're a psychiatrist?" The doctor nodded. "And I? What am I doing here?"

"You're my patient."

Ana brushed her hand over her forehead again. "I've got a headache," she said, then looked around, taking in the surgery. "That means it's over?"

Looking at her, the doctor nodded without a word.

"Where is everyone? Jelena, Buba, Bruno, David, the others? Have they been here?"

"Jelena is in the waiting room," said the Doctor.

"And the others?"

The doctor regarded her seriously. "They're here," he said. Keeping her eyes on Ana, he pointed at a thick sheaf of paper in front of him. Ana looked at him questioningly. Silently, the doctor passed her the papers across the table. Ana looked down on them without enthusiasm. She read: *They say that nothing happens by chance. Who knows what came to you on the wingbeat of that butterfly from Siberia...* Confused, she passed a hand over her eyes and kept it at her temple, pressing it as if pointing at the very centre of her pain. Suddenly, she lifted her face up: it was much brighter. "That means I didn't kill anyone!"

Before Doctor Novosel could answer, there was a knock on the door. "Come in," he said. A woman with a worried face peeped into the darkened room.

"Jelena!" Ana cried happily.

They embraced each other firmly. "You're better, thank God," Jelena said.

"Much better," Ana said. "And I remember everything. You see, I haven't become a celeb chased by the paparazzi after all... I was chased by the police instead." She halted, confused. "I mean, the doctors."

Jelena didn't know what to say.

"Now I know why I always felt there was a crowd swarming in my head," Ana went on. "I sometimes felt I was only pretending to be Ana."

Jelena held her tighter. They were silent. The doctor rang the bell. A large, middle-aged male nurse entered and touched Ana's shoulder. "Time you went back to the ward," he said. He helped her up and pointed her like a rag doll towards the door.

Ana's eyes examined his strong, hairy hand on her shoulder. "You've got a nice watch," she said. "Old-fashioned."

"Yeah," he replied with unexpected warmth. "My old Doxa."

Ana turned towards Jelena. "When will you be back?" she asked.

"Tomorrow," Jelena said. "What would you like me to bring?"

Ana halted. "I don't need anything, just a new *Moleskine* diary; my old one's full."

"Where can I get one?"

"You don't need to buy one; I've got several at home. They're in the brown dresser in the sitting room."

***

Jelena found five *Moleskine* diaries in the dresser, still in the original packaging. Underneath them she found a yellowed sheet roughly torn from a newspaper. At the bottom of the page, someone had drawn a line in pencil around an article:

Andrija Marton (65) was found dead in his apartment where he lived alone. His body was discovered when the neighbours noticed the smell of smoke and burned roast spreading from the apartment. The old man was obviously attacked while preparing a meal: carbonised remnants of meat were found in the oven, and an empty container for frozen food on the kitchen table. Everything else in the apartment was in its usual place. There were no signs of robbery. Mr Marton was killed by a single blow with a blunt object to the back of his head. The murder weapon was not found. The investigation has revealed that the only suspect, Ana Marton (30), Mr Marton's stepdaughter, had as a child been hospitalised a number of times as a consequence of brutal sexual abuse.

**

3rd October

The negotiations about the entry of Croatia into the European Union have started.

4th October

The presentation of Engdahl's book *Seeds of Destruction* – in Zagreb, because the author says food in Croatia still tastes better than anywhere else. He also says that, even if the genetically modified seeds weren't harmful – and they are -- we should continue the fight, because in the near future all the seeds on the planet, and that means the source of all food, will be in the hands of a small minority.

24th October

From Siberia, 20,000 more wild swans set off for Europe

24th October (the *Good Morning* programme)

Every hour, 700 tons of waste is discarded into the Mediterranean. Half of that waste is plastic.

8th December

Ante Gotovina arrested in the Caribbean thanks to the cooperation between Croatian and Spanish authorities.

A CLIPPING FROM THE EIGHTIES:

In 1930, the average European spent roughly 20 minutes a

day laughing; in 1980, only six minutes.

February 2006

The Muslim world up in arms because of the caricatures of Muhammed, the Prophet of God.

Bird flu spreads through Europe: sick birds found in Greece, Slovenia, Austria, Italy, France...

What was it Nostradamus said about birds dropping down from the skies and the final world war?

Afrika paprika

ABOUT THE AUTHOR

Vesna Ćuro-Tomić is one of the most interesting modern Croatian writers and possibly the most modern one among them. Her urbane, ironic gaze, self-involved, self-regarding, self-pitying and self-parodying all at once, still somehow manages to register the quotidian in all its pathetic ghastliness without losing sight of its underpinning redemptive magic. Her virtuoso mastery of narrative form is as demanding as it is rewarding, propelling the reader towards an unexpected, breathtaking end.

Born in 1954 in Sarajevo, Vesna graduated English Studies and Comparative Literature from Zagreb University. She is currently Programme Editor for Feature and Television Films at HRT (Croatian Radio and Television). In 2004, she published her first novel, the poignant yet hugely entertaining roman à clef *A Taxi to Telly*. *The Naked She-Wolf* is her first novel to be published in English.

She is married and has two children.